ABUSE
OF
POWER

Also by Nancy Taylor Rosenberg

Mitigating Circumstances
Interest of Justice
First Offense
California Angel
Trial by Fire

Nancy Taylor Rosenberg

ABUSE OF POWER

A DUTTON BOOK

DUTTON
Published by the Penguin Group
Penguin Books USA Inc., 375 Hudson Street,
New York, New York 10014, U.S.A.
Penguin Books Ltd, 27 Wrights Lane,
London W8 5TZ, England
Penguin Books Australia Ltd, Ringwood,
Victoria, Australia
Penguin Books Canada Ltd, 10 Alcorn Avenue,
Toronto, Ontario, Canada M4V 3B2
Penguin Books (N.Z.) Ltd, 182–190 Wairau Road,
Auckland 10, New Zealand

Penguin Books Ltd, Registered Offices:
Harmondsworth, Middlesex, England

First published by Dutton, an imprint of Dutton Signet, a division
of Penguin Books USA Inc.
Distributed in Canada by McClelland & Stewart Inc.
Copyright © Creative Ventures, Inc., 1997
All rights reserved

 REGISTERED TRADEMARK—MARCA REGISTRADA

ISBN 0-525-93768-4
Printed in the United States of America
Set in Goudy Old Style
Designed by Leonard Telesca

To James Dominic Nesci, welcome to our family,
and for my fabulous husband, Jerry Rosenberg.

AUTHOR'S NOTE

This was a difficult book for me to write, and many people assisted in its development. To my editor and friend, Michaela Hamilton, thank you for your tireless support and inspiration. To my publisher, Elaine Koster, and to Peter Mayer, Marvin Brown, Arnold Dolin, Lisa Johnson, Maryann Palumbo, Alex Holtz, Larry Hughes, Ellen Silberman, Peter Schneider, and all my other friends at Penguin USA, I sincerely appreciate your diligent efforts on my behalf.

I have enormous respect for the many valiant officers who risk their lives to protect our communities. Having been affiliated with a number of police agencies through the years, I found the majority of officers I worked with to be honest and dedicated public servants. Since the setting for this novel is Ventura County, and I was at one time employed by the Ventura Police Department, I want to make it clear that the characters and events depicted in this book are fictional and in no way reflect the high caliber of officers who are employed at the Ventura P.D., nor any of the other departments I have been associated with throughout my career in law enforcement.

Situations like the ones described in this novel are occurring on an ever increasing basis. Although the story I have told is fictional, I drew strictly from real-life events that have been reported by the media. I decided to undertake this project in an attempt to explain what the code of silence means, and to expose my readers to the enormous stress police officers are subjected to while performing their duties.

In conclusion, I would like to thank my wonderful family for their continued support: Forrest, Jeannie, Rachel, Chessly, Jimmy, and little Jimmy, who appeared on the scene last August. To Hoyt, Amy, Nancy; my adorable mother, LaVerne Taylor; my mother-in-law, Doris Rosenberg; my sisters, Sharon Ford and Linda Stewart; my brother, William Hoyt Taylor, and to all the other members of my family whom I love so dearly. To Irene McKeown and Alex Tushinsky for their in-house support. To my special fans: Grant Smyth, for the use of his name; Patricia

Grace Voss, for her lovely cards and inspirational letters; Mary Lou Andrea, for the fabulous quilt she made for me; and a special memorial to Robert W. Begen, who read every book I have ever written and showed up at every book signing.

chapter

ONE

Seated on a bench outside Department 22 of the Ventura County Superior Court, the male police officer was dressed in his black regulation uniform. His head against the wall, he was sound asleep. The small redheaded woman at his side wore a pink cotton blazer over a simple white dress. Her feet were encased in scuffed black flats, her knees chafed and bony.

Rachel Simmons glanced to her left at Jimmy Townsend. Testifying was no more stressful to him than writing a speeding ticket. She, on the other hand, detested going to court. How could Townsend sleep when her insides were quivering? "Wake up," she said, nudging him with her elbow when she saw two men coming down the corridor.

"What the—" Townsend bolted upright on the wooden bench. A heavyset man in his late thirties, he had unruly brown hair and a round, jowly face. His chin was peculiar, almost inverted. Only a few inches of his neck were visible. His upper body was so densely padded that his shoulders had a tendency to bunch up around his ears.

The two men stopped a few feet away. Michael Atwater was the district attorney assigned to their case. Dennis Colter was a DA as well. Rachel had attended high school with Colter in San Diego, but she doubted if he would recognize her after so many years. She glanced at Atwater, then quickly looked away.

"I don't care what Judge Sanders said," Atwater was saying. "If you plead it right, you can get an extra six years tacked onto his sentence. The oral copulation is a separate and distinct crime. Sanders has his head up his asshole. If he gives you any more problems, tell him to call me. He must have slept through the last judicial sentencing conference."

Once Dennis Colter entered the adjoining courtroom, Mike Atwater walked over to where Rachel was sitting. "We'll probably call you in about ten minutes," he told her, ignoring the officer beside her.

At six-four, Mike Atwater had the most athletic body Rachel had ever seen. A slender man, he carried most of his height in his legs. His hair was brown and neatly trimmed. He combed it straight back from his face, keeping it in place with some product that made it look as if he had just stepped out of the shower. His eyes were dark and heavily hooded. Before becoming an attorney, he had made a name for himself as a world-class runner, breaking records in the indoor mile. Everything about him was supple and loose. "You look exhausted," he said. "Did you work last night?"

"Yes," Rachel said, staring at her hands, "I work every night." She could not make eye contact with him. When she did, she became a specimen under a microscope. She raised her gaze to his slender wrists, the gold cufflinks in his starched white shirt, the clear polish on his fingernails. "I'm assigned to the graveyard shift at the PD, but I also have an extra job as a security officer at State Farm Insurance in Simi Valley," she told him. "I work there on my days off."

"I see," Atwater said, stroking the side of his face.

"Did you get the flowers?"

"Ah, yes." Rachel blushed, fidgeting in her seat. "They were beautiful. I don't know how to thank you."

"You just did," Atwater said, turning and slapping open the double doors to the courtroom.

"Flowers?" Townsend said, scowling. "Mike Atwater sent you flowers? He's an egotistical prick. I've worked with him on five other cases. In case you didn't notice, the asshole didn't even speak to me. What am I, a log or something?"

Rachel shrugged. "I have no idea why he sent them, Jimmy. All I did was go to lunch with him in the cafeteria last week when he called me to go over my testimony. The next day I got two dozen red roses. When the delivery guy rang my doorbell, I thought he had the wrong house."

"Sort of extravagant, don't you think?" Townsend said, slouching in his seat.

The doors leading into the courtroom swung open, and Rachel jumped. "Officer Simmons," the bailiff said, "they're ready for you now."

Rachel had driven to the station to pick up Townsend so he could go straight home after court and not have to return to his police unit. His house was only a few blocks from her own. The officer had been experiencing financial problems and had sold his extra car the previous month. "Where should we meet?" she asked. "I don't want to sit out here after I testify."

"They probably won't be finished with me until almost noon," Townsend said. "Meet me in the cafeteria. We'll grab some lunch."

Rachel stood and smoothed down her knee-length skirt, wishing it covered more of her legs. She was embarrassed that she had not worn hose, but when she had rushed home at eight o'clock that morning, she had been unable to find a pair without a run. She was additionally annoyed that she had not worn her uniform. Wearing it made her feel more authoritative and confident. She'd had only ten minutes to shower, though, and getting suited up took time.

She looked straight ahead as she walked down the aisle to the witness stand. She was thirty-four, but her unassuming appearance and quiet demeanor made her appear several years younger. Her fair skin was dusted with freckles, the majority of them sprinkled across her nose and cheeks. When she was frightened or angry, her eyes turned blue, shifting back to a nondescript gray when she was ill or exhausted as she was today. Her mouth was small and dainty, her cheekbones clearly defined.

Rachel took her seat in the witness stand. Once she had been sworn in, Mike Atwater stood and spoke, his voice clear and resonant. "Officer Simmons," he said, "will you advise the court where you are presently employed?"

"The Oak Grove Police Department," she said, moving the skinny microphone closer to her mouth.

"How long have you been a police officer?"

"Approximately two years."

"What did you do before you became a police officer?"

"I worked as a salesclerk at Robinson's department store," she said, her speech somewhat hesitant.

"How long did you work as a salesclerk?"

"Approximately six months," she said. "Before that, I was a housewife." She paused and coughed to cover her embarrassment. Most of the officers in the department had college degrees. Rachel had never made it past high school. Even though her grades had been good, she had not been able to save enough money to pay her tuition. "My husband was a landscape architect," she added, attempting to bolster her modest accomplishments. "I wasn't only a housewife. I handled all the books for him, made his appointments, things like that. I was his partner in the business."

Atwater circled to the front of the counsel table, then advanced to the witness box. "Why did you decide to enter law enforcement?"

Rachel blinked several times, her eyelids a pale shade of pink. On one lid was a star-shaped mole, right under her eyebrow. "My husband died three years ago. I have two children. The job paid well, the benefits were excellent, and I thought I could cut back on my child care expenses by working odd hours."

Atwater yanked on his cuffs, a jerky motion he made frequently. "So your decision was strictly financial, right?"

Rachel stared hard at him. What was it he wanted her to say? They weren't simply shooting the breeze as they had the day in the cafeteria. Every question the district attorney asked had a purpose. "I didn't decide to become a police officer strictly for financial reasons," she said, thrusting her chin forward. "I'm honest. I'm a hard worker. I've never broken the law. I decided I might be able to serve my community."

Atwater issued a shrewd smile, showing only a glimpse of his teeth. Pivoting on his heels, he marched back to the counsel table. "Before you became a police officer, were you ever the victim of a violent crime?"

Rachel shook her head in dismay. The attorney was now entering into an official court record something she had told him in confidence. No one in the department knew what had happened to her as a child. She didn't want her fellow officers to perceive her as a victim. "I—I was kidnapped while returning home from the grocery store," she said. "I was ten years old at the time." Her memories of that day came in quick, disconnected flashes. She saw the man's hands moving across her naked body. Her muscles twitched at the sound of the camera shutter clicking. Balling her hands into fists, she pressed them against her temples, trying to make the images go away.

"Please continue, Officer Simmons," Atwater said, oblivious to her distress. "Tell the court how you were rescued from the kidnapper."

"Objection," the defense attorney said. "This isn't relevant to the present case, Your Honor."

"Is there a reason for this particular line of questioning, Mr. Atwater?" the judge asked.

"Yes, Your Honor," he said. "I'm trying to establish the credibility of my witness. Her past history as a victim qualifies her expertise beyond her present position."

"Objection overruled," the judge said wearily. "Try to make your point, Counselor. We don't have all day."

"Officer Simmons," Atwater continued, "can you advise the court how you escaped from the kidnapper?"

"A woman wrote down the license plate of the car the man was driving," Rachel said. "An officer with the San Diego Police Department spotted the car in the parking lot of a nearby motel. They dispatched the tactical team, and a police sharpshooter shot and killed him." Her eyelids fluttered as the shotgun blast reverberated inside her mind. How many times had she relived that moment? The man slumping to the ground, the splattered blood, the terrible wound on the side of his head.

"A police officer saved your life, then," Atwater said, glancing in the direction of the jurors. "Isn't it true, Officer Simmons, that the man who kidnapped you had previously been imprisoned for kidnapping and raping another child?"

"Yes," Rachel said. "He served only seven years of his sentence. He was a doctor at the time of the earlier crime, so I guess the parole board took that into consideration."

"Wasn't it probable that this man would have raped you as well if the police had not come to your rescue?"

"That's possible," she said.

"Wasn't this event the impetus behind your seeking employment as a police officer?"

"More or less," she answered, folding her hands in her lap.

"What happened to you after the kidnapping?"

"I'm not sure I know what you're talking about," Rachel answered, her throat muscles tightening. She looked up at the judge, whispering, "Can I have a drink of water, please?"

The courtroom fell silent as the bailiff carried a paper cup to the witness stand. She drained it, then placed it in her lap.

"Are you ready to proceed?" the judge asked.

Rachel nodded.

"Didn't you develop a phobia of leaving the house?" Atwater asked, his voice booming out over the courtroom. "Isn't it true that you were unable to speak for almost a year following the kidnapping, that you developed a form of hysterical muteness?"

"Yes," she said.

"When you did speak, who was the first person you spoke to?"

Her face softened. "Officer Larry Dean."

"The same officer who rescued you from the kidnapper, correct?"

"Yes," Rachel said.

The defense was alleging police misconduct in what should have been a routine drunk driving arrest. Atwater considered Rachel Simmons the perfect witness for such a case—her unassuming manner, her obvious sincerity, her past hero worship of men in uniform. His eyes drifted over to the rows of jurors again. They were average, working-class people. Wealthy, sophisticated people seldom served on jury panels. The jury could easily identify with a young widow trying to support her family, particularly one who appeared as idealistic as Rachel Simmons. Her history as a victim further enhanced her credibility. "You're assigned to patrol, is that correct?"

"That's correct," Rachel said, relieved that Atwater was moving away from the subject of her kidnapping.

"Were you working on the night of April 20th, at approximately three o'clock in the morning?"

"Yes, I was."

"Can you explain why you came to stop the defendant?"

"I noticed his car was weaving," she said. "I followed him for several miles, during which I observed his vehicle cross the yellow line on four separate occasions."

"So you initiated a traffic stop, assuming this individual was under the influence? Is that correct?"

"Yes," Rachel said. Atwater had instructed her to answer the questions without elaborating. She didn't understand why the process of testifying had to be so time-consuming. She was telling the truth. No matter how many questions the attorneys asked her or how cleverly they composed them, the truth was still the truth. Why couldn't she simply tell them what had happened and leave? She had not slept in over forty-eight hours. When she went this long without sleep, she felt as if she were swimming underwater.

"Can you tell us what happened after you stopped the defendant's vehicle?"

"I asked the defendant for his license and registration," Rachel said, her voice stronger than before. "Once he handed these items to me, I proceeded to run a wants and warrants check. When the dispatcher advised me that Mr. Brentwood had an outstanding warrant for failure to appear on a drunk driving violation, I requested a backup unit."

"This is customary procedure, correct?"

"Yes," she said.

"Did you then conduct a field sobriety test?"

"Not until the backup unit arrived." She looked at the defendant. The nasty, sloppy drunk she had encountered that early morning in April had transformed himself into a clean, sharp-looking businessman with his three-piece suit, his crisp white shirt, his snappy tie. In his late forties, Carl Brentwood had graying hair and the puffy, bloated face of an alcoholic. He sold used cars at the Lexus dealership off the 101 freeway in Thousand Oaks.

"Can you advise us of the name of the officer who responded for backup?" Atwater asked.

"Jimmy Townsend," Rachel said.

"Once Officer Townsend arrived and you administered the field sobriety test," he continued, "what were your conclusions?"

"That the defendant was under the influence of alcohol," Rachel replied. "He had difficulty walking a straight line. He could not touch his nose, nor could he count backward accurately. In addition, there was a strong odor of alcohol about the defendant's clothing and person. I advised him I was placing him under arrest for driving under the influence, then informed him that he would be booked on the outstanding warrant as well."

"What did the defendant do at this point?"

Rachel cleared her throat. "He spat at me."

"Did he strike you in any way?"

"No," she said. "But after he spat at me, he proceeded to unzip his pants and urinate on my legs and shoes."

Cackles of laughter rang out from the five male spectators in the courtroom. Rachel assumed they were the defendant's friends or relatives, maybe some of the car salesmen he worked with at the dealership. She narrowed her eyes at them, wondering if they had any idea of the degradation police officers endured.

"Where was Officer Townsend when this was going on?"

"Standing about five feet away, near the rear of my patrol unit. When he saw I was encountering problems, he came over to assist me."

"Did you handcuff the defendant?"

"I assisted Officer Townsend in handcuffing him," Rachel said. "Mr. Brentwood was cursing and struggling. It took both of us to control him."

"Who searched him once the handcuffs were in place?"

"Officer Townsend," she said quickly, the attorney having carefully coached her on this area of her testimony. "I went back to my unit to order a tow truck for the defendant's vehicle."

"Did you see Officer Townsend remove a .22 pistol from the defendant's left pocket?"

"I saw . . ." Rachel stopped and sucked in a deep breath. The defendant claimed the gun was planted on him. He swore Townsend had whispered to him that he was going to pay, that no one urinated on a police officer and got away with it. Carrying a concealed weapon constituted a felony, whereas the drunk driving offenses the defendant was charged with were only misdemeanors. Jimmy Townsend wanted Rachel to say she had seen him remove the gun to substantiate his story. Atwater wanted the same thing, but during their meeting, he had insisted that he was in no way encouraging Rachel to commit perjury. He called it "realigning her memory." When Townsend had discovered the gun, she had been inside her unit ordering the tow truck. How could she swear she had seen something she knew she had not seen?

"I saw the gun when Officer Townsend showed it to me," she finally said, a slight tremor in her voice. "I didn't see him remove it from Mr. Brentwood's pocket."

Mike Atwater scowled. "No further questions, Your Honor," he said, dropping into his seat.

8

chapter

TWO

Once Rachel had been cross examined by the defendant's attorney, she was exhausted. Knowing Townsend's testimony would take at least an hour, she rode the elevator to the DA's office on the third floor of the sprawling court complex, attached to the county jail by an underground tunnel. No matter how long she had to wait, she had to know why Mike Atwater had exposed her past in court.

Several times she dozed off in the lobby waiting for the prosecutor to return. The receptionist kept watching her. Finally the young woman walked over and asked Rachel if she could get her a cup of coffee, knowing she was a police officer from her visit to the office the previous week. "Yes," Rachel said, "thank you. That would be great."

"My brother's a cop in Los Angeles," the woman said when she returned with a steaming mug. A petite brunette in her early twenties, she gave Rachel a compassionate look. "Rough night, huh?"

"They're all rough," Rachel said, resting her head on the back of the chair. Her husband had once earned a fairly decent income as a landscape architect. His illness had been long and protracted, however, and their medical insurance had not been adequate. By the time he had succumbed to cancer, the couple's savings were depleted and Rachel was deeply in debt. She'd sold their home in Ventura with the gorgeous backyard Joe had designed, exchanging it for a modest rental home in the nearby city of Oak Grove. The profits from the sale of the house had been used to pay down her debt. She had tried to make ends meet by working in a department store, but by the time she paid for child care and other related expenses, there was not enough money left to pay the rent.

Rachel closed her eyes, wishing she could clear away the painful memories. But as she listened idly to the low hum of the air conditioner, her thoughts drifted back to Atwater's questions in the courtroom. His probing into her kidnapping raised vivid images of the day her childhood savagely ended. As she continued to sit and wait, the scene replayed in her mind, from beginning to end, as it so often had.

She had been ten years old, about to step outside the front door of her house in San Diego.

The screen door slammed shut behind her, followed by the sound of her mother's voice. "Don't forget the bread," Frances McDowell shouted from the entryway.

Tapping the kickstand with her foot, Rachel grabbed the handlebars of her new bicycle, fire-engine red with chrome fenders. Her mother had bought it for her birthday the previous month. Her father had been an enlisted man in the Navy, but he had abandoned the family shortly after Rachel was born. Frances supported her three daughters by teaching piano lessons out of her home.

Rachel refused to let go of the hope that her father would come back one day. She didn't believe the things her mother told her, that he didn't want them anymore, that he probably had another family by now, other little girls who were much better behaved than Rachel and her sisters. Even though she didn't remember him, her mother kept a picture of her father on the mantel over the fireplace. Rachel thought he looked handsome in his white uniform.

The girl next door was playing jacks on her front porch. "Hey, Rach," she said, "if you let me ride your bike, I'll give you a nickel."

"No one can ride my bike," Rachel said, zipping past her.

Money was tight. Rachel had begged her mother for the bicycle. Knowing such an expenditure fell outside their budget, she had sacrificed having a gift under the Christmas tree in exchange for the promise that her mother would save toward buying her a new Schwinn.

Her red hair was fashioned in a ponytail, then laced through the back of her baseball cap. She was at the age when her teeth seemed too large for her face. Her arms and legs had recently lost their baby fat and grown into skinny twigs. When she smiled, two deep dimples sank in her cheeks, and her gray eyes sparkled with mischief. Her baseball cap was red as well as her T-shirt, and she was wearing a pair of green and red plaid cotton shorts that had once belonged to her oldest sister, Carrie.

Rachel worshipped Carrie. Her other sister, Susan, was a quiet, studious girl who kept mostly to herself, but Carrie was outgoing and fun. She was always telling jokes and making Rachel laugh. She had tons of friends, and at sixteen, boys were beginning to take notice. Carrie knew how to make herself look pretty. Her sister had promised to teach Rachel how to put on makeup as soon as she was old enough.

Rachel stuffed the bills her mother had given her into her pocket and took off down the sidewalk to the corner market. It was a beautiful afternoon, the temperature in the mid-seventies. A gentle breeze, fragrant with lilacs, washed over her face.

She loved pedaling around on her flashy new bike. The kids in the neighborhood had always ridiculed her and her sisters because they were poor. Their house was the smallest on the block, and the grass in the yard occasionally grew too high. When Rachel grew up, she was going to have enough money to hire a gardener, and her yard would be the most beautiful yard in the entire world.

At Biner's Market she walked to the back of the store, grabbed a loaf of Wonder bread off the shelf, then headed to the refrigerated section for the gallon of milk her mother had requested. The groceries would fit perfectly in the white basket attached to the handlebars on her new bike. She had even plucked a rose earlier in the day from the yard and tied it to the wicker basket with string.

A tall, dark-haired man was standing next to the dairy case. Wearing a neatly pressed pair of pants, a white dress shirt, and a polka-dot tie, he reminded Rachel of the principal at her elementary school. His hairline was slightly receding, his nose narrow at the top but full at the tip, his eyes almost the same pale shade as her own. Something about him looked familiar. Rachel decided she must have seen him in the neighborhood.

"Let me get that for you," he said, seeing Rachel straining to reach the top shelf. "Do you want skim milk or regular?"

"Regular."

"Here we go," he said, smiling as he handed the container to her. "What's your name, cutie?"

"Rachel," she said, staring at the man's hand. Her mother had told her that her father had a tattoo on his hand. She didn't know what kind of tattoo it was, though, because her father's hands didn't show in the picture. This man had a tattoo as well, a little heart with someone's name inside it.

"Rachel is a beautiful name," the man answered. "I have a daughter. She's eleven. Her name is Marjorie. How old are you?"

"Ten," she said, leaving the man and walking to the counter to pay for her purchases.

"What's it going to be today?" Mr. Biner said, seeing the girl eyeing the candy counter. A small man in his late sixties, he had graying hair and his face was heavily lined. "Your mother told me you're going to be in the spelling bee tomorrow. Didn't you win the first prize last year?"

"Yeah," Rachel said, fishing her money out of her pocket. "And I'm going to win tomorrow, too."

"That's the spirit," Biner said, smiling broadly.

The man stepped up to the counter to pay for his soft drink. "Warm day," he remarked, pulling his collar away from his neck.

"I don't believe we've met," Mr. Biner said. "Did you just move into the neighborhood? If so, I can set up an account for you. We also deliver."

"Nah," the man said, glancing over at Rachel at the candy rack. "My daughter plays with a girl down the street. I drove over to pick her up. You might have heard of the people. Their name is Marcus."

"Don't believe I know them," Mr. Biner said, closing the drawer to the cash register. "Since the new A & P opened, a lot of the folks moving into the neighborhood prefer to do their grocery shopping over there."

"See you around," the man said, exiting the store.

Rachel stepped to the counter and handed Mr. Biner a ten-dollar bill. Once he gave her the change, she placed fifty cents in her left pocket, putting the money she had to return to her mother in her right. She had already deposited thirty-five dollars in her student bank account, the profits from a summer of selling lemonade. She decided she would rather add the fifty cents to her savings than squander it on candy.

Loading the groceries into the wicker basket, Rachel began pedaling down the sidewalk to her house. It was dusk now, and the air was getting brisk.

"Rachel," a voice called to her.

She looked over and saw the man from the market. He was speaking to her from the driver's seat of a long blue car, stopped in the middle of the roadway. "Hi," she said, waving at him as she continued pedaling.

"Wait," he said, opening the car door and stepping out. "I need to ask you something."

"What?" she said, placing her feet on the sidewalk.

"Do you know where Annie Marcus lives?" he asked, his eyes darting up and down the street as if he were looking for something. "Marjorie went over to her house after school today. I drove over here to pick her up, but I forgot to bring the address with me. Annie is about the same age as you. Maybe you know her from school and can show me which house she lives in. I'm fairly certain it has blue trim."

Rachel thought for a few moments before answering. "I don't know a girl named Annie," she said. "Where is she supposed to live?"

"This is Orangetree Road, right?"

Rachel nodded. She removed her baseball cap and stuffed it into her back pocket. Now that the sun had gone down, she didn't need it.

"Maybe if I show you a picture of the house," the man continued, "you might be able to recognize it. I know it's on Orangetree Road, because I came to pick up my daughter at the same house several months ago. Now I can't seem to figure out which house it is. Stupid, huh? Marjorie is probably wondering what happened to me. Come over to my car," he told her. "I have a picture of the house in the trunk. I'm a photographer, so I snap pictures everywhere I go."

She dropped the kickstand on her bike before following the man to his car. He opened the trunk and motioned for her to come closer, holding a photograph in his hands. As soon as she stepped up beside him, the man moved behind her, tossed a pillowcase over her head and secured it with a scarf pulled tight around her neck.

Rachel felt the man's hands lifting her. She kicked out furiously. Was he teasing her, playing a trick? "Let me go," she screamed, clawing at the pillowcase. Before she knew what was happening, the man placed her in the trunk of the car and slammed the lid closed.

She shrieked, "Get me out." Her body shook in terrified spasms. She choked as her efforts to free herself caused the scarf to press tighter against her throat . . .

Someone tapped her on the shoulder, and Rachel's eyes flew open. For a few moments, she was trapped between the past and the present. She could see herself inside the trunk of the car, hear her own screams. Her eyes roamed around the lobby of the DA's office, her breath coming in short bursts.

"Did you want to speak to me?" Mike Atwater asked. "Is something wrong?"

Rachel remained silent. Focusing on the overhead light fixture, she attempted to dispel the darkness of the trunk. The memory had been so real, she could still feel the scarf around her throat. She massaged the side of her neck, then slowly pushed herself to her feet. "I'm fine," she said. "Is there somewhere we can talk privately?"

"Come with me," Atwater said, leading her through the security doors.

The interior of the DA's office was a whirl of activity. Phones jangled, word processors clicked, copy spilled out of printers. Rachel stepped aside as two harried attorneys rushed out with files clutched under their arms. The clerical staff worked in a large open room. Offices for the attorneys were positioned along the outside perimeter.

Atwater led her into his office and began rummaging through the thick stack of papers on top of his desk. Even though his mind was well ordered, his office resembled the aftermath of a tornado. Law books had been yanked from the bookcase behind his desk, then tossed here and there on the floor. Several cardboard boxes containing trial transcripts from a homicide he had handled several months ago were still stacked in one corner. His in box was overflowing with files and correspondence, briefs and motions. There were no pictures on his desk, only a glass jug of jelly beans, teetering precariously on top of an uneven mound of papers. "I know I had the damn thing," he mumbled, depressing the intercom for his secretary. "Do you have the blood-alcohol report on the Brentwood case, Marsha?"

"I put it in the file this morning," a woman's voice said over the speakerphone.

"Get me a duplicate," he told her. "I don't know what happened to it. Maybe it fell out on the way to court this morning."

After he had disconnected, Rachel grabbed his hand to get his attention. "How could you do that to me?" she demanded.

"Do what?" Atwater said, finally looking up at her.

"When I told you those things in the cafeteria, you never told me you were going to bring them up in court. You ambushed me."

"Why do you say that?" he said, sitting back. "Does it disturb you to talk about the kidnapping?"

Rachel was generally a very controlled person. Anger did not come easily. When it did, however, there was no way to stop it. "Of course it upsets me to talk about it," she shouted. "Is that why you sent me the roses, because you knew you were planning to embarrass me today?"

"Relax," he said. "I sent you the roses because I wanted to, okay? It had nothing to do with your testimony."

Rachel glared at him. With his smooth voice and slick ways, he had manipulated her. She had been impressed by his position, the athleticism of his body, the richness of his skin. She had been a fool. What would a man like Atwater see in her?

"We're going to lose the weapons charge," he said, breaking the silence. "We should be able to nail Brentwood on the two counts of drunk driving. If you had supported Townsend's story, we would have gotten the full boat."

Rachel took a seat. "I didn't see it," she said, her anger dissipating almost as fast as it had erupted. "I know you think I saw it and just forgot, but I swear I wasn't looking when Townsend found the gun in Brentwood's pocket. I patted the guy down as soon as he got out of the car, and there was nothing on him."

Atwater gave her a stern look. "A .22 is a small gun," he said. "People make mistakes."

"I didn't make a mistake," she insisted. "If you knew me better, you'd know I'm telling the truth."

"Well," he said, flashing a smile. "Maybe we should change that. I'm game if you're game." He reached over and picked up a pen. "Give me your phone number. We'll go out to dinner one night next week." He flipped through the pages of his calendar. "I guess I'll have to call you later and give you an exact date so you can get someone to watch your kids. How old are they, by the way?"

"Tracy is fourteen," Rachel told him. "Joe is three. I gave you my address and phone number last week. Don't you remember?"

For some reason, Mike Atwater found Rachel intriguing. Was it her fresh-faced appearance, her directness, the funny little expressions she made with her mouth? With the right tutoring, clothes, and makeup, she could easily be an eight. But she presented herself as a five, maybe even a three. Was this what fascinated him, her untapped potential? "I thought bringing up your past might earn us some brownie points," he said, tapping his pen on the desk. "Making a police officer appear sympathetic in the eyes of a jury these days is not always easy."

"Look," Rachel said, "I didn't mean I'm a great officer, or that I never make mistakes. That's the point. I'm so afraid for my safety that I would never miss finding a weapon during a patdown search, even if it was no bigger than a pencil."

"None of this amounts to a hill of beans now," Atwater said. "You've already testified. I only wish you'd told me about this patdown search you conducted when we went over your testimony last week. We fed right into their hands on that one."

"I know," Rachel said tensely. "When Brentwood's attorney started drilling me, I didn't know what to do other than to tell the truth. He asked me specifically if I had searched the defendant prior to the search Townsend conducted. The way you presented the question, I could hedge without actually lying. The defense attorney's question was more direct."

"I don't have much time," Atwater said, glancing at his watch. "Are you suggesting Townsend planted the gun? When we talked last week, you didn't mention anything along those lines."

"I didn't say he planted the gun," Rachel said, an anxious look on her face. "All I'm trying to do is tell the truth. No matter how the case turns out, don't you think the truth is important?"

"Police corruption is the hottest defense out there, you know?" Atwater said, nodding at another attorney standing in the doorway. "You know how many defendants we had last month who claimed the evidence was planted by the cops? A few sensational cases, and people suddenly act like there's not an honest cop in the entire country. Thank God, Brentwood isn't black. At least he can't claim he's the victim of racism. We've got three cases right now that are more than likely going to end up in acquittal because of race issues."

"I just wanted you to know that I did my best," Rachel said, rubbing her forehead. "Maybe I did see Townsend reach in and pull out the gun. Sometimes I get so tired, you know? With the extra job and all, I don't get enough sleep."

Atwater stared at her, then waved the attorney from the doorway into his office.

Rachel stood and walked out, slipping past the man who had been waiting. Mike Atwater was a strange man. One minute he was asking her out on a date, the next he was dismissing her as if he had no interest in what she was saying.

"Who was that?" Blake Reynolds asked. He was a short, wiry man in his late twenties with neatly trimmed blond hair, his eyes hidden behind wire-rimmed glasses. Carrying a file in his hands, he took a seat facing Atwater's desk.

"One of the officers from the Brentwood case," Atwater told him, plucking a jelly bean out of the jar and tossing it in his mouth. "Her name is Rachel Simmons. What do you think?"

"I don't really know all the details of the Brentwood case."

"I'm not referring to the case," Atwater said, his eyes trained on the doorway. "What do you think of her as a woman?"

The young attorney said, "Are you talking about what I think you're talking about?"

"Possibly," Atwater said. "She's fresh, cute, not too bright but intriguing. There's untapped potential there, my friend."

"I thought she was a bag lady or something," Reynolds said, chuckling. Atwater was a notorious womanizer. He had been divorced for a number of years, but to those who knew him, he behaved like a man who had never been married. He seldom dated a woman longer than a month. The women he had been associated with in the past were polished professionals, both striking in appearance and heavy on brains. He courted them relentlessly. As soon as the newness wore off, he discarded them like an old suit. Reynolds' gaze turned to the framed Mensa certificate on the wall, the track and field medals encased in glass, the Stanford law degree mounted behind Atwater's desk. Not many people would have the balls to display their accomplishments that way.

"What could you possibly see in this woman?" he asked. "She isn't your type at all."

"Integrity," Atwater said, standing and adjusting his tie. "Look around you, Blake. Integrity is in short supply these days. When you put a woman like Rachel Simmons in a police uniform, it's the same as lighting a stick of dynamite. You know what intrigues me?"

"No," Reynolds said, "but I'm sure you're going to tell me."

Atwater smiled mischievously. "How long will it be before the sparks start flying?"

Before his colleague could respond, Atwater walked out of the office and disappeared down the corridor.

THREE

Because most of the courts were in recess for the noon break, the cafeteria was crowded and noisy. After some searching, Rachel spotted Jimmy Townsend and walked over to his table. Plates were stacked on top of one another, not a morsel of food remaining. "Where have you been?" he said, cleaning his teeth with a toothpick. "I got out of court over an hour ago. I thought you'd left without me."

"Well, I see you went ahead and had your lunch," Rachel said, slightly annoyed that he had not waited. Since she had gone out of her way to give him a ride to the courthouse, the least he could have done was wait so she would not have to eat alone.

"Can you spot me a ten?" he asked. "I walked out of the house last night without any money. I had to give the cashier an IOU."

"Sure," Rachel said. When she looked through her wallet, though, she could find only seven dollars. "I'm sorry, Jimmy. Can't you put it on your credit card?"

"I don't have a credit card," he said, his face flushing.

"But I've seen you charge things before," she said.

"I have a card, okay," Townsend snapped. "I can't use it. I didn't pay the bill last month." He stood and walked over to the cashier's console.

Rachel took a seat at the table, pushing the stack of plates aside. Seeing a small white receipt, she picked it up and then realized there was not just one receipt but three. Quickly doing the math in her head, she came up with thirty-five dollars. Her eyes went to the stack of empty plates, then drifted over to Townsend. How could anyone have a thirty-five-dollar lunch in the courthouse cafeteria? The food was reasonably priced. Deciding to forgo eating now that it was so late, she walked over to the cash register to tell Townsend she was ready to leave.

"Catch you next time, buddy," he told the cashier, following Rachel out of the cafeteria.

"I thought you were supposed to be on a diet," she said, eyeing his bulging abdomen. "Aren't you worried about passing the next physical?"

"Get off my damn case," Townsend growled. "I have enough trouble at home right now. I don't need another woman nagging at me."

They exited the building and headed for Rachel's Nissan Pathfinder in the parking lot. When they reached it, Townsend paused by the passenger door. "What did you say in there? You told them you saw me remove the gun from Brentwood's pocket, right?"

Rachel opened her mouth, then closed it. "I told them the truth, Jimmy," she said, speaking to him over the roof of the car. "If I did see you remove the gun, I don't remember it."

Townsend struck the hood of the car with his palm. Rachel flinched, clutching her purse to her chest. "You made me look like a liar," he yelled. "Isn't that what you're telling me? If you weren't going to support my story, why didn't you tell me before we got to court? We could have come up with something else."

"What? You mean make up a false statement?"

Townsend lowered himself into the car. Rachel reluctantly took her seat behind the wheel. "I didn't say that," he continued. "But we can't go into the courtroom with two different versions of the same event. Don't you know how the system works by now? If we waver even an inch, the defense will rip us to shreds and the perp will walk." The more he talked, the more agitated he became. Generally an easygoing person, he had become extremely tense in recent months. His wife had become pregnant again, with their fourth child, an event the couple had not planned. The pregnancy had been troubled from the onset, and Townsend had found himself responsible for the household chores. His eating habits were out of control and his weight was soaring. "I saved your life out there," he shouted. "How do you know that asshole wouldn't have shot you? He could have palmed that .22 I found, then blown your head off the second you tried to cuff him."

"I'm sorry, Jimmy," Rachel told him, forcing herself to remain calm. "Why get into a fight about it now? I've already testified. Brentwood might still be convicted on the weapons charge. The trial's not over yet."

"He better be convicted," the officer said, shaking a stubby finger at her. "No one pisses on a cop and gets away with it. People have to learn to respect authority, Rachel. If we don't demand respect out there, we'll end up in a body bag."

They both fell silent. Rachel steered the Pathfinder up the on ramp for the 101 freeway, then became stuck in a line of slow-moving traffic. Deciding to take the surface roads instead, she exited and began winding through the hills before dropping down to the valley where the city of Oak Grove was located.

Most of the businesses in Oak Grove had new facades, and a large shopping center had been erected on the outskirts of the city where another housing development was being constructed. Rachel preferred the older section of town, where there was still an abundance of trees and the storefronts had more character. Several large software companies had recently moved into the area, erecting a triangle of skyscrapers on the land where the fairgrounds had once stood.

Rachel made a right turn onto Main Street, driving past the Majestic Theater that could no longer compete with the new multiplex cinemas that had sprung up in recent years, the toy store with its navy blue awning, the Heritage Bank, constructed out of pink brick. The Crazy Horse Saloon, the oldest structure in Oak Grove, was now a health food store, but the new owners had not replaced the hand-painted sign that dangled precariously over the front door. Oak Grove had once been a thriving agricultural community, but most of the residents were now baby boomers. The only people driving tractors these days were the developers.

When Rachel turned down Townsend's street, a blond little girl riding a tricycle shot out in front of her car. She slammed on her brakes to keep from hitting her.

"Good Lord," Townsend said, reaching for the door handle, "that's Katy."

While he leapt out of the car to corral his daughter, Rachel pulled to the curb in front of his house, a modest one-story brick rancher with a large concrete porch. She waited as he chastised his daughter for riding in the street, then returned to the car window. "She could have been run over," Townsend said, worry etched on his face. "Some of the teenagers on this block drive like maniacs."

The earlier tension between them was replaced by concern. "Where's Lindsey?" Rachel asked.

"She's restricted to bed until the baby is born," he told her. "I'm going to have to hire someone to help with the kids, Rachel. I thought we could get by on our own, but obviously we can't." He ran his fingers through his hair. "This pregnancy has turned into a nightmare. I have no idea where I'm going to come up with the money to hire a babysitter."

Rachel said, "What about your mother?"

"She has severe arthritis," Townsend said. "She could never keep up with my girls."

"I'm sorry," Rachel said. "If I can help in any way, Jimmy, please let me know."

Katy ran over to the car and tugged on her father's sleeve. "Ride, Daddy—"

Townsend scooped her up in his arms, hoisting her over his head. "How's the most beautiful girl in the world? Did you miss me, huh? Have you been taking good care of Mommy?"

"Carry me, Daddy," the child said, giggling and clapping. "Please, please."

"Not until you promise you'll never go in the street again," her father told her. "You know the rules, Katy. Daddy loves you. He doesn't want anything bad to happen to you."

Rachel saw the look of joy spreading across Townsend's face as he placed his daughter on his shoulders. She wanted to confront him about the gun. The statement he had made in the car was suspiciously close to the story Brentwood had told. But seeing him with his little girl, she knew this was not the time. Townsend was a devoted father, a man who worked hard to support his wife and children. Unlike other officers in the department, he didn't live for the excitement of the job. His father was a retired FBI bureau chief. From what Jimmy had told her, the man had groomed his son from childhood to enter law enforcement. The FBI was extremely competitive, however, and a degree from a first-class university was mandatory. Jimmy had managed to get accepted to Yale, where the FBI did extensive recruiting, but the stress of being in such an intensive academic program had been more than he could handle. His true goal had been to become a teacher. Instead of dropping down to a lesser college and earning his teaching certificate, however, he had listened to his father and joined the police department under the assumption that once he made rank, the FBI would hire him. Townsend had never risen above patrolman, though, and from what Rachel could tell, he had long ago quit trying.

"Want to come inside?" he asked. "I can make you a sandwich. I have to make the kids lunch, anyway."

"I need sleep right now more than food," Rachel told him, smiling at the grinning child on his shoulders. "Tell Lindsey I said hello. Do you need a ride to work tonight?"

"No," Townsend said. "Since Lindsey can't get out of bed, I might as well start taking the car."

Why would Townsend plant evidence? Rachel asked herself as she put the Pathfinder in gear. Brentwood wasn't an ax murderer. He was a car salesman with an alcohol problem. Waving goodbye, she stepped on the gas and drove off.

chapter

FOUR

"Where the hell is everyone?" Sergeant Nick Miller barked from the front of the room, looking at his watch and seeing it was ten o'clock.

It was Thursday night, and Rachel had just reported for duty. After dropping Townsend off, she had gone home and slept until it was time to get up and prepare dinner for her children. Tracy and Joe slept at a neighbor's house during the hours Rachel was at work.

Most of the officers arrived at the station in their street clothes and changed into their uniforms in the locker room. Rachel used those extra minutes to visit with her children or catch a bit more sleep. Whereas the rest of the officers assigned to her watch tended to linger in the locker room, gossiping and trading jokes, she was generally the last one to arrive at the station, but the first person to take her seat in the folding chairs facing the large blackboard.

Rachel picked up one of the "hot sheets" stacked on a long oak table by the door. Produced daily, the sheets listed the license plates of stolen vehicles, outstanding suspects, and other stolen property the officers were to look out for during their watch.

Officers were still straggling into the room, most of them bleary-eyed and grumpy. Metal chairs rattled, gunbelts squeaked, people coughed and fidgeted. The smell of freshly brewed coffee drifted from a pot on the back table. Someone had brought in a box of donuts, and officers were shoving them in their mouths as they gulped down their coffee. It might be nighttime to the rest of the world, but to the people assembled in the squad room, it was the beginning of a long day.

A tall, good-looking officer flopped down in a metal chair next to Rachel. "Are you coming to the watch party we're having Saturday morning?" he asked.

Considered the best-looking officer in the department, Grant Cummings was in his early thirties and had never been married. His light brown hair was always shiny and clean. He wore it long on top, but shorn neatly around his ears and neck. The shock of hair that frequently tumbled onto his forehead had a pale blond streak from the sun.

Cummings possessed a unique kind of charisma, one that worked equally well on both women and men. His laugh was boisterous, his smile playful, his hazel eyes elongated and sexy. His body was powerful, but not overly developed like those of some of the other officers. He seldom lost his cool, and was considered one of the most competent field officers in the department. He had never made rank because he had never desired to—something the officers he worked with respected. Grant was a proverbial headbanger. He loved being a street cop: butting heads, kicking asses, hauling people to jail. He had no desire to spend his days preparing schedules and reviewing reports.

Rachel was immune to Grant's charms. She was well aware he had a girlfriend, a fellow officer on their shift named Carol Hitchcock. "No, thanks, I have to catch up on my sleep." She turned her attention back to the sheets, using her ballpoint pen to jot down some of the license plate numbers on the back of her hand.

"Come on," he said, nudging her with his elbow. "It's going to be fun. We're going to the beach. We'll party until it gets too hot, then crash on the sand and sleep. When we wake up, we'll have a great tan."

"I don't think so," Rachel said. She had heard disturbing stories about the parties each watch had several times per month.

The Oak Grove PD employed 220 field officers. Sixty officers were assigned to patrol during the two-to-ten-o'clock watch, but their number dropped down to forty on the graveyard shift. If nothing major occurred, the department's response time was outstanding and things ran smoothly. Like most police departments, Oak Grove tried to divert nonemergency calls such as thefts and stolen vehicles to either the respective detective bureaus or civilian employees trained specifically to handle such calls. The fewer reports the field officers had to write, the more coverage the people of Oak Grove had on the streets.

Unlike most of her fellow officers, Rachel actually enjoyed working nights. Not only did it work out well with her kids, but once the bars closed and the drunks made their way home, the rest of the shift generally passed uneventfully. Oak Grove was a bedroom community, made up of mostly middle- to lower-income families, a great deal of them first-time homeowners. Located near Simi Valley, Moorpark, Thousand Oaks, and Ventura, the city had developed around one innovative housing development. Like Mission Viejo in Orange County, Oak Grove was one of the premier developments of tract homes in the United States.

The city wasn't affluent enough to attract criminals from outside jurisdictions, not when Beverly Hills was only an hour or so away. Other than domestic disturbances, traffic accidents, robberies, and other theft-related offenses, the most troublesome problem in Oak Grove centered around independent drug labs, most of them employed in the business of producing methamphetamine. Drug manufacturers could rent a home in an unassuming neighborhood, set up their makeshift labs, and blend into the community without notice.

The city had a few heavy-duty street gangs, and drive-by shootings were not unheard of, but nothing compared to Los Angeles and the surrounding areas. The majority of problems they experienced in Oak Grove were basic teenage nonsense: kids congregating where they didn't belong, tossing beer bottles on people's property, playing their music too loud, urinating in public.

"Where's Townsend?" Rachel asked, not finding his face among the men.

"He called and said he would be late," Grant told her. "Lindsey's not doing so good."

"Settle down, animals," Sergeant Miller yelled from the front of the room. A large man, he had unruly black hair and a barrel-shaped body, with shoulders as broad as a linebacker's. Although he was constantly harping on his officers about presenting a neat appearance, the front of his uniform was stained, and he looked as if he hadn't visited a barber in months. Now that cigarettes had been banned from the station, he habitually chewed on toothpicks.

After he had called roll and completed the unit assignments, Miller reviewed what had occurred on the previous watch. "We have an armed robbery working on the north side of town," he told them. "The suspect is a Caucasian male in his late teens or early twenties, average build, reportedly driving a cobalt blue Camaro, unknown license plate. He hit the 7-Eleven at Hemphill and Wagner. The clerk said he was wearing a dark-colored ski mask and armed with what looked like a Tec 9. According to the clerk, the gun might possibly be a toy. If the guy's a legitimate psycho, let's try not to kill him if we can help it." He paused and looked out over the room. "Around 2100 hours, we had a Jeep Cherokee stolen from Hudson Street. The license number and VIN are on the hot sheet." He clapped his hands in dismissal. "That's it, people. Hit the streets."

When Rachel walked up to the board where the unit keys were kept, the sergeant grabbed her by the arm and pulled her aside. "How's it going, Simmons?" he said, spitting out a chewed-up toothpick. "Are you having any problems working alone?"

"I'm doing fine, sir," she answered, snatching the appropriate keys off the board and clipping them to her key ring so she wouldn't lose them. Miller made her nervous. He didn't believe women made good field officers, and he had recently given her a bad performance review.

"Good girl," the sergeant said, giving her a stiff smile. Rachel headed to the parking lot behind the station to locate her unit in the pool of police cars. She went through the customary checklist, making certain everything on the car was in working order and all the required equipment was on board. When she pulled out of the parking lot and headed to her assigned beat, she let out a sigh of relief.

Until three months ago, Rachel had worked a two-person unit. Because of recent cutbacks in the budget, the officers on the graveyard watch now had to go out alone so the department could cover the city with a smaller deployment of manpower.

Sergeant Miller might have thought that she wanted to work with a partner, but he was mistaken. She hated having to shoot the bull with someone all night. After a few hours you ran out of small talk. The worst, however, was finding herself on a dark side street fighting off a horny cop. Male officers working graveyards had a problem getting laid. Having a woman sitting next to them on a slow night was sometimes a temptation too strong to resist.

Reaching the perimeter of her assigned beat, Rachel turned down a side street and slowed her unit to a crawl. It was a strange feeling being out and about when the rest of the world was sleeping. She glanced at the houses lining the streets, noting that most of the windows were dark. Her eyes searched between the houses looking for prowlers, branches moving in the shrubbery, anything that might indicate trouble. When an officer worked days, there was some sense of normalcy. The streets were filled with people going about their daily business. There were no shifting shadows, no dark alleyways, no spooky empty buildings. On graveyards, it was cops and criminals, dopers and drinkers, juveniles out for a night of pranks or street gangs looking for revenge.

A high-pitched tone signal came out over the radio. Rachel snapped to attention, reaching over and turning the volume up so she could hear better. Whenever a hot call came in, the dispatcher used an emergency signal to get the officers' attention. The piercing tone never failed to make the hairs stand up on her arms.

"Station one, 2A2," the female voice said, calling Rachel's unit number. "We have a 211 that just occurred at the Stop N Go market on Baker and Elm. Suspect's a white male driving a cobalt blue Camaro, license plate Frank—Victor—Charley—345. Code three, 2A2." She let up on the microphone for a few moments to give the officers listening time to jot down the license plate. "3A3 respond for backup, code two."

"You got anyone closer?" Grant Cummings shouted into his radio. "I'm at least ten minutes away. I just cleared the station."

The dispatcher shopped for other available units, but found none closer. Rachel suspected Grant had lingered at the station trying to organize the watch party. Shift change was a hazardous time to have an armed robbery go down. The evening watch had a habit of sneaking into the station early, and it took time for the new watch to take position, so for at least twenty minutes much of the city was wide open. Crooks were smart these days. Many of Oak Grove's robberies occurred during shift change.

"All other units be on the lookout for the suspect's vehicle," the dispatcher continued. "Use extreme caution. Suspect is armed and dangerous. He's believed to be the same person who robbed the 7-Eleven on Wagner earlier this evening."

Rachel's heart was doing a tap dance inside her chest. If you believed what you saw on television, police officers responded to hot calls all the time. In fact, though, an individual officer's beat could remain quiet for days at a time, even in a city like L.A. Rachel had drawn her weapon only on one previous occasion, and she had never fired it other than at the pistol range.

After activating her lights and sirens, she stepped on the button on the floorboard and spoke into the microphone mounted near the visor. "Station one," she yelled over the roar of the siren, "do you have a direction of travel on the suspect's vehicle?" She was flying now, the needle on the speedometer hitting seventy, then eighty, inching its way up to ninety. The side streets were coming up in what seemed like seconds as she barreled down the divided parkway, praying that she didn't hit a pothole and end up rolling the car. She saw the stained-glass windows of St. Anthony's Episcopal Church at the end of the block, then the depressing gray structure that housed the Curtis Funeral Home. She turned her head to the right, then to the left, checking for cars about to pull into the intersections.

"No direction of travel, 2A2," the dispatcher advised. "The clerk copied down the plate while the vehicle was parked in front of the market. He didn't see which way the vehicle went when it left the parking lot following the robbery. The suspect vehicle was reported stolen in Moorpark earlier today."

Not only did Rachel have to keep an eagle eye out for cars pulling into the intersections, she had to keep her eyes peeled for a cobalt blue Camaro. At night, blue could resemble black. "Shit," she said, suddenly realizing that the black Firebird she had flown past a few moments before might very well be the suspect's vehicle. Her palms were perspiring on the steering wheel. The suspect was armed. If she tried to stop him without backup, she would be putting her life on the line. Should she turn around and go back on the chance that her suspicions were accurate, or should she continue to the store to protect the crime scene and see what other information the witnesses could provide?

Rather than take the time to make a U-turn, Rachel threw the gearshift in reverse and began speeding down the street. Spotting the Firebird turning down a side street, she shifted back to drive and punched the gas pedal, fishtailing around the corner. For five miles, the vehicle didn't stop. Her hands trembled on the steering wheel.

This was it.

It had to be the robbery suspect. If not, why didn't the man stop? "Station one, 2A2," she shouted into the microphone. The license plate was not the same, but it was close enough that the reporting party could have made a mistake. "I'm in pursuit of a black Firebird, license Union—Victor—Henry 239, southbound on . . ." Rachel didn't know where she was. Elm Street was a major thoroughfare, but she was not familiar with all the side streets. Where was the street sign? The markers were all obscured by tree branches.

"Unit in pursuit, advise your location ASAP," the police radio squawked.

Finally she saw it. "Campbell Road," she yelled. "We're in the 300 block now."

She managed to overtake the speeding car. Slowing her speed, she pulled up alongside the Firebird and pointed toward the curb.

Once the Firebird stopped, Rachel checked in with the radio, reporting her exact location and requesting a backup. The driver was male, but she had not been able to get a good look at his face. Getting out of her patrol car, she adjusted her nightstick on her hip and unfastened the strap holding her gun in place. Her mouth was dry. Her pulse was racing. If the man was the robbery suspect, he might begin firing the moment she stepped up to the window. She unholstered her gun, creeping along the side of the vehicle.

"Get out of the car," she demanded, flattening herself against the car door. "Put your hands over your head where I can see them. If you move, I'll blow your head off."

She saw the man's hands moving inside the car.

"Now," Rachel yelled, terrified he was going for a gun. "Get out of the damn car."

The door slowly opened and an older man stepped out. He had white hair and Rachel could see a hearing aid in his left ear. "Was I speeding, Officer?" he said. "This is my son's car. It sometimes gets away from me."

Rachel dropped her hands to her side. "We're looking for a robbery suspect driving a similar vehicle," she said. "I'm sorry I frightened you, sir."

"You're not going to give me a ticket?"

"No," she said, rushing back to her unit. "Just watch your speed in the future. I clocked you at almost seventy."

Rachel sped off, making a right turn onto Baker Street and flooring the Caprice. Six minutes later, she saw the red awning of the Stop N Go.

Skidding to a stop in front of the market, she jumped out of the car, leaving her lights flashing and her siren yelping. Several young people were loitering in front of the store. Fearful they might decide to swipe her unit for a joyride, she locked the doors and raced inside. "Can you give me a better description of the suspect?" she asked the clerk behind the counter.

"What do you mean?" said the clerk, a reed-thin man in his early twenties with crooked teeth, his hair styled in a crew cut. "This is my first night, lady. Can you believe it? My first night on the job and I get robbed."

"Was he wearing a ski mask?" Rachel asked. "Did you get a look at his face?" She looked around the store, hoping it had security cameras, but she saw none.

"Wasn't wearing no ski mask," the clerk said, popping a handful of peanuts into his mouth. "Looked Mexican to me, but hey, what do I know? His skin was light, but I still think he was Mexican. Dude was wearing a hair net like the gangbangers wear. Had this pretty cool-looking shooter, though. Oh, he also had what looked like a tattoo under his eye, one of those teardrop jobs."

"Which eye?"

"Right eye, I think," the clerk said, scratching his chin. "I'm not really sure, you know. Once the dude pointed his gun at me, I kind of put everything else out of my mind."

"Were the kids out front present when the robbery occurred?" Rachel asked. After hearing the clerk describe the tattoo, she knew the suspect was extremely dangerous. The teardrop tattoo was known to signify how many people a gangster had killed, or to designate how many years he had spent in prison. Some gangsters had teardrops running down both sides of their faces.

"Nah," the clerk said. "Them kids just showed up a few minutes ago. Wanted to buy beer without an ID, but I wouldn't let the little farts get away with it. They've been hanging around out there trying to snag someone to buy a six-pack for them."

Rachel realized that in all the excitement she had failed to advise the dispatcher that she had arrived on the scene. This was important for several reasons. If the station attempted to raise her on the radio and she failed to answer, they might assume she was in trouble and roll more units to assist her. The second reason was so the dispatcher could clock her response time. On priority calls, the department had only so many minutes to respond. She reached for her portable radio, but it wasn't in the carrying case attached to her Sam Brown.

Rushing back out to her car, she grabbed the door handle and then remembered that she had locked her unit. Not only were the red lights and sirens still activated, but the engine was running as well. When she peered inside and saw the keys dangling in the ignition, she wanted to pound her head against the glass. She saw her portable radio resting on the passenger seat. She had forgotten to put it in the carrying case when she had left the station.

"You're an idiot," she said, cursing herself as she kicked at the tires. What was she supposed to do now? She looked through the window into the market, and spotted the pay phone on the rear wall. The three boys standing in front began laughing and jeering at her. "I'd wipe that smile off my face," she hissed as she stomped past them. "If you don't, I'll haul all three of you to jail."

"You can't do that," one obnoxious-looking youth said, five earrings stuck through the skin in his upper lip. "You're just pissed 'cause you locked your keys in the car. We ain't done nothing wrong."

"Don't push me," Rachel said, yanking open the door to the market. "I'm having a bad night, okay? If you're not careful, I'll make certain you have a rotten night too."

When Rachel picked up the phone at the Stop N Go, she dialed 911 and was patched through to the dispatcher. After advising the woman she was safe and had arrived at the market, she gave her the updated description of the suspect to broadcast to the other units.

"Hold on," the dispatcher said, "Sergeant Miller wants to talk to you. He's in the radio room."

"No, wait," Rachel said frantically, wanting to avoid speaking to the sergeant until she figured out how to break into her unit. The siren was so loud, she was afraid Miller would hear it over the phone and want to know what was going on. "Grant isn't here yet . . . I mean, 3A3. Didn't you dispatch him for backup?"

"Yes," the dispatcher said. "He should be there any minute. I don't know what's taking him so long."

She heard the sergeant wheezing when he came on the line. After twenty years of smoking, Miller had developed asthma. "Okay, Simmons," he said brusquely, "this is your chance to prove yourself. This creep hit two markets tonight. I think at this point we can rule out the gun being a toy. What I want you to do is secure the crime scene for the robbery detail. Did he touch anything while he was in the store?"

"Hold on," Rachel said. "I asked the clerk for a better description of the suspect. I just gave it to the dispatcher to broadcast. I haven't gotten around to asking him anything else." She held the phone receiver to her chest and yelled at the clerk. "Did the suspect touch anything while he was in the store?"

"Yeah," the clerk said, his expression as lackluster as before. "He touched that phone. Before he robbed me, he made a phone call. I thought something was about to go down. That's why I wrote down his license plate number."

Her eyes expanded. "This phone?" she said, pointing to the receiver in her hand.

"There ain't no other phone in here," the clerk said, shrugging.

Oh, God, she thought. This was a bad dream. What was she going to tell the sergeant? She couldn't tell him she had more than likely obliterated the most valuable evidence in the case—the suspect's fingerprints at the scene of the crime. As she stared at the flashing lights on her unit through the glass, the piercing sound of the siren made her head throb. She felt her eyes dampen with tears.

When Grant Cummings squealed into the parking lot and stepped out of his unit, Rachel felt as if she had just seen Jesus.

"I'll call you right back," she told the sergeant. "Cummings just arrived. We might have something going on. I can't talk right now." Not giving him a chance to respond, she hung up the phone.

"Did you get statements from the kids out front?" Grant said, stepping up next to Rachel with a relaxed, confident look on his face.

"No," she said, seizing his arm. "You have to help me, Grant. I locked my keys in my car, along with my portable radio. I used this phone to call the station, and now the clerk tells me the suspect used this phone. What am I going to do? When the lab analyzes the fingerprints, they may find my prints on top of the suspect's. Miller will have me fired for incompetence."

Grant Cummings's chest swelled. "Don't worry. I'll take care of this." Grabbing the phone out of her hands, he removed a handkerchief from his pocket and wiped the receiver clean, turning his back so the clerk couldn't see what he was doing.

Rachel lunged at him, trying to grab the phone out of his hands. "No," she shouted. "What are you doing? The lab might still be able to lift a few of the suspect's prints."

He pushed her aside with one hand, then went on wiping the receiver.

"I didn't ask you to wipe the phone down," she said. "You've just destroyed evidence in a felony."

"No more print problems," he said, smiling at her. "The robbery detail will just assume the perp wore gloves or the clerk was mistaken when he said he used the phone. You're in the clear, Rach." He placed one hand across his waist and bowed. "Grant comes through again. Just call me your knight in shining armor."

Rachel turned around in a small circle. "If Miller finds out what we did, he'll fire me for sure," she cried.

"No one will find out," he said, catching her by the shoulders. "Calm down. This isn't a homicide. It's no big deal, okay? Things happen. When you work the street, sometimes you have to cover your ass."

"How are we going to get into my car?" she asked, her arms locked around her chest now. "If we don't do something quick, the engine's going to overheat."

Following Grant out of the market, Rachel watched as he opened the back door to his own unit, flipped open his briefcase and pulled out a small leather case that resembled the ones used to carry manicure tools. Inside was a set of lock picks. Inserting one into the locking mechanism of the Caprice, he jiggled it, then moved on to the next pick. Within five minutes, he had the door unlocked. He reached inside and flipped the toggle switch, killing the lights and siren.

The color began to return to her face. With a hand pressed to her chest, she said, "You don't know what this means to me, Grant. You probably think I'm an idiot. I didn't get enough sleep this week. I swear, nothing like this will ever happen again."

"Listen," he said, "we all have off days now and then. No one got hurt." He positioned himself behind her and massaged her shoulders, his strong fingers digging into the taut muscles between her shoulder blades. "You need to unwind, try not to take things so seriously. Now that I gave you a hand, you have to promise you'll come to the watch party. How can you be a member of the team when you never come to our parties?"

"I-I really can't," Rachel stammered. Even though his hands felt good, she didn't feel right having Grant touch her. Out of the corner of her eye, she saw the clerk watching them through the glass. "I feel awful about what happened," she said, turning around to face him. "The DA will need the suspect's fingerprints to make the case, and because of my stupidity, you just erased them."

"So?" he said, tossing his hands in the air. "There's a million scumbags out there. If one gets off, what's the big deal? What makes you think we won't nail this guy, anyway? He'll ditch that car he stole, and we'll probably find his prints all over it."

Rachel sighed. Right or wrong, it was done.

"Meet me in back of the station at the end of the watch tomorrow night," Grant told her.

"Is Carol coming to the party?" she asked. Maybe the party would be fun if Grant's girlfriend were also there.

"No," Grant said. "She's leaving to visit her parents in Sacramento as soon as she gets off work tomorrow."

"You mean I'll be the only female at the party?" Rachel said. "I don't feel comfortable about this, Grant. Another time, okay?"

"Hey," he said, glowering at her, "do you think destroying evidence makes me feel comfortable? You don't want me to tell Sergeant Miller what happened out here, do you?"

Rachel shook her head.

Grant's face spread in a wide grin. "Then I guess you'll be coming to the party, right?"

"I guess so," Rachel said. After Grant sped off, she returned to the market to wait for the robbery detail.

An hour passed. Rachel was standing in the back of the market with Detective Tony Mancini, who was assigned to the department's homicide and robbery division. "Dust the phone for prints," he shouted to the criminologist. "The clerk says the perp made a phone call."

Mancini was a large, gruff man with ruddy skin and small watery eyes. His hair was wavy and thick, and he wore it several inches past his collar. He was wearing a tank top under his jacket, and his dense chest hair poked out from the edges of the shirt. When he wasn't on duty, he roared around town on a Harley-Davidson.

"This creep's responsible for six holdups," Mancini said, puffing on a skinny black cigar.

"How can you be certain it's the same man?" Rachel asked, waving the cigar smoke away.

"Same gun, same teardrop tattoo," Mancini said. "One of these days the clerk is going to resist, and our bandit is going to blow his head off." He flicked his ashes on the floor, a cynical grin on his face. "Robbers are idiots. They always make a mistake and get caught. What we need is a nasty little murder. Oak Grove is too quiet."

The detective had transferred to Oak Grove from the Los Angeles Police Department a year back, and from what Rachel had heard, he was already itching to return. "We have a pretty good description of the car," she said. "Don't you think we should be able to catch him?"

Mancini arched a bushy eyebrow. "He uses different wheels for every heist."

Rachel considered confessing her error. Even though she felt bad, though, she knew a confession would not put the suspect's prints back on the phone. Now that Mancini was on the scene, there was no reason for her to stay. "Keep me posted," she told the detective, heading to her unit in the parking lot.

By the time Rachel cleared the robbery call, it was after four in the morning. Jimmy Townsend called her over the radio and asked her to meet him at the Texaco station located on the border of their adjoining beats. When she arrived at the station, she saw Townsend's police car, but the officer was not inside. A few minutes later, she saw him exiting the men's room. "Did Atwater call you with the Brentwood verdict?" he asked, stepping up beside her.

"No," Rachel said. "I took the phone off the hook so I could sleep. I thought they had more witnesses to call, and the trial would run through tomorrow. What happened?"

"The bastard walked on the weapons charge," Townsend said, his voice crackling with tension. "Because of your testimony, all they were able to convict him on were two misdemeanor counts of drunk driving."

"That's too bad," Rachel said. A lone car pulled away from the pump. She looked over her shoulder at the attendant in the glass booth. Since they were parked near the rear of the station, it was dark, and the way Jimmy was looking at her made her feel uncomfortable.

"What else did you tell Atwater?"

"I don't know what you mean." Rachel was reaching for the door to her unit when Townsend suddenly lunged at her and shoved her against the side of the car.

"Atwater thinks I planted the gun on Brentwood," he snarled, his breath hot and foul. "What are you trying to do to me, woman? Do you want me to lose my shield?"

"I didn't say you planted the gun," Rachel said, cowering in fear. "I swear, Jimmy. I just told him I didn't see you remove it from Brentwood's pocket."

"You're in cahoots with Atwater," Townsend shouted, his fleshy jowls shaking like an angry dog. "That's why the asshole sent you flowers, so you'd rat me out."

"You're wrong," Rachel insisted. "The flowers had nothing to do with you, Jimmy."

Townsend stared at her, his anger slowly dissipating. "I didn't mean to shove you," he said, his voice dropping to a more reasonable level. "I just don't like DA's calling my house and suggesting I've done something illegal. Things are tough right now. I don't need any more stress in my life."

"And I do?" Rachel gave him a sour look, then climbed into her car and sped off.

chapter

FIVE

"Tracy," Rachel called to her daughter, "get your brother up while I make a pot of coffee."

It was Friday night and Rachel was in the kitchen of her home in Oak Grove. Even though the house was small, the kitchen was fairly spacious, with enough room for a good-sized table and four chairs. The cigarette burns on the white formica counter left over from earlier tenants didn't bother her, but the linoleum floor was buckled and Rachel hoped she could replace it one day. The kitchen was one of her favorite rooms, so she had tried to make it cheerful, putting up fluffy new curtains and painting the walls emerald green. The front of the refrigerator was covered with animal-shaped magnets, and dozens of receipts and snapshots were held in place on the outer door. Rachel kept a bowl of fresh fruit in the center of the butcher-block table.

The clock read a few minutes past eight, and Rachel was preparing to go to work. "Make sure Joe goes to the bathroom," she told Tracy. "I don't want him wetting his sleeping bag again."

Slumping against the counter, Rachel stared blankly out the kitchen window into the darkness. She had already forgotten what it was she was about to do. She was tired, bone tired. Every muscle in her body ached. How many hours had she slept in the past week? She couldn't remember, but she knew it wasn't enough to keep her mind alert. Appearing in court on Thursday had taken its toll, and then the confrontation with Townsend and the mess she had made of the robbery scene had caused her to lose even more sleep.

Regardless of what Townsend thought, it was more than Rachel's testimony that had caused the weapons charge to sink on the Brentwood case. She had called Mike Atwater when she got off work that morning, and the attorney had filled her in on what had happened during the remainder of the trial. Brentwood's attorney had contacted every gun dealer in Ventura County and could locate no records of his client ever purchasing a firearm. The defense had also hired a firearms expert, who testified that the .22 pistol had been modified on the street. It was well known that some officers carried throwaway guns, weapons they plucked off criminals and failed to turn in at the end of their watch. In most instances, a throwaway piece was kept inside an officer's boot, or strapped to his ankle with masking tape. Because of the officers' need to conceal them, these guns were generally .22's, like the one Townsend claimed he had removed from Brentwood's pocket.

"Joe's already up," Tracy said, walking over to her mother. Seeing Rachel in her bathrobe, she said, "Aren't you going to run tonight?"

"Too tired," Rachel mumbled. Her nightly runs had become a ritual since her husband's death. When she ran, she could organize her thoughts, rid herself of some of the stress she was under. The extra job and the day's sleep she had sacrificed to go to court on Thursday had drained her energy. Tonight she could barely walk, let alone run. She pulled out a rubber pitcher from under the sink and set about watering her plants. She touched the brownish leaves of a large fern, plucking them gently and tossing them in the trash can.

"Why don't you let me water the plants?" Tracy said. Dressed in a sweatshirt and a pair of loose-fitting jeans, the girl wore her hair layered on top, with long, uneven strands that dangled onto her forehead and cheeks. In the ravages of puberty, she had chopped off her waist-length hair when blemishes began to appear on her forehead, creating a trendy hairstyle she had designed herself to hide her skin problems. Even though Rachel thought the style was cute, the jagged strands were always in her daughter's eyes, and she wondered how she could see to do her schoolwork.

"I enjoy tending my plants," Rachel said, pouring a few drops of water into each of the small pots lined up on the ledge above the sink.

Once her mother put the pitcher away, Tracy said, "Finish getting ready for work, Mom. I'll make the coffee for you. As soon as it's ready, I'll bring it to you in the bathroom." She elbowed her mother away from the sink, then began filling the coffee pot. "Take a cold shower, okay?" She stopped and scowled, glancing at her mother's face. "You don't even look human tonight. You look like something somebody dug up."

"Thanks a lot," Rachel said, giving her a lopsided grin. "You know what they call the officers like me who work graveyards and don't rotate to other shifts?"

"Stupid," Tracy said.

"Permanent ghouls."

"Cute," her daughter said without smiling. "You have to quit the job at State Farm."

"I can't afford to do that just yet," Rachel told her. She pulled on the sash of her terrycloth robe. The State Farm job had been a godsend. If she could hang in for just a few more months, she would finally have all the medical bills paid off. She'd been dodging bill collectors for three years now.

"But it's killing you, Mom," Tracy cried, tossing the dishtowel onto the counter. "No one can work that many hours a week. What if you fall asleep at the wheel of your police car and get killed? What will Joe and I do?"

"Doctors work long hours and manage to survive," Rachel argued, carrying a few plates from the kitchen table to the sink. "I don't stay awake the entire time, anyway. After I make certain the building is secure, I generally catnap for the rest of the shift."

"There's no bed in that building," Tracy continued. "You have to sleep on the floor. Didn't you tell me they turn off the air conditioner at night, and it gets so hot inside that you can barely breathe?"

"It's not that bad," she lied, the memory of those long miserable nights far from pleasant. It wasn't only the lack of sleep, or the spookiness of being in a fifteen-story building alone all night. There were simply too many empty hours to think, to mourn, to indulge in self-pity. "State Farm pays more per hour than the PD," she said, "and I don't have to do anything but sit there. Besides, it's not forever. Once the bills are caught up, I'm going to quit."

At five-four, Rachel was a few inches taller than her daughter. Tracy had her mother's straight, regal nose, the pouty mouth, the high cheekbones. Rachel's face was oval, though. Tracy had a square jaw inherited from her father, along with his chestnut hair. Other than their appearance, mother and daughter had little in common. Rachel was an optimist, Tracy a pessimist. Rachel sometimes did things that were irrational, her decisions based on emotion rather than reason. Tracy's emotions were carefully contained, her actions calculated rather than impulsive.

Since they had moved, the girl had taken on a toughness that sometimes caused her mother concern. The neighborhood they lived in wasn't the best. Some of Tracy's friends were street urchins with little or no parental supervision. They were already chasing boys, experimenting with drugs, wearing makeup, using foul language. Rachel knew her daughter was a prime candidate for rebellion. Even though she seldom showed it, the teenager harbored a great deal of bitterness. She was angry that her father had died and left them to survive on such meager resources. While her friends worried about what they were going to buy in the mall, which movie they were going to see, or which boy they wanted to flirt with, Tracy's concerns centered on what she was going to cook for dinner, or how she could keep her three-year-old brother entertained long enough to finish her homework.

Pulling her daughter into her arms, Rachel stroked the long strands of hair back from her face. "I don't know what I'd do without you," she said. "It's not always going to be this way. I promise, honey. One of these days we're going to look back at all this and laugh." She inhaled the clean scent of the girl's shampoo. "Is your homework done? Is your lunch packed for school tomorrow?"

"Tomorrow's Saturday," Tracy said, her concern deepening. If her mother didn't even know what day of the week it was, how could she do her job? She reached out and touched her hand, tracing the blue veins with her fingers. Her skin was so pale, it was almost translucent. "If you don't hurry," she said, "you're going to be late."

Rachel rushed down the hall to jump in the shower. The house had two bathrooms, one located off the master bedroom and one located adjacent to the children's room, but neither of them had tubs, only shower stalls. The fixtures were brown and the master bathroom had no windows. Rachel had redone the floors with peel-and-stick tile that created the illusion of a marble floor. She hung her robe on a hook on the back of the door, then wiped the water spots off the mirrored cabinet with the edge of a towel. The room was painted, not tiled, and she grimaced at the mildew stains on the ceiling.

A few moments later, Tracy opened the shower door and handed her a cup of coffee in a ceramic mug. "Don't drop it," she cautioned. "If you do, you'll cut your foot. I was going to give you a paper cup, but we're all out. I'll pick some up when I go to the store tomorrow with Lucy."

"Stop mothering me," Rachel said, taking a quick sip of the coffee. "I'm a cop, damn it. Sometimes you treat me like I'm ten years old."

"Don't use profanity," Tracy said. "You're picking it up at work. Every time I say a bad word, you jump all over me."

Rachel handed her daughter back the coffee mug and stepped out of the shower, wrapping herself in a towel. Tracy was right. She had never used bad language before, but it was hard not to mimic what she heard every day. "I know what this is all about now," she said, a light coming on in her head. "You're setting me up for the pitch again, right?"

"Wh-what?" Tracy stepped back a few feet.

"You're not staying here alone all night," Rachel said, "no matter how mature you act or how many favors you do for me." She picked up a comb and ran it through her hair, then twisted the wet strands into a tight bun at the base of her neck. Her hair always looked neat when she left the house, but by the time it dried, the natural curl took hold. Wiry strands would trickle down her neck, her forehead, around her ears. "A dozen things could go wrong," she continued, finding her daughter's eyes in the bathroom mirror. "The house could catch on fire. Someone could break in. Joe could get sick during the night. We've been all through this before, Tracy. You're not staying in the house alone. That's the end of it. I refuse to discuss it again."

Tracy kicked out at a mound of dirty towels on the floor. "If some crook breaks in at Lucy's, Mom, they'll trip right over our sleeping bags. She makes us sleep right by the front door."

Rachel arched an eyebrow. "Burglars seldom use the front door."

"I hate sleeping over there," Tracy said. "I feel like Lucy's dog or something. At least let us come home and get dressed for school in the mornings. There's six people in that house, and they only have one lousy bathroom. It's disgusting, Mom. Lucy makes Joe pee in the backyard."

"You made that up," she said. "Lucy would never do that. She's been wonderful to us. She lets you stay there every night and she's never taken so much as a dime from me. How many people would do that, huh? You should show some gratitude, young lady. Right now we need all the help we can get."

Tracy gave her a look of defiance. After a few moments, though, she found herself chuckling. "How do you know these things, huh? It's the nuttiest thing. You always know when I'm lying."

"So, you did make it up?" Rachel said, heading to the bedroom to put on her uniform. "I knew Lucy would never make Joe go to the bathroom in the yard."

"Yeah," Tracy said, tossing her head. She followed her mother around as she removed a freshly cleaned uniform from the closet, then went to the bureau for her T-shirt, socks, and panties.

Most of her life Rachel had been thin, so much so that her breasts were almost nonexistent. Having purposely packed on an extra fifteen pounds during the past two years, she found the extra weight unsightly and cumbersome. Her breasts seemed like enormous blobs someone had glued to her chest. She picked up her bulletproof vest, which squashed her breasts inside like a pair of overripe grapefruits.

Tracy had to step lively to avoid a collision as her mother hurried to get dressed. Rachel's room contained a four-poster bed, a large bureau, a rocking chair, and several massive chests that had once been in the living room of their old house. Sometimes you had to turn sideways just to get from one side of the room to the other. In addition, her mother compulsively lifted weights, determined to bulk up her body. Dumbbells and barbells were strewn all over the floor. Tracy was tired of stubbing her toes on them.

Rachel stopped and stared at a rubber plant. "I think this guy needs a drink, too. Remind me to water it tomorrow."

Tracy went to the bathroom for a glass of water, walked over and tossed it at the rubber plant. "There," she said. "Now you have one less thing to worry about."

"You have to do it with love," Rachel scolded. "Plants know when you don't like them, Tracy."

"Right," her daughter said. She touched a shiny green leaf, thinking her mother's ideas about plants were crazy.

Their old house had been almost twice the size of this one. Tracy's father had inherited a houseful of furniture from his grandmother years before. The few valuable antiques had already been sold, and what remained were simply old, dilapidated relics. Her mother always talked about weeding out the clutter, yet she never did. Tracy knew her mother wanted to believe they would move back into a larger house one day.

"You should stop lifting weights," the girl said, watching as Rachel slipped her uniform shirt over the bulletproof vest. "You're beginning to look like a man, Mom."

Rachel smiled, flexing her biceps. "A little extra strength comes in handy when I end up with a nasty drunk on my hands."

"What happened with the guy who sent the roses?"

"Oh," she said, "trust me, nothing's going to come of it."

"Why not?" Tracy said. "I thought you liked him. When you got the flowers, that's all you talked about. How handsome he was, what a great body he had, how smart he was."

"He's out of my league," Rachel told her. "The flowers were just a payoff for the things I told him. Since his little plan didn't go off that well, I'll probably never hear from him again."

Leaning back against the bureau, Tracy chewed on a ragged cuticle. She had loved her mother's delicate body. Before she had become a police officer, she'd looked almost like a little girl, skinny and frail. Her neck was long, and she'd always held her head up and her shoulders thrust back. Recently her mother's shoulders had rounded, and her once graceful arms now hung at her sides like two heavy, braided ropes.

"I didn't make up how much I hate sleeping at Lucy's, Mom," she said. "Can't we please come home in time for me to get ready for school? I promise I won't disappoint you. By the time you get home from work, I'll have Joe fed and dressed for the day. Lucy just shoves him in a chair and hands him a box of Froot Loops. I'll make eggs for him. I'll give him hot oatmeal at least once a week."

"Okay," Rachel said, smiling warmly as she laced up her shoes. "You can come home to get dressed in the morning, but only after the sun comes up. This is just a trial period, Tracy. If anything goes wrong—"

"Cool," Tracy said, floating out of the room in a daze, as if she couldn't believe she had gotten what she wanted.

Once she was dressed, Rachel went to say goodbye to her son. "Hey, big boy," she said, "come and kiss Mommy goodbye." Hoisting the heavy three-year-old up in her arms, she kissed the curly hairs on the top of his head, then set him back down on the floor in a mess of building blocks. He had Rachel's gray eyes and strawberry-blond hair, a tiny dimple in his chin, and the short chubby legs of a toddler. His mother was generally able to squeeze in a few naps during the day, crashing on the sofa while Joe watched TV or played with his toys. Once Tracy got home from school, Rachel would finally stagger off to the bedroom, remaining there until she had to go to work. Because of her schedule, she was not able to give the child enough attention. Lately, he had started clinging to her every night when she tried to leave for work.

"Book," he said, thrusting a brightly colored book at her with a giraffe on the cover. "Read me, Mommy. You promised."

Rachel felt her chest constrict. "You know Mommy has to go to work right now, sweetie," she said. "I'll read it to you first thing in the morning, okay? We'll read your book. We'll watch cartoons together. I'll even take you to the park."

"Book," he said, grabbing her leg.

Rachel glanced at her watch, then squatted down on the floor beside him. After she had read three pages, she handed the book back to him. "I can't read the rest, Joe," she said, crushing him in her arms. "Be a big boy now, and let Mommy go to work."

Tears pooled in his eyes. "No," he said, fumbling with a button on the front of Rachel's uniform. Grabbing the book off the floor, he shoved it back in her face. "Please, Mommy. Read me a story."

Tracy was standing in the doorway, a tense look on her face. "Just leave," she snapped. "The longer you stay, the worse it's going to be. I'll read him the stupid book. He's tired. By the time you get to the station, he'll be sound asleep."

As the house had only two bedrooms, Tracy and her brother were forced to share a room. Grimacing at the toys scattered everywhere, the unmade twin beds, the clothes strewn on the floor, Rachel vowed to clean the room when she got home from work the next morning. Tracy helped with the housework, particularly the kitchen duties and laundry, but it wasn't right to leave all the chores for her. Even though she acted more mature than most girls her age, Rachel had to remind herself that her daughter was only fourteen and should not assume the full responsibilities of the household.

Giving Joe another kiss, Rachel stood to leave. "How do I look?" She trailed her fingers down the row of buttons on the front of her uniform, making certain they lined up perfectly with her belt buckle. Sergeant Miller was very picky about this type of thing, and she tried her best to keep her appearance and equipment in order. Her bulky Sam Brown was strapped around her waist, the holster empty. She kept her service revolver locked in the glove compartment of her car, refusing to bring a firearm into the house. "Is everything straight? My shoes aren't spotted, are they?"

"Here," Tracy said, grabbing one of Joe's T-shirts off the floor and dropping to her knees. She quickly wiped a few spots off her mother's shoes and then pushed herself back to her feet.

"Make sure you give Joe his vitamins in the morning," Rachel said. "Oh, and don't forget to take his Pooh bear to Lucy's. I don't want you coming back over here late at night."

"Please be careful, Mom," Tracy said, a glimmer of fear in her eyes. "Another police officer got killed in Los Angeles last night."

"That's why I didn't go to work for the LAPD," Rachel answered, walking over and kissing her daughter on the forehead. "You know nothing bad ever happens in Oak Grove, honey."

"There's always a first time," Tracy said, squatting down on the floor to read her brother his story.

chapter

SIX

Rachel arrived in the squad room a few minutes before ten, taking her seat while the rest of the officers were still in the locker room. Grant Cummings walked in a few moments later and sat down beside her. "I hear you and Townsend had a little spat last night."

"It was nothing," Rachel said, preferring not to discuss it.

"Ratso's got a whole case of beer iced down for the party. Meet us in back of the station at the end of the watch. You'll ride to the beach with me and Ratso."

Rachel glanced over at the officer they called Ratso. His real name was Frederick Ramone. No one besides Grant knew much about him. Prior to joining the department, Ramone had worked as a clerk in a convenience store. The department had been in a push to hire minorities, and Ratso suddenly found himself with a badge and a gun. Some people thought he was Italian because of his last name, even though the department listed him on the employment rolls as Hispanic. Grant insisted the man's ancestors were from India, explaining that Ratso had given himself the name Frederick Ramone after seeing it in a magazine. His skin was dark and his face narrow, his eyes the color of tobacco. Wherever he had come from, he had mastered the English language quite well. When he spoke, only a hint of an accent appeared.

Not everyone saw Ratso's meek demeanor as desirable, however. In a dangerous situation, he had choked. Facing a gun-wielding suspect, the swarthy officer had hesitated before pulling the trigger. Grant had taken the man out with a single shot, saving Ratso's life.

"I wish you wouldn't call Fred Ratso," Rachel said. "That's not very nice, Grant."

"Ah, shit," he said. "The guy loves it. Hey, Ratso," he called out, waving the man over. "Rach thinks I'm offending you by calling you Ratso. You're not offended, are you? You like it, don't you?"

"It's okay," Fred Ramone said, shrugging his slender shoulders. He looked down at the floor for a few moments, then returned to his seat.

Fred Ramone was a sad case. He wanted to fit in so desperately, he let people exploit him. Since the shooting incident, he had practically become Grant Cummings's slave, constantly doing his bidding, tolerating untold ridicule. Someone should stop it, but Rachel knew no one would. If you wanted to play with the big boys, her first training officer had told her, you had to keep your mouth shut and go along with the program. Fred Ramone had displayed weakness, a cardinal sin among police officers.

"Look, Grant," Rachel said. "I know I said I would come to the watch party, but I'm really tired. I think it would be better if I went home after work and tried to get some sleep."

"A deal is a deal," he said. "You're not going to go back on your word, I hope. I mean, I wouldn't want anyone to find out—"

"I'll go, okay?" she snapped. Now that Grant had something to hold over her, she knew how Ratso felt.

"I've got another damn bunion," he said, removing his boot and massaging his foot. When he dropped the boot on the linoleum floor, it made a loud thud, as if he had dropped a twenty-pound weight.

Rachel reached over and picked up Grant's boot, then scowled at him. "You've had steel loaded into the toes, haven't you?" she said, tossing it back on the floor in disgust. Boots and gloves with steel or lead loaded into the tips were outlawed by the department, but a few diehards like Grant got away with using them. It was a hard rule to enforce, unless the brass wanted to assign someone to inspect shoes and gloves at the beginning of every watch.

Rachel decided to switch seats. For some reason Grant had been all over her lately. He'd been trying to talk her into going to the watch parties for almost a year now. He bailed out of the dressing room early so he could sit next to her, knowing she was one of the first people to take her seat in the squad room. Everyone knew he was sleeping with Carol Hitchcock, a statuesque blonde seated on the far side of the room. The entire time Rachel had been talking to him, Carol had been glaring at them.

Because they were not allowed to date their fellow officers, Carol was forced to avoid Grant while they were on duty. While he exploited this situation no end, flirting every chance he got, his antics infuriated Carol. Rachel wasn't crazy about the woman, but in the mostly male world of cops, she felt the females should stick together. In addition, Carol Hitchcock had more time on the job than Rachel. The stone-faced woman had been a cop for over ten years, whereas Rachel was little more than a rookie. When Rachel wanted advice, or found herself in over her head, Carol was the first person she turned to.

Rachel stepped up behind her chair and placed a hand on her shoulder. "Want to go for breakfast with me tonight?"

"Maybe," Carol said, somewhat aloof. "What time were you thinking of?"

"You know," Rachel continued, "around four when things die down."

"Tell the dispatcher before we hit the streets," she answered. "If we don't get on the list, we won't get a break until five o'clock."

Carol Hitchcock stood just under six feet. Her height, her white-blonde hair, and her copper-colored skin made her quite striking. Her features were broad, though, and her bone structure heavy. Like Rachel, she seldom wore makeup, other than a smidgen of lipstick. She wore her pale blonde hair in a stringy-looking ponytail at the top of her head, even though she had been warned repeatedly by the brass that such a hairstyle could be dangerous. A suspect could grab her ponytail from behind and drag her to the ground. Carol said she didn't care, that by the time the perp got her to the ground, she'd have her service revolver out and blow his head off.

On her way out of the station, Rachel passed Captain Edgar Madison's office and paused in the doorway. Having grown up in Detroit, Madison was a black man with a chiseled face and large plum-colored eyes. When he smiled, his lip curled up and the pink of his gums was exposed. If an officer made a mistake or stepped over the line, they knew to expect a call from Madison within a matter of hours. Rules were his stock in trade. Laws were sealed in granite. Chief Bates used him as the department's executioner. The role fit Madison so perfectly, someone had once left a black hood on his desk. Being an African-American, Madison did not find hoods of any color humorous. He'd tracked down the culprit and suspended him for three weeks without pay.

"I'm sorry to bother you, Captain," Rachel said, "but if you have a moment—"

"Come in," Madison said, looking up from his paperwork. "I was just looking over one of your reports. You seem to be getting the hang of this, Simmons. The work you did on this rape case is outstanding."

Rachel stepped inside his office. "Really?" she said, flushing with pride. Although many of the officers found Madison intimidating, he was one of Rachel's favorite supervisors. He always seemed to have a word of praise, and his straightforward approach to police work reminded her of Sergeant Larry Dean. She wanted to tell him about the problem she had encountered with Jimmy Townsend the night before, along with the particulars of the Brentwood case. Just as she was about to begin speaking, however, Grant walked past the door on his way to the parking lot. "Do you know if our insurance covers a dermatologist?" she improvised. "My daughter's developed a problem with acne."

"Our group policy doesn't cover that type of treatment," he said. "It covers skin cancer, of course."

"I see," Rachel said. She shifted awkwardly, uncertain how to proceed.

"Is there anything else, Simmons?" Madison asked, wondering why the woman had bothered him with such a trivial request.

"No," Rachel said. How could she speak out against a fellow officer? Townsend might have shoved her, but he had at least made an attempt to apologize. When people were under pressure, they occasionally stepped out of character. With the problems Townsend was experiencing at home, she didn't feel right jeopardizing his job. "I'd better head out to the field, sir."

After she checked out her unit and pulled out onto the street, she blinked her headlights at one of the other units. Chris Lowenberg pulled up alongside her car to see what she wanted. A dark-haired officer in his mid-twenties, Lowenberg already had a wife and three young kids to support. Like Rachel, he supplemented his income by working at State Farm.

"Did you pick up our checks from State Farm?" she asked. "My bank account is seriously depleted."

"Yeah," he said, plucking an envelope off his dashboard and tossing it at her through the open window. "Look, I hate to tell you this, Rach, but we both got pink slips from the insurance job."

"What do you mean?" Rachel said. "What happened?"

"They decided to hire their own security guards, so I guess we can kiss that gravy train goodbye."

The news was devastating, but it wasn't Chris's fault. "Thanks for telling me, Chris," she said, gunning the engine and driving off. It would all work out, she told herself. She would find another job, maybe one that paid more money. Even at the end of his life, her husband had been a positive person. Nothing could be accomplished by dwelling on the negative, he had always said. Change was part of life.

Because there was a lot of activity in the field, the dispatcher could not afford to have both Carol Hitchcock and Rachel out of service at the same time for their prearranged meal break. Instead, they met at McDonald's for a quick cup of coffee, taking their portable radios inside the restaurant with them.

"Grant said you were going to visit your parents this morning after work," Rachel said. "He wants me to go to the watch party. If you were going, Carol, I wouldn't mind. I don't want to be the only female there."

"I go to all the parties," the woman said. "Maybe if you came to some of them, Rachel, you would get to know the men better. We have a lot of fun. People act different when they're out of uniform."

"You've never had a problem, then?" Rachel had heard stories about men commandeering vehicles just so they could go for a ride in a Mercedes, shooting off tracer rounds at the beach.

"Of course not," Carol said, taking a quick gulp of her coffee. "You'll have a great time. Just stay away from Grant," she added, only half-jokingly.

"What's happening with you two?" Rachel asked. "Are you going to get married?"

Carol fell silent. She had been thinking about it a lot lately. Her biological clock was ticking. She was several years older than Grant. She had begged him to marry her because she was desperate to have a child.

All her sisters had large families. The situation with Grant was far from perfect, however. There were many complexities, many areas of their relationship they had yet to sort out. She had to work with what she had, though. Even though Grant had forbidden her to tell anyone at work, they were planning to get married in the fall. "We're not living together," she said, "but we don't date other people. Why are you asking me these things? Is it because you're interested in Grant?"

"No," Rachel said. "I was just curious. I know you've been dating Grant for a number of years. Chris Lowenberg thinks you guys are secretly married."

Hearing something on the radio, Carol turned the volume up. "There's a pursuit going on," she said, sliding out of the booth. "We better get back on the streets before the dispatcher starts looking for us."

Chris Lowenberg entered the squad room at 4:40 and collapsed in a chair at the oak table where Rachel was working on her reports. "Tired?" she asked, seeing the officer stifle a yawn.

"Yeah," he said. "Losing the second job is a blessing in some ways. At least till the bills pile up again." He removed some notes from his briefcase. "I hear Grant arrested the robbery suspect from last night."

Rachel had already heard. "He tried to rob another convenience store on the west side of town," she said. "Grant stopped him five blocks from the store."

"That lucky son of a bitch," he answered, making a smacking noise with his mouth. "I would have loved to pop this jerk for two holdups. I haven't made a felony bust all month. My stats are way too low."

"I'm sure they're not as low as mine, Chris," Rachel said. "But other aspects of our job are also important, don't you think?"

"Not to the brass," Lowenberg said. "I gotta talk to the sarge. See you later."

Rachel's watch read five o'clock. Her shift ended at six. They called this the witching hour. Her mouth was parched, her breath tasted like rotten eggs. How many cups of coffee had she consumed during the night? Her stomach was gurgling and popping with acid. She had to go to the bathroom, but her legs were like dead weights, and she was too tired to get up and walk down the hall.

Ted Harriman walked in a short time later, dropping his briefcase on the table with a thud. An African-American, Harriman was a former sergeant in the Marine Corps who had spent his childhood in Georgia. He shaved his head, and his eyes bulged in their sockets. Over his lip was a neatly trimmed mustache. When he spoke, his voice resembled the smooth, clear notes of a saxophone. "Did you hear about the big bust tonight?"

"You mean the convenience store robber Grant apprehended?"

Harriman gave her a sour look. "Grant got credit for the arrest," he said. "But I'm the one who chased the guy down."

Rachel dropped her pencil on the table. "How did that happen? Carol and I heard the pursuit, but we thought it was Grant who was chasing him."

"You tell me," Harriman said, stroking his mustache. "I was driving past the market when the call came in on the robbery. I pursued the perp for about three miles. Grant heard me go into pursuit over the radio. I was about to initiate the stop when he screamed past me at about a hundred miles per hour, then forced the suspect's car off the road. I almost slammed into the back of his unit. He cut right in front of me."

"But you initiated the pursuit?"

"Doesn't matter," he said, running his tongue over his lower lip. "That arrest would have looked mighty fine in my jacket."

"Did you tell Nick Miller what happened?"

"Waste of time," Harriman said, picking his briefcase back up off the table. "Take it easy, pretty lady."

Rachel smiled. "Are you going to the beach party?"

"Grant's blowout?" he said, scowling. "They got their thing, you see, and I got mine. Cummings and his crew can keep on walking. I've got no use for their kind."

Rachel tried to finish diagramming the accident, but even with her ruler, her lines were wavy, and she kept having to erase them and start over. In frustration, she pulled the pins out of her hair and ran her fingers through it. When she consumed too much caffeine, her scalp itched and tingled.

Hearing footsteps, she looked up as Grant and Ratso entered the squad room. "You missed all the excitement," Grant said. "Did you hear I caught the robbery suspect?"

"Yes," she said.

"Finish that up," Grant said, soaring on the adrenaline of his felony arrest. "We want to take off for the beach on time." He slapped Ratso on the back. "We've got some celebrating to do, isn't that right, Ratso?"

"Grant, I—" Rachel was in no mood to go to their stupid party. The more she thought about it, the more annoyed she became that Grant was coercing her by holding the incident at the Stop N Go over her head. How could he be so childish? Why did he even care if she came?

"Don't even say it," Grant said, popping his knuckles. "You owe me, Rachel. If I hadn't caught the convenience store bandit with the gun and the bag of loot still on him, the DA would never have been able to convict him. The guy almost shot me. I'm just lucky I was able to disarm him."

"Fine," Rachel snapped, angry that he was bringing the subject up in front of Ratso. "As soon as I finish up here, I'll change and meet you in back of the station."

chapter

SEVEN

The morning sun seemed like an insult after a night with no sleep. Walking out the back door of the station, Rachel shielded her eyes with one hand while digging in her purse for her sunglasses. She had to call Lucy and tell her she wouldn't be home at her regular time, but it was still too early. Since Oak Grove was a good twenty miles from the beach, she decided to stop at a pay phone on the ride over. She kept a set of street clothes in her locker in case she had to run errands after work, and had changed into a pair of jeans and a black T-shirt bearing the police academy logo.

She spotted Grant's older BMW pulling into the secured lot where the police units were parked. Ratso was already installed in the back seat, his arm draped over a large blue cooler. Grant had purchased the BMW from a police auction in Los Angeles and had rebuilt the engine himself. He loved vintage cars and spent his free time constructing miniature models. He stuck his head out the window and waved. She walked over and climbed into the front seat.

"Maybe I should take my own car," she told him. "I've got kids at home, Grant. I might not want to stay as long as you and Ratso."

"You're hurting Ratso's feelings, Rachel," he said, already pulling out into the intersection. "You can always catch a ride home with someone else. You don't want Ratso to think you don't want to ride with him, do you? He's a sensitive fellow."

Ratso leaned forward from the back seat. His short-sleeved shirt showed sinewy arms. Grant locked eyes with him in the rearview mirror. "I've seen eight-year-old boys with arms bigger than yours. You've got to scarf up some hamburgers, boy, put some meat on your bones."

"I don't eat meat," Ratso said, thrusting his chin forward.

"Oh, really?" Grant said, cackling. "I swear I saw you gobbling up some cockroaches the other day. Maybe you should go to the grocery store now and then instead of eating whatever scurries out from under the kitchen cabinet."

"Stop it, Grant," Rachel said, turning to look at Ratso in the back seat. The man was just sitting there, a blank expression on his face. If Grant's comments were meant to be funny, Ratso didn't understand the humor. His back was straight, his hands folded neatly in his lap, his head tilted slightly forward as if he were praying. "Tell him to stop ridiculing you, Ratso. Stand up for yourself. Don't let him talk to you this way."

"You want me to leave you alone?" Grant said, a cruel tone to his voice. "Come on, buddy, say it." He slammed on the brakes, craning his neck around to the back seat. "You can get out right here if that's what you want."

The opaque, disconnected look in Ratso's eyes was replaced with a fleeting burst of anger. Rachel watched his chest expand and contract, hoping he was about to lash out at Grant and put him in his place. A corner of his lip quivered and he slowly shook his head, then turned to stare out the window.

"See," Grant said, "you need to mind your own business, Rach. Ratso and I are friends. He's the only guy I'll let wash my car."

"You make him wash your car?" Rachel said, incredulous.

"Why not?" he said. "They had a car wash at that place where he used to work. He's pretty good, to tell you the truth. Never once scratched my paint job."

After telling Grant she needed to stop at a pay phone to call Lucy, Rachel leaned back in the seat and shut her eyes, letting the brisk morning air drift across her face from the open window. Even though they were well into spring, evenings and early mornings were still chilly. Goose bumps popped out on her arms, and she rubbed them to take the chill away.

She was in a deep sleep when Grant nudged her twenty minutes later. He was steering the car into a service station directly across from the beach. "We're going to get some more ice," he said. "There's a pay phone right over there. If you need to use the john," he added, "now is the time to do it. We're going to Seaside Park, but we don't use the main beach, so it's a long walk to the public johns."

Rachel put a quarter into the pay phone. Lucy Folger and her family had moved into the neighborhood only a short time after Rachel, and the two women had quickly struck up a friendship. When Lucy was diagnosed with breast cancer, her husband had flipped out and the couple had separated. At the time, Rachel had just quit her job at Robinson's and was preparing to enter the police academy. Knowing her friend needed her, she stalled the department for over two months so she could care for Lucy and her four children while the woman underwent treatment. Her friend was cancer-free now and had recently reconciled with her husband. "Did I wake you?" she asked when Lucy answered the phone.

"Are you crazy?" Lucy answered, laughing. "Billy's been up since five o'clock. He decided to make himself pancakes and bacon. Little snot almost burned the house down. The kitchen ceiling is black now. I guess we can call it contemporary decor. It looks like a ceiling in a nightclub. What's going on? Are you still at the station?"

"No," she said. "Some of the guys twisted my arm and talked me into going to the watch party. I should be home before noon. I just wanted to let you know that it's okay to let Tracy and Joe go back to the house. Tell Tracy I'll see her there, okay?"

"No problem."

Rachel hung up, used the ladies room, and then walked back to the BMW. Grant and Ratso were waiting, the extra ice already deposited in the ice chest.

After driving south a few more miles on the Pacific Coast Highway, Grant steered the BMW into the public parking lot for Seaside Beach Park. Several of the men had already arrived and were slugging down beers in the parking lot. Most of them were wearing shorts and had already removed their shirts, leaning back against their cars as they soaked up the morning sun. It was the second week of May, and the temperature had gone from the mid-fifties of the night before to the high sixties. By noon it would probably be in the high seventies.

Rachel followed Grant and Ratso as they lugged the heavy cooler across the parking lot onto the sand, then continued down the beach to the secluded spot Grant had selected. "Do we have anything to eat?" she asked, her stomach growling as she trailed behind them. "I didn't have time to take a break last night."

"Want a Twinkie?" Jimmy Townsend said, stepping up behind her.

Rachel bristled, refusing to answer him. With the problems he was having at home, she had not expected Townsend to show up at the watch party.

"Hey," he continued, "you're not still mad at me, are you? You know, because I yelled at you the other day."

"You did more than yell at me," Rachel said in anger. "You shoved me. All I did was tell the truth. You acted as if I purposely sabotaged the case."

"I was just pissed that asshole got off on the weapons charge," Townsend told her. "Why don't we call a truce? I was out of line, Rachel. I'm trying to apologize."

Rachel turned around. She had never been one to stay angry. "Fine," she said, flashing him a quick smile. "You don't have anything more nourishing than a Twinkie, do you? My stomach feels like it's stuck to my backbone."

"Nick promised to bring hot dogs," he told her. "He isn't here yet, though. He probably stopped off at the store on the way over."

Rachel was surprised. She didn't know the sergeant attended the watch parties. She knew he was close with the troops, though, and not high enough on the ladder to be considered an outsider. Like all police departments, Oak Grove had its share of cliques. She wasn't familiar with the interior workings of the other watches, but Grant, Ratso, Hitchcock, Townsend, and Sergeant Miller hung together like glue. Even though Miller was a sergeant, Grant was clearly the leader.

"Who's watching the kids?" Rachel asked. "I thought you couldn't leave Lindsey alone during the daytime."

"I hired a nanny yesterday," Townsend told her. "The other night when I jumped on you, everything was caving in on me. Now that I've got someone to help with the kids, I don't have to worry about them so much."

By the time fifteen minutes had passed, twenty men had arrived and were laughing and chugging down beer as they trudged through the deep sand, forming a caravan behind Grant, Ratso, and Rachel.

The spot Grant had selected was lovely. Rachel found herself in an isolated cove with a small, sandy stretch of beach surrounded by tall cliffs. She walked over to the water's edge, noticing how shallow and clear the water was. Other than a few spots of tar, there was very little seaweed or other debris along the shoreline. In recent years, many of the California beaches had become so badly polluted that they were now closed to the public. Offshore drilling rigs were usually targeted as the culprits.

When she returned to where the men were gathered, Grant handed her an icy beer from the cooler. Even though she seldom consumed alcohol, she found the cold beverage refreshing. Her throat had been parched all night. Generally she stopped several times for sodas, but last night had been too hectic. She dropped down onto the blanket Grant had laid out and basked in the sun.

Jimmy Townsend spread out on a beach towel next to Rachel and lay down, his hairy belly spilling over the waistband of his shorts. "Do you remember that train accident last month?" he said, his hands behind his neck. "You know, where that fool decided to take a nap on the tracks."

"Vaguely," she said, sitting Indian style beside him. "I'm not sure I was working that night."

"It went down right before the end of our watch," Townsend continued. "Grant didn't want to write the report and get stuck working overtime. The property on the north side of the tracks falls under the sheriff's jurisdiction. When we got there, the victim was in a dozen pieces, most of them on our side of the tracks. Grant went around picking up the body parts in a plastic sack, then dumped them all on the other side of the tracks. The bastard managed to kiss the whole thing off to the SO." He laughed, his stomach jiggling. "Pretty shrewd, huh? Grant's the best at this stuff."

Rachel smiled, but she really didn't see the humor. She might have screwed up the robbery scene, but it wasn't something she'd done intentionally to get out of writing a report. She watched the waves crash onto the shore, inhaling the salty scent of the ocean. Grant had been right about one thing. She did need to relax more, get out more. Lucy was always harping on her, telling her she needed a new man in her life. Her relationship with her husband had been so complete, though, she was convinced nothing could ever come close to it.

She closed her eyes and pictured Joe. An earthy, outdoor type, Rachel's husband had been soft-spoken and gentle. Joe had seen her soul, listened to her darkest fears, kept her demons at bay. Before he became ill, they had spent their weekends backpacking high in the mountains in northern California. During the week, Joe would sit at his drafting board for hours, breaking only to eat and spend time with his wife and daughter. But there was an urgency about him, a sense of racing against time. Even before he had been diagnosed, her husband had somehow sensed his own mortality. The landscapes he designed were breathtakingly beautiful, as if he had already glimpsed the divine, and had been charged with the responsibility of leaving a model of this image behind for the benefit of mankind.

The raucous cry of a swooping gull startled her. Her eyes opened and she sat up abruptly. All around her were male cops. This was her world now. Rachel's day ended when most people's were just beginning. She was friendly with the female officers in the department, but they seldom had time to socialize outside of work. They were assigned to different watches, and like Rachel, many of the women had young children at home. Other than Lucy, she didn't have many close women friends.

Most cops had the same problem, Rachel decided, watching several officers frolic in the surf like silly teenagers. Law enforcement became a way of life, and one that could easily become all-consuming. Many police officers found it hard to talk about trivial things when they dealt with life-and-death situations on a daily basis. They could joke about picking up body parts, yet the ordinary events most people found intriguing or laughable, they saw as mundane and boring.

Being close to one another made sense. Not only did they have the job as a common denominator, but when you were up against the wall, these were the people you had to depend on.

Rachel saw Ratso sitting on the sand farther down the beach. Instead of removing his shirt like the other men, he was fully dressed and had his arms locked around his knees. She walked over and squatted down beside him. "Why are you sitting over here by yourself? Why don't you come over and talk to us? Isn't that the point of coming to a party?"

"I'm thinking," he said softly. "Sometimes it's better to think than talk."

"Are you upset about the things Grant said to you in the car?"

"No," he said, resting his chin on his knees. "I'm used to it. Words can't hurt me."

Rachel shook her head. "You don't have to take it, you know," she told him. "He's not going to stop until you say something. Why don't you talk to Sergeant Miller, tell him Grant is harassing you?"

"Things were bad for me before," Ratso said, his voice just above a whisper. "I was an outsider. The men didn't accept me. With Grant, things are different."

Rachel tilted her head. "That might be true," she said, "but don't you realize what you're sacrificing?"

"You mean my dignity," he said, looking out over the ocean.

"More or less," she said.

In reality Ratso was extremely intelligent, even though Grant and the other men didn't appear to recognize it. On the police exam he had scored one of the highest scores ever. He knew more about medicine and first aid than many of the other officers. If he came across an injured person, he could tell the paramedics what was wrong the second they arrived on the scene. His locker was crammed with library books on a multitude of subjects. Science, math, and philosophy, however, were not frequent subjects for discussion among the ranks. Rachel decided it was a strange life they led. The cost of living in southern California was high, particularly if you were trying to survive on a police officer's salary. Grant said Ratso lived in a hole-in-the-wall apartment with nothing but a bed and a refrigerator. He didn't even own a television. Unless an officer worked more than one job or his spouse also brought home a paycheck, most of their lifestyles fell below middle class. It was a bitter pill to swallow—risking your life for such a meager existence. Years before, police officers were held in high esteem by the community they served. Not so in today's world. Seldom did a shift go by that someone didn't flip Rachel the finger or shout some kind of insult. It wasn't hard to understand why many police officers became bitter.

Patting Ratso on the hand, Rachel returned to the spot where Grant was sitting. He handed her another beer, then whipped off his shirt and headed out for a quick dip in the frigid surf. She stared at the rippling muscles in his back, his strong legs. "Can I ask you something, Jimmy?" she said, turning to Townsend.

"Sure," he said, flopping over onto his stomach.

"Did you plant the gun on Brentwood? Please don't get angry at me for asking, but I'd really like to know what happened that night."

"No way," he exclaimed.

"Then why didn't I find it when I patted him down?"

"Did you grab his dick?"

Rachel blushed. "Of course not."

"That's why you missed it," Townsend said with a smirk. "Bastard had these slacks on with really deep pockets. The gun was right next to his package. I know you, Rach. I've seen you do patdowns on male suspects. You won't get anywhere near their groin area. An inch or two past their knee and you panic. You're afraid you're going to end up with something other than a gun in your hands." He laughed, cupping his hands over his genitals. "If you want to practice on me, I'll be glad to oblige you."

Rachel looked away, watching as Grant marched back across the sand. Her way of dealing with off-color remarks was to simply ignore them. Women officers who were prone to complain usually disappeared. "Brentwood just didn't seem like the type to carry a gun," she said thoughtfully. "I have no doubt the man's an alcoholic, but why would he pack a gun? And that firearms expert his attorney put on the stand thought that .22 was a Saturday night special. Brentwood makes a pretty good income, Jimmy. If he wanted a gun, why didn't he simply go to a gun store and buy one? Why would he buy an unregistered gun on the street? People don't usually do that unless they plan to use the gun in a crime. Brentwood's a drunk, not a criminal."

"How do I know?" Townsend said, trailing his fingers through the sand. "The guy sells used cars for a living. If I sold used cars, I'd probably pack a gun, too."

"You should go for a swim," Grant said, dropping down beside her on the blanket. "The water's great. I'm wide awake now. Makes you feel like a million bucks."

"I didn't bring my swimsuit," Rachel said. Looking past him, she saw that Nick Miller had finally arrived. He had brought along a small hibachi and placed it on top of a trash can. The smell of charcoal and roasting meat drifted past her nostrils. She sucked down almost the whole can of beer, then crushed the can in her fist. "I'm going for a dog," she said. "Want me to bring you one?"

"Yeah," Grant said, smearing suntan lotion on his chest. "Lots of mustard."

"Get me a couple," Jimmy Townsend said. "I don't care what you put on them."

"Your stomach looks like the Goodyear blimp," Grant said. "Don't you think you better cut back on the food, Jimmy boy? Belly fat can cause you to have a heart attack."

"Hey," Townsend said, glancing at the taut muscles in his friend's abdomen, "food is like sex for me. As long as you keep chasing women, pal, I'm going to eat."

Grant smirked. "Did your wife cut you off?"

"Nope," Townsend said, looking away, "her doctor cut me off. No sex until after the baby is born. This pregnancy hasn't been a heck of a lot of fun, let me tell you."

"Vasectomy time?" Grant asked.

Townsend felt like his genitals had just contracted inside his body. "Don't even say that word around my puppy dog, okay? He has a thing about knives."

"Tell you what," Grant continued. "Every time you feel like eating, go to the bathroom and whack off. You're about to explode, my friend. If you don't shed some of that blubber, you won't pass the physical this year."

Rachel had had enough of their banter. She kicked off her shoes and walked over to the hibachi, letting the warm sand drift between her toes. The sergeant was wearing a tank top, jeans, and a cowboy hat. From the look on his face, he was already well on his way to getting bombed. His eyes were heavy-lidded, his jaw slack. She wondered if he had started drinking even before he left the station.

"Well, look what the cat drug in," he said, wiping his hands on his jeans. "Since when did you start coming to these affairs?"

"It's kind of fun," she said, smiling. "I'm usually asleep by now, so I seldom get a chance to see the sun."

The sergeant pulled a slim flask from his back pocket. "Take a swig," he said, handing it to her. "It'll clear out the cobwebs."

Rachel tried to push the flask away politely, but the sergeant pushed it right back at her. "What's in there?" she asked, sniffing.

"Jack Daniel's," he said. "Guaranteed to make all your problems go away. Go on, take a swig. It'll be good for you."

She took a swallow, and the liquor burned its way down her throat. "Whew," she said, handing the flask back to him. "That's strong stuff. If I'm not careful, I'm going to get smashed."

"That's the whole point," he said, belching.

She gave him a chastising look. "I thought the point was to spend time with each other. You know, like the family everyone's always talking about."

"The family that plays together stays together," Miller said. "Didn't you ever get drunk with your husband? You know, go out dancing or something and tie one on?"

"Not really," Rachel said, painful memories flooding her mind. "Joe was too sick to go out dancing."

"The whole time you were married?" he asked, tilting his head.

"Sometimes it seems that way," she answered, moving her feet around in the sand. "He was diagnosed three years after we were married. The cancer went into remission for almost seven years, but he wasn't the same person. When it came back, it took him three years to die. Bad years, if you know what I mean."

The sergeant turned the hot dogs on the grill, using a stick he had found in the sand. "I thought if you made it five years, you were in the clear," he said, thinking of all the years he had smoked. "Isn't that what the doctors always say?"

Rachel sighed. "Don't believe everything you hear. My husband's dead, so I guess the five-year marker doesn't always apply."

A gunshot rang out, and both Rachel and Miller jumped. "Shit," he said, squinting off toward the surf. "Rogers is trying to shoot fish again. Tell him to knock it off," he shouted to one of the men closer to the water. "If he doesn't, I'm going to take his gun away and shove it up his idiotic asshole."

Alcohol and guns were a lethal mix, but Rachel knew better than to say anything. It wasn't her place to tell the sergeant he should make the men leave their guns in their cars.

She got the hot dogs loaded onto a paper plate, but when she started back to where Grant was waiting, they slid off the plate into the sand. "What a klutz," she said, turning back to get more. Coupled with her exhaustion, the booze was getting to her. Her vision was blurred, and she had a queasy sensation in the pit of her stomach. She had to eat something quick, or she'd get sick and make a fool of herself. By the time she returned to the spot where the sergeant had the hibachi set up, though, Miller had jogged off toward the water to make good on his threat to Larry Rogers.

Rachel lifted the lid of the cooler, thinking she would cook more hot dogs herself. Only a few empty wrappers remained inside. She started walking back to where Grant and Townsend were waiting, then suddenly sank to the ground on her knees. It was as if someone had stuffed her head full of cotton. She lost consciousness, tumbling face-first onto the sand.

chapter

EIGHT

The dream was intensely erotic. Rachel moaned in pleasure, moving her head from side to side. Joe's face was floating somewhere above her, back in the days when he was handsome and healthy. He had worn his hair long, grazing the top of his shoulders. When he made love to her, his hair would brush across her face and tickle her nose. "Just relax," a deep voice said.

The place between her legs was wet and throbbing. Her body felt hot, her skin on fire with passion. She inhaled Joe's aftershave, the smell of the sun on his skin. "I love you," she whispered, reaching up to run her hands through his hair. But instead of Joe's long hair, her fingers found short bristles above bare ears. Her eyes sprang open. When she saw Grant Cummings on top of her, her face twisted in fury. "What the—"

"Be still, baby," Grant said, placing his hand over her mouth.

His eyes were rimmed with red, his breath reeking of beer. Rachel could feel his erection poking at her through his clothing. She sank her teeth into the fleshy part of his hand, causing him to yelp in pain. "Get off me," she snarled, trying to push herself to a sitting position.

Her T-shirt was shoved up to her neck, along with her bra. Grant's other hand was crammed inside her jeans, his fingers probing her genitals. She seized his hand and yanked it out, twisting his wrist in the process. "If you don't let me up this second," she yelled, "I'm going to gouge your eyes out."

Grant laughed drunkenly. "Don't fight me, baby," he said, mashing his lips against her teeth. He reached down and fumbled with his zipper. "Come on, you know you want me. You've wanted me from the first day you saw me."

Out of the corner of her eye, Rachel saw Nick Miller watching them from a few feet away. He was leaning back against his cooler, blurry-eyed and intoxicated. His shorts were unzipped, and a corner of his T-shirt had come out. A cigarette dangled out of one side of his mouth. Other than Miller and Ratso, the other officers must have gone home.

Rachel brought her knee up and connected with Grant's groin. When he rolled off her, he pulled his knees up to his chest. "You're going to regret this, bitch."

"You perverted maniac," she shouted, springing to her feet. She kicked Grant in the side with her bare foot. He was holding onto his balls and groaning. "How could you do this to me?" she continued, quickly pulling her shirt down and zipping up her pants. "I wish I had your steel-toed boots right now. If I did, I'd kick what brains you have out the top of your head."

She started to march off, then became enraged when she saw the smirk on the sergeant's face. Storming over to him, she shouted, "You sat right there and watched him. You make me sick. How could you let him do that to me? This is a public beach. You're supposed to be a role model to these men. Instead, you're as disgusting and perverted as they are."

"Hey," he said, catching her arm in a steely grip, "be a sport, kid. You wanted to be a part of the team, didn't you? Well, this is the team. You finally passed the initiation test."

"I could report you, you know," she said, her body shaking. "I could get your stripes. Maybe I'll pay a visit to Internal Affairs and let them know what goes on at your nasty little parties."

His eyes narrowed, the muscles in his face locking into a scowl. "I wouldn't make threats if I were you," he said, removing the cigarette from his mouth and staring at it. Because of his asthma, he wasn't allowed to smoke anymore. Someone must have given him the cigarette, but he had never gotten around to lighting it. "I hear you made a righteous mess of that robbery two nights ago," he continued. "Grant told me you locked your keys in the car with the engine running. What kind of dumbass stunt was that, huh? You want to start running to Internal Affairs, Simmons, you better remember that two can play the same game."

All the blood drained from Rachel's face. Grant had promised to keep quiet about her stupid mistake if she came to the beach with him. She turned and stomped off toward the parking lot. A few moments later, the sergeant's words replayed in her mind. Initiation test. Didn't he say she had passed the initiation test? What did that mean? Had they all fondled her? She stopped and looked back at the drunken officers on the beach. Had they done more than fondle her? Had Grant or one of the other officers actually had sex with her?

What if she got pregnant?

Rachel didn't take birth control bills. She started jogging along the damp sand at the water's edge, tears streaming down her cheeks, wanting to put as much distance between herself and her fellow officers as she possibly could.

Rachel had been sitting on the curb in front of the Texaco station for over forty-five minutes, waiting for Lucy to come and pick her up. She had sand in her hair, her eyes, and her pants, and the abrasive grains were stuck to her back, itching like fire ants. She'd left her shoes on the beach, and the bottoms of her feet were blistered from the sun-baked asphalt. By the time she'd walked the three miles to the gas station in the afternoon sun, it was two o'clock. The reason her skin had felt so hot earlier was not passion. She'd sustained a severe sunburn from being in the sun so long without sunblock. She could still taste the putrid mix of Jack Daniel's and stale beer in her mouth. Entering the small convenience store attached to the gas station, she bought a package of Tylenol and a cold soda, then returned to wait on the curb.

In only eight hours' time, Rachel knew she would have to walk back into the squad room and face the same men. And Grant had gone back on his word and told the sergeant what had happened at the scene of the Stop N Go robbery. For all she knew, he had told everyone at the watch party. She could imagine them all gathered around, laughing and hooting as Grant told them how she had foolishly locked her keys in her unit. Had he told the sergeant about wiping down the phone as well? Had he changed the story and claimed she had done it?

Her stomach roiled as she thought of the leer on Grant's drunken face when she woke to find him on top of her. The gleam in his eye, the cruelty in his expression—she had seen that look before, that awful last day of her childhood, her last glimpse of the kidnapper before he drew the pillowcase over her head and threw her into the trunk of his car . . .

The car had bumped and rattled as it sped over the city streets. Rachel rolled to one side when it careened around a corner. A few moments later, the tires hit a large bump in the roadway, and she popped up in the air, striking her head on the trunk lid. Kicking and thrashing, she became so hysterical that she vomited. The pillowcase was suffocating her. She kept sucking the fabric into her mouth.

A few moments later, the vibrations beneath her stopped. Rachel heard what she thought was the car door opening and closing. Some time passed, and she heard heavy footsteps approaching. When the man opened the trunk, he said, "If you're quiet, nothing will happen to you."

Rachel struggled in her kidnapper's arms, then fell limp with exhaustion. His arms were like steel rods. She knew she could never free herself. When the man finally removed the pillowcase, she was weak and disoriented. As her eyes adjusted to the light, she saw a bed, a green vinyl chair, and a small desk located in the corner near the window. The drapes were closed, and the room had a stale, musty odor.

Clasping Rachel's hands, the man dropped to his knees in front of her. "You're so beautiful," he said, a strange, pleading look in his eyes. "Don't be afraid. I promise I'm not going to harm you. I've never seen a girl as pretty as you before. I'm just going to take a few pictures of you. When I'm finished, I promise I'll take you home to your mother."

Rachel glared at him, too frightened to speak. Her face was caked with vomit, her pulse pounding in her ears. When the man had removed the pillowcase, vomit had spilled down the front of her red T-shirt. He used a damp towel to clean her.

"I have a little girl of my own," he said, placing a finger under her chin. "I would never hurt a child. Look at this, Rachel." He picked up a doll off the floor and showed it to her. "If you do what I say, you can take the doll home with you. Isn't she the most special doll in the world? I bought her for my own little girl, but I've decided to let you keep her instead."

Rachel stared at the doll as something fluttered just outside her memory. The face and hands were made out of fine china, and the doll had real eyelashes and silky red hair. Her fingers trembled as she reached out to touch the pink satin dress embossed with rhinestones. Underneath the dress was a real lace petticoat. On the doll's feet were tiny, removable slippers. "I want to go home," she said, her voice hoarse from crying. "It isn't right to put someone in the trunk of your car. I was scared. When my mother finds out what you did to me, she'll come after you with her belt."

"Please forgive me," the man said, a contrite expression on his face. "I didn't mean to scare you. You're just so pretty, and I love little girls with red hair. I'm a photographer, remember. I only want to take some pictures of you for a magazine assignment I'm working on. If you stay calm and let me take the pictures, I'll give you the doll to take home with you. You know you want her. I could tell by the way you looked at her. Think of how jealous your friends will be when they see your beautiful new doll."

Rachel shoved the man in the chest. "Take me back," she said. "I don't want your stupid doll. I have to get my bicycle before someone steals it."

Something in the man's eyes changed. Grabbing Rachel by the arm, he tossed her onto the bed, then began ripping her clothes off. She kicked wildly. "No," she screamed, holding onto the waistband of her shorts. A moment later, the man had her shorts off and was yanking on her panties. Terrified, she urinated on the bed. Once her panties were off, he pulled her T-shirt over her head.

Her attacker stuffed a handkerchief in her mouth and secured it with masking tape. Using the scarf from before, he tied her hands behind her back, then propped her in the green vinyl chair with the doll beside her. The shutter clicked repeatedly as the man snapped pictures of her naked body with a Polaroid camera, the flash causing black spots to dance in front of her eyes.

An hour passed as Rachel sat shivering. The muscles in her arms were strained and throbbing. The handkerchief was shoved so far down her throat that she kept gagging on it, but there was nothing left in her stomach to regurgitate. The man smelled awful. He had touched her in places where no one was supposed to touch her. She wanted her mother. She wanted to go home. She knew now that the man didn't have a little girl, that everything he had told her had been a lie. He was going to kill her. And after he killed her, he was going to cut her up in tiny pieces.

Just when the man was squatting down to snap another picture, Rachel heard a loud voice call out, "Police. We know you have the girl, Richardson. Send her out and you won't get hurt."

The man raced to the window, pulled back the drapes and peered out. The room was suddenly lit from the glare of a powerful spotlight. Rushing to the opposite side of the room, the man removed a revolver from an Army duffel bag, then raced back to the window. "I have a gun," he shouted, flattening himself against the wall. "Leave or I'll shoot the girl."

"There's only one way out," the same voice said over the bullhorn. "It's over, Richardson. Your parole officer is here. He says if you put the weapon down and send the girl out unharmed, he'll do everything he can to keep them from sending you back to prison. Don't force us to come in after you."

The man paced inside the room, perspiration soaking his face and clothing. Every few moments he would walk to the window and peek out, then return to pacing again.

"All we want is the girl," the voice said. "We don't want any bloodshed, Richardson."

Rachel had no idea how much time passed. The man was cursing and mumbling under his breath. The voice outside droned on as the police officers tried to reason with him. Her eyelids fluttered and then closed. When she awoke, the man was untying her.

Holding the big gun against her head, he positioned Rachel in front of his body, pushing her toward the door. "I'm coming out," he shouted. "If anyone gets near me, I'll kill the girl."

When the man flung the door open, Rachel was struck by a gush of cold air. It was night now, and the police officers had the beams of their headlights focused on the door to the hotel room. All she could see was a circle of white light. Beyond the light was inky darkness. The man had his arm around her waist. Her feet were dangling in thin air, the top of her head grazing his chin. She could feel the hard metal of the gun against her temple, the man's arm squeezing her insides like a boa constrictor.

Rachel's body stiffened. She couldn't go outside without her clothes on. The man was afraid, too. She could feel his heart thumping against her back. Twisting her slender body sideways, she managed to slip out of his arms and tumbled to the ground.

A loud shot exploded in her ears, and the man collapsed beside her.

Rachel stared at him, screaming in terror. Part of the man's head was gone. Her hair was soaked with his blood, her skin speckled with red splotches. Scrambling to her feet, she raced blindly into white light and into the open arms of a police officer.

"It's okay, baby," Sergeant Lawrence Dean said, crushing her to his massive chest. "Get a blanket," he said to an officer standing beside him. "The poor kid doesn't have any clothes on."

Gently peeling the masking tape off Rachel's face, the sergeant plucked the rag out of her mouth, then cradled her trembling body under the folds of his nylon parka. Sirens blasted in the distance. Feet thundered past them. While Dean tenderly rocked her in his arms, Rachel stared up into his face. She tried to speak, but no words came out. Her tongue felt swollen and heavy. Her body contracted into a tight ball, her fist pressed against her mouth.

"It's over now, honey," Sergeant Dean told her, his eyes crinkling with kindness. "He was a bad man, so I don't want you thinking about what happened to him. Bad people get what's coming to them."

Craning her head around, Rachel looked at the man on the ground. His eyes were open but his body was still, his arms and legs twisted beneath him.

Turning back to Sergeant Dean, she committed his face to memory: his clear eyes, the fine lines darting out around them, his soft padded lips. With the tips of her fingers, she reached out and touched the badge pinned to his police uniform.

Rachel had her head buried in her hands when she heard a horn honking. Its repeated blasts caused her to surface from her memories. When she looked up, she saw Lucy's head protruding from the driver's window of her station wagon. "Good Lord," her friend exclaimed, "what happened to you? You look awful."

Half in a daze, Rachel circled to the passenger side of the car and got in. She tossed a diaper and several fast food wrappers into the back seat. Lucy Folger was a petite woman with a kind face and an easy smile. She had lost her hair while undergoing chemotherapy and radiation treatments, but it had finally started to grow back and Lucy was very proud of it. Although her once thick hair was now stringy and sparse, she refused to wear a wig. She was a simple woman with a large heart. Tracy might complain about her from time to time, but both the kids adored her. "Who's watching the kids?" Rachel asked, knowing Lucy's husband had to work on Saturdays.

"Tracy," the woman answered, turning sideways in the seat. "Want to tell me what happened? Where's your car? Couldn't one of the other officers give you a ride home? It's not that I mind coming to get you, Rachel. I just want to know what's going on. You sounded so distraught on the phone, I was afraid you'd been in an accident."

Rachel took a deep breath, then proceeded to tell her neighbor what had transpired on the beach. "I'm so ashamed," she said, sniffing back tears. "I should have never gone to their awful party. I only did it because Grant said if I didn't go, he'd tell the sergeant what happened at the market. The bastard told him anyway."

Lucy fired up the wagon and pulled out onto the Pacific Coast Highway. "They can't get away with something like this," she said, cutting her eyes to Rachel. "That's attempted rape, isn't it? Just because they're police officers doesn't mean they're above the law. They can't jump your bones and get away with it."

"It might be more than attempted rape," Rachel said weakly. "For all I know, one of them had sex with me."

"I doubt that," Lucy said, touching her hand. "Surely you'd know if someone had sex with you. Didn't you only have a couple of beers? Isn't that what you told me? I don't think you were drunk so much as exhausted. Don't make it out to be worse than it was."

"The sergeant got me to drink some Jack Daniel's," Rachel told her. "I think that put me over the top. The last thing I remember was the hot dogs sliding off the plate. The watch ended at six, Lucy, and we probably got to the beach around seven. When I woke up, it was one o'clock. My pants were unzipped, and my T-shirt was pushed up to my neck. I was out for a long time. There's no telling what they did to me."

"Report their asses, then," Lucy barked, outraged by the things her friend was telling her.

"I can't," Rachel said. "You don't understand, Lucy. I'd lose my job for sure. They'd claim I was drunk . . . that I just made it all up. Then the sergeant would retaliate by bringing up the mess I made of the robbery the other night. How do I know what Grant told him? They could classify me as incompetent and dismiss me. Even if I manage to get Internal Affairs behind me, I'd end up the loser." She began trembling again. "I can't afford to lose this job. I need this job. I haven't even paid off all of Joe's hospital bills yet."

"You should have filed for bankruptcy," Lucy said, steering the car up the ramp to the freeway. "I've told you that a dozen times, Rachel. How could anyone expect a woman with two kids to pay such enormous bills?"

"Filing for bankruptcy is similar to going on welfare," Rachel said, dabbing at her eyes with her fingers. "I'm not going to put my kids into that kind of a life. After Carrie and Susan left home, Mother had no choice but to go on welfare. I'll never forget the looks people gave me when I paid for our groceries with food stamps."

Lucy sighed in frustration. They had covered this topic many times. She hated to see her friend buried under a mountain of bills when there was a legitimate way for her to obtain relief. "Bankruptcy," she said, "is nothing at all like going on welfare. No one looks down on you. No one will even know."

"I'll never be able to buy another house if I do what you say," Rachel told her. "I have to get Tracy her own room, Lucy. She's a teenager now. She needs her privacy."

Exiting the freeway, Lucy stopped at a red light and pulled Rachel into her arms. "It makes me sick to see you this upset. I wouldn't be alive today if it wasn't for you."

"That's silly," Rachel said. "I didn't cure you, Lucy. The doctors did."

"When Glen left me, I was on the verge of committing suicide," she continued. "It takes more than medicine to cure someone, Rachel. You cleaned my house, took care of my kids, cooked our meals. You helped me to be strong. Without you, I would have never survived the chemotherapy. Don't you think I know the truth? If you had entered the police academy when you were scheduled to, you wouldn't have fallen so far behind with your bills."

"You've more than paid me back," Rachel told her. "I worry you're overdoing it by taking care of Tracy and Joe for me while I'm at work. I've been thinking of switching to days and putting Joe in day care."

"I feel like a million bucks," Lucy insisted, her face spreading in a warm smile. "The kids only stay with me at night. Having a couple of kids sleep on the floor in your living room isn't exactly taxing. Tracy is a gem. She always helps me get my brood bathed and in bed. There's no reason for you to pay for day care. With Glen working late so many nights, Tracy is great company for me."

"I don't know if I can continue working with the men on my watch," Rachel said, staring out the window. "What happened today on the beach brought back everything from the kidnapping. I thought I had finally pushed it from my mind, but now it's all coming back again." She sucked in a deep breath.

"Calm down, sweetie," Lucy said. "We'll get you home, get you in a hot shower, then we'll figure out what to do about these awful cops."

chapter

NINE

When Rachel left Lucy's house with Tracy and Joe, she saw a red car parked in her driveway. A moment later, Carrie's long legs unfurled from the driver's seat. "Where have you been?" her sister said, yanking her sunglasses off. "I've been calling the house all morning. I finally decided to drive over here and see what was going on. Didn't you remember I was coming today?"

Carrie was an attorney. She lived in San Francisco and specialized in civil litigation. Rachel had completely forgotten that she had said she would be passing through Los Angeles that morning on her way back from a business trip. Dressed in a white linen suit, nude hose and stiletto heels, Carrie had her hair dyed jet black and cut severely to frame her face at her jaw line. Her skin tone was fair, similar to Rachel's.

"I'm sorry," Rachel said, walking over and embracing her. "How long can you stay? Have you had lunch?"

Carrie glanced at her watch. "I was going to spend the morning with you, but now we'll have to cut our visit short. My plane leaves at four, and I have to return the rental car." She squatted down to hug Joe, then leaned over and gave Tracy a peck on the cheek. "You're growing up, kid. You look about sixteen now. Got a boyfriend yet?"

"She's only fourteen," Rachel said, taking in her sister's polished red fingernails, her perfect makeup, the expensive designer suit she was wearing. Carrie was a sophisticated, accomplished woman. Rachel looked down at her rumpled jeans, her stained T-shirt. She still felt light-headed, and the sun was burning her eyes. "Why don't we go inside? I'll make a pitcher of lemonade."

"I brought some stuff for the kids," Carrie said, removing several boxes from the trunk of the car before following her sister into the house. Her nose was small and dainty, her eyes almost as dark as her hair. She wore smoky taupe shadow and her lipstick was a vibrant shade of coral. Her eyebrows were slender arches that darted up and down when she talked.

Tracy and Joe ripped into the packages in the kitchen. Carrie had bought Tracy a white leather miniskirt. Joe got a set of Mighty Morphin Power Rangers and three dinosaur figures, along with several playsuits that he instantly tossed aside. "This is the coolest skirt I've ever seen," Tracy exclaimed, racing to her room to try it on.

"Don't I get a kiss, Joe?" Carrie said, watching as the little boy played with the toys. He toddled over and planted a mushy kiss on her forehead, then squatted back down on the floor. Carrie turned her attention to Rachel. "You look like hell."

"Gee, thanks," Rachel said. "You always say the nicest things. And I didn't say one word about your new hair color. If I look like shit, then you look Japanese."

"Hey, I tell it like it is," her sister said, removing an earring and massaging her ear. "You're working too hard. You're going to get sick if you don't cut yourself some slack. Look at the bags under your eyes. Don't you ever sleep?"

"I'm fine," Rachel said, preparing the lemonade and carrying the pitcher to the table. "You look like you've lost another twenty pounds. Are you trying to starve yourself to death?"

Carrie laughed, a deep, hearty sound that filled the room. "Since I'm divorced now, I have to stay in shape to cope with the competition. I turned forty last month, remember? It isn't easy for a forty-year-old woman to find a man."

"I thought you wanted to be independent, do your own thing. Isn't that what you told me when you and Phil got divorced?"

"I can do my own thing and still want a man now and then," Carrie told her. "In case you haven't heard, single people do occasionally have sex. What about you? Are you still living like a nun, going to bed with Joe's picture under your pillow?"

"I didn't divorce my husband," Rachel said, scowling. "He died, Carrie. Don't you think that's a little different?" She could never tell her sister what had happened on the beach that morning. Their lifestyles were worlds apart. Carrie spent her days in courtrooms and skyscraper office buildings. She had a private secretary to cater to her needs, maids to clean her apartment, a big fat paycheck at the end of every month. Rachel eyed the dirty dishes stacked in the sink. To her sister, the way she lived must be depressing, reminiscent of childhood days with their mother.

"You can't be in love with a dead man, sweetie," Carrie said. "It's been three years. It's time to move on with your life. Find yourself a successful guy. You're attractive enough. All you have to do is fix your-self up a little, start thinking like a woman for a change."

Carrie sometimes came across as strident, but Rachel knew she loved her. Her sister had fought long and hard to get where she was in life. Her drive had become incorporated into her personality more out of necessity than by design. The soft-faced young girl with the wavy brown hair who used to sit on the piano bench beside their mother and sing show tunes seemed light-years away. Rachel had never seen her sister perform in the courtroom, but she was certain she was a fine attorney. Carrie had left home while Rachel was still in high school, and put herself through college by working as a waitress. After she had married, her husband had supported her and looked after their son while she attended law school. The boy was now in his first year at U.C. Berkeley. Carrie had once said the only thing she regretted in life was not having more children, particularly since she'd had so little time to spend with her son during his early years.

Tracy was eavesdropping from the doorway. She waited until the women stopped speaking, and then walked in and twirled around in her new leather skirt. "It's wonderful, Carrie. It looks just like a skirt I saw in *Cosmopolitan* the other day. It's mod, isn't it? All the magazines say mod is coming back."

"You've got a fashion plate on your hands, Rachel," Carrie said, smiling.

"Yeah, well," Rachel said, thinking the skirt was far too short but not wanting to say anything to spoil her daughter's happiness, "Tracy might be a fashion plate, but there's not a lot of room for fashion in our budget these days."

Carrie slumped in her seat. She hated that Rachel was so hard up for money, but when she offered to help her get out of debt, she consistently refused. In many ways, she thought her sister was a martyr. Ever since the kidnapping, she had walked around as if she were carrying a cross on her back. Carrie had never been certain if the adversity Rachel experienced was natural or if she drew it to her through some kind of strange negative energy. "I'll go through my closet when I get home," she said. "I've got some cute things I never wear that might look great on Tracy. I'll pack up a box and put it in the mail as soon as I get home."

Carrie used the bathroom, then said she had to take off for the airport. "How about a trip to San Francisco this summer?" she said to Tracy, clasping the girl's hands. "We can ride the cable cars, go to the beach. I'll take you shopping, have my hairdresser work on your hair."

The girl's face came alive, then quickly fell. "Who would watch Joe?"

"Right," Carrie said, frowning. She might be able to entertain Tracy, but she could not handle a toddler with the demands of her law practice. "Maybe next year, okay?"

Tracy nodded silently. Rachel stood in the doorway until her sister had driven off, then headed to the back of the house to go to bed.

Once Tracy had prepared the evening meal and placed it in the refrigerator, she grabbed Joe's hand and led him out the front of the house, quietly closing the door behind her. The day had turned out to be fairly warm, and she was dressed in a halter top and a pair of cut-off shorts. She had not yet developed real breasts. She had pimples and a few months back had begun to have periods, but the thing she wanted most had not yet happened. Glancing down the front of her halter top, she shook her head, then yanked on her brother's hand to get him to walk faster. If a girl didn't have boobs, she was still a baby. She didn't feel like a child, act like a child, or think like a child. She thought it was time for her body to catch up with her mind.

A battered green Datsun was parked at the curb. Smiling at the long-haired boy in the driver's seat, Tracy pushed back the seat and lifted her brother into the car.

Matt Fitzgerald's blond hair was styled like a surfer's, long and shaggy. At sixteen, he was a good-looking young man with clear skin and large hazel eyes. His father was a prominent local dentist, and his mother worked as his receptionist in Ventura. When Tracy had first seen him leaning against the wall at the video arcade near her house, it was as if he had stepped right out of one of her teenage magazines. Everything about him seemed perfect. But things were not always as they appeared, Tracy had learned that day. Matt had been born with a birth defect, a deformed left hand.

"Do you have to bring the kid?" he asked.

"You know I have to bring him," Tracy said, her voice laced with bitterness. "My mom's sleeping. If she's not at work, she's sleeping. That's the way it is."

"It's okay," Matt said. "I just thought we could be alone for a change." He glanced in the back seat at the boy. "Yo, Joey," he said, "how's it hanging, big guy?"

"Don't call him Joey," she snapped.

"Why?"

"Because his name is Joe," Tracy said, the words catching in her throat. "He was named after my dad."

Matt scooted over in the seat. "I can tell you loved your dad very much," he said softly. "What was he like?"

Tracy rested her head on his shoulder, then looked up at his face. "Now that I think of it, you remind me a little of my dad."

"How's that?" Matt said, tentatively draping an arm over her shoulder.

"He had long hair like you," she told him. "And he loved the out-doors. You're crazy about the ocean. My dad was into dirt and plants." She nestled her head into his armpit. "You even smell like my dad."

"I probably have BO," Matt said, smiling down at her. "I didn't shower after I went surfing today."

"Whatever it is, I like it," Tracy said, tickling his armpit with her nose. "You smell fishy, like the ocean."

"When do you have to be back?"

"Probably around eight," she told him. "Let's go to the park over by the high school. That way, Joe can play in the sandbox."

"Ice cream," the toddler said, kicking the back of the seat. "You promised, Tracy."

"It's too close to dinner," his sister said. "I'm taking you to the park, so shut up."

Matt repositioned himself in the driver's seat and cranked the ignition with his good hand. Once they reached the park, he removed a blanket from the trunk and placed it on the lawn. Patting her brother on the rump, Tracy steered him in the direction of the playground. As they sat down, Matt reached over and pulled on a strand of her hair, then bent down and tried to kiss her.

"Don't do that!" she said, shoving him away. "I don't want to be your girlfriend. I just want us to be friends." Seeing his disappointment, she tried to explain. "If we start going out, you'll want to have sex. I don't want to get pregnant. I already have Joe. I don't need any more kids to take care of."

"It's not that," Matt said, a shattered look on his face. "You're afraid I'm going to touch you with my hideous hand." He curled up on his side, his deformed hand hidden inside his T-shirt. It was smaller than his other hand. The fingers were short and thick, as if they had not completely formed at the time of his birth.

Tracy crawled to the other side of the blanket. Matt rolled over onto his stomach, refusing to look at her. She reached beneath him and pried his bad hand out, then placed it in the center of her chest. "See, I'm not afraid for you to touch me," she told him. "Your hand might be a little different, but I swear, it doesn't matter. I like people who are different. Who wants to be the same as everyone else?"

Matt turned onto his side again, gazing longingly at her face. A few moments later, Tracy felt his stunted fingers on the edge of her halter top. "That's enough," she said. "Just because you have a bad hand doesn't mean you can feel me up. There's nothing there anyway, in case you haven't noticed."

Matt sat up. "Why are you so moody today? Did you have a fight with your mother?"

"No." Tracy thought of Carrie's invitation. "Look, I saw my aunt today. She's a hotshot lawyer in San Francisco. She wanted me to come and stay with her this summer. She said she'd take me shopping, show me the sights." She brushed a jagged strand of hair off her forehead, remembering how Carrie had promised to take her to her hairdresser. "I can't go, of course. What do I ever have to look forward to? Just another miserable summer chasing after Joe. Can you blame me for not wanting to get knocked up?"

"Is Joe your kid?" He had wanted to ask her this question ever since he met her. "I've heard of that kind of thing. You know, a young girl getting pregnant and having a kid, and her mother pretending it's hers."

"No, stupid," Tracy said, punching him in the side. "If Joe was my kid, I would have only been eleven years old when I had him. Sometimes it feels like he's my kid, though," she added. "Joe was born a few weeks before my father died. I spend more time with him than Mom does. My mother purposely got pregnant, even though she knew my dad was going to croak. She said she wanted something to remember him by." She busied herself pulling a tuft of grass. "That doesn't make a lot of sense, does it? I mean, she had me. I'm his daughter."

"Bummer," Matt said. "Guess she wanted a boy."

"I worship Joe," Tracy continued, her face softening as she watched the child play in the sandbox. When she took her brother to a public playground, she never took her eyes off him. She knew how easily children could get hurt. Her mother had also taught her about child molesters, people who lurked around playgrounds and preyed on innocent children. "I just know we wouldn't be so hard up for money if Mom hadn't had him," she continued. "And I can't ever do anything with my friends. When I'm not in school, I have to babysit. Mom keeps promising it's going to be different, but I know it's not."

"Maybe it will," Matt said. "You never know. Your mom could win the lottery or something."

"Yeah," Tracy answered, tossing a blade of grass at him, "and I still believe in Santa Claus."

Matt fell back onto the blanket. Tracy leaned over and impulsively kissed him on the mouth.

He reached for her, but she pulled away. "It was only a kiss," she said, her face flushed with excitement. "I decided I owed it to you for acting like such a bitch."

"Oh, yeah," Matt said, grinning. "Maybe next time you'll be in a really bad mood."

"Never know," Tracy said in a playful tone.

"You only want to be friends, huh?" he asked, arching an eyebrow. "I mean . . . I don't want to be pushy or anything, but there's some good-looking chicks at the beach."

"I guess I changed my mind," she said, her heart pounding in her ears. "I kissed you, didn't I?"

Tracy got up and walked toward the sandbox to get Joe. Her very first kiss. She had thought it would be awkward, dumb, one of those things everyone tells you will be so great but turns out to be nothing. She saw Matt watching her from the blanket. Did he know she had never kissed a boy before? The wind whipped her hair back from her face, and she sighed in pleasure. She had no right to feel sorry for herself. She glanced down at her hands, imagining how difficult it would be to have a disability like Matt's. Kids were cruel. They probably made fun of him, treated him like a freak. Seeing the confident smile on his face, though, Tracy wondered if Matt was really as sensitive as he made out. He was outrageously handsome, and she could not believe girls were not attracted to him. She adjusted her halter top, remembering how soft his touch had felt on her skin. Boys knew how to get their way, and sixteen-year-old guys like Matt had nothing but sex on their brains. She would have to be careful.

"Hey, slugger," Tracy said to Joe, straining as she picked him up and balanced him on her hip. "Because you've been such a good boy, I'm going to buy that ice cream cone you wanted." She planted kisses all over his face. "Are you my best friend, huh? Are we a team?"

Although Tracy wished she wasn't saddled with her brother all the time, she knew she would be miserable without him. When they didn't have to sleep at Lucy's house, Tracy sometimes brought Joe into the bed with her and cradled him in her arms. When her father died and they had been forced to move from their old neighborhood, Tracy had been devastated. She had missed her father, her friends, her school. Even though Joe was only a baby at the time, she could see traces of her father in his face and in the expressions he made with his eyes. Her mother had crazy notions about what happened to people when they died. Rachel had told her one time that her father's spirit might have somehow returned in little Joe. Tracy didn't believe in all that spiritual stuff, but if her mother wanted to think that way, she didn't see how it could do any harm.

"I loves you," Joe said, hugging her tight around the neck.

"I love you too, pumpkin," Tracy answered, setting him back on his feet. "Now, let's go and get that ice cream cone."

chapter

TEN

When Tracy woke her mother up at nine o'clock Saturday night, Rachel was drooling on her pillow. The girl dropped down beside the bed and dabbed her mother's mouth with a tissue. "You're drooling again," she said, placing a hand on her forehead. "Not only that, you're burning up. I think you have a fever. You must be getting the flu or something."

"It's just the sunburn," Rachel said. When she stood, the room spun and she sank back on the edge of the bed. "I think I need to eat something. Can you make me a sandwich while I jump in the shower? I'd really appreciate it."

"I made a meatloaf and some mashed potatoes," Tracy said. "I'll pop you a plate in the microwave." She started to leave the room and then stopped. "Maybe you should call in sick tonight, Mom. I'm worried about you. If that was a party you were supposed to be at this morning, it certainly doesn't look like you had any fun. What really happened out there?"

Rachel waved her away, then headed to the shower. It was the fifth shower she had taken since coming back from the beach. Her skin was burning, her eyes were red and swollen, and the mere thought of seeing Grant Cummings made her sick. Grant was an animal, all right, but at least he was fairly obvious. It was the conversation she'd had with the sergeant that still had her reeling. Had he really meant the things he'd said? If she filed a complaint about what had transpired on the beach, would he attempt to get her fired for incompetence?

Once she had showered and dressed in a fresh uniform, Rachel ate some of the food her daughter had prepared for her. When she had had enough, she carried the plates to the sink and began loading them into the dishwasher.

Tracy lounged against the doorframe with studied nonchalance. "The cheerleader tryouts are next week," she said. "Sheila Ross wants me to try out with her. We've been practicing routines during the lunch break."

"That's great," Rachel said, pleased that her daughter was interested in school activities.

"I probably won't make it," Tracy continued. "But if I do, I'll have to go to practice every day after school, as well as cheer at all the football games." Her voice dropped. "Maybe I should forget it."

Rachel felt her heart skip a beat. "It's not for this year, though, right?"

"No," Tracy said, chewing on a fingernail. "But Mom, how would you manage without me? You don't get enough sleep as it is. Besides, the uniforms are really expensive."

"Look," Rachel said, wiping her hands on a dish towel, "I don't want you putting your life on hold because of Joe. If you make cheerleader, we'll figure something out."

Tracy decided to change the subject while she was ahead. "Some man called for you," she said. "He didn't want to leave a message. Is there something going on that I don't know about?"

Rachel walked over and kissed her forehead. "It was probably a wrong number," she said. "In case you haven't noticed, your mother's not exactly a femme fatale."

"You could be," the girl said, glancing at her watch. "Carrie was right, Mom. You just need to fix yourself up, maybe wear a little makeup. It's early. Give me a few minutes. I want to try something."

"Maybe some other time." Rachel headed to the back of the house to tell Joe goodbye. But when she came out of his room, her daughter grabbed her hand and pulled her into the bathroom. Relenting, Rachel sat down on the commode. "What are you going to do to me?"

"Be still," Tracy said, a handful of pencils in her hand. "I'm going to give you some eyebrows. All redheads need to wear eyebrow pencil and eye liner. If you don't, you look washed out."

"How do you know these things?" Rachel said as her daughter used a light brown pencil to fill in her eyebrows.

"I watch the fashion channel," she said. "Close your eyes, Mom. I'm going to give you some liner, then put on some mascara. When I'm finished, you'll look like a model."

"Please," Rachel said, recalling how Carrie had given her makeup sessions so long ago. "I'm not in the mood for this tonight, honey. Where did you get the money for this stuff, anyway?" She picked up one of the pencils off the counter. "When I worked at Robinson's, pencils like this cost almost ten dollars."

"I buy them at Woolworth's," she said. "You can get a dozen pencils for ten dollars if you know how to shop. Look at yourself now, Mom. See how pretty you look."

Rachel glanced in the mirror, then quickly looked away. "I'm not in the market for a man, Tracy," she said. "Is that what this is all about?"

"Why not?" her daughter said, scowling. "Dad's been dead for three years. Before that, he was sick all the time. Maybe if you married a rich guy like Carrie said—"

Rachel shook her head. They were getting desperate, all right. "I've got to go," she said, rushing out of the house.

Rachel timed her entrance into the squad room to the very last minute, waiting outside the door until she heard the sergeant begin speaking. She stepped in and was looking for an empty seat when Ratso stuck his foot out and tripped her. Falling onto her knees, Rachel heard several of the men laughing. She stood and glared at Ratso, who had an idiotic grin on his face. For the first time, she saw why Grant had chosen his nickname. When he smiled, his teeth protruded and he looked just like a rodent. Did he fondle her as well? The thought made her shiver with repulsion. Deciding to forget about finding a seat, Rachel stood along the wall in the back of the squad room.

When the sergeant called her name during roll call, Grant gave her a devious smile, then stood and grabbed his balls in a mocking gesture. Rachel flipped him the finger.

Once Sergeant Miller had stopped speaking, she walked to the front to pick up her unit keys, purposely stepping on his foot. "Oh," she said, "I'm sorry, Sergeant. Did I step on you?"

"Damn," he growled. "You're as clumsy as an ox, woman."

"Oh, really?" she said, smiling in satisfaction.

"Hey," he said, jerking his head toward the corner of the room, "get over here."

"What?" she said, staring up into his rugged face. Gravity and too many slugs of Jack Daniel's were making his face sag. "Are you going to threaten to have me fired for stepping on your foot?"

"You better knock off the bitchy attitude, Simmons," he said, a slight wheeze rattling inside his chest. "I won't tolerate insubordination on my watch, especially from a ditsy broad like you. We're here to work. Now get your ass in gear and do your damn job, or your next performance review will be even worse than the last one."

"What happened this morning wasn't right," she said. "I just want you to know that I hold you personally responsible. I'm not going to report it, but I'm not going to forget it."

"Get over it, Simmons," Miller snapped, turning to speak to one of the other officers.

Rachel quickly exited the squad room. So much for the happy family, she decided. If the events on the beach were what it took to become a part of their team, she would just as soon remain an outsider.

The first few hours of the watch passed uneventfully. Rachel rolled for backup on a family disturbance on the south side of town at 11:16. By the time she and Ratso arrived, the couple had stopped fighting and things seemed to be under control. Rachel spoke to the wife in the kitchen while Ratso stepped outside to talk to the husband. Bonita Cervantes was a curvaceous blonde with an inch of black roots showing at the base of her scalp. Her husband, Jesus, was dark and muscular, his biceps decorated with tattoos. A thin stream of blood oozed out of the corner of Bonita's mouth, and her lower lip was swollen.

"She's fucking around behind my back," Jesus told Ratso in the front yard, agitated and angry.

"I see," Ratso said. "How did you discover this?"

"I caught her, man," he said. "I followed her to a motel and caught her fucking some dirtbag biker dude from the bar up the street."

"Did you strike her?"

"Yeah, I belted her," Jesus said, clenching his fists at his sides. "She was cheating on me, man. She's my damn wife. I can't let the bitch humiliate me like that. Shit, the whole neighborhood probably knows she's screwing around on me."

"Go stand beside the police car," Ratso said, tilting his head toward his unit parked at the curb.

"Are you going to arrest me?"

"I need to confer with my partner," he explained, opening the door to enter the house. Pulling Rachel aside, he said, "Does she want to swear out a complaint?"

Rachel shrank away from his touch, trying to clear her mind of the incident on the beach and concentrate solely on the task at hand. "She's afraid of him, but I'm trying to talk some sense into her."

Ratso shot the woman a look of disgust. "She was unfaithful."

"So?" Rachel said. "What difference does that make? It doesn't give him a right to beat her."

Ratso dropped his eyes. "She is his wife. She disgraced him. He was only doing what any man would do."

"Are you saying what I think you're saying?" Rachel said, a muscle in her eyelid twitching. "That he has the right to punish her? What is she? His possession? Is that the way you see it, Ratso?"

"This is a personal matter between two married people," he told her. "We have no right to interfere."

"I don't know where you grew up," Rachel told him, "but in this country, a man is not allowed to beat his wife no matter how many men she sleeps with." The incident at the beach again passed through her mind and her anger intensified. "Do you believe in taking advantage of an unconscious woman as well? I'm disappointed in you, Ratso. I thought we were friends." Remembering how he had tripped her at the watch meeting, she gave him a quick jab in the side with her elbow. "Next time you trip me, I'm going to whack you with my baton."

Rachel walked off to talk to Bonita again. Ratso stared at her back, seething. A few moments later he walked outside onto the porch and kicked a clay pot, cracking it into several pieces.

"What are you doing?" Jesus yelled from the curb. "I paid good money for that pot."

Ratso stomped down the sidewalk to his unit. "Get out of my way," he said, lashing out with his arm and knocking him aside. While Jesus mumbled profanities, Ratso climbed into his car and sped off.

* * *

When Bonita Cervantes refused to swear out a complaint, Rachel knew there was nothing more she could do. She handed the woman her card and cleared, driving back to her assigned beat.

Pulling off onto a tree-lined street, she killed the engine and closed her eyes. The police radio made it impossible for her to fall into a deep sleep. She didn't believe in sleeping on duty. All she wanted to do was rest. Some of the men who worked residential beats like the one she covered went so far as to drive to their homes, relaxing in their easy chairs in front of the TV while they monitored their calls over their portable radio.

Because it was a pleasant night, she left the window rolled down, thinking the fresh air might revive her.

Never would Rachel have dreamed that she would one day be driving around in a police car, a gun strapped to her side. The picture Mike Atwater had tried to portray in the courtroom had not been entirely accurate. It was true that the kidnapping had been a monumental event in her life. For years after that awful day, Rachel had been afraid to step outside of the house unless her mother or one of her sisters was present. Her fear had imprisoned her, taken her voice away. She winced, recalling the many times during that year that her mother had slapped her.

As her thoughts drifted, she could see the small house in San Diego clearly. She recalled the sound of the kitchen cabinet opening and shutting. Her mother kept a bottle of vodka hidden behind the cans of soup and vegetables. Before the kidnapping, she had drunk only during the day when the girls were at school. Because Rachel would not leave the house, the school system had been forced to provide home tutoring for her as well as a speech therapist. While the tutor worked with Rachel in the living room, her mother sipped vodka in the kitchen out of a teacup. As soon as the tutor left, she would tear into her daughter.

"Speak," Frances had shouted, slapping Rachel hard across the face. "There's nothing wrong with you. The man didn't rape you. All he did was touch you. You can't stay here in the house every day. How can I teach my students?"

Rachel's mother had been an accomplished pianist. Prior to the kidnapping, the house had been filled with music. Every afternoon, Frances would sit down at the piano and play for her daughters. She knew the score of almost every Broadway musical. Carrie would memorize the lyrics and belt out the songs while she sat next to her mother on the piano bench. Rachel would twirl around the floor, pretending to be a dancer. Susan was the only one with an interest in the piano. Frances was a stern teacher, though, and Susan had finally given up, realizing she could never play to her mother's satisfaction.

After Nathan Richardson swept through their lives, the music stopped. With each day the house seemed to get darker and the family's finances leaner. Frances stopped wearing makeup, then stopped getting out of bed in the morning, leaving Rachel to fend for herself until the tutor arrived. Knowing her daughter derived a small amount of pleasure from sitting in front of the living room window and watching the other children play, her mother insisted the drapes be kept closed.

The only thing Rachel had to look forward to were the weekly visits from Sergeant Larry Dean.

Yes, the man had become her hero, her savior, the only person who had managed to break through her wall of silence and get her to communicate again. But the thought of emulating him and becoming a police officer had never once crossed her mind. She had sought employment as a police officer out of financial need, not idealism.

Without realizing it, Rachel had her arm dangling out the window. While she was lightly dozing, she felt something sticky and wet on her hand. Bolting upright in the seat, she was certain she'd been stabbed and the warm liquid she felt was her own blood.

What she saw was a huge black Labrador standing by the window of her police cruiser. The animal had been licking the salt off her skin. Either that, she thought, or the beast had been humping her arm. "Great," she said, rolling up the window and engaging the ignition. In a twenty-four-hour period, she had not only been accosted by a gang of horny police officers, but a Labrador had tried to have his way with her as well.

Just then she heard the dreaded tone signal and cursed under her breath, spinning the volume knob as high as it would go.

"3A3, 4A2, 2A2, and 5A," the dispatcher said. "Units respond to a report of juveniles fighting on the corner of Main and Fairmont across from the Majestic Theater. Approximately twenty juveniles are involved. One individual is reportedly armed with a gun. Respond code three."

Grant was the first to acknowledge the call. "Station one," he shouted into the radio, his siren blasting in the background. "Can't you give us a description of the juvenile who's packing? It might keep us from getting shot out there."

"No can do," the dispatcher said. "We received the report from an anonymous caller. Like it or not, this is all we've got."

Rachel flipped the toggle switch for her red lights and sirens, and started rolling code to the area. She checked in with the other officers responding, asking them to advise her of their approach routes. More than one unit rolling code to the same location was extremely dangerous. A few years back, two units had been involved in a head-on collision under similar circumstances. Both officers had been killed instantly.

When she arrived in the area of Main and Fairmont, she saw approximately twenty juveniles assembled in the street in front of the old theater. Beer bottles were flying through the air, and rowdy youths were yelling and shouting. Some of the kids were wearing Oak Grove letter jackets, and she spotted several Simi Valley jackets as well. Evidently it was some sort of school rivalry. She saw three police cars parked at the end of the block near the Heritage Bank and quickly came to a stop behind them. Leaping out of her unit, she pulled her nightstick out. She saw Jimmy Townsend wrestling with three youths and raced over to assist him.

Grabbing one burly male by the back of his shirt, she tossed him to the ground and straddled him, then flipped him over onto his stomach, pulled his hands behind his back, and snapped on the handcuffs. A few feet away, she spotted Grant kicking a boy wearing a yellow shirt. Directly across from them, Ratso had another teenager on the ground and was furiously slamming his head into the pavement. Rachel had heard about Ratso's temper, but she had never seen it firsthand. "Look at Ratso, Jimmy," she shouted at Townsend. "The kid's going to be brain damaged. I think I saw blood coming out of one of his ears. As soon as you get your man hooked up, you better get over there and stop him."

"Stupid punks," Townsend snarled, wrenching his suspect's hands behind his back and then shoving him onto his face on the ground.

Someone tossed a beer bottle at Grant Cummings, barely missing his head. He growled like an angry bear, leaving the boy wearing the yellow shirt and rushing off to find the youth who had tossed the bottle.

Rachel knew they needed more manpower. Four officers were not enough to handle twenty teenagers. "Station one," she said on her portable radio, panting and out of breath, "we need more units out here. We've got a mini-riot on our hands, and we're getting pelted with beer bottles."

While she listened to the dispatcher try to free up more units, a beer bottle smashed into the back of her head. For a few moments she was certain she was going to pass out. Blood spilled down her forehead, trickling into her nose and mouth. She reminded herself that head wounds always bleed profusely, and that the wound was probably less serious than it appeared. Feeling the cut with her fingers, she decided it wasn't deep. Looking around, she saw that Ratso was dragging the dazed looking young man he had been beating to his police unit. Grant had a boy wearing an Oak Grove letter jacket by the arm and was about to handcuff him when someone called, "Look out! He's got a gun!"

Whirling around, Rachel saw the boy with the yellow shirt that Grant had been kicking earlier. He was standing, chest heaving, with a gun in his hand. Grant seized the juvenile he was about to cuff by the shoulders and pulled him in front of him, using him like a shield. Almost in the same instant, the youth in the yellow shirt squeezed off a round. The boy Grant was holding jerked as the bullet struck him in the chest. Grant dropped the injured boy to the ground, whipped his gun out, and returned fire. Shots were popping all around.

Rachel unholstered her weapon, but the juveniles were rapidly dispersing, running from the area in a dozen directions. The boy who had fired the shot was on the ground. She couldn't tell if he had been hit, or if he'd just dropped to the ground for cover.

"Send an ambulance," she screamed into her portable radio, racing to the injured youth and kneeling beside him. "We have one kid with a gunshot wound to the chest. We may have more injuries. I can't tell yet."

The boy appeared to be in his mid to late teens. He had sandy blond hair and an oval face. His eyes were open and he appeared to be conscious, but Rachel had no doubt that his injury was serious. A trickle of blood oozed out of the corner of his mouth. A singed hole was burned into the front of his letter jacket. Blood was gushing out of the hole and pooling around him.

"It's going to be okay," she told him, unzipping his jacket and ripping open his shirt so she could get a better look at the wound. She tried to keep the panic out of her eyes and maintain a calm, steady voice as she stared at the small, dark hole made by the bullet. "Try to relax if you can. The more you fight it, the worse it will be. The ambulance is on the way. You're going to be fine."

"Mo-mom," he stammered, his eyes flashing with fear. "I can't . . . breathe. Please . . . help . . . me."

Rachel leaned over, cupping the side of his face with her palm. He was only a few years older than Tracy. She picked up his clammy hand and squeezed it, using her free hand to support his head. "It's okay, honey. Hold on. Be strong. You can do it."

She heard a gurgling noise inside the boy's chest. His eyes opened wide, and he almost raised himself to a sitting position. A second later, his body shook violently, and he fell back. His eyes remained open, but his hand went limp and his head rolled to one side.

After listening for a pulse and hearing nothing, Rachel frantically pried the boy's mouth open and began administering CPR, ventilating and then compressing his chest. The wound was so close to his sternum and there was so much blood, her hands seemed to sink into his flesh. She kept repeating what they'd taught her at the academy. He's already dead. You can't hurt him. If you do nothing, he'll be dead forever.

She didn't know how long she'd been administering CPR when she felt a paramedic's hand on her shoulder.

"You're exhausted," the paramedic said, trying to pull her away. "Let us take over now."

Still on hands and knees, Rachel moved aside. The paramedic continued the compressions for a few more moments, then stopped. "He's gone," he said. "I think the bullet punctured a lung, and he drowned in his own fluids."

"No," she cried, crawling back to the boy's side. "He can't be dead. He's so young." She lunged at the boy's body, thinking if she could just get his heart beating, they could patch him up at the hospital. The paramedic grabbed her around the waist from behind and pulled her away.

"There's nothing you can do," he said, waving his partner over with the stretcher. "From what the other officers told us, you've been trying to resuscitate him for over twenty minutes."

Rachel sat on her knees. Her hands and uniform were smeared with the boy's blood. She peered up at Grant, Ratso, and Jimmy Townsend huddled around her in a small circle. "Are you happy now, Grant?" Townsend said, watching as they loaded the boy's body onto the stretcher.

"What did you say, huh?" Grant snarled, grabbing Townsend by the neck. "Say another word and you're dead."

"Take your hands off me," Townsend said, struggling to pry Grant's fingers off his neck.

Kneeling forward, Rachel placed her forehead on the cold asphalt, her shoulders shaking as she sobbed. No one had ever died in her arms before. She'd seen dozens of dead bodies during the past two years, both adults and children, but she'd never held a dying teenager, never had one look at her and call her mother with his last words.

Flashes of the shooting passed through her mind, Grant pulling the boy in front of him just as the other boy fired the gun. It had all happened so fast. Had she really seen Grant using an innocent bystander as a human shield?

Rachel's mind flew back in time. She saw the circle of brilliant light in front of the Easy Eight Motel, felt the cold gust of night air brush across her naked body. Nathan Richardson had held her in front of him, using her as a shield against the police officers' guns he knew were waiting for him. The man had been a kidnapper and a pedophile, though, a far cry from a police officer.

The rest of the men who had responded were marching their youthful prisoners to their respective police units. Grant reached down and offered his hand to Rachel. When she ignored him, he dropped it back to his side. "Pretty hairy scene," he said, the muscles in his face jumping. "I'd already patted that kid down. I don't know where he got the damn shooter. I guess one of the other kids handed it to him just before he started firing. We're just lucky someone else wasn't killed out here." He stopped and popped his knuckles, looking off into space. "I took a shot at the little prick, but I missed. He was smart. As soon as he fired, he hit the deck."

Rachel slowly raised her eyes, making no attempt to mask the hatred she felt for Grant Cummings. Through the fabric of his uniform, she could clearly see the outline of his bulletproof vest.

"Come with us," one of the paramedics said to Rachel. "You can ride in the ambulance. You need to get that injury on your head treated. I think you're going to need a few stitches."

"I'll drive myself," she said, her eyes still trained on Grant. Could she have been mistaken? It was dark. With only one streetlight illuminating the area, it was hard to see anything that well. As Grant turned to speak to Ratso, though, her doubts disappeared. She knew what she had seen. Grant had purposely positioned the boy to protect himself. Seeing the sharp edge of his bulletproof vest pushing against the fabric of his police uniform, Rachel felt her blood begin to boil. Grant had broad shoulders and a narrow waist. When he wore his vest, his physique became more squared off and bulky.

Rachel didn't speak. While the men were conversing among themselves, she stood and walked back to her police unit.

chapter

ELEVEN

"You can use this phone," the ER nurse said, directing Rachel to a seat behind the counter at the reception station. The clock on the wall read 1:05. "Just make sure you keep it brief."

Once she got Sergeant Miller on the phone, she said, "I've got the victim's ID. His name is Timothy Hillmont." She stopped speaking, her fingers trembling on the boy's school identification card. He was just fifteen years old. He wouldn't turn sixteen for nine months. "Listen, I need to talk to you," she said before the sergeant had a chance to respond. "Something awful happened out there tonight." She craned her head around, seeing all the people assembled in the waiting room behind her. Every bed in the ER was full, and dozens of people were still waiting to be seen by a physician. "I don't want to talk over the phone," she continued. "I'll tell you what happened when I get to the station."

"How's your head?" he said. "I hear you got clobbered with a beer bottle."

Rachel fingered the bandage at the back of her head, trying to rearrange her hair to cover it. "Five stitches," she said. "Nothing serious. Do you have a pen? I'll give you the boy's address so you can send someone over to notify his parents. According to his ID, they live on Ridge Road. Several reporters have been snooping around here at the ER, trying to find out what went down. If you don't get someone to the kid's house right away, his parents are going to hear the news on television."

"You're at Presbyterian, right?" the sergeant asked.

"Yes," she said, propping her head up with one hand. "Why?"

"Ridge Road is only a few miles away," Miller told her. "Go ahead and handle the notification. When you're finished, I'll speak to you in the conference room."

"Can't someone else do it?" she said, dreading the thought of facing the boy's parents.

"What's the big deal?" he barked. "You've made death notifications before. Sometimes you act like a fucking rookie. I've got my whole watch tied up at Juvenile Hall booking prisoners, or back at the station writing reports. You're it, Simmons."

She cupped her hand over the receiver. "I've never made a notification on an officer-involved shooting," she whispered. "Don't you think someone else should handle it, maybe a lieutenant or a captain? You know, someone who wasn't involved. What if the parents start asking questions?"

Sergeant Miller's voice took on a sharper edge. "This is *not* an officer-involved shooting. I don't know where you come up with this stuff. We didn't take the kid out. One of the rioters shot him. Weren't you there, Simmons? Don't you know what happened out there?"

"I know more than you think," Rachel said, slamming the phone down in his ear.

By the time Rachel pulled up in front of the Hillmont residence on Ridge Road, it was 1:45 Sunday morning. She spotted a light burning in the back, but the rest of the house was dark. Even though she had handled other death notifications, she had never gone out alone, and never when the victim had been as young as this one. She reached for the door handle to exit the car, then froze. Were the parents awake, she wondered, just sitting in there waiting for their son to come walking through the door? She felt that by remaining in the car, she was somehow delaying their misery. A dozen questions raced through her mind. Did they have other children? Had the boy ever been in trouble before? Was there a father inside the house, or was the mother a single parent like herself?

"God," she exclaimed, her fingers tightening on the steering wheel. She was the messenger of death, a speeding missile set to destroy the lives of people she had never met. She remembered the phone call from the hospital the night Joe had passed away. How could she ever forget it? It had been the one night she had left the hospital to spend time with her daughter. She had promised her husband she would be by his side at the end. It would be many long years before she would rid herself of the guilt.

She walked up the narrow brick walkway, lined with blooming rose-bushes. Everything about the house seemed surreal. It was all too perfect, almost like a page ripped out of a magazine. The manicured yard, the flowers, the little white fence around the front yard, even the way the moon was dangling right over the rooftop, as if she could reach up and grab it. This was the kind of house she dreamed of purchasing someday.

The image of Grant pulling the boy in front of him kept appearing in her mind. Had he acted on instinct? Did he forget he was wearing his vest? Or was the fearlessness he usually exhibited nothing more than a cleverly concocted act? Was Grant Cummings the coward she suspected he was—a man who would sacrifice another person's life in order to protect himself?

She rang the bell and waited. After some time had passed, she heard a woman's high-pitched voice, then a few moments later, she heard heavy footsteps. A tall, distinguished-looking man with graying hair and puffy eyes cracked the door open and peered out at her. He was dressed in a bathrobe.

Rachel took her badge out of her back pocket and held it up close to his face. "I'm Officer Simmons with the Oak Grove PD," she said. "May I come in? There's been . . ." She started to say *an accident*, but it didn't apply. The door opened wider, revealing a dark-haired woman in her middle fifties with her hand pressed over her mouth. Dressed in black stretch pants and a long overblouse, Liz Hillmont had a pair of reading glasses perched low on her nose.

"Oh, my God," she exclaimed, "it's Tim, Larry. Something's happened to Timmy."

"Maybe it would be better if we spoke inside," Rachel said, moving forward a few steps into the doorway.

The man's brows furrowed. "Yes, of course," he said, stepping aside and motioning for Rachel to enter.

The mother was already crying, tears streaming down her face.

Rachel pictured her in a back room of the house where she'd seen the light burning, reading a book as she waited for her son to come home. "He's dead, isn't he?" she said.

"Yes," she said, having to cough the word out like a piece of dislodged meat. "I'm sorry." It was as if the woman had known in advance. She didn't ask if her son had been arrested, or if he'd been injured in a traffic accident, the first things that should have popped into her mind. Rachel suspected that with the weird premonition that all mothers seemed to possess, the woman had known her son was dead the moment Rachel stepped onto her porch.

They were standing in the small entryway, the front door still open behind them. As Mrs. Hillmont collapsed into her husband's arms, Rachel caught the scent of roses floating past her in the night air. She thought of funerals and the sickening, too-sweet smell of flowers. These people would be there soon, she thought, selecting a gravesite, a funeral home, sobbing as they watched their son's casket lowered into the ground.

"How did it happen?" the father said, his arm around his wife's waist.

"There was a fight in front of the Majestic Theater," Rachel said. "One of the boys had a gun."

"D-did he suffer?" the mother said, her words catching in her throat. With one hand she clutched her husband's robe, as if she would slide to the ground if she released it.

"No," Rachel said. "It was very quick. The bullet punctured his lung. I was with him when he died." She started to tell the woman that her son had asked for her, but she knew it would only intensify her agony. Later, she thought.

"Where is he?" the father said.

"His body is still at the hospital right now, but they'll be transferring him to the medical examiner's office in the next hour or so," she told him. "We'll need one of you to confirm his identity. He was carrying his school ID on his person, but we still need a relative to officially confirm it's your son. We can either go to the hospital right away, or—"

"We'll go now," the mother said, a frenzied look on her face. "Wait here while I get my purse."

The woman could not give up hope that the police were mistaken. Rachel could read it in her eyes. Once his wife had left the room, Mr.

Hillmont coughed several times in what Rachel thought was an attempt to keep from crying. His grief was etched on his face, though, and his skin had turned an ashen shade. "Does he . . ." He stopped, sniffed, then continued. "Does he look bad? I mean, maybe Liz shouldn't see him. He's our only son, you see. We had another son, but he died."

"The bullet entered here," Rachel said, pointing to one side of her chest. "His face isn't disfigured. I think it's better if your wife sees him now, though, rather than wait and have to make the identification later. A hospital is a better environment than a morgue, don't you think?" As soon as the words were out of her mouth, she wanted to snatch them back. A hospital was a place where they took sick people. A morgue was strictly for the dead. Accepting the death of a loved one happened over a period of time. No one could instantly absorb the finality of such an event.

The man slumped against the wall, grabbing his chest. Rachel was afraid he was having a heart attack. After a few moments, he seemed to snap out of it. "Excuse me," he said stiffly, "I'll need to get dressed."

Rachel stood at the pay phone in the women's locker room. It was after eight in the morning, and she was on the phone with Tracy. "I can't come home for a while," she said, knowing her daughter was alone at the house.

"Why not?" Tracy said. "I was supposed to go to Magic Mountain today with Sheila and her parents. They're on their way over here to pick me up right now."

"Ask Lucy if she'll watch Joe until I get there," Rachel said, having forgotten about her daughter's plans.

"I just saw her drive off in the station wagon to go to church."

"You'll have to stay with Joe until I get there, then," Rachel said, sighing deeply. Her head was throbbing, but right now it seemed to be the least of her problems.

"Sheila and I planned this a long time ago," her daughter said. "You promised me I could go. Why can't you come home? Are you going to another beach party? Maybe I'd like to go to a party too, but I'm always stuck looking after Joe."

"I'm not going to a party," Rachel said, trying not to take offense at her daughter's sarcastic tone. "A young boy was killed last night. I have to work late to finish my reports."

"Why did you even have Joe?" Tracy shot out. "You never spend any time with him."

"I-I . . ." Rachel was speechless. Her daughter had never spoken to her this way before. When she finally collected herself, she realized she was listening to a dial tone.

Grant Cummings, Sergeant Miller, Jimmy Townsend, Fred Ramone, Rachel, and Ted Harriman were all assembled around the conference table, located a few doors down from the chief's office. Whenever a major incident occurred, Chief Bates insisted that the officers involved be put through a debriefing session before they sat down to write their reports. The chief felt it was better to find out where their stories differed before the men put them into writing. Among the cities in Ventura County, Oak Grove had the lowest crime rate. The cases they presented to the DA seldom fell apart during prosecution. Chief Gregory Bates was certain the debriefing he put his officers through was partly responsible for the success of their cases in the courtroom.

In a symbolic gesture, Rachel had taken a seat at the end of the table, far away from the other officers. She sat stiff-backed and sullen, her eyes glued to Grant Cummings's profile.

The scene at the hospital had been worse than Rachel had anticipated. Mrs. Hillmont had appeared fairly composed on the ride over. Rachel had the impression that she was a strong person. When she'd seen her son's body, though, the woman had become hysterical, throwing herself on top of him and screaming that she wanted to die. The men from the medical examiner's office had arrived shortly thereafter, compounding the tragedy. They had other stops to make, they said. They wanted to take the body immediately, and insisted that Rachel get the mother and father out of the room, even if she had to physically restrain them. Rachel had refused, ending up in a shouting match with the two morgue attendants while Mrs. Hillmont screamed and cried over her dead son's body.

She took in the men assembled at the table. Everyone had changed into street clothes, basically T-shirts and jeans. She had worn her only set of extra clothes to the beach the day before, and had nothing left in her locker to wear. She was still dressed in her blood-splattered uniform, her hair hanging in thick, matted strands to her shoulders.

Everyone in the room, with the exception of Sergeant Miller, had been present at the Majestic Theater. Although additional units had responded as well, they had not arrived until after the shooting and were not included in the debriefing. The sergeant had been having breakfast at Denny's when the fight had broken out.

Ted Harriman was seated directly across from Grant Cummings. Knowing how he felt about Grant, Rachel linked eyes with him across the table. She knew Harriman was honest, and that the ex-Marine was not afraid to speak out if the situation called for it. If he could substantiate Rachel's story, it would make things a lot easier.

Jimmy Townsend was slumped in his seat, his arms resting on his ample abdomen. Rachel recalled his bitter comment to Grant while the paramedics were working over the boy. She knew he had witnessed the shooting. He had been only a few feet away from her at the time. Would he tell the truth? It was a difficult call.

"Okay, troops," Sergeant Miller said, "let's go through the events of last night step by step. Who was the first unit on the scene?"

Grant raised his hand.

"Grant drives like a maniac," Townsend said, scowling and jumpy. "That's why he always gets there before everyone else."

"When you're in trouble, Jimmy boy," Grant snapped, "you never mind me exceeding the speed limit. I've bailed your fat ass out about fifteen times in the past year alone."

"We're not here to discuss who gets to the scene first," Miller said, sensing the tension mounting in the room. "The sooner we get our stories together, the sooner we'll be able to get out of here and go home. What was happening when you got there, Grant?"

"You know," he said, glancing over at Rachel, "it wasn't a complex situation, Sarge. Just your typical gang of rowdy kids. It's getting close to graduation time, so they're already out drinking and raising hell. We've had problems at the Majestic before. When they were showing the *Rocky Horror Picture Show*, we had fights there every Saturday night."

"How many kids do you estimate were out there?"

"I'd say twenty, maybe twenty-five," Grant continued. "As soon as I arrived, I dove in and tried to see what I could do to contain the situation. The shooter—what's his name? Donald Trueman, right? He was punching another kid in the gut. When I tried to stop him, he took a swing at me. I got him on the ground and was about to cuff the little bastard when this bottle sails right past my head."

"Who was the bottle thrower?" Miller asked, leaning back in his chair.

None of the officers present on the beach the day before had fully recovered. Now that it was mid-morning with hours left before they would see a bed, the sergeant and everyone else in the room looked as if they were on their last legs. Ratso kept nodding off; Jimmy Townsend had to kick him several times under the table to wake him up.

"As far as we can tell, the bottle thrower was the kid who got shot," Townsend offered, glancing down at his notes. "His name was Timothy Hillmont. I checked our records, and he's never been arrested or cited before. Perhaps you should ask Rachel what she found out. She notified the family, right?"

"Did you witness the actual shooting?" the sergeant asked.

"*Nada*, Sarge," Townsend answered, rubbing the dark stubble on his face. "I was busy dodging bottles and wrestling kids. I heard the shot, and then everything just turned to worms. Grant was firing at the shooter. I saw the Hillmont kid on the ground. When I saw Rachel on the ground beside him, I thought they'd shot her as well. She had blood on her face, blood in her hair. I squeezed off a couple of rounds, trying to take down the shooter. We all thought we'd nailed the little sucker," he said, pausing and chuckling. "Guess we need to spend more time at the pistol range. At least we didn't shoot each other."

Townsend's chuckles made Rachel's stomach turn. "You're lying, Jimmy," she said. "You saw what happened out there. Do you think I didn't hear what you said to Grant? Maybe you wouldn't think it was so funny if it was one of your kids who got killed tonight."

Townsend's face flushed in anger. "I don't know what you're talking about," he said. "And I refuse to let you call me a liar." He pushed his bulky body out of the chair, his shoulders bunched up around his ears.

Rachel was faster. She stood and kicked her chair aside, curling her finger and challenging him. "You got the best of me the other night," she said, yanking out her baton. "Maybe we should even the score."

"That's enough!" Miller shouted, grabbing Rachel's baton and placing it on the floor by his chair. "One more outburst, and I'll place you both on suspension."

"Rachel's the one making all the trouble," Townsend said, squeezing himself back in his chair.

"Jimmy, I want you to interview the other kids," Miller said, wanting to bring the meeting to a close as soon as possible. "Ratso, I want you to pull all their records, and see if any of the rioters have ever been in trouble before."

The sergeant bypassed Ratso for the moment, zeroing in on Ted Harriman instead. "What was your involvement in this incident?"

"I was the last unit to arrive, sir," Harriman said in his Georgia drawl. "I gathered up some juveniles on the perimeter of the problem area. Since I had three of them in tow, I really couldn't jump back in at that point and give the rest of the crew a hand. Like Townsend, I heard the first shot, but I didn't see the actual shooting go down."

Rachel's face fell. If Harriman said he had not witnessed the shooting, she had to believe he was telling the truth. Outside of Chris Lowenberg, Ted Harriman was the only man on her watch she felt she could trust. Staring at his rich mahogany skin, she thought about Captain Madison. Since the captain had not been present during the incident, Rachel doubted if there was anything he could do for her.

"Ratso," Nick Miller said, "what did you see out there?"

"Ah," he said, looking at Grant, "you mean the shooting, Sergeant?"

"What do you think we've been talking about?" Miller said, his voice thick with sarcasm.

"I saw the boy with the yellow shirt pointing a gun at Grant," he said. "I dropped down for cover. I didn't see what happened after that."

Rachel's voice seemed to come out of nowhere. "I saw it all," she said. "Why don't you ask me what happened?"

The room fell silent.

"When I got there," she said, "Grant had Donald Trueman on the ground and was kicking him in the ribs. In case you're not aware of it, Sergeant, Grant has steel loaded into the toes of his boots."

"That's a bold-faced lie," Grant said. He yanked off one of his boots and tossed it on the table with a loud thud. "Check it yourself, Sarge. She's out of her frigging mind."

Sergeant Miller reached over and felt the end of Grant's boot, then handed it back to him. "There's nothing there," he said, glancing over at Rachel. "It's just a heavy boot, Simmons. Granted, it might be heavy enough to do some damage, but it's not outside of department regulations."

"He must have changed them already," she said, grimacing. "He always wears steel-toed boots." She narrowed her eyes at the other men. "They all know it. They just won't admit it. They probably have steel in the toes of their boots as well."

"Forget the fucking boots," the sergeant shouted, spitting the toothpick out of his mouth without realizing it. He didn't like the way things were shaping up. He was responsible for the officers on his watch. If the shooting was reviewed by the brass and his troops' conduct was determined to have been less than stellar, he would be the person who would end up taking all the heat. He was attempting to make lieutenant, and the test was only two months away. His climb up the ladder had not been swift, nor had it been easy. He was not about to kiss off his career over a shooting incident involving a gang of kids. "What do you think happened out there, Simmons?" he asked, a pained look on his face. "The situation appears fairly simple to me. One dumbass kid shot another dumbass kid. Happens all the time."

"It's not what I think happened," Rachel said forcefully, "it's what I *know* happened. I was standing only a few feet from Grant. While Grant was kicking Donald Trueman, another kid threw a beer bottle at him. I'm not sure if it was Timothy Hillmont who threw the bottle, or someone standing close to him. Grant left Trueman on the ground and went chasing after Hillmont. He had Hillmont by the arm and was about to cuff him when someone yelled, 'Look out! He's got a gun!'"

She paused and sucked in a breath. Grant had caused a young boy to lose his life. There was no way she was going to let him get away with it. As Lucy had pointed out the other day, just because they were police officers didn't mean they weren't accountable for their actions. "A second after the person warned us about the gun," she said, "I saw Grant grab Hillmont by the shoulders and position him in front of his body, using him as a human shield. As soon as the kid caught the bullet in the chest, Grant dumped him on the ground and began firing at the shooter."

Grant leaped to his feet. "You're a damn liar," he said, waving his arms in protest. "You know what this is all about, Sarge. She's still pissed about what happened on the beach. She's making up this silly story to get back at me."

The room plunged into silence again. Jimmy Townsend looked down at his notepad. Sergeant Miller rubbed his bloodshot eyes. Ratso straightened up in his seat. They'd never seen an officer accuse another officer of so much as fudging on a parking ticket. If something went wrong in the field, the men made it right before they reached the station.

Rachel stared into Grant's eyes without flinching. "Trueman wasn't aiming at Hillmont," she said. "He was aiming at Grant because Grant had just kicked the shit out of him with a pair of steel-toed boots. You saw the emergency room report, Sergeant. If what I'm telling you isn't true, how did this kid get four of his ribs broken?"

"Well," Miller said slowly, "any number of things could have caused the boy's injury. He could have been hit with a bottle, another kid could have punched him or kicked him." A slight tremor appeared in his voice. "Do you realize what you're saying, Simmons? These are extremely serious charges."

"I realize that," she said, adrenaline coursing through her veins. "The Hillmont boy was only fifteen. He'd be alive right now if Grant hadn't acted like a coward. Why did he need to use the kid as a shield? He was wearing his bulletproof vest. The kid was completely defenseless. For all practical purposes, Grant killed that boy." She stopped and took a breath before spitting out the next sentence. "Since when are we allowed to use bystanders, or even prisoners, for that matter, as a shield to protect us from a bullet?"

Grant paced next to the conference table, a vicious look on his face. Rachel felt herself perspiring and blotted her forehead with a napkin off the table.

"I guess you'd rather one of us get killed than some punkass kid off the street," Grant growled. "I never pulled that kid in front of me. If you saw anything, it must have been an optical illusion."

Ratso, who generally never said so much as a word during the squad meetings, suddenly spoke up. "Rachel got hit on the head before the shooting even went down, Sergeant. You know," he continued, "maybe it affected her vision. She was bleeding pretty profusely when I saw her. She could have had blood in her eyes."

"You lost it out there," Rachel said, glaring at the dark-skinned man. "I saw him trying to smash a boy's head open on the pavement like a watermelon. What was that all about, Ratso?"

"The kid was resisting arrest," he said. The rage she had seen during the riot sparked momentarily in his smoky eyes.

"He was in handcuffs," she said. "How could he resist when he was already on the ground and cuffed? You beat him because you wanted to beat him. I didn't know you were like that, Ratso. You've been hanging around Grant too long. You're beginning to act just like him."

"You are mistaken," he answered. "The suspect was fighting me, trying to flee. I didn't do anything out of line."

"Shut the fuck up, Ratso," the sergeant snarled, knowing the more serious problem involved the charge that Grant Cummings had used the Hillmont boy as a shield. "Cummings and Simmons, I'll see you in my office. The rest of you start writing. No one's allowed to leave the building until we agree on what happened last night."

Three pairs of red-rimmed eyes turned to Rachel. Even Ted Harriman looked annoyed. "Fucking women," Townsend mumbled as Rachel walked past him.

chapter

TWELVE

Rachel followed the sergeant down several corridors to the opposite side of the building, Grant stomping along a few feet behind them. When they reached his office, Miller pointed to a chair in the corridor, grunted at Rachel, then waved Grant into his office and slammed the door.

"She's full of shit," Grant said, slouching in a chair.

"Be quiet," Sergeant Miller hissed, taking a seat behind a small metal desk. "Give me some time to think this through." For a long time, the sergeant stared over Grant's head. The tiny room was about the size of a broom closet, and it wasn't even *his* office. He had to share it with the sergeants from the other watches. If he made lieutenant, he'd have a private office all to himself.

He braced his head in his hands, trying to come up with a reasonable way to defuse the situation. Picking up his copy of the California Penal Code, he tried to figure out what type of offense they might legally charge Grant with for using a bystander as a shield. It certainly violated every rule within the department, but he was also concerned that Grant's actions constituted a prosecutable felony. They could charge him with wrongful death or manslaughter, he decided, but he didn't see how they could classify it as murder. Grant surely didn't intend for the boy to die, and intent was a required element in a homicide. If Grant had done what Rachel said, he decided, he must have done it instinctively, like a person who raises his hands to his head when he believes someone is about to hit him.

Did he believe Rachel was telling the truth? Absolutely. After two years of attempting to turn her into a competent police officer, he had learned enough about Rachel Simmons to know that she wouldn't lie. He also knew she could have been mistaken. She was an inexperienced officer who had never been in a situation where gunfire was exchanged. Whatever Rachel believed she had seen, however, was what she would testify to in a court of law. She had made this clear with the Brentwood case. Another officer would have supported Townsend's statements, whether he had actually seen him remove the gun or not. That's the way things were done in a police department. Police science wasn't specific. Lawyers were specific. Cops had simply learned to give the lawyers what they wanted. If cops didn't doctor their stories now and then and present a unified front, every other person they took to court would go free.

As a whistle-blower, Rachel Simmons could easily become the department's worst nightmare.

When Chief Gregory Bates had transferred from Simi Valley to Oak Grove ten years before, he had taken a force of poorly trained and marginal officers and made it into one of the finest departments in the county. Unlike the LAPD, Oak Grove had previously had an unsullied reputation. In the five years he had been sergeant, not one officer had been formally charged with brutality or the use of excessive force. If there were racist cops among the rank and file, they had learned to keep their prejudices to themselves.

Snapping the penal code shut, Miller knew the problem was as serious as any he had ever faced in his career. If Rachel went to the press with her accusations about Grant Cummings, the entire department would stand in disgrace. The media hungered for stories about police brutality and misconduct. Bad cops sold newspapers and kept tabloid television shows in business. Once the cat was out of the bag, the Oak Grove Police Department, despite its previous record of excellence, would be known all over the county for its brutal and sexist cops.

Things had gotten out of hand at the beach.

If the situation had involved only Grant Cummings, it would not be so bad. Instead, it involved the core group of troublemakers that Miller had tried to keep out of sight of the brass. Working graveyards played with a man's mind, and Miller had a tendency to get bored during the long, slow nights. He had moved too close to Grant's group, having been friends with the man since the police academy. When they were younger, the two men had traded off girlfriends and shared wild times. He gave Grant a harsh look, wishing he'd had the foresight to have him transferred off his watch. "Was it you or Townsend who decided to put Valium in Rachel's beer?"

"Townsend," Grant said, scratching the side of his face. "It was just a prank, Sarge. She's so tight-assed and prudish, we thought it would be fun to see her smashed out of her mind."

"Well, I hope you enjoyed yourself," he barked. "That little prank, as you call it, might ultimately cost you your shield."

"Nah," Grant said, shaking his head. "I guarantee she never knew what hit her. What's she going to do to us? As far as anyone will ever know, she was drunk as a skunk. If she didn't want to get down and dirty with us, why did she come to the watch party?"

The sergeant spread his elbows out on the desk. "She knew what was happening when she woke up, though. Right, asshole?" Once Rachel had passed out, they'd all acted like a bunch of sex-starved hyenas, taking turns fondling her breasts, cracking jokes about her, shoving sand down her jeans. Ratso had said she reminded him of one of those blow-up dolls they sell in sex stores—limp and lifeless, her mouth open for business.

As far as the sergeant knew, none of the men had gone so far as to have intercourse with her, but they were all involved in what would be viewed by the public as disgusting and vile behavior. They had all been active participants, himself included. What would his wife think, his children? His oldest son was about to go to college. His twin daughters were just entering high school. They had always looked up to him, treated him like a god.

"What's all the talk about the beach for?" Grant said, his jaw thrust forward. "I'm not about to take the blame for what went on out there. I was the last man to have a go at her, remember? From what I saw, you had a bang-up time playing with her tits. Ratso's even got a picture of you making out with her." He gave the sergeant a knowing glance. "You know, I thought you might want a souvenir for your scrapbook."

"I should wring your lousy neck," the sergeant shouted, furious. "If you're telling the truth and you do have pictures, the prints along with the negatives better be in my hands by tomorrow night or you'll be the sorriest motherfucker to ever walk the face of the earth. Are we clear on this?"

Grant didn't answer. He had suspected the photos would come in handy when he'd instructed Ratso to take them. He never thought he would need them this quickly, though. "I swear I didn't shove that kid in front of me. If I'm lying, then why don't the other guys corroborate Rachel's story? It's a crock of shit, that's why. That woman's dangerous, Sarge. She's not fit to be an officer. She needs to go in for a psych evaluation, pay a visit to the department shrink or something. Look how she screwed up that robbery."

"Locking her keys in the car with the engine running was a dumb stunt, Cummings," Miller said, "but I don't think it can compare to the allegations she's making about you."

"It was more than the car keys," Grant told him. "She also locked her portable radio in the car, so she had to use the pay phone to check in with the station. She didn't think of asking the clerk if the suspect had touched anything in the store until it was too late." He paused and laughed. "The only thing the guy touched was the damn phone. By then Rachel had covered up the suspect's fingerprints with her own. She begged me to help her, so I did. And this is the thanks I get. First she kicks me in the balls. Now she's making up crazy stories about me, trying to say I was responsible for that kid's death."

"Let's back up a minute," the sergeant said, acid bubbling back in his throat. "Tell me again about the fingerprints. What exactly are you talking about?"

"I wiped the phone down for her," he said. "She was afraid she'd get canned if the truth came out. I felt sorry for her. I bagged the perp the other night, so what the hell difference does it make?"

"You destroyed evidence," Miller shouted, spit flying from his mouth. "And you have the gall to sit here and admit it to my face."

"Hey," Grant said, as calm as before, "you want to shitcan me, go ahead. I'm one of the best officers you have and you know it. Before you made sergeant, I bailed your ass out a few times, too. Have you forgotten the drug bust on Morningside Road? You read the numbers on the search warrant wrong. We ripped apart the wrong house and the old fart who lived there had a heart attack. The department was sued over that incident, remember? Because you thought it might keep you from getting your stripes, I took the fall for you."

"Get out," the sergeant said, pointing toward the door. "You're a loose cannon, Cummings. You're not fit to carry a badge."

"No problem," Grant said, standing and striding to the door. "Just remember one thing," he said, glancing back. "If I go down, I'm taking a lot of people with me. Since you might be one of them, I suggest you find a way to keep Rachel Simmons in line."

Picking up a toothpick from a box on his desk, Sergeant Miller shoved it between his teeth. What he needed was a cigarette, maybe a stiff drink. Crossing the room, he opened the door and tilted his head, indicating Rachel should come into his office.

Instead of taking a seat, she stood in front of his desk.

"Sit down," he said.

"I don't feel like sitting down."

"Fine," he said, placing his palms on top of the desk and glaring at her. "I'll stand, too."

Rachel dropped into the chair.

"Okay," Sergeant Miller said, slowly lowering himself into his seat, "let me make something perfectly clear here, Simmons. What you said in the briefing room could cost Grant Cummings his shield. Are you aware of that?"

"Timothy Hillmont is dead," she said. "I don't think Grant's problem compares to his."

"None of the men's statements support your version of what happened out there," he went on. "How can you be certain what you saw when you'd just been hit over the head with a beer bottle? As Ratso pointed out during the meeting, your visual perception could have been less than accurate."

"I know what I saw," Rachel insisted, her voice ringing with conviction. "I didn't receive a concussion. It was only a scalp wound. I was in no way impaired. I was looking directly at Grant when the boy fired at him. Townsend saw what Grant did. He just won't admit it because of their friendship. For all I know, they all saw it. Even Ratso is turning into an animal. Cruelty is contagious. If you ask me, Grant Cummings is the source. I guess the men figure if Grant can beat the crap out of people, they can too."

Oh boy, Miller thought, running his fingers through his already disheveled hair. The woman who had once been so submissive, almost scared of her own shadow, had suddenly developed a king-size set of balls. He could see it in her eyes, read it in her body language. He had to find a way to get her to back down. If he didn't, the whole disgusting mess might surface. "Let's try to discuss this rationally," he said. "Say Grant did what you said. I don't believe he did, but just for the purpose of conjecture, let's pretend everything happened exactly as you said."

"Pretend!" Rachel shouted, rising a few inches from her chair. "Now we have to *pretend* I'm telling the truth. My word no longer has any value."

"Okay, okay," Miller said, holding up a palm, "maybe I used the wrong word. Calm down. You said Grant was holding Timothy Hillmont by the arm. That means the boy was standing beside him, right?"

"Right," she said, kicking her leg back and forth.

"If the boy was standing right beside Grant, then he could have easily been hit by the bullet no matter what Grant did or didn't do. Do you agree on this point?"

She ran it over in her mind before speaking. "Possibly," she said, "but I doubt if the Hillmont boy's wound would have been fatal under those circumstances. When Grant moved him in front of his body, he caused the boy to take a direct hit to his chest. The bullet punctured his lung."

During his many years as a cop, Nick Miller had done some outrageous things, but he had never once been called on the carpet. His record was flawless, his chances to move up the ladder excellent. Was this where it all stopped? Was a scrawny, freckled-faced woman going to be the one to finally take him down? "Do you really believe Grant did this on purpose?"

"Of course," she said, nodding. "He did it to protect himself at the expense of the kid. I don't know if he forgot that he was wearing his vest, or what was wrong with him. I only know what I saw."

After a number of strained moments had passed, Miller shifted to another tactic. "Have I treated you fairly since you joined the department?"

Rachel blinked several times, not certain where the sergeant was going. "Not always," she said. "I thought my last performance review was unfair. You rated my performance below average in almost every category. I've been here every day on time. I always try to do my job to the best of my abilities. I've never had a citizen's complaint filed against me, and my response time has always been in line with department policy." Since they were putting everything on the table, she decided she might as well speak her mind. "The detective bureau has commended me on my reports on numerous occasions. Even Captain Madison praised me the other night over a rape case I handled. I don't know what I did to deserve such a lousy review, other than the fact that I'm a woman."

"I wasn't really referring to your performance review," Sergeant Miller said, chastising himself for coming down so hard on her. In many ways, Rachel's statements were true. She wasn't a bad officer. She had an outstanding memory, and her writing skills were as good as anyone's in the department. Her reports were concise and cohesive, painstakingly detailed and consistently accurate. He'd just never been fond of women in patrol. A field officer had to be aggressive, cunning, alert to his or her environment. Rachel Simmons was not aggressive. "I mean," he went on, "have I given you the proper field training?"

"Yes," she said, pushing a shock of red hair back behind one ear. "I don't have any complaints in that area."

"Being a member of this department is the same as belonging to a closely knit family," Miller continued, his tone less confrontational than before. "Families look out for one another, take care of one another, sometimes even bend the rules for each other. When you had a problem the other day with some fingerprints, someone helped you resolve it. Isn't that true?"

Rachel's jaw dropped. "Are you referring to the robbery?"

"Yes, I am," he said.

"You can't possibly condone what Grant did," she said, her eyes enormous. "He tampered with evidence in a felony."

"He didn't tamper with evidence to save his own neck, though," the sergeant pointed out. "Right?"

"No," she said, flicking the ends of her fingernails. "He did it for me, but I swear I never asked him to wipe down that phone. I knew I'd screwed up, and I guess I just panicked. You'd been all over me the past month. I'd just lost my side job with State Farm. When I asked Grant to help me, I don't know what I expected him to do."

"With your recent performance review," Miller said, arching an eyebrow, "and the incompetent manner in which you handled the robbery, the personnel review board might consider this sufficient grounds for dismissal."

Rachel leaned forward in her seat, a hand pressed into her abdomen. "What are you saying?"

"I think you get the gist," he answered, fiddling with some papers on his desk.

She gripped the arms of the chair. "You want me to lie, right?"

"I didn't say that."

"I need this job," she said. "I have two kids to support. You're trying to blackmail me into covering up what Grant did with the Hillmont boy. How can I sleep at night if I don't tell the truth? I'm the one you sent to tell this boy's parents he was dead. Do you know how terrible it is to lose a child? Don't these people have a right to know what really happened to their son?"

"Well," the sergeant said, his voice just above a whisper, "sometimes a person has to compromise their standards. The world is not an easy place, Simmons. Do you get my drift?"

"Can I go now?" Rachel said, standing.

"Are we in agreement?"

"I guess so," she said, holding onto the back of the chair. "I lie or I lose my job. Isn't that the nature of our agreement? Since I can't afford to lose my job right now, I have no choice but to lie."

"Good," Miller said, brushing his hands over his face. "It's been a long night, Simmons. Go home now and get some sleep. You can come in later this afternoon and finish your report."

"I'm starting my days off," Rachel told him, a nasty, metallic taste in her mouth. "I'd rather not come back to the station. I've had enough of this place for one day."

"Finish the report at home," he said. "Just drop it by when you're finished. Leave it in my box."

chapter

THIRTEEN

At ten o'clock Monday morning, Mike Atwater's secretary received a call from Bill Ringwald, the elected district attorney of Ventura County.

Five minutes later, Atwater stuck his head in the door of Ringwald's office. "My secretary said you wanted to see me," he said. "I have a hearing at ten-thirty. Do we have enough time, or would you rather I come back later?"

"Come in," Ringwald said, a solemn look on his face. "I have a meeting myself this morning. We have to talk now."

Because of his position, Bill Ringwald had one of the coveted corner offices with floor-to-ceiling windows. Spacious and well-appointed, the room contained a large maple desk with a polished surface, two high-backed leather chairs facing Ringwald's desk, and a small conference table in the far corner. In his late fifties, Ringwald was a large, intense man with dark hair and a round face. His hair was combed carefully to cover his bald spot, then held in place with spray. His skin had a yellowish cast and was creased with heavy lines. An avid sailor, he had spent too many weekends baking in the California sun.

Ringwald's predecessor, Harvey Ledderman, had managed the agency like a Hollywood studio, cultivating a stable of star prosecutors. With the exception of Mike Atwater, Ledderman's top men had all abandoned the agency for greener pastures. They were now considered the legal elite of Ventura County. Many of them had large, prestigious law firms. A number had seats on the bench. One had even gone on to become a State Supreme Court justice.

For Atwater, though, the rewards of being a star prosecutor had not yet fully materialized. The attorney was still searching for the perfect case—one that would give him the widespread notoriety he craved. Ringwald had seen it before in other attorneys of Atwater's stature. Their eyes took on a frenzied look; they jumped on sensational cases the minute they came into the agency, thumbing their noses at crimes that weren't newsworthy enough. They became almost like ambulance chasers, showing up at crime scenes, cultivating contacts in the police departments, developing cases through the use of paid informants.

"Did you hear about the shooting Saturday night in Oak Grove?" Ringwald asked.

"The football player, right?" Atwater said, sitting down in one of the leather chairs. "Wasn't it some kind of school rivalry that got out of hand? As I understand it, the boys involved were on either the Simi Valley football team or were members of the Oak Grove team. Simi Valley won the state championship."

Ringwald stared off into space. "I've known Larry and Liz Hillmont since Larry first got a seat on the City Council." He paused, releasing a low sigh. "The man worshipped that boy. They had another son. He died of some rare disease when he was about ten years old. Liz was in her forties then, and didn't think she could get pregnant again."

Atwater fiddled with his ear. "The paper said the Hillmont kid might have had a chance to play college ball."

"Tim was a good kid," Ringwald said, thinking of his own son and the heartache his friends were suffering. "There's no indication he used drugs. He might have had a beer now and then, but the Hillmonts claim they never once saw him drunk."

"Well," he said, deciding Ringwald had called him in only to commiserate. "I only know what I read in the paper this morning. Sounds like the boy was in the wrong place at the wrong time, Bill. Sad, but with teenagers, these things sometimes happen." He glanced at his watch, then stood and walked toward the door.

"I'm assigning you to prosecute the Trueman boy for the shooting," Ringwald said.

The attorney turned with a scowl. "You don't need me to try this," he said, leaning back against the door. "It's an open-and-shut case. Dozens of police officers witnessed this crime. Even Blake Reynolds could try it. In ability and comprehension, he's about a seven now. When you brought him on board, I pegged him as never making it past a five."

Ringwald shook his head. The attorney's habit of constantly rating people was demeaning. "I don't want Reynolds," he said, looking him squarely in the eye. "Larry Hillmont has served this city for almost ten years. He deserves the best we have to offer."

Atwater's chest expanded. "I appreciate the praise," he said, "but isn't it a waste of talent? The paper said the suspect is a juvenile. I don't try juvenile cases."

"Trueman is sixteen," Ringwald told him. "With a crime this serious, we're fully justified in trying him as an adult. I know we don't have murder one, but I want this kid to go to prison for as long as possible. That's one of the reasons I want you to prosecute the case. Trueman isn't a gang member, and as far as we know, he has no prior criminal history." He plucked the newspaper off his desk, glancing at the article. "We're talking the quarterback on the Simi Valley football team. You know how these things go, Mike. Like you pointed out, the team just won the state championship. Can you imagine the support this kid will have from the community?"

"Are the police reports in yet?" Atwater asked.

"No," he said. "Trueman's in custody, though, so we'll have to arraign him by tomorrow at the latest. I spoke with Sergeant Miller at the PD earlier this morning, and he assured me they would have the reports in by late this afternoon."

A double homicide was on the burner, an insurance salesman who had gone berserk and killed his estranged wife and young daughter. Atwater had been anticipating it for several months, anxious to get his hands on something meaty and challenging. He knew it wasn't the case he needed to cap off his career as a county prosecutor, though. An insurance salesman from Ventura would not draw national attention and make him a household name. He had another situation that might be the ticket, but he would have to be patient and nurse it along. In the interim, he could not afford to waste his time trying juveniles.

The Ventura PD was putting the finishing touches on the double homicide, on the verge of making an arrest any day now. If Atwater got involved in the Hillmont matter, the case he wanted to try might fall through his fingers. "The Scarpella case is about to come in," he said. "The crime is horrendous and the evidence marginal. I just tried Brentwood, a mammoth waste of time. We convicted him on two drunk driving counts, both of them misdemeanors."

Ringwald gave him a cold stare. He respected the attorney's skills in the courtroom, but his ego sometimes ballooned beyond reason. "What are you trying to say?" he said, the muscles in his face tightening.

"If you promise to assign me Scarpella when it comes in," he said, "I'll agree to handle the Hillmont case."

"Let me tell you something," Ringwald snapped, leveling a finger at him. "You will try whatever case I tell you to try. I realize you've had carte blanche around here for years, but it's time for you to come down off your high horse and do as you're told."

Atwater looked as if the man had just struck him. His head jerked back. His hooded eyes flashed in outrage. Without speaking, he spun around and stormed out of the office.

When Tracy got home from school Monday afternoon, the house was spotless, the furniture in her room had been rearranged, and a chocolate cake was baking in the oven. She found Joe, dressed in clean dungarees, plunked down in front of the television set in the living room watching cartoons. Giving him a quick kiss on the top of the head, Tracy headed to the back of the house to find her mother.

Rachel was on the floor in her room lifting weights, her clothes soaked with perspiration. "Hi, baby," she said, dropping the barbell on the floor. She stood and rushed over to embrace her. "Did you see your room? I cleaned out your closet. I even did some work on your drawers. Don't you like the beds that way? It makes the room look a lot bigger."

"Thanks," Tracy said, pushing her mother back and studying her face. Her eyes were lined with dark circles, but she seemed to be bursting with energy. "I thought you were going to leave Joe with Lucy today, try to get caught up on your sleep. I heard you walking around in here all night last night. Are you on speed or something?"

"Of course not," Rachel said, laughing that her daughter would even suggest such a thing. "I went to the store and picked up two great-looking steaks for us. I thought we'd cook them on the grill. You know, have a little barbecue. I even bought some paper plates so we can eat outside."

"MOM," Tracy shouted, her hands on her hips. "Will you please slow down a minute? How many cups of coffee have you had today?"

"I don't know," Rachel said, picking the weights off the floor and lining them up in a neat row against the back wall. "What difference does it make?"

"You're wired," her daughter said. "I've seen kids on drugs who are more mellow. What's going on? Why are you acting like this?"

"Nothing's wrong," Rachel lied, patting her face with a towel. "I just wanted to get some things done around the house. Now that I lost the State Farm job, there's no reason for you to do all the housework. I'll have my days off to spend with Joe. You can go out with your friends."

"You didn't tell me you lost the State Farm job," Tracy said. Even though she had pressed her mother to quit, she knew they needed the extra income. She had been wearing the same clothes for over a year. The kids at her school made fun of her. She hemmed them, dyed them, added different accessories she scrounged from her mother, but they were still the same clothes.

"Oh, didn't I?" Rachel answered, folding the towel neatly and placing it on the edge of her bureau. "Well, it's for the best. You were right, honey. Working two jobs was too much for me, and it wasn't fair to you and Joe. We hardly saw each other."

"It's more than that, isn't it?" Tracy said, her stomach churning. "Something's wrong. I can tell by the way you're acting. When Dad died, you didn't stop cleaning for a month. You finally collapsed from exhaustion and ended up spending a week in the hospital."

"Sit down," Rachel said, sitting on the edge of the bed and patting the spot next to her. She had been anguishing about the incident with Grant and the Hillmont boy ever since it had occurred. If she let the house go and moved to an apartment, she felt certain they could get by even if she lost her job at the department and had to secure employment elsewhere. Tracy was very attached to her school and friends, though, and Rachel wanted to test the waters before she decided what she would say in her report. "What would be the worst thing that could happen to us?"

"I don't know," Tracy said. Her mother had played this game for years. She believed a person had to visualize the worst and learn to accept it. If you could do this, her mother had always preached, then the other problems you encountered would seem insignificant. "I guess if you were to get killed."

"I'm not going to get killed, okay?" Rachel said, taking her hand. "Now, what's the second worst thing that could happen?"

"This is stupid," Tracy said, jerking her hand away. "I'm not like you, Mother. You believe bad things can be turned into good things. Bad things are just bad things. The world is full of bad things, bad people, bad diseases."

Rachel put a finger under her chin. "Come on, think."

Her daughter sighed. "If you lost your job, okay?"

"I could always get another job," Rachel countered. "It's not like the income I earn at the PD is such a tremendous salary. I could probably make the same amount of money working as a waitress in a busy restaurant."

"We talked about that when Dad died," Tracy said. "If you work as a waitress, we won't have any medical benefits. Dad *had* insurance, remember, and we still ended up owing thousands of dollars to hospitals and doctors."

"That's because his insurance didn't cover certain chemotherapy drugs," her mother explained. "If a person doesn't have insurance or is too poor to pay their medical bills, the government will pay for their treatment. We might have been better off if we'd had nothing . . . no insurance, no savings account, no house."

"Now we're going on welfare?" Tracy cried. "You promised no matter what happened, you'd never make us go on welfare."

"I'm not suggesting we go on welfare," Rachel said, attempting a laugh. "If I lose my job and have to work as a waitress, we'll just have to make certain we don't get sick."

"Right," the girl said facetiously. "Look what happened to Dad. A person has to have medical coverage. Even I'm old enough to know that."

Rachel took a deep breath, then slowly let it out. "What if we had to move to an apartment? How would you feel about that?"

"Would it be in the same school district?"

"I don't know," her mother said, dropping her eyes. "I haven't checked the price of apartments around here yet. Lucy says the rents are considerably lower in Simi Valley." Seeing the look on her daughter's face, she added, "It might not happen. I just want us to be prepared in case it does. Things haven't been going that well at work lately."

Tracy buried her head in her hands. When her father died, she had been uprooted, ripped away from her friends at a time when she had needed them the most. Now when she had just befriended Matt, starting her very first relationship with a boy, her mother was telling her they were going to have to move again. Life sucked. Some mornings when she opened her eyes, she wanted to turn around and go back to bed, maybe never wake up again.

"Why is life always just one problem after another?" she cried. Leaving her mother sitting on the bed, Tracy raced down the hall to her room and slammed the door.

After she had bathed Joe, Rachel put him to sleep in her bed. Tracy had refused to come out for dinner, and was still holed up in her room with the door locked. The steaks had gone into the freezer. She was about to heat up some soup for herself when the phone rang.

"Is this Rachel?" a man's voice said.

"Yes," she said. "Who is this?"

"Mike Atwater," he answered. "Have you already had dinner?"

Rachel glanced over at the pot of soup bubbling on the stove. "Is that an invitation?"

"Do you like Chinese?" he asked. "There's a great restaurant about a block from the courthouse. They make the best Peking duck in town."

Rachel looked at her watch. It was almost eight o'clock. "Are you still at work?"

"I've been going over some police reports," Atwater said. "The shooting incident in front of the Majestic Theater, to be precise. When I stumbled across your name as one of the principals, I decided to call and invite you to dinner."

"Why?" she asked, suspicious.

"Why does anyone call a lovely lady and ask her to dinner?" he said, chuckling. "I want to enjoy your company."

"Are you sure?"

"Absolutely," he said. "Why don't we meet at the China Palace in thirty minutes, unless you'd prefer to have me pick you up at your house?"

"Are you trying to get information out of me?" she said. "If so, tell me now."

"What information?" Atwater said. "If you're referring to the shooting, I have everything in the reports. I noticed your report hasn't been turned in yet. I assume it will come in tomorrow." He lowered his voice. "I didn't call you to talk shop. Are we on for dinner or not?"

Rachel reached over and turned off the stove. She would have to shower, change, try to look presentable. She knew she couldn't talk to Atwater about the situation with Grant Cummings, at least not until she knew what she was going to write in her report. Since the attorney had ambushed her in the courtroom, however, she decided to let him treat her to a decent meal. "Give me the address, make it an hour, and you've got a date."

"Tracy," Rachel yelled through the door, "I'm going out for a few hours. Joe's already asleep in my bed. If you're hungry, there's a pot of soup on the stove. All you have to do is heat it up."

"Go away," the girl shouted.

"I can't leave until you come out," she said, wondering if she would have to call Atwater back and cancel. "You can't hear Joe with the door closed." She leaned her head against the wood. "I have a date, Tracy. The attorney who sent me the flowers asked me to go to dinner with him."

The door swung open. "He's not married, is he?"

"Of course not," Rachel said.

"Great," Tracy said, looking her mother up and down. "You're not going to wear that, I hope."

Rachel glanced down. She had on the same pink blazer and white dress she had worn to court. "Why?" she said. "Does it look bad? I don't have many street clothes. This is one of my best jackets."

"It's hideous," Tracy said, grabbing her mother's hand and leading her down the hallway. "And you need to fix your hair, put on some makeup."

"Gosh," Rachel said, smiling broadly, "you sure made a rapid turn-around. I thought you weren't speaking to me."

While Rachel carried Joe back to his own bed, her daughter searched through her closet. "This," she said when Rachel returned, holding a black knit dress on a hanger.

"I hate that dress," her mother said. "I haven't worn it for years. Since I've gained weight, it makes me look fat."

"Take off that terrible thing," Tracy told her. "You'll look fabulous in this, probably better than you did when you were thin. Wait," she added, dropping to her knees to search for the right shoes on the floor of her mother's closet. "You have to wear high heels. Men love women in high heels."

"Let's not get carried away," her mother said, laughing. "I'm only going for the free meal."

Tracy stood, her upper lip trembling. "Don't say that."

Rachel saw the desperation in her child's eyes and her stomach twisted. "Come here," she said, walking over and embracing her. "I can't marry someone just to solve our financial problems. You wouldn't want that, would you?"

"I don't know," the girl said, sniffing back tears.

Rachel brushed the strands of hair out of her face. "We're going to be okay," she said. "Please, try to believe me. I'm going to take care of us. Whatever I have to do, I'll do."

FOURTEEN

When Rachel walked through the door of the China Palace, Mike Atwater was already seated in a chair in the reception area. Wearing the black knit dress her daughter had selected, nylons and high heels, she felt awkward and self-conscious. The restaurant, located in a strip shopping center, was tacky and cramped. Several people were waiting for takeout orders, and only a few tables were set up in back of the restaurant. "I guess I'm overdressed," she said, smoothing down her short skirt. "I don't go out for dinner that often."

"You look great," he said, smiling. "Don't worry, we're not going to eat here. I've already ordered our food. It should be ready any minute."

"Oh," she said, caught off-guard, "where are we going? Back to the courthouse?"

"My house is only a few miles from here," Atwater said. "It's a beautiful night. I thought we'd eat outside, get some fresh air."

Rachel looked toward the back of the restaurant. "This place isn't so bad," she said, uncomfortable with the thought of going to his house. "Why don't we just eat here?"

Atwater picked up their takeout order. "Trust me," he said, taking her elbow and steering her toward the door, "you'll love my yard."

"Okay," she said, slipping away from him, "I'll follow you in my car."

* * *

Mike Atwater's house was located on a tree-lined street near Ventura College in an older, quiet neighborhood with mature trees and manicured yards. From the attorney's grandiose style, Rachel had expected him to live in a palace. He drove a new Mercedes. He dressed in the finest clothes. From her perspective, everything about him seemed extravagant and pretentious. When he pulled into the driveway of a modest stucco house, Rachel was surprised.

Inside, the floors were Spanish tile, the furniture casual, the colors muted and earthy. The focal point of the living room was a large stone fireplace. Silver trophies from his track and field days were lined up on top of the mantel. Even though the house had a cozy feeling, there were no pictures, no knickknacks other than the trophies, no personal items strewn around. To Rachel, it looked more like a hotel room than a home.

"I saw you run once on television," she told him, walking over to study the trophies.

"You're kidding," he said.

"No," she said, smiling shyly. "I was in high school at the time. You were fabulous. I always wondered why you didn't make the Olympic team. You broke the world record in the indoor mile."

"Yes," Atwater said, remembering the excitement of that day. "I held the record for all of thirty days, then Damian Washington took it. When the Olympic trials came up that year, I was suffering from a hamstring injury. By the time they came up again, my window of opportunity had passed."

"That must have been difficult to accept."

Atwater shrugged. He didn't want to dwell on the subject. "Would you like to see the rest of the house?"

"Sure," she said, following him down the hallway. He led her to a spare bedroom, crammed full of electronic equipment and computer terminals. Papers were strewn everywhere. The trash can had spilled over onto the carpet. The windows were covered with black paper, fastened with masking tape. The room was so cluttered and dismal, Rachel felt claustrophobic.

Atwater rubbed his chin. "I've been trying to sell off some of my securities and reorganize my stock portfolio. If I had a window in here, I'd never get anything done."

The next room he showed her was his bedroom. It was stark, containing only a bed. For an end table, he used a wooden crate.

"As you can see," he said during their walk back to the living room, "I don't care much for indoor living." He motioned toward the French doors leading into the backyard. "Go outside and make yourself comfortable. I'll get some plates and open a bottle of wine for us. We'll eat in the gazebo." He darted into the kitchen, then returned with two candles and some matches. "Maybe you can light these," he said, handing them to her. "I have electricity in the gazebo, but candlelight is nicer, don't you think?"

Rachel passed through the French doors into a paradise of lush greenery. The patio had a lattice-style roof, and Chinese wisteria crept down the columns. She inhaled the sweetly fragrant lilac-blue flowers, plucked one off, and brushed it past her nose.

The Santa Ana winds had kicked up. It was balmy and breezy, the temperature in the high seventies. On the right side of the yard was a black-bottomed pool, surrounded by natural boulders. The gazebo was located on the left, and in the center of the yard was a stone walkway lined with lush plants and blooming perennials. Rachel spotted a yellow cactus dahlia, dozens of purple liatris, orange lilies, and white acidanthera with black centers.

The gazebo was constructed out of wrought iron, but tented with white canvas, the ends of the fabric tied back like curtains around the supporting columns. Atwater had developed an entire living area inside the gazebo. There was a fire pit, an entertainment center containing a television and stereo, a daybed with dozens of colorful pillows, two padded recliners, and a small round table with four chairs. Seeing twin candelabras on the table, she placed the candles in them and lit them with a match.

When Atwater came out with their food, Rachel said, "You must have a great gardener. I was married to a landscape architect, and I have to admit I'm impressed."

"You're looking at the gardener," he said, smiling as he set up their plates at the table. He left and returned with the bottle of wine and two glasses.

Atwater had discarded his jacket and tie, and had rolled up the sleeves of his dress shirt. Several buttons on his shirt were open, and Rachel's eyes drifted to his chest. He wasn't hairy like most men. Joe's chest had looked like the national forest. The skin on Atwater's chest and forearms was a burnished copper, hairless and smooth. Glancing at his face, she didn't see one wrinkle.

"The yard's so perfectly balanced," she continued. "Don't tell me you designed it yourself?"

"Ah, yes," he said, beaming. "Now, are you ready to eat?"

Dinner passed quickly. They were both famished, and the duck was everything he had promised, moist and succulent, wrapped in little pancakes and smothered in plum sauce. Once Atwater had refilled their glasses with wine, he stood and directed Rachel to the recliners. "We can watch TV if you want," he said, stuffed from the meal. "I seldom use the house. When the weather is good, I generally sleep out here."

"I'm not much of a TV person," Rachel said, taking a sip of her wine. "Besides, I should go home soon. The past week has been hectic."

For a long time, they sat in silence. Rachel didn't feel the need to talk as she did with most people, and from what she could tell, Atwater felt the same. "You're not what I expected," she said softly.

"Oh, really?" he said, arching an eyebrow. "How's that?"

"I don't know how to explain it," she said. "I pictured you living in a different environment. You know, fancy furniture, expensive artwork. I certainly didn't peg you as the type to putter around in the garden."

"See," he said, chuckling, "you've learned something. Never judge a book by its cover. This," he added, sweeping his hand toward the yard, "is my oasis. When I retire, I want to move to Bali, where I can live in a house with no walls."

"I had a yard like this once," Rachel said, cutting her eyes to him. "I doubt if I'll ever have one again, though."

"Why is that?"

"I can't afford it," she said, brushing a wispy curl back from her face. "All I'm trying to do right now is survive."

He turned sideways on the recliner, reaching over to clasp her hand. "One way or the other, Rachel, we're all trying to survive," he said. "You may not believe that, but it's true. Money isn't the answer, having a certain kind of car, house, whatever. Possessions are just toys. Sure, it's nice to be able to pay your bills, but money doesn't guarantee happiness."

Spoken like a person with a fat paycheck, Rachel thought. "I'm sorry," she said, slipping her hand out of his. "I didn't come here to talk about my problems. Tell me about yourself. Have you ever been married? Do you have any children?"

"No children," he said, looking away.

"But you were married once, right?"

"Briefly," he said.

Atwater had become so guarded, Rachel's interest was piqued. "What happened, if you don't mind me asking?"

"My wife was a pathological liar," he said, straightening up in his recliner. That was all he was willing to reveal. The rest was too embarrassing. The three years of his marriage had been a nightmare. His wife had been arrested repeatedly for shoplifting. She had papered the town with bad checks. Even five years later, he was still struggling to get out from under the mountain of debt she had created. He had expended thousands of dollars on therapy for her, but nothing had been accomplished. When he discovered that his wife had been having an affair with another attorney for more than a year, the marriage had finally crumbled. He had been so weary at that point, he had given her everything, knowing his emotions were too ragged to withstand a protracted divorce. She had taken the furniture, the appliances, the house he had built several years before he had met her.

"I'm sorry," Rachel said, seeing she had upset him. "I shouldn't have brought up bad memories. Because my husband died, I'm always curious about people who get a divorce."

"Divorce can be similar to death," he said quietly. "It's only that way, though, because we make it that way. We feel compelled to link ourselves with other humans, thinking this is the only way we can fulfill our emotional needs and fit into society. Then when the relationship dies, it becomes like an amputation. Even if the limb is diseased, it still hurts like hell when they chop it off."

"Did you love her?"

"Yes, I did," he answered. "You can love someone and still not be able to live with them. Since my divorce, I've loved a number of women."

"But not enough to marry them?"

"No," he said, shifting his position on the recliner. "I don't mind living alone. It's something you grow accustomed to, not having to deal with another person's problems, the constant demands on your time, their annoying little habits."

They fell silent again, gazing out over the yard. Her thoughts turned to the shooting incident at the Majestic Theater, the report still unfinished on the dining room table. If she lied about what she had seen and signed her name on the report, she would be committing perjury. She felt compelled to go along, do what the other officers asked. She couldn't put Tracy through another move, a new school. If she could convince herself she was doing it for her child, compromising her ethics might go down easier.

"Can I ask you something?" Atwater said. "It's something I've been curious about since we talked in the cafeteria. You told me this Larry Dean, the police sergeant, was responsible for getting you to speak again, but you didn't tell me how he managed to get through to you. After a year of not speaking, he must have said something remarkable."

Rachel coughed nervously. "I don't usually talk about that time in my life, remember?"

"I'm sorry," he said quickly. "I was insensitive. Sometimes my curiosity gets away from me."

"No," she said. "I asked you about your marriage, so your question is fair. To tell you the truth, I'd probably be better off getting some of this stuff off my chest. Since you already know most of it, you might as well know the rest." She paused and stretched her arms over her head. "Larry Dean was an incredible man. Like a lot of children who are sexually abused, I blamed myself for what happened. I despised Nathan Richardson for what he had done to me, but at the same time, I convinced myself that I was just as guilty as he was. I'm not certain if it was something he told me in the hotel room that I suppressed, or if it was simply that things became twisted around in my mind."

"I'm not sure I understand," Atwater said. "Why would you feel guilty?"

"I wanted the doll," Rachel said, the words slipping out without thought. "I can't believe I said that," she said, a startled look on her face. "I didn't want his awful doll. I was terrified. What he did to me was perverted and disgusting."

"What about Larry Dean?" Atwater reminded her.

"I can't remember all the things he said to me," Rachel said, still shaken by her spontaneous statement about the doll. "In essence, he told me that I felt guilty because I had let Richardson trick me into walking over to his car. He said I had convinced myself that I should have fought harder to get away from him, that I should have realized Richardson's story about finding the house where his daughter was visiting was a lie. My mother also told me about the other child he had kidnapped, describing how he had raped her. I guess I developed a case of survivor's guilt. Mother had a habit of reminding me how lucky I was that Richardson had only fondled me, instead of raping me like he did the other girl he abducted."

"Let's talk about the doll," Atwater said, fascinated. "The doll was symbolic, I believe. It represented wealth, indulgence, something your mother couldn't give you at the time. Maybe you didn't want the doll when Richardson offered it to you, but you longed for it later, after he was dead. Because you associated the doll with Richardson and you knew he was evil, the doll and your desire to possess it became evil as well."

Rachel stiffened. Atwater was moving too close to the fire, poking around in her subconscious. She had been trapped inside the house for almost a year following the kidnapping. The doll had become incorporated into her fantasy life. She realized now that she hadn't wanted to possess the doll in the pink satin dress. She had become the doll. She had stopped speaking because dolls didn't speak. They didn't have to speak. And dolls did not die. They could break, but they did not bleed when you stabbed them, nor could they cry. Rachel had not shed one tear following the kidnapping. "I'd better go now," she said suddenly.

"We can talk about something else, Rachel," Atwater said. "It's still early. Why don't you stay? I'll open another bottle of wine."

"I can't," Rachel said, standing. "It's been a lovely evening, but I should go home. Like I said, it's been a busy week."

Pushing himself to his feet, Atwater caught her hand and pulled her into his arms. He didn't kiss her. He simply held her. "It feels right with you here," he whispered. "I don't say that to many women. I'd like it if you stayed, Rachel."

Rachel trembled in his arms. How long had it been since she had been held? The way he smelled. The hardness of his body. Without thinking, she let her hands roam to his chest. Ever since she had seen him, she had wanted to touch him, feel his skin beneath her fingers. She couldn't continue living in the past. Joe was dead. The memories were fading. Even her daughter knew she needed a man in her life. Was Mike Atwater the right one? She doubted it, but for some reason, she no longer cared. "Make love to me," she whispered, looking up into his eyes.

"Let's go inside the house," he said, a surprised but eager look on his face.

"No," she said, tilting her head toward the daybed. "Over there."

The attorney took her hand, leading her the few feet to the daybed. Positioning himself next to her, he leaned over and kissed her on the mouth. It wasn't a probing kiss, not even what Rachel considered a passionate kiss. It was sweet, nice. The wine had relaxed her. A mild breeze washed over her face. He stroked her arms, her face, trailed his fingers across her collarbone. There was no sense of urgency, no rush toward intercourse. After twenty minutes, they were both still fully clothed. "Are you sure this is what you want?" he asked. "If not, we can stop now."

"No," Rachel panted. "I want to be with you." Reaching over, she unbuttoned his shirt, then pressed her lips against his chest. Since her husband's death, she had stifled her emotions the same way she had done as a child, transforming herself into an inanimate object. She wanted to feel her body again, experience sex again. Atwater was nice, but she knew she could never love him. She didn't have to love him. All she had to do was desire him, and she did.

He gently pushed her onto her back. His hands drifted under the hem of her knit dress, caressing her knees, her thighs, the gentle curve of her hips. His fingers found the edge of her pantyhose, and he slowly pulled them down to her ankles, then carefully slipped them off her feet. Rachel giggled when he sucked her toes. A bolt of electricity made its way to her groin, though, as if her toes were directly linked to her sex organs. She shivered in delight. She had never slept with a man other than her husband. Joe had been a tender lover, but their lovemaking had always been rushed. Sexually, her husband had been naive. In all the years they had been married, he had never given thought to what it took to please a woman. As long as Rachel didn't complain, Joe assumed she was satisfied. She had learned to take pleasure from the intimacy of the act, the touching, the merging of their bodies.

Atwater's hand drifted up her thighs to the place between her legs. Rachel tensed. After a few moments, her anxiety passed and she found herself swimming in pleasure. Her mouth fell open. Her body bowed upward to meet his fingers. She sat up and laced her fingers through his hair, then slipped his shirt off his shoulders. "Your skin," she said, her palms roaming over his hairless chest. "I've never felt anything like it."

She reached for his zipper, but he pushed her hand away and ducked his head under the hem of her dress. Rachel fell backward onto the daybed. She yanked the dress over her head, wanting to feel the night air on her nipples. What she was doing was reckless, crazy, exciting beyond words. Her children were home alone. The report was waiting to be completed. Decisions had to be made.

The moment seized her. The soft strokes of his tongue were both pleasure and torture. She tried to stop herself, hold back. She was on a runaway train, out of control, speeding through the universe. Experiencing such intense pleasure was frightening. "Oh, God," she cried, her body exploding in a powerful orgasm. "Stop, please stop."

Their skin was slick with perspiration, glistening in the flickering candlelight. He stood and dropped his pants. His body was more beautiful than she had imagined, a burnished statue of perfection. His stomach was ridged with taut muscles, his legs powerful but not muscular, the high-performance tools of a runner. His shoulders were broad, his waist narrow. Crawling back onto the bed with her, he pulled her on top of him and stared deep into her eyes. "You're beautiful," he said. "You're the most natural and spontaneous woman I have ever known."

Feeling him slip inside her, Rachel suddenly panicked. "I can get pregnant," she told him. "I don't use birth control."

"I'm sterile," he told her.

"AIDS," she panted. "You have to use something."

Atwater slipped out from under her and headed to the house. Rachel stared at the ceiling of the gazebo, thinking she had ruined it for him. A few moments later, he returned and she immediately pulled him down on the bed beside her. Wrapping her fingers around his penis, she slowly stroked it. Once he became aroused again, she bent over and sealed her lips around it.

He turned her over onto her stomach, taking her from behind. Reaching around her waist, he stroked her breasts, then moved down her abdomen to the place where they were connected. Rachel climaxed again, the pleasure so overwhelming, she began to sob.

"Am I hurting you?" he asked.

"No, no," she cried, grabbing his hand and pressing it hard against her genitals.

He didn't cry out. He simply stopped with a strange little grunt. Rachel slapped onto the bed in exhaustion, her body as limp as a dishrag. He collapsed on top of her, lifting her hair and kissing the nape of her neck.

"Am I crushing you?" he whispered.

"No," she said. "Don't move. I like the way it feels having you on top of me. That way, I know I'm not alone."

They remained that way, still and silent. Rachel felt safe, protected, satiated. Would he continue to see her? Would people find out that she had slept with him? Did he think she was cheap, easy?

Did she really care?

Pleasure was still coursing through her body. Her skin tingled with warmth. She opened her eyes and stared out over the yard. The candles had burned out. The only light was coming from the spotlights trained on the various trees and shrubbery. He had called the yard his oasis. She must accept the evening in the same way. Only an oasis, an isolated moment of pleasure.

Rachel dropped her head back to the daybed. He stirred, then moved to a position behind her, aligning his body with hers. She found his hand and placed it between her breasts. Wrapped in his arms, her eyes closed and she slept, dreamless and peaceful. They did not awake until the sun streaked in through the sides of the gazebo.

chapter

FIFTEEN

Rachel was standing in the entryway of Mike Atwater's home about to leave. "I'll call you," the attorney said, "either later today or—"

She reached over and put her finger against his lips. "It was wonderful," she said. "Let's leave it at that."

Surprise registered on his face. He had expected a demand for commitment, particularly from a woman like Rachel. Most of the women he bedded were sophisticated, independent women who accepted the attorney for what he was—an attractive escort, a competent lover, a brilliant conversationalist, everything but a potential husband. "Does that mean you don't want to see me again?"

"No," she said. "Of course I'd like to see you again. Last night was very special to me. Whether you believe it or not, I don't jump into bed with men. I just don't want you to feel obligated."

"This is ridiculous," he said, grimacing. "Why would I feel obligated?"

"Because I slept with you," Rachel said. "I didn't do it to please you, Mike. I did it to please myself."

Atwater laughed, but it was more like a nervous reflex. "Are you trying to say you used me?"

"I guess so," Rachel said, shrugging. She wondered if this was the way men felt after they seduced a woman. Hadn't she been the aggressor? He might have set the stage, but she had been the one to make it a reality. She felt like calling Sergeant Miller and informing him that she could take charge of things, that she wasn't the passive person everyone seemed to think she was. She had indulged herself in a way she had never dreamed possible. Instead of feeling guilty, she felt powerful, competent. The feeling was similar to locking herself in the bathroom with a box of chocolates, eating them all, and never gaining a pound. With so little pleasure in her life, why should she deny herself something that had no apparent consequences? He had used protection. She would not get a disease, nor would she get pregnant.

"I'm not sure how I should feel right now," Atwater answered, a thoughtful expression on his face. "If it had been someone else last night, would you have slept with him as well?"

"No," she said, reaching over and tousling his hair.

A smile played at the corner of his mouth. "Then I guess I have some pride left, right?"

"Right," Rachel said, chuckling with delight.

He put on his prosecutor's face. "What are you looking for from me?"

"Nothing," she said. Giving him a quick peck on the cheek, she opened the door and stepped out into the brisk morning air. She took a few steps down the walkway and then stopped, turning around to face him again. "I figured out what Larry Dean said to me."

"What?"

"He told me that since Richardson had kidnapped me, nothing bad would ever happen to me again. He said the chances were one in a million that I would ever be a victim of another crime."

"Interesting," Atwater said, watching as Rachel got in her Path-finder and drove off.

Rachel made it home by six o'clock. Tracy and Joe were still asleep when she slipped into the house. She felt so invigorated that she put on her shorts and running shoes and went out jogging. Her rubber soles smacked against the pavement. The morning air was refreshing. She didn't feel tarnished in any way. She felt strong, focused, ready to tackle whatever came her way.

When she reached the end of her street, she jogged into a large abandoned orange grove. Even though the trees still produced a small crop of fruit, most of them fell to the ground and rotted. The neighborhood kids used them like snowballs, gathering up the squishy oranges and hurling them at each other for fun. Lucy said the property had recently been purchased by a developer, and another tract of houses would soon spring up.

Rachel imagined herself loping along inside Mike Atwater's body. Her legs were too short, her arm movements not well synchronized with her legs. When she had run track in high school, she had been the slowest girl on the team. She had watched Atwater compete on television during that time and had marveled at the economy of his movements, the length of his stride, his incredible speed.

Would he run with her?

She set aside thoughts of the attorney, concentrating on her present dilemma: What to say in her report about Grant using the Hillmont boy as a shield. She decided she would do what Grant and Nick Miller wanted, withhold the truth of what she had witnessed in front of the Majestic Theater. Turning in Grant would not bring the Hillmont boy back to life.

Running always cleared her mind, enabled her to see things more logically. If she went after Grant, she would be going against the entire department. Even if the sergeant didn't get her fired as he had threatened, she would be treated as a traitor by her fellow officers. Spending the night with Atwater had made her see that her life still held meaning, opportunity. She felt as if she had finally stepped over the line, from the dead to the living.

"You're up?" Rachel said, seeing her daughter in the kitchen when she returned to the house.

"When did you get home last night?" Tracy asked, picking at a pimple on her chin. "I waited up until midnight."

"Oh," Rachel said, pouring herself a glass of water, "I'm not certain what time it was. I was so tired when I got home, I went straight to bed." Removing the rubber pitcher from underneath the sink, she filled it and walked around the kitchen watering the plants.

"You did not," the girl snapped, certain her mother was lying. "I just looked in your room and your bed hasn't been slept in. You spent the night with that lawyer, didn't you?"

Rachel had always been truthful with Tracy, but she wasn't certain her sex life was something she should discuss. "We just talked," she said. "It was nice."

Tracy's face came alive. "You like him, don't you? What was his house like? What kind of car does he drive? When are you going to go out with him again?"

Rachel held up a hand. "Slow down," she said, smiling at her daughter's enthusiasm. "I'm not going to marry the man. I may never see him again. No one knows how things like this are going to work out."

"Humph," Tracy said, staring at her mother's face. "You look different. I don't know what that guy did to you, but you don't look the same."

Rachel gave her a quick hug, then headed down the hall to wake her son for breakfast.

For most of the day, Rachel sat at the dining room table trying to complete her report. She kept writing and rewriting, ripping up the pages and tossing them in the trash. Exposing the truth might not bring the Hillmont boy back, but failing to report that Grant had kicked the shooter while wearing steel-toed boots created another problem. If Grant had not kicked Trueman, the boy might not have fired the gun. In itself, she didn't see this as a defense against murder. It did explain the Trueman boy's anger, however, and Rachel knew it might be considered a mitigating circumstance in determining his punishment if he was ever convicted.

Jimmy Townsend had been assigned the task of interviewing the other juveniles who were present that night. She headed to the phone in the kitchen, calling Townsend's house and asking his wife to tell him to stop by as soon as he woke up. After the words they had exchanged during the debriefing, Rachel wasn't certain if he would come.

Had one of the kids seen Grant use the Hillmont boy as a shield? Surely one of them had witnessed him kicking Trueman on the ground. From what they had learned thus far, the gun had not belonged to Trueman, but had been handed to him by another juvenile.

She stopped and placed her head down on the table. The situation could turn into a nightmare in the courtroom. She was an awful liar. Telling the truth was easy. Lying required finesse. On the rare occasions when she uttered an untruth, Rachel became flustered. A strong defense lawyer could rip her to shreds.

Joe toddled over with a miniature truck in his hand. He ran it down her shoulder. *"Vroomm, vroomm,"* he said, balancing the toy on the top of her head. Rachel moved and the tiny truck tumbled to the floor. "Come here, sweetie," she said, hoisting him into her lap. She cradled his head to her chest, rocking him in her arms. Some day she would have to teach him right from wrong. Would she tell him it was all right to distort the truth, lie to save yourself at the expense of others? She felt a heavy sensation in the pit of her stomach.

Joe scrambled out of her arms, retrieving his toy and running it back and forth on the wood flooring. Watching him, Rachel thought back to her childhood. Carrie had been her primary role model, teaching her younger sister about values, morality, decency. Rachel remembered all the nights she had crept into Carrie's room, then cuddled in her bed as her sister tried to explain the basics of life. Years later, she had understood why Carrie had taken on such a maternal role. When Rachel was fifteen, her sister had told her the truth about their mother.

"Mother used to be a prostitute," Carrie had said. "Didn't you notice that her students were all men? She never taught them to play the piano, Rachel. That's why we had to go on welfare, because after the kidnapping she couldn't turn tricks anymore with you in the house."

Their mother's drinking had consumed her, turning her into a wasted shell. No more tinkling piano keys. No more show tunes and family sing-alongs. It was as if someone had tossed a dark shroud over the house. As soon as her sisters finished school, they left home and moved to Los Angeles, leaving Rachel to struggle with her mother alone. Six weeks after she graduated from high school, Rachel came home to find her mother dead in the living room from a mixture of tranquilizers and booze.

By then she and Joe, whom she'd met at a nursery where she worked after school, were already seeing a lot of each other. Without his love, she knew she would not have survived. Her husband had resisted the marriage. He was still a college student, determined to earn his degree. They had made it work, though. Rachel had taken a job as a waitress. In addition, she typed all Joe's reports, conducted most of his research. Joe worked two jobs, carrying a full college curriculum at the same time. When he had finally stepped onto the stage to accept his diploma, Rachel had felt as if she were up there with him. She had never given consideration to her own future, never realized that she would one day regret her lack of education and feel inferior because of it. Rachel and her husband had been a team. Whatever Joe accomplished, she accomplished. When he died, much of her self-esteem had died with him.

She felt as if her entire childhood had been built on lies. The little house in San Diego with the frilly white curtains. The baby grand piano in the living room. The picture of her father on the mantel in his white Navy uniform. Toward the end, her mother had finally told her the truth. The man in the photo was not Rachel's father, although he had lived with her mother for a few years and Carrie and Susan remembered calling him Dad. Frances was not certain who had fathered any of her children, only that each of the girls had been sired by a different man. Rachel's sisters became her half-sisters. The man she had thought was her father became her mother's boyfriend, possibly her pimp. The people on the block didn't look down on them because they were poor, or because their yard was not well-kept like the other yards in the neighborhood. They shunned them because Frances was a prostitute. Everyone had known but Rachel.

She looked over at little Joe, then quickly placed the blank pages of her report back in her briefcase. She could not give her son expensive toys, private schools or fine clothing. All she had to give him was herself. When he looked at her, she wanted to see respect mirrored in his eyes. She was not prepared to sell her soul just yet. Before she fell, she would at least put up a fight.

Jimmy Townsend stopped by Rachel's house after dinner. Instead of talking in the house where the kids could overhear, she led him into the backyard, indicating he should take a seat in one of the plastic lawn chairs. "I know you saw what Grant did last night, Jimmy. Why are you denying it?"

He fixed her with a steely gaze. "You're being foolish, Rachel. If you persist with this, I guarantee you're going to regret it."

"Is that a threat, Jimmy?"

"Of course it's not a threat," he said, trying to get his mammoth body comfortable in the unyielding chair. "You're bringing the heat down on all of us, though. What do we need this kind of shit for, huh?"

"You saw it, didn't you?" Rachel said, refusing to let up. "What does Grant have on you? He's holding something over your head, I bet. I've seen how he operates. He waits until someone makes a mistake, then he jumps in and fixes it for them. He controls people that way. Haven't you seen how he's influencing Ratso? Ratso's turning into another Grant. I saw him smashing that kid's head against the pavement. You know he was only mimicking Grant."

"Ratso's a good guy," Townsend said. "He just doesn't know how to stand up for himself. You have to draw lines with Grant. If you don't, he'll squeeze you dry."

"I know you saw what Ratso did," Rachel argued. "I yelled at you to go over and stop him. Don't you remember?"

"No," he said. "There was a lot going on out there, Rachel. I remember you saying something to me about Ratso, but I forgot what it was you said. Lately, my memory isn't the best."

"Great," she said, swinging her leg back and forth. "Suddenly everyone involved in the Majestic Theater incident has a terrible memory. Pretty convenient, isn't it, Jimmy?"

Townsend was wearing a light blue shirt and sweat pants. Dark stains appeared under his arms. "Right after you called the house, Lindsey went into premature labor and I had to take her to the hospital. The doctor's afraid the baby is going to be born too soon. I can't leave her alone now even at night. I'm going to have to hire a nurse."

Rachel tilted her head. "I don't understand what this has to do with Grant. You're talking in circles, Jimmy."

"Okay, okay," he said anxiously. "Grant loaned me a few thousand dollars to hold me over until the baby is born. I've tapped my father too many times. Now that he's retired, he's living on a fixed income and can't afford to help me out as much as he did in the past." His voice took on a pleading tone. "We've had plumbing problems this year. The engine on Lindsey's Escort blew up and I had to sell it for salvage. Our grocery bill alone takes almost my entire salary. We have a lot of mouths to feed."

Rachel pinned him with her eyes. "So you did see it?"

Townsend pushed himself to his feet, adjusting the worn elastic on his sweatpants. "You're making a serious mistake, Rachel. Drop this before it comes back and bites your head off."

He started to leave through the side gate, but Rachel called out to him, "Why does Grant do these things? I bet this isn't the first time he's hurt someone."

Townsend returned to the patio, resting his back against one of the pillars. "Why? I'll tell you why. Because he knows he can get away with it. I remember when I first started on the job. I was terrified of breaking the rules. During the day, the brass were always breathing down your neck, just waiting for you to fuck up so they could call you on the carpet and rip you a new asshole." He stopped and took in a deep breath. "Once I transferred to graveyards, everything changed. So a guy gets carried away in a stressful situation and pounces on someone a little too hard. There's no one around to see you, report you. If the perp complains, it's their word against yours. Once you get away with one thing, you become convinced you can get away with anything."

"What did the other witnesses say?" Rachel asked. "Did they see anything?"

Townsend shook his head. The look on his face said he had said more than he had intended to say. "I have to go."

"If I come forward and tell the truth about Grant," Rachel asked point-blank, "will you back me up?"

Townsend didn't answer. He stared at her a long time, then turned and waddled out the side gate.

Grant Cummings had just begun his scheduled days off. When Rachel arrived at the station Tuesday night, she was relieved that she wouldn't have to face him for several days. Still, people were whispering about her behind her back. Other officers simply avoided her, walking right past her as if she didn't exist. When Carol Hitchcock asked her to have breakfast with her, Rachel immediately agreed.

The dispatcher gave them permission to eat at 3:10. Rachel met Carol in the parking lot of Coco's restaurant near her assigned beat. "How was your trip?" she said, locking the door to her unit in the parking lot.

"Fair," Carol said, as they walked toward the entrance to the restaurant. "My dad has cancer. From the way he looked, I don't think he has much time left."

"I'm sorry," she said. "I didn't know." They walked to the door in silence, entered and were seated. Slipping into a booth, Rachel dropped her napkin in her lap. Other than a few truck drivers at the counter, the place was empty. "I have some books on cancer if you're interested."

"Oh, yeah?" Carol said, waving the waitress over. "That's right, your husband died of cancer. Sometimes I forget. You seem too young to be a widow. What kind of cancer did he have?"

"Lymphoma."

"Why did you get pregnant?" Carol asked. "Didn't you have a baby right before he died? Townsend said you got pregnant after the doctors told you he was terminal. Is that true?"

"When Joe first found out he had cancer," Rachel explained, "he insisted that we go to a sperm bank. We'd planned on having a large family. We already had Tracy, but Joe had always dreamed of having a son, and the doctors told him the radiation treatments would make him sterile. He didn't want me to get pregnant while he was undergoing treatment, though, because he needed me to be strong enough to care for him. When the doctors told us he wasn't going to make it, I was artificially inseminated."

"That's crazy," Carol said. "Didn't you care that your son would grow up without a father?"

Rachel shrugged. "Joe was able to see his son before he died, so I guess it was worth it. He was with me in the delivery room, although he was so ill by then, they had to bring him in on a gurney. He said it was one of the greatest moments of his life, that seeing his son born took away his fear of death."

Carol was silent for a long time. Finally she said, "My dad has prostate cancer. It's spread to his liver now. He waited too long to get treatment."

"It's terrible, I know," Rachel said, reaching out to touch her hand. The waitress set her coffee down, and she almost drained the entire cup. Her first day back was always difficult. If she slept the night before, she could not sleep during the day. By the time morning arrived, she felt like the walking dead. "Joe was in college when we met. I was a senior in high school. Once I laid eyes on him, it was all over for me. I never wanted to be out of his sight. Even toward the end when things were awful, I wanted to be with him."

"What did he do?"

"He was a landscape architect," she said, finishing the coffee and waving the waitress over for a refill.

"You mean he designed people's yards?"

"He did more commercial property than residential. You know, hotels, office buildings, apartment complexes. He was very talented. He knew every plant, every shrub." Rachel recalled the beautiful home they had lived in. Even though the house was not large, the yard had been a virtual paradise. A small artificial stream snaked through the property. They even had a bridge. She used to hold Tracy's hand as a toddler, walking her back and forth across the bridge.

Once her coffee had been refilled, Rachel ordered eggs and bacon. Carol settled for an order of wheat toast and a slice of cantaloupe.

"I heard what you said about Grant and the shooting incident," Carol said after the waitress delivered their food.

"It wasn't just a shooting incident," Rachel told her, shoving a spoonful of eggs into her mouth. "The kid died, Carol."

"Well," she said, blinking, "Grant didn't kill him. Aren't they going to charge the Trueman kid with murder?"

"Maybe voluntary manslaughter," Rachel speculated, taking a quick bite out of her toast. "They can't prove specific intent, so I don't see how first or second degree murder can apply. Because Trueman's sixteen, though, they may decide to try him as an adult. That means he'll go to prison if he's convicted."

"Whatever," Carol said, pushing her plate away without touching her cantaloupe.

Rachel was tempted to tell her what had happened on the beach. If she could convince Carol that Grant had tried to sexually assault her, she might believe what she had seen him do to Timothy Hillmont. Carol was in love with him, though. It didn't take a genius to see it. Telling her Grant had fondled her would be like waving a red flag to a bull.

"I want you to stop spreading lies about Grant," Carol said, her voice escalating. "I know you didn't mention it in your report, but the entire station is talking about it. Grant might try to make sergeant some day. These are the kind of rumors that can destroy a person's chances to advance in the department."

"My report," Rachel said, flabbergasted at what she was hearing. "Who told you about my report?"

"Well, I mean, I—" Carol knew she had made a mistake. Before she had started sleeping with Grant, she'd had a long term affair with Nick Miller. Even though they were no longer lovers, the sergeant still confided in her on a regular basis.

"Miller told you," Rachel guessed.

"Grant's a good officer," Carol said, leaning forward over the table.

"You don't know how upset he is by all this. When someone gets killed on his watch, he goes home and cries like a baby. I know you think I'm making this up, Rachel, but it's true. He really cares about people. He'd never put an innocent person's life in jeopardy."

"Give me a break," Rachel scoffed, finding it difficult to believe Grant Cummings cried over anyone. "The man packs steel in the toes of his boots. He wears sap gloves, Carol. He loves to punish people. What does he call it?" She stopped and mimicked Grant's voice, " 'This asshole needs an attitude adjustment.' That's what he always says before he beats the crap out of someone. Don't tell me you don't know what he's like."

"Sometimes you need an edge," Carol said huffily. "It's us against them."

"Don't start with that crap," Rachel said, her temper erupting. "Our job is to *serve* people, not brutalize them. I grew up believing police officers were the most honorable people in the world. Am I crazy or did something go wrong? Is every person who doesn't carry a badge now considered our enemy? Maybe we should drive around in armored tanks. Then if anyone looked at us the wrong way, we could just mow them down on the spot."

"I was idealistic too when I first joined the department," Carol said, staring off into space. "I was going to save babies from drowning, arrest bad guys, leap tall buildings with a single bound." She brought her fist down on the table, causing the silverware to jangle. "You know what we are?" she said. "We're trash, scum under their feet. We risk our lives for fucking peanuts. Gangsters are getting rich, cutting records about killing cops. Most of us can't even pay our damn bills." She pointed out the window of the restaurant. "You think the people of Oak Grove care about us? They care about us about as much as they care about the dogcatcher, the garbage men, all the stupid little people who clean up after them. If we don't look out for ourselves, no one will."

Something inside Rachel snapped. She might have taken the job out of desperation, but she was determined to perform her duties in an honorable and forthright fashion. If people didn't respect police officers today, it was because they had failed to earn respect. They were becoming legally sanctioned gangsters. Her childhood was behind her, but Sergeant Larry Dean had been an outstanding role model—a man of valor and integrity. Rachel refused to allow her career as a police officer to become a sham.

"I've got a news flash," she said, placing her palms on the table. "For all I care, you can blab it to everyone in the department. I haven't filed my report yet. When I do, I'm going to tell the truth."

Carol's look of anger changed to alarm. "What are you going to say?"

"That I saw Grant use Timothy Hillmont as a human shield," Rachel told her. "And I saw him kick Donald Trueman senseless, the primary reason the boy picked up the gun and started shooting."

"You were mistaken," Carol said, her voice cracking. "You'll destroy Grant if you go through with this. He'll be brought up on charges. His future will be destroyed. The job is his life. You know that, Rachel. Everyone in the department knows it."

Rachel slowly shook her head. "I know what I saw."

"What about me?" she said. "Don't you know what this is going to do to my relationship with Grant? We have plans, Rachel. We're trying to build a life together." She sniffed back tears. "My father's dying. Now you're trying to ruin the man I love. My whole life is coming apart. If you won't drop this for Grant's sake, then please . . . do it for me."

"I'm sorry," Rachel said. A second later, a light came on in her head. She knew how Grant operated. He never did his dirty work himself. "Grant put you up to this, didn't he?"

"Grant has a lot of friends in this department," Carol shouted in fury. "As of today, you have none." She slid out of the booth, reached into her pocket and pulled out a handful of money. Tossing the bills in Rachel's face, she turned and stormed out of the restaurant.

SIXTEEN

At 4:15 that morning, Rachel was dispatched to respond to a complaint of loud music in the 400 block of Maple Avenue. "Don't you have a house number?" she asked the radio operator. "Maple is a long street."

"Since the reporting party lives at 453 Maple," the male dispatcher advised, having already given Rachel the complainant's address, "it's got to be somewhere close if she can hear the music, don't you think?"

A strange noise came over the radio. Rachel bristled, knowing it was the other officers clicking their microphones. Before Ratso had aligned himself with Grant, the officers had clicked their microphones at him when he uttered something foolish over the radio. Rachel had opened her mouth without thinking. Loud music calls never came in with an exact address, particularly at this hour of the morning. It was getting close to the witching hour, though, and almost every officer on her watch had said something silly at one time or the other. But Rachel was no longer one of the guys. Even Carol Hitchcock was now her enemy. She had turned on a fellow officer. She realized that any mistake she made, no matter how insignificant, would now be subject to ridicule.

Maple Avenue was part of the Windermere tract. The houses were similar in size and appearance to the one Rachel rented on the south side of the city. Constructed out of brick and wood, they were single-story residences. Even though the exterior facades were different, the interiors of the homes were all the same. Adjusting the volume on her radio and rolling down the window in her unit, she slowly cruised the tree-lined streets. Most noise complaints were a waste of the taxpayers' money. By the time an officer responded, the offending party had turned the music down and gone to bed. Hearing what sounded like the Rolling Stones blasting at a deafening level, Rachel hit the brakes and steered her unit to the curb.

The yard was overgrown with weeds. The paint on the house was cracked and peeling. As she approached the front porch, she picked up the scent of rotting garbage. Three overflowing trash cans stood by the side of the house. She was glad she didn't have these people for neighbors. They had managed to get the garbage out of the house, but they were too lazy to drag the containers to the curb so the trash collectors could pick them up.

The front of the house was dark. Before ringing the bell, Rachel checked in with the station via her portable radio to let the dispatcher know she had arrived at the scene. Placing her ear to the door, she tried to determine if there were people inside or if someone had just left the house without turning the stereo off. The pounding bass of the Rolling Stones drowned out all other sounds.

Removing her flashlight, she flicked it on and trained the beam toward the ground. Seeing a few flecks of red on the concrete porch, she bent down to get a closer look. Reaching down with her fingers, she tried to see if the spots were wet. A slightly reddish stain appeared on the tips of her fingers. She sniffed it, knowing blood generally had a distinctive odor. Unable to identify the substance, she wiped her hands on her thighs.

Rachel was reaching for the doorbell when she suddenly dropped her hand. The hairs on the back of her neck were standing straight up. She turned and looked back at her police unit, then let her eyes travel up and down the street. In the academy, the instructors had taught her to listen to her instincts, never to take a premonition lightly. A good cop learned to smell trouble from several miles away.

She started to call for a backup unit, but was afraid if she did so without a good reason, she would never live it down. If she was too chicken to ring a doorbell and ask someone to turn down the music, she didn't belong in a uniform.

Rachel rang the bell. She waited. She rang the bell again. The people were probably asleep, she decided. In the Windermere houses, the bedrooms were located in the back. Walking past the rotting garbage, she approached a six-foot wooden gate leading into a back-yard, secured with an industrial-size padlock. Grabbing the top of the gate, Rachel hoisted herself up so she could check the yard for dogs. She didn't want to dance a jig with a Doberman pinscher. She'd already had that pleasure back when she was a rookie, and she had a scar on her calf to prove it. "Woof, woof, woof," she barked over the top of the fence. "Come and get it, doggie." Hearing nothing, she tossed her leg over the fence, hanging on until she felt the ground under her feet.

The grass in the backyard was even higher than in the front. It came to Rachel's knees, and she reminded herself to notify the fire depart-ment. Tall grass was a serious fire hazard, and the occupants deserved to be cited. Besides, she didn't know what was brushing up against her legs. Snakes lived in high grass. She was more terrified of snakes than she was of Doberman pinschers.

She peered through the nearest window into darkness. Generally she did not enter someone's backyard without another officer present. People could easily mistake you for a burglar and start shooting.

"Station one, 2A2," the portable radio squawked near her ear. "We've just received our third complaint of loud music on Maple. Have you located the house yet?"

"I'm at the house now," Rachel advised. "The address is 489 Maple. The situation should be resolved in about three minutes."

Standing near the window, she shouted, "Police. This is the Oak Grove Police Department. Answer your door. We've received numerous complaints about your music." She paused, sucking more oxygen into her lungs. "If you don't turn the music down, I'm going to cite you for disturbing the peace."

Rachel listened, but all she heard was another Rolling Stones song blasting from somewhere inside the house. Looking to her left, she saw a sliver of light coming from what she thought should be the smallest of the three bedrooms. When she walked over, she put her face to the glass and saw the back of a person's head through the transparent curtains. The room was too dark to determine if it was a male or a female. The light wasn't inside the room itself, she decided. From what she could tell, it was coming from the hallway. The person's hair was dark, and cleared the ears, and he or she was sitting in an upholstered recliner.

From the bureau mirror, she saw the reflection of a TV flickering on the far side of the room. She pounded on the glass. No response.

It had to be a drug overdose, Rachel decided, or possibly a heart attack. Either that, or the person was in a drunken stupor. Knowing she couldn't take a chance of ignoring a legitimate medical emergency, Rachel tried the window and found it unlatched. Lucky break, she thought, hoisting it up so she could crawl through.

The curtains had hidden a great deal. Boxes and clothes were strewn all over the floor. As soon as her feet hit the floor, Rachel saw what appeared to be a broken glass right below the windowsill. "I'm a police officer," she announced loudly to the silent form, gingerly making her way across the room. "Are you okay? Are you sick?" She reached down to her side and unsnapped the strap holding her gun in place, resting her hand on her revolver.

As Rachel circled to the front of the chair, her heart was racing like a steam engine. She whipped her gun out of the holster, then dropped her arm back to her side. She knew the girl in the chair was dead. Her throat was slit from ear to ear. It was as if she had vomited blood down the front of her shirt, or someone had tossed it on her from a bucket. As Rachel moved closer, she could see the girl's severed vocal cords and what appeared to be the back of her spinal cord. Bloody pools had formed on the floor. She inhaled the putrid odor of human excrement, the overwhelming stench of death. One more inch, she thought, and the girl would have been decapitated.

"Oh, God," Rachel said, bending over and regurgitating her break-fast into a pile of gore.

"Station one," she said a few moments later, "I-I need backup fast. Send me a couple of units, and advise the sergeant to respond as well." She was not allowed to say she had a homicide over an open radio frequency. If she did, the press would pick it up over the police scanner and arrive on the scene before the medical examiner and the homicide detectives. If she'd been in her unit, she could have used her scrambler. For years they had used police codes for such calls, but the news media had memorized all the codes. She listened as the dispatcher called the units on the adjoining beats, Carol Hitchcock and Jimmy Townsend, advising them to respond for assistance.

Something moved behind her. Before Rachel could turn around, an enormous weight landed on her back, slapping her to the floor in a sloshy puddle of blood. Her portable radio flew out of its pouch, landing on the floor a few feet away. Her attacker's body odor was rancid and foul. Rachel knew it had to be a man, as the person's musculature was too well developed for a woman. She tried frantically to throw him off, grunting as she strained.

"You fucking bitch," he shouted. "I told you not to take my stuff. Didn't I tell you I'd kill you if you took my stuff, huh? Didn't I, huh? Didn't I?"

"Let me up," Rachel pleaded, trying to get her hand on her gun. The man had a knee positioned in the center of her back, and was using his hands to press her head against the floor. She couldn't panic. The other units would be here in a matter of minutes. All she had to do was keep the man talking and pray he didn't still have the knife that he'd used to slit the girl's throat. "You're strung out," she said, her mouth so close to the floor that her words were muffled. "You need help. If you go to the hospital, they'll give you some really good dope . . . bring you down. I can help you. I promise. All you have to do is trust me."

"You're lying," the man said, seizing a handful of her hair.

The portable radio squawked a few feet away. Rachel heard the dispatcher asking Carol Hitchcock her ETA. The radio operator spoke her call signals again and again, trying to raise her. "Advise your ETA, 3A4," the dispatcher asked Jimmy Townsend. "The sergeant's responding from the station. He's a good fifteen minutes away. Something must be wrong with Hitchcock's radio. I can't get a response from her."

Rachel choked on her own saliva. In fifteen minutes, she could be dead, butchered like the woman in the chair. Both Townsend and Hitchcock should be here by now. When they'd first received the call, they had been only a few minutes away.

The man released her hair, and Rachel lifted her head, able to see his face for the first time. She gasped in horror, knowing instantly that he was psychotic. His hair was long and filthy, his face smeared with blood and what looked like feces. But it was his eyes that told the story. His pupils were no larger than the head of a pin. Oozing sores covered his face and arms. Wearing a Harley-Davidson T-shirt, he grinned at her with rotting yellow teeth. Only one drug could drive a person this far—methamphetamine. On the street it was known as speed, crystal, crank, meth. After repeated use, the drug became toxic, exiting the body in open sores.

Rachel saw a shiny object on the floor a few feet away. When she realized it was a bloody butcher knife, she stretched out her fingers, but the weapon was several inches outside her grasp. Just then the man moved, and she managed to scramble to her knees. As she did, however, she heard the creaking of leather. The man had yanked her gun out of the holster.

An explosion reverberated in her eardrums. She collapsed on the floor, certain the man had shot her.

When she got the courage to raise her head, Rachel saw that the man was shooting wildly. Bullets were striking the adjacent wall, the ceiling, the floor. When he fired at the television, the picture tube exploded and sparks and glass flew through the air.

Carol Hitchcock's voice finally came out over the radio. "Station one," she said, "I'm on a traffic stop. I may have a drunk driver. I can't clear until I've given him a field sobriety test."

Rachel's muscles locked into place. They weren't coming. This was their revenge because she had threatened to expose Grant. The man had the muzzle of the gun pressed to the center of her back now. On the radio she heard Jimmy Townsend advising the dispatcher he had a flat tire. The radio operator called other units, but they either didn't answer or they claimed they were tied up on other calls and were unable to clear.

Catching the man's reflection in the mirror, Rachel saw he was smiling at himself and posing with the gun. She lunged for the knife. The man was a homicidal maniac. She couldn't wait for her fellow officers to respond.

Once the knife was in her fingers, she gritted her teeth and plunged it into the man's right kneecap, praying she had struck a nerve. A psychotic was often unable to feel pain. The man looked down at her with a demented grin. He didn't flinch. All he did was shift his weight to his uninjured leg.

Then he pointed the gun at her.

Rachel rolled her body to the side just as the man fired. The bullet seared its way into the wood flooring only an inch away from her abdomen. Raising the knife again, she drove the blade into his thigh.

At the same time, she waved her free arm from side to side, trying to prevent the man from getting a clear shot at her head.

As she withdrew the knife and thrust it into him again, Rachel sobbed hysterically. She had been transformed into a killer. She saw the awful face of Nathan Richardson, remembered his coarse hands on her body. All the bitterness of a lifetime seemed to converge into that one moment. When she struck her attacker's femoral artery, blood gushed out and struck her mouth, her eyes, saturated her hair. The gun tumbled from his hands to the floor. Rachel seized it, and trained it up at his face. The man's head fell back against the wall. For a few moments he was motionless, then his body slowly slid to the ground.

Rachel didn't check to see if his heart was beating. She didn't care. She refused to touch him again. His blood in her mouth tasted like rusted metal. She spat onto the floor, choking back another spasm of nausea.

Picking up her radio, she gasped, "Station one, I've just stabbed a man. Maybe now you can get me some help. I have a female DOA with her throat slashed. The man may still be alive. Dispatch an ambulance and notify the medical examiner. While you're at it, call Captain Madison at home and advise him to respond as well. I have some things to discuss with him."

"I'm en route," Miller shouted in the radio. "What do you need the captain for? It's five o'clock in the morning, Simmons."

"Station one, I'm rolling too," Carol Hitchcock said. "I just cleared my traffic stop. I'll be on Maple in less than ten minutes."

Rachel listened as Townsend, Ratso, Rogers, Harriman and the rest of the officers on her watch checked in with the station. Her eyes drifted over to the partially decapitated corpse, the unconscious man she had stabbed, the bullet holes, the pools of blood on the floor. With the mention of the chief, the cockroaches had decided to crawl out of their hiding places. For forty-five minutes, she had been trapped in a room with a deranged killer, waiting for her fellow officers to come to her rescue. They were too late, a lifetime too late. Picking up the portable radio, she hurled it across the room.

While Rachel was waiting for the units to arrive, she checked the residence for other suspects, then returned to the back of the house to find a bathroom and wash the blood off her hands. Entering what should have been the master bedroom, she saw what appeared to be a makeshift lab. Bunsen burners were set up on a long oak table. Chemicals used to manufacture methamphetamine were stored in a metal cabinet. The windows were boarded up with sheets of steel, and a steel overlay had been hammered over the wooden doorframe leading into the bedroom, the front of the door secured with four deadbolts. As the house itself was not alarmed, she decided the occupants didn't care if a burglar broke into the main section of the house as long as their drug lab was safe.

Opening off the room was a small bathroom, containing only a commode and a sink. The tub had been removed, and boxes of supplies were stacked underneath the shower nozzle. Rachel stepped inside and turned the faucet on in the sink. Once she had washed her hands and splashed cold water on her face, she looked for a towel. Not finding one on the towel racks, she opened the cabinet underneath the sink.

Inside were cardboard shoe boxes stuffed to the brim with cash. Rachel had never seen so much money before in her life. Squatting down on the floor, she grabbed a handful of bills and crushed them to her chest. She could solve all her problems. She could pay off Joe's medical bills, then set the rest of the money aside for Tracy's and Joe's college tuition.

How much was here?

Rachel quickly counted the boxes and came up with nine. Most of the bills were tens and twenties, and some of them were bundled and secured with rubber bands. Flipping through one of the bundles, she decided each bundle had to contain at least five thousand dollars. The total must come somewhere close to fifty thousand. With fifty thousand dollars, she could own the world, establish a new life. If she acted fast, no one would ever know. All she had to do was carry the cardboard boxes out to her car and lock them in the trunk. Before the watch ended, she could stop where her Pathfinder was parked on the street and transfer the money.

Rachel stared at the bundles of cash. The man had almost killed her. Her fellow officers didn't care what happened to her. It wasn't as if she were stealing from an individual. The money would be confiscated and end up in the city's coffers.

Sirens rang out in the distance. Now they were coming! Now! Now! She didn't need them now. She didn't want them now. She had money . . . green money, beautiful money. She brought the bills to her face and inhaled the ink. It smelled like salvation, freedom. Finding it had to be an omen, a gift from God, payback for all the misery she had endured.

If she took the money, she would never have to risk her life again, never face a madman again.

The sirens were getting closer. Rachel couldn't risk taking the shoe boxes out to the car now. She would have to bury them somewhere, maybe in the backyard. Her pulse was pounding. Her palms were sweaty.

She didn't have time to bury them.

The sirens were getting closer, only a few blocks away now. Rachel decided she would have to hide the money, then come back later and retrieve it. She stacked several of the boxes in her arms, then bent down to get more. Catching a glimpse of her image in the mirror, she saw her eyes flashing with greed, her face ugly and contorted. The boxes fell from her arms, the bundles of cash spilling out onto the bathroom floor.

chapter

SEVENTEEN

The front yard of the residence on Maple Avenue was roped off with yellow evidence tape. Jimmy Townsend and Carol Hitchcock were stationed outside the house for crowd control. Once the ambulance had picked up the injured man, police officers and criminologists from the county crime lab began streaming in and out the front door of the residence. Members of the media had been allowed to set up their equipment on the front lawn, even though they were not allowed access to the residence.

A reporter from the local television station stood with a microphone in her hands, staring into the lens of a minicam. Mary Standish was a thirty-year-old blonde with classic features and a trim physique. She wore an expensive jacket with a gold pin on the lapel, jeans and tennis shoes. When the cameraman gave her a cue, she began speaking into the microphone. "We're here on Maple Avenue, where the partially decapitated body of a young woman was discovered approximately an hour ago."

"You've got a hair sticking up on the left side of your head," the cameraman told her.

Seeing a long-haired man in a leather motorcycle jacket lifting the yellow tape and approaching the front of the house, Mary Standish stopped fiddling with her hair and rushed over, shoving the microphone in Tony Mancini's face. She recognized the detective from the recent robberies. "Can you tell us what happened? Has the victim been identified yet? Someone mentioned a struggle. Is the killer still at large?"

"No comment," Mancini said, walking over to Jimmy Townsend.

The detective was puffing on a slender black cigar, and his teeth were stained from tobacco. "Get these people out of here," he said. "If they're not here in an official capacity, they don't pass beyond the tape. This is a crime scene, asshole."

Townsend shrugged. He enjoyed seeing himself on TV and had hoped the reporter might ask him a few questions. Mancini glared at him, then disappeared inside the house.

Rachel was seated on a tattered, filthy sofa in the living room. She was silent and sullen, refusing to speak to anyone until the captain arrived.

Sergeant Miller met Mancini at the door, and led him to the bedroom where the woman's body was located. Once he had examined the corpse, Mancini walked through the house, checking out the drug lab and giving instructions to the various crime scene technicians. "The chick's been dead over eight hours," he told Miller once he returned to the living room. "From the sores on her arms, I'd say our little sweethearts were serious speed freaks. If the guy hadn't slit her throat, the woman would have died in a few months anyway. When you get to this level of toxicity, there's not a whole hell of a lot they can do for you."

"Do you think they were in this alone," Miller asked, "or do you think they had partners?"

Puffing out a stream of cigar smoke, Mancini said, "We have no way to know, of course, but my guess is that they were in it alone, at least as far as the drug lab. They were probably heavy users, humping to raise enough cash to support their habits. Suddenly they got smart and decided to cook the shit themselves. So they ditch L.A. and rent themselves an unassuming house in Oak Grove. Quiet neighborhood. Mostly families. Because they're a couple, they don't raise suspicions. They keep a low profile, never deal product locally." He glanced around him at all the debris and clutter. "You ask me, these people probably never left this house. There's receipts where they had groceries delivered. We also found a stack of Federal Express envelopes in the other room. They probably shipped the speed back to L.A., and had a contact there who peddled it for them on the street."

"What makes you think they moved here from Los Angeles?"

"The fellow Simmons stabbed studied chemistry at UCLA," Mancini said. "Found a textbook with his name in it on a table in the lab." He shifted the cigar to the other side of his mouth. "Don't see no suitcases full of cash, though. Even if their distribution network was located in L.A., where's the loot? People like this don't use banks."

Rachel's mouth fell open. "Th-the money was in the bathroom," she said. "In the cabinet under the sink."

Miller jerked his head around. "We already searched under the sink. Nothing's in there but a bunch of empty shoe boxes."

Rachel ran down the hall to the bathroom, pushing several crime scene technicians out of her way. She stared at the bathroom floor. The boxes were scattered on the tiles, completely empty. She dropped down on her hands and knees and searched behind the commode, thinking at least a few of the bills might have become lodged there when she dropped the boxes on the floor. Had she been hallucinating?

Nick Miller was standing in the doorway. Mancini stepped up behind him. "What did you see in here?" the detective asked, his voice nasal and gruff.

"These boxes were full of money," Rachel said, gazing at them on the floor. "I didn't have time to count it, but I'm certain there was close to fifty thousand dollars." She picked up an empty box, then dropped it. "Where did it go?"

With his broad shoulders, Miller nudged Mancini out of his way. "When did you find the money?"

"Right after my last radio transmission."

"The guy you stabbed never regained consciousness?"

"No," Rachel told him.

"No one else was inside the house with you?"

"No."

"What did you do after you found the money?"

"I heard the sirens pull up in front of the house," she said. "I wasn't certain if it was the ambulance or one of the officers arriving. I wanted to direct the paramedics to the injured man, make certain they didn't disturb the crime scene."

Miller and Mancini exchanged tense looks. The detective removed the cigar from his mouth, letting a stack of ashes tumble onto his jacket. "Did you come back in here after the ambulance arrived?"

"No," Rachel told him. "Sergeant Miller arrived right behind the ambulance, then Townsend and Hitchcock. Ratso was here for a few minutes, but the sergeant ordered him to clear."

"Who's Ratso?" Mancini asked, shoving the cigar back in his mouth.

"Fred Ramone," Miller told him. "I told him to clear because we needed him back on the street. I'm almost positive he didn't go into the rear of the house. We spoke briefly in the living room, then Ratso left out the front door."

"Was the back door unlocked?"

"There isn't a back door," Rachel told them. "There should be a side door near the garage. I never checked it. It's on the opposite side of the house, if this house follows the same floor plan as all the other Windermere properties."

They left the bathroom, passing into the kitchen. The side door leading out of the house opened onto an enclosed utility porch. Mancini pulled on a pair of rubber gloves. The door didn't have a deadbolt. It locked with a small lever above the door handle. The only way the detective could be certain the door was unlocked was to try to open it from the outside. He walked out and closed the door, then opened it and stepped back inside the kitchen. "Well, we answered that question," he said. "Your man could have left through the front, Miller, then circled around and reentered through the kitchen. While you were busy with the stiff in the front room, he snuck into the bathroom and bagged the loot."

"That doesn't sound like Ratso," Rachel said. "He's a smart man, but more book smart than streetwise. Whoever did this had to size up the situation immediately, figure out they were running a drug lab. If not, why would they assume there was money in the house?" She turned to Miller. "Did you tell Ratso about the lab?"

"I don't remember," Miller said. "This is your fault, Simmons."

Rachel placed a hand over her chest. "Why is it my fault? I didn't take the money."

"If you hadn't got a bug up your ass and refused to tell me what was going on here," Miller yelled, "I would have secured the money the second I arrived, before someone had a chance to get their grubby hands on it."

Mancini asked, "Did Townsend and Hitchcock have access to the bathroom?"

"No," Miller said. "I had them remain outside for crowd control. As far as I know, neither of them came inside the house."

"How many paramedics responded?" Mancini asked.

"Two," Rachel said.

"Did one of them leave your presence for any length of time?"

Rachel rubbed her forehead. "One of them went outside to get something. I think they had trouble getting an IV in the man's vein. I heard them say they needed a smaller needle."

Several of the crime scene technicians had overheard part of the conversation and had stopped working to listen. Miller pulled Mancini outside onto the porch area. Rachel followed, closing the door leading into the kitchen. Miller said, "How do we know one of the crime techs didn't swipe it?"

"Maybe you swiped it, Miller," Mancini said, his beady eyes shining like marbles. "You were one of the first officers on the scene."

"Maybe it was never there, asshole," Miller shouted. "Simmons has a problem. She has a tendency to tell stories."

"The money was here," Rachel insisted. "I didn't make it up. Someone stole it."

Miller flew into a rage. "Can't you keep your damn mouth shut, woman?" he barked. "Are you trying to rip this department apart? This case is fucked anyway because of you."

"Where's the captain?" Rachel said. She had done nothing wrong. She refused to let Miller bully her. "Why isn't he here by now? It's been over an hour since I asked the dispatcher to call him."

"Forget the captain," Miller said.

Rachel was furious. He had overruled her request. "I'm going to call the captain myself," she said. "I made a valid request. You had no right to cancel it."

"Listen," Miller said, his voice dropping to a more reasonable level, "you handled this situation like a damn rookie. Why would you crawl through a window, huh? You entered this man's house illegally. When this case gets to court, the judge could exclude every piece of evidence we've collected and this maniac will go free."

"That isn't true," Rachel said, her voice quavering. "I saw the woman in the chair through the window. I thought it was a medical emergency, that she'd overdosed on drugs or had a heart attack."

"It doesn't work that way," Miller said. "You couldn't see her throat through the window. The woman's chair was facing away from you. For all you knew, it was just a woman asleep in a chair in the privacy of her own home. We have no right to enter under those circumstances. You entered this house without the benefit of a search warrant. Didn't you learn anything in the academy?"

"But the neighbors called in," Rachel argued. "I was dispatched to this house."

"They called in about loud music," Miller told her. "They didn't call in a medical emergency or a homicide. They didn't even give you a specific house number."

"What if the woman had been alive?" Rachel said. "She could have bled to death. I had to go inside to find out what was wrong with her."

Mancini began plotting how they should proceed. None of the problems they had encountered were out of the ordinary. Drug money frequently vanished from crime scenes. When he'd worked for the LAPD, hundreds of thousands of dollars disappeared every year into the hands of corrupt cops, opportunist ambulance attendants, crime scene technicians, and other related law enforcement personnel. In many ways, stealing drug money was a guilt-free crime. Some cops viewed it along the lines of a bonus.

"Here's how it goes down," Mancini said, his eyes trained on Rachel. "You came here to investigate a report of loud music. When no one answered the door, you went to the side of the house and looked in through the window. You saw a woman sitting in a chair with her throat slashed, her clothing covered in blood. Thinking she was still alive, you entered to render emergency medical treatment."

"That isn't true," she said, shaking her head. "Miller just told you I couldn't see the woman's face. All I could see was the back of her head."

"Do you have learning disabilities?" Mancini yelled. "Do you want this murderer to go free? You heard what the sergeant just said. If they suppress all the evidence because of an illegal search, what are we going to use to convict this bastard? We're talking the murder weapon, the drug lab. Without that bloody knife, we don't have shit. The perp will claim someone else broke in here during the night and slit his lady's throat."

"He tried to kill me," Rachel said, her eyes expanding. "He took my gun away from me. Didn't you see the bullet holes in the walls and furniture? He was shooting everywhere, firing randomly. He's a deranged psychotic. Anyone in their right mind would know he's the man who killed that woman."

Mancini smirked. "Ever heard of protecting your property? The man you stabbed paid the rent on this pad. You were the intruder, Simmons. How did he know you were a cop? He could say he thought you were the killer."

"I'm wearing my uniform," she said. "How could he not know I was a cop?"

Mancini played the devil's advocate. "It was dark. He was spooked. All he saw was an intruder dressed in dark clothing. His girlfriend had just been brutally murdered. The guy thought his life was in jeopardy, so he fought you, disarmed you. The way I see it, you'll be lucky if the guy doesn't sue you for stabbing him."

Rachel's mind was spinning. How could something so obvious be turned into something so convoluted? "I announced myself as a police officer the second I entered the house. No," she said, correcting herself, "I announced even before I entered the house."

Mancini spat a piece of cigar scum out of his mouth. "Your word against his, babe."

"What about the missing money?"

"What money?" Mancini said, a blank expression on his face. "I didn't hear anything about missing money. What about you, Miller? Anyone mention money to you?"

"Not a word," the sergeant said.

Rachel took a few steps backward. "We aren't going to do anything? You can't be serious. There was fifty thousand dollars in those boxes. I saw it with my own eyes."

"What do you suggest we do?" Mancini said, glowering at her. "Come on, Simmons, I want to hear how you think we should handle this situation. Should we haul in every cop that set foot inside this house? Should we search their cars, their lockers, their homes? You'll be the first person in the hot seat. Shit, you had plenty of time to stash the loot before the others showed up. How about calling a press conference? Then we could tell the whole community what kind of crooked bastards police their streets, how they can no longer feel safe in their homes." He dusted the ashes off his leather jacket. "It's Christmas, okay? Someone just got an early visit from Santa."

For a few moments, Rachel just stood there, too stunned to move. She felt a violent wave of nausea, as if she had been forced to eat contaminated food. She saw herself holding the bills in her hand, crushing them to her chest. She had to get away. She had almost caught their disease. If she stayed, they would extract every ounce of decency from her, drawing it out a drop at a time until there was nothing left.

"May I clear, sir?" Rachel asked Sergeant Miller.

The sergeant ignored her, stepping a few feet away and whispering something to Mancini.

"I'm talking to you," she shouted, her arms stiff at her side. "I need to go for an AIDS test. I swallowed some of the suspect's blood when I stabbed him."

"Stop by the hospital," Miller said. "I'll speak to you later at the station."

"Absolutely, *sir*," she said, hissing out the salutation.

"Are you being insubordinate, Simmons?" Miller said.

Rachel didn't answer. Spinning around, she marched past the crime scene technicians in the living room. When she exited the front of the house, she ran into Jimmy Townsend and Carol Hitchcock on the steps.

"Thanks for being there when I needed you," she said, shoving them out of her way. "It's nice to know I have such good friends."

"I warned you," Townsend said. "Cops don't stab each other in the back, Rachel. We're all in this boat together. Maybe after tonight, you'll understand what we mean."

"Wait," Carol said, concerned that things were getting out of hand, "I want to talk to you."

"Forget it," Rachel snapped, continuing on to her unit.

chapter

EIGHTEEN

Rachel was swaddled in a blanket, seated on a sofa in the doctors' lounge at Presbyterian Hospital, clasping a mug of coffee with both hands. It was 9:20 Wednesday morning, and Mike Atwater had just walked into the room.

The prosecutor had responded to Rachel's 7:00 a.m. call with mixed feelings. He was horrified by the ordeal she had been through, but he wasn't sure if the situation would amount to anything. A few cops failing to respond for backup was not a crime. During their phone conversation, however, Rachel had alluded to a more serious problem. She claimed one of the officers involved in the shooting at the Majestic Theater had used the Hillmont boy as a human shield. Since Ringwald had insisted he try the case, a police scandal might work out quite nicely. The only way it would fly, though, was if Rachel's story turned out to be cohesive and factual, and there were other witnesses who could corroborate her statements in the courtroom.

"Captain Madison never came," she said as soon as she saw him. "Sergeant Miller wouldn't let the dispatcher call him. At least the man I stabbed didn't test positive for AIDS. They gave me a test to be certain. They said it could take up to six months for the virus to show up. They'll have to test us both again."

"From what you told me on the phone," Atwater said, sitting down in an orange plastic chair across from her, "Madison might not be the best person to spill your guts to right now."

"Why?" Rachel asked. "Shouldn't he know what's going on? Maybe I should call the chief, then."

"I've been around this element a lot longer than you have," the attorney said. "Police departments are closed environments, similar in some ways to cults. What trickles down to the bottom usually starts at the top."

"I have no idea what you're talking about," she said, shaking her head in confusion.

"The things you've mentioned wouldn't occur if the chief and the higher-ranking officers didn't condone them, or at least look the other way. Corruption thrives where it resides, if you know what I mean." He stood to get himself a cup of coffee. "How many people were involved in this?"

Rachel tracked him with her eyes. "Are you talking about last night, or the shooting at the Majestic Theater?"

"They're both related, right?" he said, returning to his seat with his coffee.

"Grant Cummings wasn't on duty last night," she said, pulling the blanket more tightly around her. "They did it for Grant, though. When I told Carol Hitchcock that I was going to tell the truth about the Hill-mont shooting, they decided to teach me a lesson."

"You can forget last night," Atwater said. "How could we ever prove that these officers intentionally didn't respond for backup? That's not a crime, anyway. It's a disciplinary problem."

Rachel told him about the money she had found in the shoe boxes. "I think pocketing fifty grand constitutes more than a disciplinary problem, don't you?"

"Do you have any idea who took it?"

"The guy I stabbed certainly didn't take it," Rachel tossed out. "The only people inside that house were law enforcement personnel."

"I'll get in touch with Internal Affairs," he said, "have them initiate an investigation."

"What about Grant? He used that kid as a shield. The Hillmont boy should be alive, Mike. There was no reason for him to die."

"We're looking at another tricky situation," Atwater said, his expression troubled. "If the other officers aren't willing to testify that what you said is true, it will be your word against theirs. That's a heavy burden to carry. Are you sure you're up to it?"

"After tonight," Rachel said, "I'm willing to take on the whole department. There's more that I haven't told you." She swallowed her pride, then poured out the sordid details of the party on the beach.

"Sounds like sexual harassment," he said, twirling his cufflinks. "You'll have to hire an attorney and sue the department. I can't help you with civil matters, Rachel."

"Why is it sexual harassment?" she argued. "I wasn't on duty when it happened. It had nothing to do with my job. Grant Cummings tried to rape me. And the sergeant, Ratso, Jimmy Townsend, they were all involved. If they didn't actually fondle me, they certainly did nothing to stop it."

Mike Atwater had an uncomfortable sensation in the pit of his stomach. He stared at Rachel's face, trying to read her. The events she had described were outrageous. If they came out in the open, the media would go wild. He could already envision the headlines. Sex. Brutality. Missing drug money. Bad cops. The recipe was ripe, a wicked brew of sensationalism. Even though he was excited by the possibilities of such a situation, he had to make certain Rachel would be able to go the distance. "Are you willing to swear out a criminal complaint against Grant Cummings?"

"Yes," Rachel said.

"Well," Atwater said, "I guess the attempted rape is the best place to start. I'll contact the Attorney General's office and advise them of the other matters you told me about, as well as notify Internal Affairs of the missing drug money. Since I'm prosecuting Donald Trueman, I can see if any of the other witnesses support your story." He stood and glanced at his watch. "I have to be in court in twenty minutes. Why don't I get the complaint typed up and drop by your house later tonight for your signature?"

"I'm on duty tonight," she said. "Should I take a sick day?"

"Sounds like a good plan," he said.

"When will they serve Grant?"

"Probably tomorrow," he said. "Look, once this goes down, all hell is going to break loose. You're going to be besieged by the media. The way you've described these officers, Rachel, I'm not certain it's safe for you to go back to work."

"You mean I'm not going to have a job," she said. "Isn't that what you're trying to tell me?"

"It could come to that," Atwater said, taking a seat beside her again. Rachel closed her eyes against welling tears, and he gently touched the star-shaped mole on her eyelid. Memories of their lovemaking passed through his mind, and he leaned closer to kiss her.

Rachel pushed him away. "Will I get paid?"

"I can't make any promises," Atwater told her, becoming all business again. "I'll do whatever I can to keep you on the payroll. If Personnel finds a way to cut you loose, you'll have to do what I said, hire an attorney and file a lawsuit."

As Rachel watched him get up to go, a tear inched its way down her cheek. How would she pay her bills? Her career as a police officer was over. She could move to another state, but she knew her reputation would follow her. Once she signed her name on the complaint, there would be no turning back. "Bring the papers over around seven," she said. "I should be awake by then."

Grant Cummings was in his townhouse in Ventura. Located only a few blocks from the beach, his home had a living room with a towering ceiling, a small study, and two large bedrooms in the upstairs loft. He kept everything clean and perfectly ordered. When he had visitors, he insisted they leave their shoes in the entryway.

Ratso was sitting on the floor in the kitchen cleaning Grant's thirty-piece gun collection. He had not slept since the day before. When Grant had called him that morning, he had reluctantly agreed to come over. Instead of working alongside him as he had promised, Grant had spent the morning on the beach while Ratso slaved away on his kitchen floor.

Walking into the room, Grant opened the refrigerator and removed a cold beer. "Don't get that gun oil on my floor."

Ratso nodded. His eyelids were so heavy that he could barely keep them open. He was hungry and thirsty, but Grant had not offered him food or drink. He dropped an antique revolver on the floor. "I'm concerned about the things Rachel said about me. What's going to happen, Grant?"

"Nothing," the other man said. "You're with me, bud. You know I take care of my people."

"I can't afford to be the subject of an investigation," Ratso continued. "I'm afraid, Grant."

Grant was unconcerned about Ratso's fears. Riding herd on so many people was sometimes a pain in the ass. Everyone came to him with their problems. He didn't mind helping them, but he expected to be compensated. Everything in life came with a price. "Once you clean up this mess," he said abruptly, "you can go home. Just make sure you put the guns in the right slots in the gun cabinet."

Two beige leather sofas faced each other in the living room. In the center of the room was a glass cocktail table covered with newspapers. When the phone rang thirty minutes later, Ratso was gone and Grant had his shirt off, his upper body burnished by the morning in the sun. He was squatting on the floor next to the table, constructing a model of a '57 Chevy. "Yo," he said, picking up the portable phone off the table. "You got me. Speak, or forever hold your peace."

"It's Carol," she said. "I just got off the phone with a clerk at the DA's office. Rachel is filing charges against you for attempted rape."

"Nah," he said, laughing. "Why are you kidding around about something like this? You're a case, Carol."

"I'm not teasing, Grant," she said. "My friend says she just typed the complaint. I went to breakfast with Rachel last night like you said, but she refused to back down about the Majestic Theater incident. What is she talking about now? What have you done to this woman?"

"Rachel's insane," he said, holding up the model car to check the placement of the bumper he'd just glued on. "I didn't do anything to her. Are you serious? Does she really think she can get away with this shit?"

"I swear," Carol said. "First she accuses you of using the Hillmont kid as a shield. Now she's accusing you of attempted rape. This time you've made a mistake, Grant. You played around with the wrong woman."

"I didn't play around with anyone," Grant lied, his voice booming out over the room. "No one's going to believe Rachel's ridiculous stories. She doesn't have any proof. She can file all the charges she wants. I guarantee you nothing is ever going to come of them."

Carol fell silent. Finally she said, "You might be wrong, Grant. I think we all underestimated Rachel, including Miller. Last night when we ignored her requests for a backup, she asked the dispatcher to call the captain out at five in the morning. When Miller put a stop to it, she evidently ran straight to Mike Atwater at the DA's office."

Holding the miniature door to the model in his free hand, Grant crushed it to smithereens. "I'll talk to you later," he said, slamming down the phone.

Jimmy Townsend met Grant Cummings in the men's locker room prior to the Wednesday night shift. The other officers were already in the squad room. "We need to talk," he said.

"Shoot," Grant said, strapping on his holster. "The watch meeting is due to start any minute, so you'll have to make it fast."

"Two of the witnesses from the Majestic Theater incident claim they saw you kicking Donald Trueman after he was already on the ground."

"So?" he said. "They were rioting. What good is their word? They're a bunch of punks. No one is going to take a kid's word over mine."

"I wouldn't be so sure about that if I were you," Townsend said. "The kids I interviewed are all football players. They come from good families. They make decent grades." He stopped speaking as Ted Harriman walked past them. After the former Marine exited the locker room, he continued, "At least no one saw you pull the Hillmont kid in front of you. You lucked out on that one, Grant. If Rachel keeps her mouth shut, you should be in the clear."

"Where have you been?" Grant shouted. "She's already gone to the DA's office. She's saying I tried to rape her at the watch party. They're preparing a warrant for my arrest right now."

"No," Townsend said, aghast. "I don't believe you. Rachel never said anything about what happened at the watch party. All she mentioned was the problem with the Hillmont boy."

"If I end up taking a fall for attempted rape," Grant growled, "you're going to be right there with me."

Townsend's jaw dropped. "What are you saying?"

"You know what I'm saying," Grant said, shoving the heavy-set officer against his locker. "You drugged her, Jimmy boy. You played with her tits just like everyone else did. Why should I be the only one to pay the price? You're one of the fuckers who blew the lid off this thing. If you and the rest of the crew had responded for backup last night when Rachel was in trouble, she wouldn't have gone running to that prick Atwater."

Townsend felt his stomach rolling. "We did it for you, Grant," he said. "We thought if we taught her a lesson, Rachel would learn not to flap her mouth about her fellow officers. How did we know she would run to the DA?"

"Whatever," Grant said, tossing his hands in dismissal. "But don't forget, you've got a few skeletons in the closet, too. You hang me out to dry and I'll make certain those old bones find their way to the surface."

"We have to stop her," Townsend said, horrified at what he was hearing. "I have a family, Grant. You know how difficult things have been for me at home lately. I don't need any more problems, particularly when it comes to my job. We always stand up for each other. Isn't that what you're always preaching?"

Grant thought for a moment. "Tell you what," he said, a sinister look in his eyes. "Once we clear the station, meet me in the parking lot of the Holiday Inn on Center Street."

Lucy invited Rachel, Joe and Tracy to her house for an early dinner that evening, then insisted on keeping Joe for the night, hoping Rachel could get a decent night's sleep.

"Someone's coming over," Rachel told her daughter once they returned from Lucy's. Both of them were sipping iced tea at the kitchen table. "Do you have a friend you could stay with?"

"It's the guy, isn't it?" Tracy said, clapping her hands in excitement. "See, I knew he would fall for you. Before you know it, you'll be getting married."

"It's business," Rachel said, grim-faced and weary. "He might be the same man I went to dinner with, Tracy, but he's not coming over to socialize."

"I don't understand," the girl said, her face showing her disappointment.

"I know," Rachel said. "Something happened last night. Mike Atwater is helping me sort it out. I think under the circumstances, it would be better if we spoke privately."

"What happened?"

"I stabbed a man." Rachel took a drink of her iced tea, her throat so parched she could barely swallow. "He murdered his girlfriend. He surprised me and got my gun away from me. I had no choice. I stabbed him in self-defense. If I hadn't, he would have killed me."

"You killed someone?" Tracy said, her eyes enormous.

"No," she said. "The man was injured, but he's alive."

The girl reached her fingers across the table to touch her mother's hand. "It must have been terrible, Mom," she said. "Why didn't you tell me before now?"

"It's part of my job," Rachel said. Job? she asked herself. Right now, she didn't know if she would ever put on a uniform again. "Look," she went on, "I may ask for a leave of absence from the department until some of the things I mentioned are cleared up. It's nothing to worry about. They're still going to pay me."

"Are you sure you're all right?" Tracy said.

"I'm fine," she said. "Do you know someone you can stay with for a few hours? If not, you can go next door with Lucy, maybe give her a hand with Joe."

"Sheila Ross," Tracy answered. "She already asked me to spend the night with her so we could practice our cheerleading routine. I told her I couldn't because it was a school night. Should I call and see if her mother can pick me up?"

"Yes, please," Rachel said, burying her head in her hands.

NINETEEN

By ten o'clock, Rachel had signed the complaint against Grant Cummings. Mike Atwater insisted she give a formal statement, and had set up a tape recorder in the living room. Once they were finished, Rachel asked him politely to leave.

"No problem," he said, bristling at her aloofness. "Was it something I said? Your kids are away. I thought we—"

She gave him an icy look, then escorted him to the door. "I need to be alone now, Mike," she said. "I have to figure out what I'm going to do, how I'm going to support my family. I haven't even told my daughter what's going on yet. I only told her I stabbed a man last night, and you were helping me with the paperwork."

"I wouldn't write off the job so fast," he said. "Once Cummings is in custody, it should be safe for you to return to work."

"I thought you knew everything there was to know about police departments," Rachel said, tilting her head. "Isn't that what you told me this morning? I'll never be safe now. Last night they abandoned me, forced me to deal with a madman alone. If I hadn't got my hands on that knife, I'd be dead right now. How can I go back on the street?" She stopped and ran her fingers through her hair. "Besides, Grant will make bail. They'll never keep him in custody."

"You're probably right," Atwater said, stroking the side of his nose.

"But I doubt if the department will take him back as long as he's facing a felony conviction."

"What about the sexual battery?" she asked. "You're charging Grant with attempted rape, but the sexual battery charge I saw on the complaint is only a misdemeanor. You're going to let him plead to the lesser offense, aren't you? I'm about to destroy my life, and Grant is going to skate."

Atwater stared at her. She wasn't simply a fresh-faced woman anymore, sexy and appealing. She had become every prosecutor's nemesis. Rachel Simmons was now a victim. "It's common procedure to plead both counts," he told her. "If the jury finds the evidence insufficient on the attempted rape, they can still deliver a conviction on the sexual battery." He stopped and looked her squarely in the eye. "We have no intention of entering into a plea agreement with this man, Rachel. We're only trying to assure ourselves of a conviction on one of the counts. Any conviction is better than none, don't you think?"

"But why are you giving the jury a choice?" Rachel argued. "You know they'll go for the lesser offense. They always do."

"Look," he said, "I had to push Bill Ringwald into accepting this case on any level. You've admitted you were drinking when this happened. All we have is your statement. There's no physical evidence. From what you've told me, none of the officers on the beach will support your story. That means no corroborating witnesses. I'm going to do everything in my power to put Cummings behind bars, Rachel, but there are no guarantees here."

It wasn't what she wanted to hear, but at least he was being straight with her. "When will they arrest him?"

"I'll send a marshal to his house first thing in the morning," Atwater told her. "Ringwald doesn't want him served on the job. We're going to have a media frenzy when this goes down. My suggestion is for you to keep your mouth shut, no matter how much the reporters pester you for a statement. Since we're still investigating the allegations you made about Grant and the Majestic Theater incident, there's no reason to expose you to the media just yet." The attorney knew that timing was crucial. The media wanted exclusive interviews, inside information, inflammatory details. If Rachel went to press prematurely, she would seem too accessible, and the story would be old news before he was ready to go public with his own press conference.

"Fine," she said.

"Try to get some rest," Atwater said, clasping her hand.

Rachel leaned over and pecked him on the cheek. "Call me when Grant is in custody," she said. Once the attorney had stepped through the doorway, she slid the deadbolts into place, then headed to the back of the house to go to bed.

Sergeant Miller had the radio operator call Fred Ramone in the field and advise him to report to his office. "Have a seat," he said when Ratso walked in. He pointed to the chair in front of his desk.

"What's wrong?" Ratso said with an anxious look. He was so nervous, he accidentally knocked the metal chair over. Picking it back up, he slowly lowered himself into the seat.

"I just saw the medical report on the kid you arrested in front of the Majestic Theater," Miller said, taking a toothpick out of a box on his desk. "He suffered a brain hemorrhage. He's in intensive care. His parents are demanding a full investigation."

"I didn't hurt that boy," Ratso lied, his face blanching. "I swear, Sergeant. He must have got hit on the head with a bottle. Bottles were flying all over the place."

"That's not what Rachel Simmons says," the sergeant answered. "She claims she saw you smashing the boy's head against the sidewalk. If she tells the same story to her new pal at the DA's office, you're going to be in one heap of trouble. The injured kid's parents are loaded. His father is president of Stanford Insurance."

Ratso's fear simmered into rage. "Rachel's lying. You know that, Sergeant. Grant told you she was lying. She's angry about what happened on the beach."

"She's sworn out a complaint against Grant for attempted rape," Miller told him, spitting the toothpick out of his mouth. "For all I know, we're all going to be charged as co-conspirators. You better see if that 7-Eleven you used to work at has any openings, Ratso. You might be back in the job market."

"I didn't work at a 7-Eleven," Ratso said, glowering at him. "I worked at a mini-mart with a car wash. I was the manager. I supervised a number of employees."

"Yeah, well," the sergeant smirked, fiddling with one of the drawers to his desk, "I guess you can get your executive position back then, because this gig is about to expire."

"What's going to happen to Grant? He knows I didn't hurt that boy. He'll stand up for me."

"If Rachel doesn't recant her story to the DA, Grant might be working with you at the car wash."

Ratso went to the men's room and locked himself in a stall. His heart was racing. His stomach was tumbling over and over like a beach ball. If they investigated him for beating the boy, they might uncover the truth. No one knew about his past except Grant Cummings. Grant had protected him, looked out for him, given him status with the other men. Even though he despised him, Ratso knew this was the way the world worked. They had reached an agreement over a year ago when Grant had stumbled across some private papers in his apartment. If Grant was on the verge of being fired, would the men ignore him again and treat him like an outsider? If Grant's word was no longer any good, who would defend him against the charges of brutality Rachel was alleging?

Dropping his pants, he squatted on the toilet, letting his bowels explode into the bowl. Grant Cummings was a despicable man. Ratso had allowed him to control him through threats and intimidation, accepting his abuse because he felt he had no alternative. Even though the men treated him like he was an idiot, he was a proud man with a refined mind. He stood and walked to the sink, washing his hands like a surgeon.

Staring at his watery brown eyes in the mirror, Ratso slowly formulated a plan. In this land of plenty, people didn't understand about survival. His country was twice the size of California but had almost four times as many people. Although human life was grossly abundant, resources were limited.

Ratso didn't mind hurting people as long as it served a higher cause. When he had beaten the young boy in the parking lot of the Majestic Theater, he had also lifted his wallet. He had pocketed several hundred dollars to send to his sisters in Peshawar.

Without his support, Ratso's sisters would die. Two were already dead. One was missing. His three remaining sisters were living in seclusion. They were older, and without a father to arrange their marriages, their lives had no value. As a child he had weaved carpets, chained to his loom in a filthy hovel. He had traveled to this country in the belly of a tanker. He had worked hard and studied diligently, learning the language and customs so he could blend in without notice. Even though he had drifted away from the teachings of Islam, he would pray to Allah for strength to complete his mission and preserve his livelihood.

Heading to the locker room, Ratso made sure no one was around, then unlocked the padlock and removed a large object wrapped in newspapers and tied with a string. As he was carrying the package out of the back door to the police station, he ran into Ted Harriman.

"What you got there, bro?" Harriman said. "The sergeant assigned me a unit that must be in the garage. I can't find it in the parking lot."

"Evidence," Ratso said. "I'm taking it to the crime lab."

"Do you know what's going on with Rachel? She wasn't at the watch meeting tonight. Is she sick?"

"I don't know," Ratso said, brushing past him and continuing on to his police car.

chapter

TWENTY

Once Mike Atwater had left, Rachel undressed and went to bed. After tossing and turning for over an hour, she decided to give up. Before she had gone to Lucy's for dinner, she had napped for several hours on the living room sofa. She knew she needed more sleep, but she couldn't relax. The murder victim's partially decapitated body kept appearing in her mind, as well as the deranged look in the madman's eyes.

The Santa Ana winds had pushed the temperature into the mid-eighties, and even after eleven o'clock, the bedroom was stifling. She dressed in shorts and a T-shirt, then went out the front door. Bending over, she slipped her keys in the side of one of her running shoes.

As she took off down the street at a fast clip, her muscles were cold, stiff. She knew she should stretch, but she never did. The moment she laced up her shoes, she was ready to fly. Even though she called it jogging, she had never really been a jogger. She was a sprinter. She wanted to go fast, see the sidewalk flying up to meet her, feel the wind in her face.

Elmhurst Road was a dead-end street, but it opened into the abandoned orange grove. Rachel loved running there. The dirt cushioned her stride, and the spaces between the orange trees made a perfect jogging path.

The moon was out, yet Rachel failed to see the police car parked at the edge of the grove with its lights off. She was deep in her thoughts, trying to think of solutions, wondering where she might apply for a job. Carrie could float her for a few months if they cut off her salary, but she knew her sister couldn't carry her indefinitely. Susan had married a carpenter and moved to Oregon. They led a comfortable life, but their income was modest and they had four young children to support.

Rachel hadn't phoned in sick. While Atwater was taking her statement, Sergeant Miller had called on the answering machine, demanding that she report to the station. Atwater instructed her not to return his call, telling her that he would contact Captain Madison himself and tell him that she was ill. Because the DA might ultimately charge Miller as a co-conspirator in the attempted rape, he preferred that Rachel didn't speak to him outside of an attorney's presence.

The moonlight was casting eerie shadows over the orange grove. Rachel was certain something had moved behind her. Was it a dog?

When she turned around, Grant Cummings jumped out from the row of orange trees. He seized her by the throat and forced her to the ground. "Don't move," he muttered, staring down at her. "If you move so much as a muscle, I swear I'll kill you."

"What are you doing?" she said, trying to remain calm. Grant was on duty, dressed in his uniform. He couldn't torment her for long. The dispatcher would start looking for him. "It isn't going to change anything, Grant. I've already given the DA a formal statement."

"You'll take it back," he said, "tell them you made it up."

"I can't do that," she told him. "They recorded it. You're wasting your time, Grant. You're only making things worse."

"I'm not going to let you ruin my life," he snarled, the muscles in his jaw locked. "Don't you know why I pulled that kid in front of me? Black Talons. Are you such an idiot you've never heard of them? If the Trueman kid had Black Talon ammo loaded in that shooter, it would have pierced my vest and killed me. Why do you think they call them cop killers?"

"Why would a kid like that have Black Talons?" Rachel said. "He was just a teenager, Grant. His parents are shattered. How would you feel if it were your son? You know Timothy Hillmont didn't deserve to die."

"And I do?" he said, kicking dirt at her. "If Hillmont hadn't decided to get in a rumble out there, he wouldn't have been shot. Why should I lose everything I've worked for just because some high school punks wanted to mix it up over a football game?"

Rachel eyed his gun belt, wondering if she could disarm him. But she knew Grant had lightning-fast reflexes. If she went for his gun, he would shoot her in a second. "Why don't we discuss this like two rational adults?" she said, propping herself up with her arms. "We can go to my house. I'll make a pot of coffee. We'll talk this thing through, see if we can come up with some solutions."

"No," Grant shouted, his body trembling with rage. "You have to learn who's in charge. That's the problem with fucking women like you. You've forgotten the basics. The man wears the pants. The man gets the respect. Didn't you have a daddy? Didn't he teach you about respect?"

A trickle of saliva ran down the corner of his mouth. His face was contorted, his skin purple and blotchy.

Until that moment, Rachel had never considered that Grant might physically harm her. She knew now that she had been mistaken. The rage she saw was beyond anger, something he must have bottled up inside him for years. "I respect you, Grant," she lied, knowing she must outwit him. "Let me up and we'll talk. Maybe I can withdraw the charges like you said. I didn't understand about the Black Talon ammo. I mean, I knew about them, but I forgot."

"You're trying to trick me," he yelled. Seeing Rachel trying to push herself to her feet, he threw himself on top of her, his impact so heavy that it crushed the breath out of her. They rolled in the dirt. Grant grabbed a corner of her T-shirt, causing it to rip. He clawed at her chest, tearing her bra apart.

"Stop," she screamed, as his rough hands squeezed her breasts. "What are you doing?"

"You need to be taught a lesson," Grant snarled, his hand darting inside the elastic waistband of her jogging shorts.

She decided to go for his gun in the holster, terrified he was going to rape her. She managed to touch the metal, but Grant wrenched her hand away, removing the gun and tossing it into the row of orange trees. Pulling back his fist, he slugged her with tremendous force, connecting with her chin and jerking her head back.

Rachel lost consciousness. She awoke to blinding pain. Grant was beating her with his fists, pummeling the soft tissue in her abdomen and breasts, slamming into the narrow bones in her rib cage.

"I'll teach you," he shouted, sweat dripping off his forehead onto her face. "You hear me? Respect."

The pain was sickening. "Please, please," she whimpered pathetically, "I'll take back my statement. I'll do anything you tell me to do."

"You're damn right you will," he barked. "If I ever see you talking to that prick Atwater again, I'll come back and beat you to a bloody pulp. Do you understand, bitch?"

"Yes," she moaned. "Whatever you say, Grant."

His large hands encircled her neck. He laughed insanely. Wind was whipping through the groves, howling and whistling. Rachel could smell rotting oranges, the rich scent of the soil. He was high on power, feasting on her fear as he squeezed the breath out of her. When he removed his hands from her throat, Rachel thought it was over. Grant stood, though, kicking her onto her back.

"Get on your knees," he said, unzipping his pants and pulling out his penis. "Suck it."

Tears streamed down her face. The tip of his boots had savagely battered her side. She twisted her body, trying to relieve the pain, certain her ribs were broken. He yanked her to her knees. "Please, Grant," she begged, kneeling in front of him, "don't make me do this. I'll take back my statement. I swear. I'll do anything you ask of me."

"Suck it," he said, grabbing her head and forcing her face to his groin. "If you bite me, I'll snap your neck like a twig."

Rachel tried to do what he said. She was so repulsed, though, that she leaned over and vomited. The contents of her stomach spewed out onto Grant's pants and shoes.

"Look what you've done to my uniform," Grant shouted, jumping back. "You haven't learned your lesson yet, have you? You still haven't learned about respect."

She picked her torn T-shirt off the ground and tried to wipe the vomit from his pants leg. Grant kicked her in the abdomen, knocking her back to the ground. "I'm going to stink now, whore."

Mucus dripped from her nose. Her insides felt as if they had been ruptured. Bile rose in her throat. Grant seized her by the hair and dragged her through the dirt. He was going for his gun. She had to stop him. If she didn't, she would soon be a corpse among the rotting oranges.

Rachel locked her hands around Grant's at the root of her hair, and pried back his fingers to break his grip. Scrambling to her feet, she spun around and kicked him in the shins, knocking him off balance. She took off at a dead run, but pain made her slow. Grant caught her from behind. They tumbled to the ground. He pummeled her with his fists again. Rachel struck back but her blows only enraged him.

As he brutally beat her, she clenched her eyes shut, trying to retreat inside her mind, praying Grant would come to his senses before he killed her.

Finally his rage was spent. Rolling off her, he stared up at the moon, his breath ragged. Rachel was lying still beside him, unable to move.

"You'll be watched," he told her, still panting. "If I hear you've been talking to anyone outside of your kids, you can expect another visit from me. I'll be listening to every phone call you make. You will not call that prick Atwater. You will not report what happened out here, nor will you seek medical treatment. Tomorrow, you will go to Nick Miller and withdraw the ridiculous story you told about me. Miller will then take care of our little problem with the DA's office." He turned his head to Rachel. "Look at me when I speak to you, bitch."

Rachel turned her eyes to him.

"If I have to come back," Grant said, standing and dusting off his uniform, "I won't be looking for you. I'll be looking for that pretty little daughter of yours. You might not be able to suck for shit, but young girls are fast learners." Once he had zipped his pants, he walked into the row of orange trees to retrieve his gun, then returned to stand over her again. "You better get on home now," he said, placing the gun in his holster. "Several women have been attacked in these orange groves. If I were you, I'd find another place to jog."

chapter

TWENTY-ONE

With a hand pressed into her abdomen, Rachel staggered back to her house. She had retrieved her torn T-shirt and tied it around her chest. Slamming the door and bolting it behind her, she collapsed on the floor in the entryway. Grant's parting remarks played over in her mind. "I'll be looking for that pretty little daughter of yours." Her eyes went to the phone, and she fought the urge to call Atwater, Lucy, anyone.

Lifting her head off the floor, she looked at the door. She distinctly remembered locking it when she left, but it had not been locked when she returned.

She limped down the hall, checked her daughter's room and saw the window had been shattered. Someone had been inside the house. The intruder must have gained entrance through the window, then exited through the front door. She knew there was no way Grant could have broken into the house prior to the attack in the orange grove. Once he had left her, she had come straight home. Someone else had been in the house. Who? Why? It couldn't have been a burglar, because her television and stereo had not been taken.

She went to the medicine chest in the bathroom, pulling out all the prescription bottles and reading the labels. She had to stop the pain. Seeing a label that read codeine, prescribed for a sprained ankle several years back, Rachel poured out the four remaining pills and tossed them in her mouth, flushing them down with a glass of water. For all she knew, the beating had caused internal injuries. She could not go to the hospital, though. Grant had forbidden it.

Returning to the living room, she picked up the phone. Grant had said he would know about every phone call she made. If his statement was true, he had to have a way to monitor her calls. She unscrewed the receiver, plucking out a minuscule microphone.

Someone had bugged her house.

Grant had an accomplice, a co-conspirator. She knew it had to be another cop. He would have never trusted anyone else. Were there other monitoring devices? She pulled the cushions off the sofa and tossed them on the floor. She went through the kitchen cabinets, rummaged through her bedroom drawers, checked underneath all the tables. In a large potted fern in the dining room, she discovered another small microphone sitting on top of the dirt.

Rachel had no doubt now that Grant would follow through on his threats. He had friends at his beck and call. Unlike the average criminal, Grant's minions had guns, badges, radios, access to electronic surveillance equipment. More than anything, though, they had the power of authority. If Grant sent someone for Tracy, he could walk right into her school, flash his badge, and no one would be able to stop them from taking her off the premises.

Now that she had removed the bugs, could she call Atwater and report the assault? Would they be able to make the charges against Grant Cummings stick? There were no witnesses, no evidence other than the bruises on her body. Even if Grant was behind bars, she decided, her family would not be safe. Grant could simply call on Jimmy Townsend, Carol Hitchcock, Ratso, Sergeant Miller. They would do anything he asked of them. Were they covering for Grant right now?

Picking up the phone, Rachel called the dispatcher, telling him she needed to ask Grant something about a report. "Where is he now? Is he on a call?"

"Yeah," the male dispatcher advised. "A burglary. Someone broke into Evans Hardware on First Street."

"How long has Grant been on the scene?"

"For over an hour now," the dispatcher said. "He should be clearing any minute."

"Is Grant the only officer you dispatched?"

"No," he said. "Carol Hitchcock rolled for backup. The reporting party thought the suspect might still be in the area."

Carol was Grant's alibi. The woman probably had no idea what Grant had intended to do. "Did you locate the responsible party at the hardware store?"

"No," he said. "They must be out of town."

Without saying goodbye, Rachel replaced the phone in the cradle. Grant was shrewd. He had covered his tracks like a pro. With no independent party present at the hardware store, Grant would have an airtight alibi should she try to press charges against him over the attack. At the time of the crime, Grant would claim he was performing his official duties. With another police officer to back up his story, no one would believe Rachel. And Carol was a woman, which would give her statements greater credibility. How could anyone believe that a female police officer would lie to cover up a savage beating committed against another female officer?

Grant's plan had been brilliant. Once he had arranged an alibi, he had set out to destroy her. She buried her head in her hands, her body shaking in terror.

If she withdrew the charges as Grant had insisted, how could she be certain he wouldn't still come after her daughter? He had enjoyed overpowering her, brutalizing her, degrading her. She had seen the pleasure in his eyes, heard it in his voice.

She walked to the window and peered out at the street. Were Grant's minions out there somewhere? Were they watching her even now?

Heading to the back of the house, Rachel turned on the shower, removed her clothes, and let the water pound her back and buttocks. Could she move away, disappear, take the kids some place where Grant could never find them? Susan and her husband lived in a remote area in Oregon that would be perfect. The closest city was almost an hour's drive away. But how would she support herself? She didn't even know if Susan would be receptive to having them stay with her for a short time. Since their mother's death and the revelation that the girls didn't share the same father, Rachel and Susan had drifted apart. Only Carrie had tried to keep the family together. She sent gifts at Christmas, remembered the kids' birthdays. If she asked anyone for help, she decided, it would have to be Carrie.

"God help me," Rachel prayed, turning her face into the hot spray. She lathered her body from head to toe with soap, wincing as she felt the extent of her bruises. The assault played over in her mind, along with the things Grant had said to her. His references to the previous rapes in the orange grove had been strange. The incidents he was referring to had occurred five years back, before she had moved into the neighborhood. Both victims had been joggers, and for the first six months she had lived there, Rachel had refused to run in the groves for this reason. Concerned also for her daughter, she had pulled the crime reports out of the archives to familiarize herself with the particulars. Grant had not been the reporting officer. If her memory served her correctly, he had not been involved in the incidents in any official capacity. The victims had described the rapist as tall and muscular, wearing dark clothing. He had leapt out of the row of orange trees and blindfolded them before they had a chance to get a look at his face. He had not ejaculated, one of the primary reasons the police had never been able to identify him.

She felt the tender spots on her abdomen, her ribs, her thighs. By tomorrow morning she would be black and blue, but with her clothes on, no one would know she had been beaten. She probed her face with her fingers. There wasn't a mark on it. Grant's actions had closely paralleled those of a practiced batterer. He knew just how to hurt her, where to hit her, what spots on her body to avoid. His blows had bypassed sensitive organs such as her spleen and kidneys. He had wanted to punish her, but not enough that she would require medical treatment. Had he raped those other women? Could Grant Cummings be a sex offender? Had he been hiding behind the badge for years, committing horrendous crimes and getting away with them?

She remembered an evening last summer. The temperature had been in the nineties, but Carol Hitchcock had shown up for work in her long-sleeved winter uniform. Rachel had touched her arm, and Hitchcock had screamed. She claimed she had hurt herself by bumping into a chest of drawers while rushing to get to work. Rachel suspected now that her story was a lie, that Grant had beaten her.

She turned off the shower, holding onto the nozzle for support. Her mouth tasted like cotton from the codeine tablets, and her stomach was cramping so severely that she could barely stand upright. Her reason suddenly evaporated, buried under a wave of uncontrollable rage. She exploded, kicking out the glass in the shower door.

Grant was a monster, a brutal animal who had to be purged from society. She had already danced with the devil. Once in a lifetime was enough. Nathan Richardson had been the essence of evil. Prior to kidnapping Rachel, the former physician had kidnapped and raped a six-year-old girl in an attack so brutal, the child had almost died. Nonetheless the parole board had released him in only seven years, setting him free so he could steal Rachel's childhood.

Even though Richardson was dead, he had haunted her for years, chasing her through the labyrinths of her subconscious, the delicate china doll always in his hand. She saw the doll's pink satin dress, the tiny shoes on its feet. "I know you want her," Richardson's voice said. "I can tell by the way you looked at her."

She would die before she would let Grant get his hands on her daughter.

When Rachel looked into her past, there were no sun-filled days, no childish laughter, no romps in the park. Like a sponge filling with water, the kidnapping and Richardson's violent death had swollen to such enormous proportions that they had squeezed everything else out of her mind.

It was as if Grant Cummings and Nathan Richardson had merged into one person. She returned to the morning on the beach, Grant's face looming over her, the stale odor of beer on his breath, his coarse hands roaming over her body. "You know you want me," he had said. "You've wanted me since the first day you saw me."

Nathan Richardson had used Rachel like a shield to fend off the sharpshooter's bullets. Grant had used the Hillmont boy in exactly the same fashion. She rubbed her forearms, thinking that she wouldn't mind Grant's brain splattered all over her skin the way Richardson's had been.

She stepped out of the shower, walking across the shattered slivers of glass. Even though her feet were cut, she felt no pain. She had moved beyond pain. Rage was driving her now, pushing her along with a frightening momentum.

With her towel, she rubbed a spot in the steamy mirror and looked long and hard at her tormented image. "Respect, huh?" she said. Imagining it was Grant's face instead of her own, she picked up a bar of soap and hurled it at the mirror.

Rachel dressed in a pair of jeans and a cotton shirt. Returning to the bathroom, she picked through the bottles of pills scattered on the floor, finally finding what she wanted. Morphine. Joe's doctor had prescribed it for him in the final months. Only one pill was left. She swallowed it without water.

Heading to the kitchen, she made a pot of coffee, then went to sit on the living room sofa in the dark. The night passed in agonizing slowness. Several times her eyes closed. As soon as she fell asleep, she felt Grant's fists pounding her body and bolted upright, her clothes soaked in perspiration.

Every hour or so, Rachel would walk to the kitchen, glance at the clock on the wall, refill her coffee mug and then return to the living room to continue her vigil. If she didn't contact Nick Miller as Grant had demanded and recant her story about the attempted rape on the beach, she had no doubt that he would come after Tracy. She knew Grant well. He was not the type of person who made empty threats.

chapter

TWENTY-TWO

The graveyard watch was trickling into the parking lot of the police station; the majority of the morning watch had already cleared to drive to their respective beats. Only a few stragglers were lingering inside the station, munching on donuts and gulping coffee.

Grant and Townsend arrived a few moments later, entering through the rear door to the station and heading down the corridor to the men's locker room.

Townsend leaned back against his locker and spoke in an undertone. "Do you think you talked some sense into Rachel? I mean, this whole thing is making me a nervous wreck. I did what you said, Grant, but I'm telling you right now that I don't feel good about it. Other than the Brentwood incident, I've never had a problem with Rachel, and even then it wasn't entirely her fault."

"It's over," Grant said, his face still flushed with excitement. "Rachel's going to contact Miller today and retract her statement."

"I hope you're right," Townsend said, opening his locker and removing his street clothes. "How can you be sure, though? What did you say to her to make her change her mind? Just telling her we would be monitoring her phone calls couldn't have done it. Why would that make her back off? We're the ones in the wrong here. Rachel doesn't have anything to hide."

"I said I took care of it," Grant said. "Don't you trust me, Jimmy?

Haven't I always taken care of things? When you need money, I always come through. I know you can't pay me back. Have I ever asked you to pay me back?"

"You've asked me to do things I didn't want to do," Townsend told him, slamming the door to his locker. "Everyone pays you back, Grant, one way or the other."

Grant laughed, causing a shock of sun-bleached hair to tumble onto his forehead. "Do you need a ride home? The rest of the crew got tied up on that three-car pileup on Cliff Road. If you need a ride, you better wait for me. Those guys could get stuck out there for hours." He peeled off his uniform, wadding it into a ball and shoving it into the bottom of his gym bag. All night long he had endured the stench of Rachel's vomit. He couldn't wait to jump in the shower.

"I brought the car today," Townsend said, a worried look on his face. "No one's with the kids right now. The woman I hired doesn't work on Friday. I've got to get home."

"Can't your parents give you a hand?"

"No," he said. "My mom is crippled with arthritis, and my father's pissed because I got Lindsey pregnant again. He says a man isn't supposed to bring a child into the world unless he can support it. It's not like I'm a slacker or anything. I go to work every day. My father thinks I'm a hog. He accused me the other day of spending my entire paycheck on food."

Grant whipped his towel across Townsend's fleshy midsection. "Your father might have a point."

Townsend yanked the towel out of his hands and tossed it on the floor. "You don't understand," he said. "No one understands." Before Grant could respond, he turned and rushed out of the room.

After Grant had showered, he wrapped a towel around his waist and padded back to his locker to put on his street clothes. Hearing something rattle behind him, he turned around, thinking it was one of the other officers. Not seeing anyone, he dropped his towel and reached for a pair of clean undershorts from his gym bag. Just as he bent over to step into them, a loud shot rang out.

A bullet seared its way into the base of Grant's spine. His body was propelled forward into his locker. Images from his past flashed in his mind. He saw his father's rugged face floating in front of him. "Bend over, son," the image said. "This will teach you to respect your elders."

Grant screamed in terror, his fingernails scraping the metal door. His heart throbbed in his ears. Blood gushed from the gunshot wound, then splashed onto the tile flooring. When he heard the crack of his father's razor strap, he clenched his eyes closed and let the darkness take him. Almost in slow motion, his body slid down the front of the locker and crumpled onto the floor.

Hearing what appeared to be a gunshot from the squad room where they were finishing their reports, Ted Harriman and Chris Lowenberg drew their service revolvers and raced into the locker room. They saw Ratso sandwiched between the rows of lockers, kneeling over Grant.

"Call an ambulance," Ratso shouted, his uniform soaked in perspiration. "He's in shock. He's losing blood fast. He stopped breathing. I had to resuscitate him."

"What the hell happened?" Lowenberg asked, sloshing through a pool of Grant's blood.

"Rachel Simmons shot him," Ratso said, panting. "I tried to catch her but she got away. If I had continued chasing her, Grant would have died. She must have been hiding in here somewhere."

Ted Harriman shoved his gun back into the holster. "Did you see the actual shooting?"

"I saw Rachel with a gun in her hands," Ratso continued, leaning over to check Grant's pulse again. "Grant had already been shot by the time I got here. I chased her down the hall, then came back to check on Grant. She ran out the back door to the station."

"I'll get Sergeant Miller and have an ambulance dispatched," Harriman said. "Check the parking lot, Lowenberg."

"We can't wait for the ambulance," Ratso cried in panic. "Grant's going to bleed to death. Help me carry him to my car."

Harriman instructed Lowenberg to order the ambulance, then squatted down beside Ratso. When he didn't see an entry wound on the front of Grant's torso, he slipped his hands underneath him. "I think the bullet is lodged in his spine," he said. "We can't move him without a back board. I'll go see if we have anything we can use in the squad room."

After Harriman left the room, Ratso saw Grant's eyelids flutter and then open. He placed a palm in the center of his chest. "You're going to be okay, my friend," he said. "Rachel shot you. I saw her running away."

Grant's lips moved but no words came out.

"Don't worry," Ratso continued. "By the time they get you to the hospital, Rachel will be in custody."

As soon as Grant had been loaded into the ambulance, Sergeant Miller pulled Ratso aside in the parking lot under a large shade tree. "You saw Rachel Simmons with the gun in her hand. You're certain? Is there any way you could have been mistaken?"

"Absolutely not," Ratso insisted. "She looked right at me, Sergeant. She must have shot Grant only seconds before I ran in there. I heard the shot. It had to be her. No one else was in the locker room. I'm your eyewitness. The DA shouldn't have a problem proving the case. What other reason would Rachel have had to be inside the men's locker room? She wasn't even on duty last night."

Miller walked around in a small circle, then stopped and smiled. "To be perfectly honest, Ratso, I've never liked you. Don't take offense, but there's something about you that makes my skin crawl. Right now, though, I feel like kissing you. Do you realize what this means?"

"I saved Grant's life," Ratso said.

"More than that. It means Rachel has no case." He slammed his fist into his opposite palm. "Who's going to believe her stories now, huh? She's a felon. She shot a fellow police officer. In the back, no less. What a fucking bitch. I knew her story about Grant using the Hillmont kid as a shield was bogus." He slapped the smaller man on the shoulder. "You're a hero, Ratso. You not only saved Grant's life, you solved our problem with Rachel. Good work, pal. You finally made your mark around here. I'll make certain you get a commendation. Believe me, if the chief knew what kind of trouble was brewing with Simmons, he would probably promote you to detective."

"Detective?" Ratso said. He would give anything to make detective. He had never thought he could rise above patrol officer. There would be no more fetching and groveling, no more degrading remarks. Grant would never expose his past. How could he? Ratso had saved his life.

"Hey, man," Miller said, "I owe you one." He felt sorry for Grant, but not deeply enough to dampen his relief. When it came down to clutch time, a man had to look out for himself. "I didn't sleep yesterday thinking about this mess. What can I do for you? Buy you a beer?"

Ratso smiled, exposing his protruding front teeth. "I don't like beer," he said. "But if you want, you could wash my car for me."

Miller stared at him a few moments as if he were insane. "Forget it, dickhead," he said. "You're not that big of a hero."

chapter

TWENTY-THREE

When Tracy unlocked the front door of the house at eight o'clock Thursday morning, she found her mother sitting on the sofa in the living room. The drapes were drawn and the room was pitch black. "Why are you sitting in here in the dark?" the girl asked, knowing something was wrong. Her mother had always hated a dark house. Even at night, she seldom closed the drapes.

"Come here," Rachel said. "I didn't know where to call you. I was worried about you. I couldn't sleep. I even drove around trying to find Sheila's house."

"Why would you be worried about me?" Tracy said, finding her mother's behavior strange. "Don't you want me to open the curtains, get some light in here? Maybe when I get home from school this afternoon, we can take Joe to the park and let him get some fresh air."

"No," she said, seeing Tracy reaching for the pull to the drapes. "People are watching us. Don't stand near the windows."

Her stomach fluttering with apprehension, Tracy took a seat on the sofa next to her mother. "Did something happen?" she asked. She picked up her mother's hand, finding it cold and clammy. Her eyes were sunken, burning with intensity.

"I'm going to send you and Joe to San Francisco to stay with Carrie for a few days," Rachel said, her voice tinged with panic. "I don't want you in this city. It isn't safe."

"I'm not going anywhere," her daughter said. "You're scaring me, Mom. Why are you saying these things?"

"I can't explain right now," Rachel said. "You have to trust me. Go to your room and pack your bag. Throw some clothes in for Joe. I'm going to call Carrie, then see if I can find a flight leaving this afternoon."

"I'm not leaving you," Tracy told her, becoming teary-eyed. "If something's going on, I want to be here so I can help."

Rachel captured her face in her hands. "Listen to me," she said. "What's going on right now is serious. I don't want you involved."

Tracy was sobbing now. "I don't understand," she cried, her shoulders shaking. "Why are you so afraid? Why do we have to go to San Francisco? I'm supposed to be at school in thirty minutes."

Her mother seized her, hugging her tightly against her chest. "Everything's going to be fine if you just listen and do what I say."

"But the cheerleader tryouts are next week."

"What day are the tryouts?"

"Tuesday."

"I'll try to get you back by then," Rachel told her, "but I can't make any promises right now."

The girl stood, wiping her teary eyes with her fingers. After a few moments, she went to her bedroom to pack.

Rachel dialed Carrie's number and got her answering machine. She was leaving a message when she heard cars screech to a stop outside, followed by the sound of muffled voices. Dropping the phone, she raced to the front of the house and peered out through a crack in the drapes. Mike Atwater was standing on the sidewalk in front of her house. He was wearing a tank top and a pair of running shorts, and his hair was disheveled. Rachel wondered why he was not dressed for work, and suspected someone had paged him while he was taking his morning run. Sergeant Miller was speaking to him, along with Captain Edgar Madison.

The contingent of men headed up the sidewalk. Why were they here? Had they come to force her to recant her statement about the shooting at the Majestic Theater? If so, why would Captain Madison and Mike Atwater be present?

Tracy came into the living room and walked over to her mother, taking her hand and clasping it tightly. Her back was straight, and her eyes had taken on a fierce, protective look.

Rachel was weak and in pain. Black spots danced in front of her eyes. The mere sight of a police uniform filled her with loathing. Leaning against her daughter, she whispered, "Open the door."

Thirty minutes later, Rachel and Tracy were seated side by side on the sofa. Captain Madison and Mike Atwater had taken the two chairs, leaving Miller standing in the back of the living room. After Captain Madison advised her that Grant had been shot and a witness had identified her as the shooter, Miller stepped forward and read Rachel her Miranda rights off a plastic card. She agreed to speak to them without an attorney.

"Grant was shot in the back," Miller told her. "He's alive, but the doctors aren't optimistic. If the bullet severed the nerves in his spine, he'll be a paraplegic."

"How could someone say I shot him?" Rachel exclaimed. "Even if I had wanted to, I wouldn't have had the nerve." She directed her next statement to Captain Madison. "Maybe one of Timothy Hillmont's friends came after Grant. They may have seen him using the boy as a shield." She thought of the beating she had endured. Could she tell them what Grant had done to her? Absolutely not. She was not a fool. If she told them the truth, she would establish a motive for shooting him. He had been shot at a little before seven in the morning. She didn't have an alibi.

Atwater leaned forward in his seat. "After I left here last night, you went straight to bed?"

"Yes," Rachel said.

"Where was Tracy?"

"She spent the night with a friend."

"I see," Atwater said, giving Tracy a fleeting smile. Many of her features were similar to her mother's. There was a sharper edge, though. He could read it in her eyes. "You didn't wake up until your daughter came home this morning?"

"That's right," Tracy said, her voice booming out over the room. When she got excited, she had a tendency to talk too loud. "Mom never gets enough sleep. I had to shake her this morning to get her to wake up. I got home a few minutes before seven. I had to come back from Sheila's house early so I could get ready for school."

Rachel's body stiffened. She cut her eyes to her daughter. Why had she made such a statement? Sheila's mother must have driven her home. Tracy was foolishly spinning a tale that she would not be able to substantiate. It might give her a few hours, a day at the most. When the truth came out, Rachel would look even more culpable.

Atwater looked over his shoulder at Miller, then linked eyes with the captain. Tracy moved closer to Rachel on the sofa. "Did you look at your watch when you got home?"

"Of course," the girl said, holding up her wrist so they could see she was wearing a watch.

"What was the name of the girl you spent the night with?" Miller said, a small note pad in his hands.

"Sheila Ross," she told him. "Do you want her address and phone number?"

"Yeah," the sergeant said.

"Wait," Rachel said. "I don't want my daughter involved in this. Go in the other room, Tracy."

"She has to be involved in this, Rachel," Atwater said. "She's the only person who can swear you were here at the time Grant Cummings was shot. Don't you understand how serious this is? We have an eye-witness who saw you with the gun in your hand inside the locker room."

"Who?" Rachel demanded.

"We're not prepared to release that information at this time," Captain Madison said.

Atwater stood, motioning for Miller to follow him into the kitchen. In a low voice he said, "Your man made a mistake, Miller. Rachel was here with her daughter at the time of the shooting. You heard the girl in there. What reason does she have to lie?"

Miller made a smacking noise with his mouth. He detested Mike Atwater. As far as he was concerned, the district attorney was a pompous prick who treated cops like uneducated baboons. If he had not taken Rachel's word and filed a case against Grant, none of this would have happened. "How about keeping her mother out of prison, Atwater? Isn't that a pretty good reason? Ratso's a cop, for Christ's sake. The man knows what he saw."

"Okay, okay," Atwater said, holding up a palm. "Track down this Ross girl and verify Tracy's statement right now. If Rachel's alibi falls apart, I might take these allegations more seriously."

"There are other DA's," Miller told him. "My officer was shot in the back. You're damn right you're going to take these allegations seriously, or I'll demand they take you off the case."

"Let's slow down," Atwater said, determined to control the situation. "Any number of things could have happened. This whole thing smacks of a setup, if you ask me." He paused, finding it suspicious that the same men Rachel had named in the beach assault were now accusing her of a serious crime. "Your officers have been harassing this poor woman ever since the day she put on a uniform," he said. "In case you aren't aware of it, Rachel's got a ton of dirt, enough to put half your department behind bars."

"Setup, my ass," Miller said, stepping up in the prosecutor's face. "No one had a bone to pick with Cummings outside of this broad. Don't tell me you think one of my men set her up. Any idiot would know that doesn't add up. We have an eyewitness who placed her at the scene of the crime. This is a slamdunk, Atwater."

Atwater's body grew tense. "Are you calling me an idiot, Miller?"

"If the shoe fits," he said.

"There's a window broken out in the kid's room," Captain Madison said, walking into the kitchen. "The shower door is busted out in the master bathroom as well."

The three men returned to the living room. "What happened to the bedroom window?" Atwater asked, dropping back down in a chair.

"I don't know," Rachel said, a vacant look in her eyes. "Is something wrong with it?"

"It's shattered."

"One of the kids on the block probably broke it," she told him. "Tracy, was your window broken when you left last night to go to Sheila's house?"

"No," the girl said, shaking her head.

Rachel shrugged, staring down at her hands. The less she said, the better.

"Tell me about the shower door," Atwater said. "It's broken as well."

"I slipped," Rachel said. "After the incident on Maple Avenue, I was so tired, I passed out in the shower and fell against the door. It happened last night, after Tracy had already left to go to her friend's house." She took off her shoes and showed them the cuts on her feet. "This is an older house. I guess they didn't use shatterproof glass in the shower."

Miller went to the kitchen and called the Ross family. "This is Sergeant Miller with the Oak Grove PD," he said. "I need to ask you some questions about Tracy Simmons."

"Wait a minute," a groggy female voice said. "I'll go get her."

"Tracy Simmons is here," Nick Miller said, confused. "Did she spend the night at your house last night?"

"Yes," Madeline Ross said. "What's going on? My husband and I had to go to a company banquet last night. I was asleep when you called."

"How did Tracy get home?"

"I don't know," she said. "Do you want me to get my daughter?"

"Yeah," he said.

A few moments later, the woman came back on the line. "I didn't realize how late it was," she said. "The girls must have already left to go to school."

Sergeant Miller copied down the phone number for the school, disconnected and then dialed the number, asking the office to call Sheila Ross to the phone. After ten minutes had passed, the girl came on the line and Miller began shooting questions at her. "You didn't see Tracy this morning?"

"No," Sheila said, "I guess she got up and went home while I was still sleeping. She does that sometimes."

"When did you see her last?"

"About midnight when we went to sleep."

"You didn't wake up when she left the house this morning?"

"No," the girl said.

"We'll be in touch," Miller said, replacing the phone on the cradle. For a long time, he just stood there, staring off into space. It might appear that Rachel had an alibi for the time in question, but in reality, she had nothing. No one could substantiate the exact time Tracy had left the Rosses' house. Any jury would realize a daughter might lie to protect her mother. With the father dead, Rachel and her daughter had to be extremely close. Did the girl know the truth? She was only a kid. In most instances, teenage girls cracked easily during interrogation.

Returning to the living room, Miller said, "I'm taking the girl down to the station for questioning."

The captain looked up, but he remained in the same position, his arms folded over his chest.

"I can't let you do that," Atwater said. "She's a minor, Miller. You can't interrogate a minor outside the presence of her parents. Surely you realize that."

"She's not under arrest," Miller countered. "I have an obligation to question her. Since her mother is our primary suspect, how can I get a straight answer with Rachel in the same room?"

"It's okay," Tracy said, looking over at Rachel. "I don't mind going with him. They can ask me all the questions they want." She turned back to the men. "My mom didn't shoot anyone. She was right here with me."

"I will not allow my daughter to leave the house," Rachel said, knowing Tracy was in over her head. "If you want to question her, you'll have to get a court order."

"Want to play hardball, huh?" Captain Madison said, his voice gruff. A master at body language, he decided Rachel might be putting on a good show, but something was clearly troubling her. Her skin was ashen. Her eyes were haunted. She had her arms wrapped around her waist, and on several occasions, he saw her wince as if she were in pain. She kept her hands folded in her lap, a good way to control the jitters. Her daughter was a nervous wreck as well, her eyes darting back and forth from the men to her mother.

"All I know," he said, standing and directing his statement to Mike Atwater, "is I have an officer who may never walk again. I find this kind of problem extremely distasteful. Officers accusing one another of crimes. Shootings in the station house." He turned and faced Rachel. "I'll take your badge and gun now. Until we get to the bottom of this, I'm going to have to suspend you."

"Aren't you being somewhat hasty?" Atwater said. "I mean, until we know more, is it wise to suspend her?"

"Wise?" the captain said, his upper lip recoiling. "I'm not sure if it's wise, Atwater, but it's department procedure to suspend an officer facing criminal charges."

"I'll have to go out to the car," Rachel told him, fishing her shield out of her pocket and handing it to him. "I keep my service revolver in the glove box."

"Just give me your car keys," Madison said. "I'll get the gun on my way out, then leave your keys on the floorboard."

"Fine," she said, going to the other room to retrieve her purse.

Once Rachel had returned and handed over her car keys, Mike Atwater walked the captain to the door, then stepped outside to speak to him privately. "I don't have enough to sanction an arrest without conferring with Ringwald," he said. "Since Cummings is alive, my advice is that we wait until he wakes up and see what he says. Have your men canvas the area near the police station to see if anyone saw a black Pathfinder like Rachel's at the time of the shooting. It might also be a good idea to check the neighbors here as well, see if one of them saw Rachel leave the house this morning. Once they dig the bullet out of Cummings, send it to ballistics and see what they make of it." He started to step through the door and then stopped. "Rachel might have a point about the Hillmont boy. One of his football buddies might have decided to seek revenge against Grant for using the kid as a shield."

"That's just fine and dandy," Madison said, squinting in the morning sun. "But what if the shooter comes back to finish the job? Whoever shot Cummings must have cooked up a pretty good mad, don't you think? Besides, this was an inside job. The shooter had to have a key to gain entrance to the station. The front doors are kept locked until nine, when the support personnel arrive."

"Post a guard outside his door," Atwater suggested.

"About the missing drug money that you mentioned to Internal Affairs," Madison said, brushing his hand under his nose. "Officer Simmons had the greatest opportunity. She was inside the house for over an hour before the other units arrived."

"That's asinine," the attorney said. "If Rachel took the money, why would she have insisted that I report it to Internal Affairs?" He tilted his head toward the house. "Fred Ramone and Nick Miller were present on Maple Avenue. Maybe one of them is your thief. And don't forget the paramedics and crime scene technicians who were working inside that house."

Edgar Madison would do more than put a guard on Grant Cummings's hospital room, he decided, as disturbed over the stolen money as he was by Cummings's shooting. He despised thieves, particularly those who carried a badge. Before Rachel had joined the department there had been no accusations of misconduct, no looting of crime scenes, no shootings inside the station. Police departments didn't disintegrate overnight, and Madison didn't believe in coincidences.

Had Grant Cummings somehow found out that Rachel had taken the cash from Maple Avenue? Had the woman shot him to keep him from reporting what he knew?

Unlocking the Pathfinder with Rachel's keys, Madison checked the ammo clip on her service revolver, but none of the rounds were missing. She would be placed under twenty-four-hour surveillance. If Rachel Simmons so much as hiccuped, he would have his men hook her up and haul her ass to jail.

chapter

TWENTY-FOUR

Rachel, Joe, and Tracy were on Rachel's bed in the master bedroom. It was a few minutes past ten. Joe was stretched out on his mother's lap sleeping. Rachel was propped up on the bed with several pillows. While the boy slept, she gazed at his face and softly stroked his hair away from his forehead.

"What's going to happen now?" Tracy asked, curled up at the foot of the bed.

"I don't want to think about it," Rachel told her.

"You have to think about it," the girl argued. "If we don't, we won't be prepared."

She had told Tracy the truth. The only thing Rachel held back were the threats Grant had directed toward the girl. "You shouldn't have lied, Tracy. Lies always come back to haunt you."

"If I hadn't lied, they would have taken you to jail," she said. "That man beat you, Mom. He's the one who should be in trouble, not you."

"Well," Rachel said, her eyes filling with pain as she lifted Joe off her stomach and placed him in the center of the bed, "I guess he got his punishment, Tracy. The doctors believe he's going to be paralyzed."

"But the cops think you're the one who shot him," Tracy said, shoving her hair off her forehead. "How can they get away with something like this? Who is this person who saw you? How could he see you when you weren't there?"

"See, honey," her mother said, "this is the kind of damage you can cause when you don't tell the truth. That's why I won't allow you to continue your deception about being in the house with me this morning. How did you get home from Sheila's house? Eight miles is a long way to walk."

Tracy avoided her mother's eyes. "I got a ride with a friend."

"None of your friends can drive," Rachel answered. "Why can't you just tell me the truth? If someone drove you home, that person is going to eventually come forward. When you testify under oath in a courtroom, a lie becomes a crime. They call it perjury, and perjury carries a substantial penalty."

"Are they going to send you to prison?"

"I don't know," Rachel told her. "It's possible. The way things have been going, anything is possible."

Tracy chewed on a fingernail. "What will Joe and I do?" she said. "Where will we go?"

"I don't think we need to worry about that right this minute," Rachel said, sighing. Knowing how her daughter's mind worked, she added, "You could stay with Carrie or Susan if I have to—" She couldn't say the word *prison*. It was beyond comprehension that she would end up behind bars, that she would be separated from her children for a crime she didn't commit.

"I don't even know Susan," Tracy shouted, causing Joe to wake up and whimper. Rachel picked up the child and deposited him in his bed in the other room. Once her mother returned, Tracy continued. "The only time I saw Susan was at Dad's funeral. Carrie's okay, but I don't want to live with her. I'd have to go to a brand-new school, leave all my friends again. I'd rather die."

"Don't say that," Rachel said, climbing back into the bed.

"I'm sorry," Tracy said, weeping again. "It's just that everything is always wrong. First Dad dies, then this happens to us. It seems like we're always in this big hole that we can't ever get out of. Maybe we should all kill ourselves. Then we would be with Dad. We could be reborn into a different life."

Rachel's eyes filled with tears. "We're going to be all right," she said. "Whatever happens, we'll survive. Please, honey, I can't stand to see you this upset."

Tracy crawled up on the bed, resting her head on the pillow beside her mother. "Nothing should happen to you," she said, her eyes focused on the ceiling. "We'll just have to figure out a way to make them believe you. If they knew all the bad things this Grant guy has done, maybe they would put him in prison instead of you." She turned her head, meeting her mother's gaze. "He was a police officer. He had a gun. Can't they understand that there was no one for you to go to, no one who could help you? Who do people call when they're in trouble or someone hurts them? They call the police. You couldn't do that because they're all rotten." She shook her head from side to side. "It isn't right, Mom. You didn't do anything wrong."

"I know," Rachel said, touching a strand of her daughter's hair. "But life isn't always fair, honey. Sometimes we have to play the hand we're dealt."

"No," Tracy said. "I don't believe that. You're a good person. You always try to do the right thing. They're not going to put you in prison. I won't let them." She got up and started walking toward the door. "I'm going out for a walk."

"No," Rachel called. "You can't leave the house."

"Why?" Tracy said, giving her a look of defiance. "That Grant guy is in the hospital. He isn't going to hurt anyone. I need to get some fresh air."

"Please don't leave," her mother insisted, picking up the remote control. "It's late. Come back to bed with me. We'll watch TV. Maybe there's a movie on we haven't seen."

Tracy threw her hands in the air. "I can't stay here, Mom," she said. "If I don't get out of the house, I'm going to go crazy."

Rachel's voice was firm. "I forbid you to leave the house, Tracy. You don't understand. It's not just Grant I'm afraid of. There are others. Other officers. They could be watching our house right now. That's why I refused to let you go down to the station with Sergeant Miller."

"Why should I listen to you anymore?" her daughter exploded. "If you go to prison, I'll end up raising Joe by myself. I hate you. Why did you even have him? All you ever do is make things worse for us."

"Don't go near the orange grove," Rachel pleaded, trying not to react to her daughter's hurtful words. "If you're determined to go out, promise me you'll at least stay on the portion of the sidewalk that's well lit."

Before her mother could stop her, Tracy raced down the hall to her room. After she had placed a call to Matt Fitzgerald, she ran out the front door.

Tracy met Matt on the corner near her house. Leaping into the passenger seat of his green Datsun, she said, "Drive. I don't care where you go as long as it's not here."

"What's going on?" the shaggy-haired boy asked. "How did you get out of the house so late at night?"

"I walked out."

"Is your mother asleep?"

"No," she said. "I just told her I was leaving and left. There wasn't much she could do about it. All this parenting stuff is crap. What's she going to do? Chain me to my bed? From now on, I'm going to do anything I want to do."

"Whew," he said, letting out a low whistle. "Your mother doesn't know you're with me, I hope."

Tracy was staring out the window. "My mother was attacked. The man who attacked her was a police officer. He beat her up in the orange grove down the street from our house."

"You're not serious," he said, shocked. "When did this happen?"

"Last night when I was at Sheila's," she told him. "This morning someone went down to the police station and shot the man who attacked her. The police think my mother did it. I told them she couldn't have done it because I was with her at the house." She turned and put a hand on his shoulder. "All you have to do is tell the police you dropped me off at the house before seven o'clock."

Matt took his foot off the gas and let the car come to a stop in the center of the roadway. "I only gave you a ride home. If I get messed up with the police, my mother will kill me. You didn't tell them my name, I hope."

"No," Tracy said. "Not yet."

"What does that mean?"

"My mother wouldn't let the police question me, but when they do, I'll have to tell them how I got home."

"I was asleep in my bed at seven," Matt told her. "My dad's out of town, but for all I know, my mother saw me. What was it? Almost eight o'clock when you called me and asked me to pick you up at Sheila's house?"

"Then you have to make your mother lie," Tracy said, her fingers tightening on him. "If you don't, my mother won't have an alibi."

"Now you want to get my mother involved in this," Matt exclaimed. "No way, man. My mother's scared shitless of the cops. She got busted for drunk driving last year and spent three days in the pokey."

"So what?" Tracy shouted. "My mother may end up in prison. I'm not going to let them do that to her." She began slapping out at him with both hands. "You have to do this! You have to!"

"Stop," Matt said, deflecting her blows with his forearm. "What's wrong with you? What did I do?"

"You have everything," Tracy cried, slumping back against the seat. "All I want is a normal family. Why can't I go surfing every day after school like you? Why can't I come home and do my homework or talk on the phone with my friends? I'm sick of cooking and taking care of Joe. The cheerleader tryouts are next week. How can I try out for anything now? My mother is about to go to jail. My life is ruined."

"Calm down," Matt said. "You're getting carried away. Your mother might be in some trouble, but I don't think your whole life is ruined." He placed his deformed hand on the steering wheel, grimacing at the sight of it. "Your problems will go away. I'll have this forever."

"I'm sorry," Tracy said, tears streaming down her face. "You don't know what it's like, though. Your dad's a dentist and makes gobs of money. Your mother cooks your meals, cleans your room, stuffs money in your pocket all the time. Even if I did make cheerleader, my mom can't afford to pay for the uniforms." She glanced at his hand. "Your hand isn't that bad anyway. Most of the time you keep it hidden so no one even notices."

Matt drove around the block, waiting for Tracy to calm down. After a few minutes had passed, he pulled to the curb and parked. "What will you do if your mother has to go to prison?"

"We'll have to go live with one of my aunts," Tracy said, her eyes dark with bitterness. "One of them lives in some kind of wilderness area in Oregon. They don't even have running water," she told him. "As for my other aunt, I like Carrie, but I don't want to leave my school. If my mother tries to make me, I'll run away. I'd rather live on the streets."

"That's crazy," he said. "Hey, maybe you can come and live with me. My mom's cool. She's always taking in stray dogs."

Tracy narrowed her eyes at him. "She wouldn't take in a three-year-old like Joe, though. A kid isn't the same thing as a dog."

"Probably not," he said.

"I didn't think so," she said, glowering at him. A few moments later, her face softened. "Will you talk to your mother?"

"I don't know," he said, taking a deep breath.

"Let me tell you what to do," Tracy said, turning sideways in the seat. "First, you've got to find out if your mother saw you in the house at seven o'clock this morning. If she was still asleep, you don't have to ask her to lie. Just tell her that you picked me up at Sheila's house and drove me home. Make certain you mention the time. I told the police I was back in the house before seven."

"This is your problem, not mine," Matt told her. "If the police find out I'm lying, they could put me in jail. My dad wants me to go to dental school. I'll never be accepted if I have an arrest record."

Tracy slid across the seat, tugging on his sleeve. "If you do this for me, I'll do something nice for you," she said, her voice soft and seductive. "You know you want it. All boys want to have sex. Are you still a virgin? Don't you want to tell your friends you had sex with a girl?"

Matt knocked her hand away, cranking the ignition of the car. "You're talking silly," he said. "You're just trying to con me into doing what you want. I'm taking you home."

"Fine," Tracy snapped. "But when the police call, you know what to say, right?"

"Yeah, sure," he said, flooring the accelerator and speeding down the road. "All I have to do is say I gave you a ride home. I'll tell them I don't know what time it was because I wasn't wearing a watch. That way, I won't get in trouble."

"Wrong," she said. "You have to tell them it was before seven o'clock or it won't mean anything. You know what the reward is now. Do we have a deal or not?"

Matt felt blood racing to his groin. Tracy was sitting so close, he could smell the almond-scented conditioner she used on her hair. Draping his arm over her shoulder, he gave her a quick kiss on the cheek. She was the first girl who had accepted his deformity. When he was with her, he felt handsome and confident. Most of his friends had already had sex. "I guess we've got a deal, then," he said, winking. "A guy would be a fool to turn down something this hot. Seven o'clock. No problem. When do I get my reward?"

"After you talk to the police," Tracy said, removing his arm from her shoulder and returning to her side of the seat.

chapter

TWENTY-FIVE

Mike Atwater stopped by Rachel's house at nine o'clock Monday morning, a newspaper tucked under his arm. When she opened the door, he didn't say hello. He simply walked in and quickly closed the door behind him. "Have you looked outside?"

"No," she said, heading for the windows. When Atwater had rung the doorbell, she had been taking a shower in the children's bathroom. She was naked under a thin nylon robe.

"Stand back," he told her. "The minute they see you, they'll storm the front door."

A reporter for the local paper was waiting in his car at the curb. A mini-van containing a camera crew from one of the TV stations had pulled up right behind Atwater.

"Why don't they just ring the doorbell?" Rachel asked. "They saw you come in just now. They have to know I'm home."

"I think the reporter is waiting for a photographer to arrive," Atwater said, pacing in the entryway. "They want to get a shot of your face when you open the door. The people from the TV station just got here. It takes them a few minutes to set up their equipment."

"So?" Rachel said, shrugging.

"Where's your daughter?"

"At school," she said. Eyeing the newspaper in his hand, she asked, "Was Grant's shooting in the paper this morning?"

"Front page," he said, unfurling the paper.

She started to reach for it, then dropped her hands back to her side. Reading it would only upset her. "Did they mention my name?"

"No," he said, tossing the paper down on the coffee table. "They only said another officer was listed as one of the suspects. Obviously, though, someone at the department is talking. If not, why is the media suddenly camped out on your doorstep?"

Rachel turned and headed to the kitchen. Atwater had no choice but to follow her. "Grant Cummings was shot with his own gun," he said. "The shooter must have been hiding in the men's locker room. Cummings probably placed his revolver in his locker when he went to take a shower."

"Did they find any evidence?" she asked, pouring them both a cup of coffee. "You know, fingerprints, fibers, forensic stuff?"

"Nothing significant," he said, slicking back his hair. "I haven't seen the final reports, though. The results from the crime lab won't be complete for several days."

Rachel pulled out a chair and took a seat at the kitchen table, motioning for Atwater to do the same. "Where do we go from here?" she said. "How do you fit into the picture?"

"I'm going to try the attempted rape," he said. "I spoke to Bill Ringwald last night at home. He thinks we should move forward with it. Since no arrests have been made on the shooting incident, we really don't have a case yet to prosecute."

Rachel felt as if a black cloud had lifted. "You're still going to prosecute Grant, even after what happened?"

"I don't see why not," Atwater said, with a small smile. "Getting yourself shot doesn't preclude you from being prosecuted for a crime. We'll have to give the man a chance to recover, though, before we can bring the case to trial. I'm still going to have Cummings arrested, either tomorrow or the next day. If we have to arraign him in the hospital, we will. We've done it before."

Rachel fidgeted in her seat. She had a strong urge to tell Atwater the truth. "Don't you want to ask me anything?" she said, tapping her fingernails on the table.

"I'm not sure I know what you're talking about," Atwater said, a puzzled look on his face.

"Aren't you curious?" she said. "Don't you want to know if I shot him or not?"

"No," he said, bracing his head with his hand. "Does that answer your question?"

"I guess so," Rachel said.

Atwater cleared his throat before speaking. "Carol Hitchcock is a viable suspect," he told her. "One of the clerks in our office lives in her apartment building. She confessed this morning that she had leaked information to Hitchcock regarding the attempted rape complaint against Cummings. I guess when she saw he had been shot, she got spooked. Maybe Hitchcock went crazy when she heard what Grant had done to you. She was working last night. She could have left the station, then returned a short time later to shoot him."

Rachel arched her eyebrows, wondering if his statement might be true. "I don't look anything like Carol. Do you think the witness actually saw Carol in the locker room, and then decided to shift the blame to me because I was causing trouble at the department?"

"I don't know," Atwater said, toying with the salt shaker. "I only know one thing that might discredit their eyewitness."

"What?"

"The man who swears he saw you with the gun in your hand was one of the men at the beach."

Rachel's jaw dropped. It could only be Ratso, Townsend, or Sergeant Miller. "Who?"

"I can't tell you yet," Atwater said, taking a sip of his coffee.

Rachel carried her cup to the kitchen counter, gazing out the window into the backyard. Her grass was too high. Now that she wasn't working, she would have time to mow it and weed the flower beds. The green foliage suddenly melded into another image. She saw Grant's face looming over her in the orange grove. She shook her head, knowing she was hallucinating, suffering from sleep deprivation. She had been surviving on caffeine for days now, consuming one cup of coffee after another. Her heart was beating at an erratic rate. Her head was throbbing, her scalp tingling. She held her hands in front of her and saw that they were shaking.

The attorney was watching Rachel from across the room. Light was filtering through her nylon robe and he could see the outline of her body: her soft, rounded hips, the gentle slope of her waist. But something else also captured his attention. Dark shadows seemed to cover her torso from her shoulder blades to her knees. He blinked, thinking it was an aberration, something to do with the light.

Standing and walking over to where she was standing, Atwater put his hands on her waist. All night long he had thought about her, dreamed about her. How had he stooped so low? His plan to further his career at Rachel's expense now seemed despicable. Even the reporters camped out in her yard held no interest for him.

Without thinking, Atwater let his hands roam to her breasts. Rachel caught hold of his thumb and bent it backward, causing him to cry out in pain. "Don't touch me," she said.

"I'm sorry," he said, shaking his hand. "I just wanted to hold you. Christ, you almost broke my thumb."

"I don't want to be held," she told him. The doorbell rang in the front of the house. As if on cue, Joe began crying in the other room. "Go see if you can take care of my son. I need to get dressed. There's some crackers in the cabinet by the sink. He's hungry. I was about to give him breakfast when you came."

"No problem," Atwater said. He started to walk off and then stopped, glancing back at her. "I have to warn you, I know nothing whatsoever about kids."

"You'll do fine. Don't worry, it won't take me more than a few minutes," Rachel said, leaving him and heading to her bedroom.

She looked through the clothes in her closet, wanting to look her best. The only thing suitable was the black knit dress she had worn on her date with Atwater. Putting on her underwear, she slipped the dress over her head, then went to her daughter's room to get her makeup. She didn't want to look washed out in the photographs. She wanted to look strong and confident.

When she looked into the kids' room, Atwater was sitting on the floor with Joe. Both were covered with cracker crumbs. When the boy saw Rachel, he began crying. She knelt down beside him, kissing him on the top of the head. "It's okay, Joe," she said. "Mike is a nice man. Why don't you show him your coloring book?"

"I can't stay much longer," Atwater told her, an anxious look on his face. Just then, Joe leaped in his arms and hugged him around the neck. "Hey, guy," he said, "you're strangling me."

"He likes you," Rachel said, picking up the eye liner pencils off Tracy's bureau and leaving to go back to her room.

Once she had made up her face, Rachel brushed her hair, then clipped on a pair of gold earrings. Returning to Joe's room, she told Atwater he could leave now.

"Are you going out?" he asked, wondering why Rachel was so concerned with her appearance.

"I'm going to talk to the reporters," she said. "Didn't you hear them ringing the doorbell?"

"I wouldn't do that," he said, standing and sitting Joe down on the floor. "You'll be opening a can of worms, Rachel. The media can twist things around. You might think they're your friends, but trust me, all they care about is a story."

She plucked her son off the floor and headed to the front door, Atwater tagging along behind her. "The more people know," she told him, balancing the heavy three-year-old on her hip, "the safer my family will be. Grant isn't the only one with a grudge against me, you know. It's the whole department."

"It's your decision," Atwater said, turning to leave out the back of the house.

Rachel flung open the front door. Camera shutters clicked. Microphones were shoved in her face. She took a deep breath and then said, "I'm speaking to you today so you will know the truth. A number of officers I worked with at the Oak Grove Police Department are brutal and corrupt, more concerned with enforcing the code of silence than performing their duties in the community."

A man with a mini-cam on his shoulders stepped up, and Rachel turned to face the camera. "An officer by the name of Grant Cummings tried to rape me. I additionally saw him use Timothy Hillmont as a human shield, causing the boy to take a bullet in the chest. My sergeant, along with several other officers, threatened me and forced me to withhold this information. As you probably know, Hillmont died from this injury. Grant Cummings is the person responsible for his death."

"Did you shoot Cummings?" Mary Standish said, jumping up so Rachel could see her.

"I'm not here to answer questions about the shooting," Rachel answered firmly. Joe reached over and grabbed a handful of her hair.

Rachel pried his hands off, placing him on his feet and taking hold of his hand.

A male reporter with bushy hair said, "Where did the attempted rape occur?"

"At the beach," Rachel said.

"Were you on duty at the time?"

"No," she said. "It happened during a watch party."

"Are you certain Grant Cummings was the man who tried to rape you?"

"Absolutely," Rachel said.

The questions came at her like bullets now. "Were there any witnesses?"

"Other officers were present," she said. "They knew what was happening. They did nothing to stop it."

The sensationalism just went up another notch. Reporters were pushing each other aside to get a better position. "Tell us their names, Rachel," someone shouted.

"Jimmy Townsend, Sergeant Nick Miller, and Fred Ramone."

Rachel watched as the reporters scribbled the names on their notepads.

Joe attached himself to Rachel's leg. "I'm hungry, Mommy."

"You have to be quiet a few more minutes," Rachel told him, patting him on the head.

"Timothy Hillmont is the football player who was shot in front of the Majestic Theater, right?"

"Yes," Rachel said. "He would be alive today if it hadn't been for Grant Cummings. Cummings is a coward and a predator. I have reason to believe he's sexually assaulted other women besides myself. Now that I've come forward, maybe his other victims will speak out as well."

"If this guy was so bad, why didn't the department get rid of him?" the bushy-haired reporter asked. Before Rachel had a chance to answer his first question, he shot another one at her. "You mentioned the code of silence. What exactly were you referring to?"

"Threats, intimidation, failure to respond for backup when an officer is in trouble," Rachel explained. "Police officers protect one another, cover up each other's mistakes and bad deeds, even if innocent people suffer as a result. Anyone who attempts to break through this wall of silence is in great danger. I know," she added, "because that's what happened to me."

"Do you know who shot Cummings?"

Rachel shook her head. "I have nothing more to say. I've given you what you wanted. Please respect my privacy now." She picked up Joe, closed the door and bolted it.

chapter

TWENTY-SIX

Grant Cummings's hospital room was dark and dreary, located in a wing of Presbyterian Hospital that had no outside windows. For security reasons, orderlies had moved him from intensive care as soon as his condition had stabilized. Carol Hitchcock had been at the hospital since she first heard Grant had been shot, sleeping in a chair next to his bed. Her clothes were rumpled, her face haggard. At eleven-thirty, she left the room to get a bite of lunch in the hospital cafeteria. When she stepped back into the room, he moaned, then opened his eyes. "Grant," she said, hurrying to his bedside. "I've been so frightened. Don't move, baby. I'll get the nurse."

His hand snaked through the guardrail, seizing her by the wrist. Even though he was heavily sedated, his grip was strong. "Where am I?" he asked, his speech slurred from the narcotics. "What did you let them do to me?"

"You're in Presbyterian Hospital," Carol told him, gently brushing his hair back from his forehead. "You were shot. Don't you remember what happened?"

"I remember everything," Grant said, although his memory was seriously impaired. He didn't remember the shooting or the seconds following it before he lost consciousness. But he did recall the words Ratso had said: "Rachel shot you. I saw her running away." He saw Rachel's eyes full of hatred during the attack in the orange grove, and it was easy

216

to picture her standing behind him seconds before he was shot. Bending over to step into his shorts, he had seen a glimpse of slender legs encased in a police uniform. The images in his mind came into sharper focus. "That fucking bitch shot me. Rachel Simmons. She shot me in the back. I saw her through my legs."

"The bullet entered your lower back, Grant," Carol told him, stroking his arm. "They had to operate. Try to be still. You don't want to rip the stitches out. The bullet lodged in the base of your spine. Tomorrow they're going to put you in some kind of brace."

Grant's eyes flashed in panic. He couldn't feel his legs. He tried to wiggle his toes, but nothing happened. He grabbed the railing, attempting to pull himself up. "My legs," he shouted. "Something's wrong with my legs."

Carol pressed her hand over her mouth. How could she tell him he would never walk again, that the bullet had damaged the nerves beyond repair? The surgeon had said Grant was lucky. If the bullet had severed the nerves higher up on his spine, he would have been left a quadriplegic. "I'll get the doctor now."

"Why can't I feel my legs?" Grant yelled, eyes wide with terror. "Help me, Carol, I can't move my legs."

Carol rushed to the door.

"Don't leave me," he called.

Returning to his side, Carol pressed the call button for the nurse. "May we help you?" a woman's voice said a few moments later.

"Yes," Carol said, "get the doctor in here right away."

"Is something wrong?"

"He's awake," she said, glancing at Grant and then quickly averting her eyes. "He has no feeling in his legs."

"The surgeon who operated on this patient is no longer at the hospital," the nurse said in a flat voice. "We'll have to call his office and ask him to come over."

"Then call his frigging office," Carol shouted. Grant looked panic-stricken. Seeing him this way tore her apart. He was her rock, her warrior. He had also been her tormentor, but she couldn't think about that now. Whatever he had been in the past was over. It was as if Grant's spirit had left his body, and a helpless child had taken its place. She leaned over the bed, her voice heavy with emotion. "It's going to be okay, honey. Just hang tight. The doctor's on his way."

"It's never going to be okay," Grant said, sobbing. "She did this to me. I want her to pay."

"She'll pay, Grant," Carol said, a look of steely resolve on her face. "Believe me, we'll make certain Rachel is punished."

"I think there's something on TV that you should see," Barbara Weinstein told her boss, sticking her head in the door of Bill Ringwald's office at a few minutes before noon. The secretary seldom took lunch outside the office. She had a small portable TV about the size of a transistor radio. Instead of eating out, she brought food from home and watched her favorite soap opera at her desk.

"Oh, really?" Ringwald said, setting some paperwork down on his desk. He flicked on the small television located on his credenza. Swiveling around so he could see the screen, he said, "What channel?"

"Channel Four," she said, dropping down to his visitor's chair. "They did a promo for the noon news a few minutes ago. Rachel Simmons, that police officer from Oak Grove, is going to be on television. It sounded pretty sensational. She's blaming the officer who was shot the other day for Timothy Hillmont's death."

"Grant Cummings?"

"Yes," she said. "I'm fairly certain that was the name they mentioned."

"Call Larry Hillmont at the City Council chambers," Ringwald told her. "They have televisions over there. Make sure he sees this."

While Barbara rushed out of the room, Ringwald leaned back. The male news anchor came on and began speaking. "Shocking revelations were made this morning by a thirty-four-year-old police officer and mother of two. During an interview this morning at her residence, Rachel Simmons alleged widespread corruption inside the Oak Grove Police Department. After accusing a fellow officer of attempted rape, Simmons went on to say that the officers at Oak Grove are more concerned with enforcing the code of silence than serving the needs of the community."

They cut to the tape of Rachel standing on her front porch, little Joe fidgeting in her arms. Ringwald was riveted. If the woman was lying, she was doing a bang-up job of it. She looked straight at the camera. She didn't blink. She never hesitated for a second. She named names, places, details. She spoke of threats and intimidation, sordid activities, co-conspirators. When she mentioned the incident at the Majestic Theater, Ringwald bolted upright in his chair and pressed the intercom button. "Get the Attorney General's office on the phone," he said.

"What should I tell them?" Barbara asked.

"Tell them the lid just blew off the Oak Grove Police Department," he said, picking up his private line to call Mike Atwater.

A problem of this nature could be far-reaching. When an investigating agency such as a police department fell under public scrutiny for misconduct, dozens of unrelated cases could be affected. Within hours, defense attorneys would begin revising their trial strategies, claiming their clients had been railroaded by corrupt Oak Grove police officers. If their clients had confessed to crimes, they could now say the confession was forced through violence and therefore invalid. Every Oak Grove officer who took the witness stand would be put through the wringer.

Ringwald knew that situations like this followed a predictable pattern. The city flew into an uproar. The media gobbled up the story like candy. The corrupt cops would ultimately be weeded out, and the Oak Grove Police Department would end up with a new chief of police.

"Atwater," he barked when the attorney came on the line, "the shit just hit the fan. Get down to my office this minute." He disconnected, then picked up the line that was blinking to tell the Attorney General what was unfolding.

"Larry Hillmont is on line three," Barbara said over the intercom. "Should I tell him to hold until you finish speaking to the AG?"

"No," he said. "Tell him I'll call him later."

"He's insistent," she said. "He says he's going to have his attorney sue the Oak Grove Police Department. He's also demanding that you arrest Grant Cummings for causing his son's death."

Ringwald sighed. "I don't care what Hillmont says," he answered. "Tell him he'll have to wait his turn. By next week, half the people in Oak Grove will be filing lawsuits against the police department."

Mike Atwater called Rachel at home at four-thirty, after spending Monday afternoon sequestered in Ringwald's office. An hour after Rachel's appearance on TV, Captain Madison had stormed into the meeting, demanding her arrest.

"Grant Cummings is conscious," Atwater told her. "He was bending over at the time of the shooting. He swears he saw you between his legs."

"What's going to happen now?" Rachel paced the living room, clutching the portable phone to her ear.

"I'm trying to stall, but Captain Madison is forcing us to file a complaint against you. When you spoke to the media this morning, you turned it into a war. I tried to warn you, Rachel, but you refused to listen."

"I told the truth," she said. Looking out the window, she saw several reporters standing around a white television van.

"I believe you," he said. "Shit, even Ringwald believes you. Nothing you said on television, however, can excuse your actions if you actually shot this man."

"I didn't shoot him," Rachel said.

"Just listen," Atwater said. "The bullet severed the nerves in Cummings's spine. He'll recover, but the doctors say he's going to be paralyzed from the waist down. No matter what kind of allegations you've made against Cummings and the police department, we have to take action. Don't you understand? The man's injuries are too serious."

"Do whatever you have to do," she said, resigned. "You know where to find me." She started to hang up, but Atwater began speaking again.

"We decided to arraign Cummings on the attempted rape tomorrow morning. I had a marshal serve him about two hours ago at the hospital. The judge has agreed to conduct the arraignment in his hospital room."

"Do I have to be there?" Rachel had no desire to confront Grant. Even in his injured condition, he could be dangerous.

"No," he said.

"Fine," she said, slamming the phone down.

Later that afternoon, Rachel called her sister in San Francisco, telling her what had occurred in long, rambling sentences. "I'll jump on the next plane," Carrie said without hesitation. "Don't bother picking me up. I'll take a cab to your house."

"You don't have to come right away," Rachel said. "Even if they arrest me tonight, my neighbor can help me out. I'm more concerned with the future, Carrie. If I have to go to prison, I'll have to make some kind of arrangements for the children."

"I'll take them," she said. "Put that out of your mind. Besides, we're not going to let that happen. Have you hired an attorney yet?"

"No," Rachel said. "Why can't you represent me? You're a lawyer."

"I want you to have a first-rate defense," Carrie said. "I don't practice criminal law, Rachel. I have some money saved, plus I have a line of credit established with the bank. If I need to, I can get a loan. We'll hire the best lawyer we can get."

"I can't take your savings," Rachel told her. "For all I know, you'll be throwing your money away. Grant has positively identified me, along with another eyewitness. What if I'm convicted? You'll need that money to take care of the kids while I'm in prison."

"Let me go," Carrie said. "I'm getting on the next plane. Don't do anything until I get there."

After Mike Atwater concluded his phone call to Rachel, he rushed down the hall to Bill Ringwald's office. "I don't want her arrested," he said from the doorway. "This woman has been through hell, Bill. Can't we stall the PD until we get to the bottom of this mess?"

Ringwald looked up in surprise. He had never encountered a situation like this before, where two individuals were both defendants and victims simultaneously in the same judicial district. He had to manage the situation with a clear head, maintain order, assign the appropriate prosecutors. If not, the Attorney General's office would step in and seize control, and he'd end up a hapless bystander in his own agency. He took in Atwater's unusual state of agitation. "Are you involved with this woman, Mike?"

Atwater removed an invisible speck from his sleeve. "Involved?" he repeated. "I-I mean, there are different levels of involvement. I'm not engaged to her. There's no long-term relationship."

Ringwald sensed the evasion. "Greg Bates informed me you sent Rachel Simmons flowers a few weeks ago." He stopped and rubbed his eyes. "An officer named Jimmy Townsend told him, one of the men Rachel indicated was involved in the fiasco at the beach. What was that all about?"

"It was nothing," Atwater hedged, avoiding Ringwald's gaze. "I felt sorry for her, that's all. She's a widow, struggling to support two kids on a police officer's salary. After I dragged up her past in the Brentwood matter, I felt I owed her something."

Ringwald was growing increasingly impatient. "What past?" he demanded.

Atwater took a seat and told his boss about Rachel's childhood kidnapping and Nathan Richardson's death at the hands of the police sharpshooter. "Dennis Colter went to high school with her," he said. "He says the kids treated her like she was some kind of freak. Not many ten-year-olds end up with a guy's brains splattered all over them, so I guess Rachel might have come across as a little strange back then. There were some rumors floating around about her mother as well."

"What kind of rumors?"

"That her mother was a prostitute passing herself off as a piano teacher."

"Good Lord," Ringwald said. "You know this could hurt her case, don't you?"

"Which one?"

"The attempted rape against Cummings," he said. "The defense will try to paint her as some kind of party girl, claim she willfully submitted to Cummings's advances, then decided to cry rape."

"That's ridiculous, Bill," Atwater said. "Promiscuity isn't a genetically inherited trait."

Ringwald gave him a harsh look. "You're not sleeping with her, I hope. If you are, now's the time to tell me."

The question had been posed in the present tense. After the way Rachel had reacted to his advances that morning, Atwater was certain their sexual relationship was over. "No," he said, feeling he could make such a statement with honesty, "I'm not sleeping with her. I admit I intentionally struck up a friendship with her, Bill, but not for the obvious reasons."

"Go on," Ringwald said, sitting at rapt attention.

"During the Brentwood trial," Atwater said, "Rachel hinted that the gun found in Brentwood's pocket might have been planted by Townsend. I handled another case involving Jimmy Townsend last year that I thought was somewhat suspicious."

"Which case are you referring to?"

"I don't recall the defendant's name," he said. "It was a Hispanic man, though, and if I remember correctly, he worked as an orderly in a nursing home. Townsend shot him when he allegedly saw the guy reaching for a gun during a routine traffic stop. The defendant swore the gun was a plant." He paused and frowned. "The man had a family, Bill, and his employers and co-workers spoke highly of him. Since he went to prison, I felt I had a responsibility to find out if the poor bastard was framed."

"Where does Officer Simmons come into the picture?"

"I thought I might be able to use her as a mole to feed us information from inside the police department," Atwater said haltingly. "I had no idea it would get this big."

"Is this why Simmons came forward?" Ringwald asked, narrowing his eyes. Before the attorney could answer, he added, "I wish you would have spoken to me before you decided to run a covert operation out of this agency."

"Look," Atwater snapped, "I never told Rachel that I suspected there were problems inside the department. When she told me about the assault at the beach, I was shocked. You know I'm a competitive man, Bill. I'd give my right arm to try a case that could earn me the kind of notoriety some of the prosecutors in L.A. have right now. Hell, some of their people are celebrities. Their pictures are in all the magazines. They've signed publishing contracts."

"Fine," Ringwald said, although he still harbored suspicions. Atwater was a cold bastard in many ways. He had never seen him this emotional. "With what's happening at the PD," he said, "I suggest we keep our own house as clean as possible. Have you researched the Hillmont case like I asked?"

"Yes," Atwater said, relieved to be off the subject of Rachel. "I'm not certain what we can charge Cummings with for using the kid as a human shield. Hillmont may have to sue him in civil court for wrongful death, maybe some type of dereliction of duty. I've never had a case quite like this before. I have no idea how we should proceed."

"What about involuntary manslaughter?" Ringwald suggested, having already given it considerable thought.

"The absence of malice fits," Atwater said, walking over to Ringwald's bookcase and pulling out the current penal code. "Section 192 (b) seems to be the most appropriate. The language reads as follows: 'In the commission of an unlawful act, not amounting to a felony; or in the commission of a lawful act which might produce death.' " He paused and looked up. "Cummings was trying to arrest Hillmont, so that could be construed as a lawful act which might produce death. I'm not sure a judge will buy it, however, as the majority of arrests do not produce death."

"Read the whole section," Ringwald said.

Atwater continued, "'In the commission of a lawful act which might produce death, or without due caution and circumspection.' How do you interpret it, Bill?"

"I think we can make it work," he said. "I know Larry Hillmont well. The man buried his son Saturday. He will never be satisfied with a cash award, even if he enjoins the police department in a lawsuit and taps into their liability policy."

"The term of imprisonment on this is two, three, or four years," Atwater told him, shutting the book and replacing it on the shelf. "Since your defendant is now paralyzed, you know his attorney will argue for the lowest possible term. If Cummings is sentenced to two years, he'll be out in twelve months. My bet is he'll never see the inside of a prison, at least not as a result of this crime. A man in a wheelchair can garner a great deal of sympathy."

Ringwald scowled but had to agree with Atwater's assessment. "Your attempted rape is never going to fly," he said, his eyes focused on a spot over Atwater's head. "Your best bet is to offer him a guilty plea on sexual battery, with the promise of no jail time." He waved a hand to cut off Atwater's protest. "We're wasting our time trying to prove attempted rape. As I understand it, all Cummings did was fondle the woman. Before his attorney gets through with Rachel Simmons, she'll look like the town tramp. That party on the beach sounds like it was a drunken orgy. Factor in her past and this stuff you just told me about her mother, and you'll be looking at an acquittal."

"I don't want to accept a plea," the attorney said adamantly. "I've already promised her we would take the case to trial. Sexual battery is only a misdemeanor. That would be a slap in the face to this woman."

Atwater was definitely too involved. "I'm assigning Blake Reynolds to handle the Cummings shooting," he said, jotting down notes on a pad. "He'll work up the pleading right away, then have one of our men go out and arrest Simmons at her home. You'll handle the attempted rape case against Cummings, as well as the involuntary manslaughter of the Hillmont boy." Ringwald sighed, feeling as if he were speaking out of both sides of his mouth. How could they fight for the rights of these individuals as victims, then turn around and prosecute them as defendants? It was a convoluted situation. Getting the paperwork rolling and assigning the proper prosecutors was a beginning, but things were going to get even more muddled along the way.

"Why don't we just cite Simmons to appear in court," Atwater argued, pacing in front of Ringwald's desk. "Don't insist that they book her into the jail. She's not going to flee. She doesn't have adequate resources to go into hiding. Besides, she has two minor children. Women with small children never run to avoid prosecution."

"I'm not so sure about that," Ringwald said. "She fled the scene of the crime. It takes a lot of nerve to shoot someone inside a police station. Don't underestimate this woman, Mike."

Atwater was outraged. "How can you believe Rachel's allegations against Cummings and the police department and still feel we should prosecute her for attempted murder? She didn't shoot this man. Her daughter swears she was at home with her when the crime went down."

"I don't have a choice," Ringwald said, choosing to overlook Atwater's outburst. "If I give Simmons preferential treatment, or even hint that we might offer her immunity, it'll look like we're buying her testimony in the Hillmont matter. We'll end up impeaching our own witness. The AG strongly cautioned me against taking this line of action. They'll be launching a major investigation into the corruption allegations at the police department. They may need to rely on this woman's testimony as well."

They were hanging Rachel out to dry, Atwater thought, his stomach bubbling with acid. She had become a pawn in a high-stakes game of politics and governmental agencies. Careers would be made, while those less fortunate would stand in disgrace. Rachel's future, her safety, along with the emotional needs of her children, would not be considered by those in power.

He had thought that after so many years as a prosecutor, he was too jaded to get passionate about victims. But he was wrong. He believed in Rachel Simmons. She believed, simply and completely, in justice. And she was being punished for her integrity.

Atwater spun around and stormed out of Ringwald's office, mumbling profanities under his breath. Regardless of the outcome of the various cases, Rachel would be destroyed, consumed by the criminal justice system she had fought so valiantly to protect.

chapter

TWENTY-SEVEN

Carrie arrived at three o'clock Tuesday morning. The sisters chatted briefly; then Rachel put her to sleep in her bed, and took the living room sofa for herself. She awoke the next morning to the doorbell ringing. Looking through the drapes, she saw more reporters camped in her front yard. She had already given them her statement. She refused to speak to them again.

"I won't be home until late today," Tracy said, stepping up beside her mother at the window. She was already dressed for school.

"Why?" Rachel asked.

"The cheerleader tryouts are this afternoon," she said, staring out at the reporters. "Why won't they leave us alone? How are you going to drive me to school?"

Her mother pulled her into her arms. "I'm sorry things have been so tough, baby. With Carrie here, it should be better."

"When did she get here?" Tracy asked. "When I went in your room this morning, I saw Carrie asleep in your bed. You didn't even tell me she was coming."

"I called her the other day," Rachel said. "She got in late. I wanted her to sleep in my bed so you and Joe wouldn't disturb her this morning."

Tracy started to ask how long Carrie was going to stay. The house was too small for so many people, but she knew her mother needed all the support she could get. "I have to leave now," she said. "Sheila and I want to practice our routine before first period. She's bringing one of her outfits for me to wear."

Rachel felt a pang of regret. "Are the other mothers coming to the tryouts?"

"I guess," Tracy said, shrugging.

"Do you want me to come?"

Tracy shook her head. "I don't think that would be a good idea, do you? All I need is to have those stupid reporters show up at my school during the tryouts." Her tone became accusing. "The kids are already talking, Mom. They replayed your interview on the evening news last night."

"Okay, I'll stay out of the way." Rachel went to the kitchen to call Lucy and ask if she would mind driving Tracy to school. "Put everything out of your mind," she told Tracy, replacing the phone in the cradle. "Just concentrate on the tryouts this afternoon. I'm sure you and Sheila will do great. I'll keep my fingers crossed for you." She brushed the strands of hair off the girl's forehead, then kissed her. "Will they announce the results today?"

"No," Tracy said. "Before they announce the winners, they have to check their grades and make certain they're eligible. Can I spend the night with Sheila tonight?" she continued. "I know it's a school night, but I can't stand being in the house with those people outside. Last night when I was getting ready for bed, I saw this ugly reporter spying on me through the window."

"Why didn't you tell me?" Rachel asked. "I'll report them for trespassing."

"Who will you report them to, Mom?" her daughter asked. "The police department? Do you really think those people are going to help us?"

"No, you're right," Rachel said. "Stay at Sheila's tonight. But be sure and call me later and tell me how the tryouts went." She watched until the girl disappeared inside her neighbor's house.

At 5:15 Tuesday evening, Carrie and Rachel were peering into the freezer, trying to decide what they were going to prepare for dinner. "I haven't been to the store in almost a week," Rachel said, reaching for a frozen hen. "We could cook this, but we'll have to thaw it first."

Carrie nudged her aside and removed a head of lettuce out of the vegetable bin. "Sounds good," she said. "I'll make us a salad as a snack, then we can eat the rest of our meal later."

Rachel placed the hen in the microwave, hitting the defrost button.

"I can't stop it," Atwater said. "I want you to know that I'm breaking the law by telling you this, but Madison went over my head and got a bench warrant for your arrest. The best thing to do now is cooperate with them."

The news was not unexpected, but still Rachel felt its impact like a blow. "When will they come for me?" she asked.

"It usually takes several hours to process the paperwork," he said. "If the marshal comes for you tonight, you'll have to spend at least one night in jail. They won't set bail until the arraignment."

"What about Grant?" Rachel said, glancing over at her sister as she carried their salad plates to the kitchen table.

"The preliminary hearing will be held in two weeks," he told her. "The doctors say Cummings should be able to come to court by then, even though he'll be confined to a wheelchair."

"There's also the shooting at the Majestic Theater," she said. "Will Grant face the music for using the Hillmont boy as a shield?"

"We're working on it," Atwater said. "The boy's father is on the City Council. When the family saw you on TV yesterday, they demanded we prosecute. We may get to the bottom of this, Rachel. Don't lose hope. We're going after Cummings on several different counts now. We'll nail the bastard on one of them."

She could tell he was uncertain. She had no witnesses to back up the attempted rape charge, and there was conflicting testimony on what had happened at the Majestic Theater. Would Grant get off scot-free? "He attacked me," she blurted out. "He jumped me in the orange grove after you left my house Wednesday night. He beat me and tried to force me to orally copulate him."

"What are you saying?" Carrie shouted, jumping out of her chair. "You've just given them a motive."

"I want him to know the truth," Rachel told her, covering the mouthpiece of the phone with her hand. "Don't you think some of the things I said on television would provide them with a motive? You saw the tape this morning, Carrie. Think about it."

Carrie tried to wrestle the phone away from her sister. "You're a fool," she said. "Don't you realize this man is a prosecutor?"

Atwater was appalled. "Cummings attacked you? Why didn't you tell me this before now?"

Rachel leaned her forehead against the wall. "Grant threatened to rape Tracy if I reported it," she said, trembling as she remembered that night. "He demanded that I go to Sergeant Miller the next morning and recant my earlier statement. He had someone bug my house, Mike. I found a monitoring device inside my phone, another one in a planter. He said if he found out I was talking to anyone other than my kids, he would come after my daughter."

"Do you still have these monitoring devices?"

"I guess so," Rachel told him. "I'll have to figure out where I put them, though."

"Stay put," Atwater said. "I'll send one of our investigators over right now. Were you injured?" He remembered the dark shadows he had seen under her robe the previous day.

"Yes," Rachel said, touching a tender spot near her ribs. With the pain came a new wave of doubt. "It doesn't matter, though. Grant has an alibi. No one will believe me."

"My person will escort you to the hospital," he said, his prosecutor's expertise kicking in. "I want them to document any injuries you sustained. Do you still have the clothes you were wearing? Was there any exchange of blood? If so, we might be able to identify Cummings as the assailant through DNA testing."

"No blood," she said. "Besides, I've already washed the clothes I was wearing."

"Rachel, how could you do that? You not only withheld the truth from me," Atwater exclaimed, "you destroyed all the evidence. Damn it to hell, woman, don't you know what you've done? This is a nightmare, a frigging disaster." He stopped speaking, trying to calm himself. "Turn the clothes over to my investigator. Maybe there's still some hairs on them or some other type of forensic evidence."

"Okay," Rachel said.

"First thing in the morning," he added, "I'll come over and take down a full statement." Something else came to mind. "One of your neighbors claims they saw you driving off in the Pathfinder around the time Grant was shot. Were you in the house the entire night or was that a lie?"

"I was home when Grant was shot," she answered, her voice shaking. "I-I drove past the station earlier, Mike, but I swear I didn't shoot him."

"You what?"

"Since Grant demanded that I report to Nick Miller the next day and retract my statement," Rachel explained, "I knew I had to get down there around six or the sergeant would have already left for the day. All I did was drive past the station. I didn't stop. I didn't go inside. Once I realized I couldn't do what Grant wanted, I drove around a few more minutes, then came back to the house."

The line fell silent. "It doesn't look good, Rachel," Atwater said. "What you've basically told me is that the man beat you and tried to force you to orally copulate him only hours before someone plugged him with a bullet. With an eyewitness who can place you in the locker room and Grant's statement that you were the shooter, coupled with the motive you've just provided, a conviction is looking more likely. Do you understand what I'm trying to tell you?"

Rachel had already thought it through. "Someone is trying to frame me. It has to be one of the men, don't you see? No one else would have access to the locker room. All the doors to the building are locked at that time of the day. The only way to get inside is to use a key." She related her suspicions that Grant had used an accomplice, another officer who had burglarized her home and set up the monitoring devices. "Can your investigator lift prints?" she asked, thinking of the glass in the broken window.

"No," he said, "but I'll send someone who can."

"As long as they don't work for the PD."

"You've placed me in a terrible position," Atwater said. "You should never have told me these things, Rachel. I'm not your attorney. As a prosecutor, I can't withhold information made during a spontaneous admission. At present, you're the primary suspect, the only one with a reason to harm this man."

"I've told you the truth," Rachel said calmly. "Whatever happens, I'll have to deal with it."

The attorney told her he would talk to her the following day and disconnected. Pacing his office, he thought she was a foolish, impulsive woman, too naive to comprehend the game. In her mind, it was about guilt or innocence, right versus wrong. She didn't understand that criminal proceedings were basically a battle of wits and finesse, that half the things said under oath were lies, that no one gave a rat's ass about the truth these days. He slammed his fist down on his desk, causing a jar of jelly beans to tumble to the floor.

He glanced at his watch. Ringwald had already left for the day. At least, Atwater thought, he would have the night to sort through his thoughts before he was forced to tell Ringwald about the beating in the orange grove. Shoving all the papers on his desk into his briefcase, the attorney snapped it shut and walked out of the office.

"Is that it?" Rachel said, getting up off the examining table in the emergency room at Presbyterian Hospital. The investigator Atwater had sent was waiting outside the room.

"That's it," the young doctor said, ripping off his rubber gloves and tossing them in the trash can. "Those bruises on your torso are pretty severe. I thought you might have suffered internal injuries, but nothing showed up on the X rays. Stay in bed for the rest of the week, give your body a chance to heal. Do you need anything for pain?"

"No," Rachel said. Grant Cummings was in the same hospital. Even though he was incapacitated, the thought that he was only a few floors away was unnerving.

Once she put her clothes back on, she stepped outside, where the DA's investigator was waiting. Paul Firestone was a tall man in his early thirties with blotchy skin and a prominent nose. He had arrived at her house with a criminologist employed by the county crime lab. Leaving the expert to search for fingerprints and other evidence, he had escorted her to the hospital. "I have to wait until the doctor hands over the evidence," he said.

"What evidence?" Rachel said. "There isn't any evidence outside of the bruises."

"We need to document them," he said. "We'll use the examination room. I brought a Polaroid camera with me."

Firestone led her back inside, said a few words to the doctor, then waited until the physician had walked out. "I'm sorry," he told Rachel, "but I'll have to ask you to take off your blouse."

She hoisted herself onto the table, staring straight into his eyes without blinking as she undid the buttons on her shirt for the second time and slipped it off her shoulders. From her shoulder blades to her knees, she was covered in ugly bruises, some a deep purple, some so dark her skin appeared black.

"If you don't mind," Firestone said, "could you please stand over by the wall there? I want to show the contrast against the white paint. I feel terrible asking you this, but could you please remove your bra? I see some bruises around your breasts."

Rachel did as he said. The plaster was cold against her bare back. Firestone asked her to raise her arms out to her sides. The shutter on the Polaroid clicked. She remembered Nathan Richardson sitting her in the chair, the china doll propped up beside her, the camera clicking relentlessly. She suddenly panicked, wrapping her arms around herself. "I can't do this."

"I'm sorry," the investigator said. "If we don't document these injuries—"

"I know. Just give me a minute." Rachel backed up to the wall again, her hands stretched out. She felt as if she were facing a firing squad.

"Turn around, please," Firestone said. "I need to get some shots of your back. Pull your pants down past your buttocks."

Rachel faced the wall, her fingers trembling on the zipper of her jeans. Sliding her underwear down with her pants, she stood still until the camera stopped clicking. "Can I turn around now?"

"Yes," the investigator said. "I'll wait outside until you get dressed."

Rachel and Paul Firestone headed to his county car in the hospital parking lot. The sky was dark, the stars hidden behind a thick layer of smog, the air sticky and warm. A red Camaro was pulling out onto the street, but the driver suddenly slammed on the brakes, screeching to a halt in the middle of the roadway. Carol Hitchcock had been on her way home to get a change of clothing. Seeing Rachel, she left the engine running in her car and leapt out.

"I thought that was you," she yelled. "Grant is paralyzed because of you. He'll never walk again. What are you doing here? You shouldn't be allowed to step foot on the hospital grounds after what you've done to this man."

Firestone stepped in between the two women, placing an arm across Hitchcock's chest. "Go to the car," he told Rachel, but she didn't move.

"I could arrest you right now for probable cause," Carol shouted.

"You're not going to arrest anyone," the investigator told her. "Go to the car, Officer Simmons. Let me handle this woman."

"I'm a cop," Carol said, fishing her badge out of her purse and shoving it in his face. "I have firsthand information that this woman shot Grant Cummings. I'm fully within the law by placing her under arrest. Captain Madison assured me the DA's office is cutting an arrest warrant, but I can take her into custody right now on probable cause."

"I'm here because he attacked me, Carol," Rachel said, refusing to leave. "The night he asked you to cover for him at the hardware store, he jumped me in the orange grove by my house and beat me senseless. He tried to force me to orally copulate him. He even threatened to come back and rape my daughter."

"He did not," the woman spat at her. "You just got smashed and made an ass of yourself at the watch party. Why don't you admit it? We know you shot Grant. Ratso saw you leaving the locker room. He saw you with the damn gun in your hand. Why do you have to persist with this stupid rape shit?"

"I'm not referring to what happened at the watch party," Rachel said. "I'm talking about Saturday night when he asked you to provide an alibi for him. Did you think Grant simply dropped by to have a conversation with me? I don't know what kind of story he told you, but his intent was to beat me into submission. If I didn't recant my statement, he threatened to come back and rape my daughter."

Carol pressed against Firestone's arm. "You're lying," she said. "Grant was going to marry me. Now he'll spend the rest of his life in a wheelchair."

"Did Townsend plant the bugs in my house or did Ratso do it?"

"What bugs?" Carol exclaimed, thinking she was talking about insects. "You're insane. You should be in a mental institution."

"Grant beats you, doesn't he?" Rachel said, her speech rapid-fire. "I remember the day last summer when you came to work in your winter uniform. You wore long sleeves so you could cover up the bruises. You're a strong woman, Carol. Walk away while you still can. Grant might be paralyzed, but he still has fists."

Carol Hitchcock's mouth fell open. "I-I don't have to listen to this garbage," she stammered.

Rachel lifted her blouse and exposed the ugly bruises on her torso. "Do you still think I'm making this up?"

Carol placed her hand over her mouth, then spun around and jogged back to her car.

chapter

TWENTY-EIGHT

After Rachel returned from the hospital, Carrie suggested she spend the night in a local hotel and surrender to the authorities the following morning. She knew if they came for Rachel that evening, her sister would have to spend the night in a jail cell. A prisoner could not be released until he or she was arraigned in front of a judge and bail was set. Since Carrie knew she would have to come up with Rachel's bail money as well, she wanted to buy time so she could make arrangements for a transfer of funds from her bank in San Francisco. The two women were sipping sodas at the kitchen table.

"Is this fat Coke?" Carrie asked.

"What does that mean?"

"You know, not diet."

"You won't even drink a regular Coke anymore?" Rachel asked, concerned that her sister was going overboard with the dieting. At five-seven, she was three inches taller than Rachel and weighed almost twenty pounds less.

Carrie frowned. "Why should I drink something that's loaded with calories?"

"You're terribly thin," Rachel said, squinting at her. "And I liked your hair better when it was brown."

"Hey," Carrie said, "a woman's got to keep up her appearance if she wants to snag a man. Guys in their forties don't date forty-year-old women, Rach. They want girls in their twenties. That leaves me with the old farts in their sixties."

"Why would you want a man who is attracted to you only because of your appearance?" Rachel asked, plucking an orange out of the bowl on the table. "Besides, you make a good living. You don't need a man to support you."

"When Phil and I first separated, I thought it might be fun to be single again," Carrie said. "I had my work, and Brent and I were very close. When he moved out to go to college, everything came crashing down on me." She stopped and rubbed her eyes. "I get depressed some-times. Every time I look in the mirror, I see another wrinkle. Pretty soon, no man will want me."

"I doubt that," Rachel said, walking over and touching her shoulder. She had thought Carrie's fixation with her appearance was mere vanity, but she had been wrong. Her sister seemed insecure, and the bouts of depression she had mentioned were troubling. "You're smart, beautiful, outgoing," she told her. "Look at all you've accomplished in life. Besides, you'll be gorgeous even when you're sixty."

"Thanks," Carrie said, placing her hand on top of Rachel's. "I didn't come here to talk about my problems."

Rachel glanced at her watch. Would a marshal ring her doorbell any minute with an arrest warrant? She went to the wall phone to call Lucy. "I need to borrow your car," she said. "I know the PD has me under sur-veillance, because I spotted one of the undercover officers parked down the street."

"Glen had to work the late shift tonight," her neighbor said. "What if I need to go somewhere?"

"You can use the Pathfinder," Rachel told her. "I'll leave the keys on the floorboard. Is your car in the garage?"

"Yes," Lucy said.

"I'll come through the back door," Rachel said, replacing the phone in the cradle. "I don't know if I should do this," she told her sister, returning to the kitchen table.

"Why?" Carrie said.

"They're going to arrest me eventually. Why shouldn't I let them take me now?"

"You're not going to go to jail," Carrie said. Walking to the sink, she poured out her soda and filled the glass with water. "You have a witness who will testify as to your whereabouts at the time of the crime."

"I refuse to let Tracy testify," Rachel said. "She's lying, Carrie. They'll rip her to shreds on the stand."

"Your concerns are unfounded," Carrie told her. "Tracy's testimony will be fairly simple. I've given it a lot of thought, and I don't think they can trip her up."

Rachel tensed, locking her arms over her chest. "I'm not going to allow my daughter to perjure herself."

"You don't have a choice," Carrie said, turning around to face her. "They have both the victim and an additional witness who will swear you shot this man. Two of the most important elements in proving a criminal case are motive and opportunity. Since you told Atwater that Cummings had beaten you the night before he was shot, they know you had ample motive. If Tracy's testimony can keep them from establishing opportunity, you might still have a chance to be cleared."

"You've changed," Rachel said, peeling the orange and dividing it into quarters. "Wasn't it you who always told me how important it was to be honest? When I stole that candy bar from the market, you marched me over to the manager and made me confess. I wet my pants, remember? I was certain they were going to take me to jail."

"You were only seven years old," Carrie said, smiling at the memory. "I knew they wouldn't do anything to you. I only wanted to teach you a lesson."

The phone rang and Carrie answered it, then handed the phone to her sister. "The tryouts were great, Mom," Tracy said. "Sheila thinks we're both going to make it. The judges loved our routine, and we didn't make one mistake."

Rachel smiled proudly at this news. "Are they going to announce the winners tomorrow?"

"Yes," Tracy said. "They're going to make us wait until fifth period, though."

"Can you stay at Sheila's another night?" Rachel asked, hoping she would be out of jail by the following afternoon.

Tracy whispered something to her friend, then came back on the line. "Sheila says it's fine."

After she had hung up, Rachel stood next to her sister at the kitchen counter and gazed out the window into the yard. After some time had passed, she said, "Do you still see Phil?"

"God, no," Carrie said, a scowl on her face.

"Why did you guys split up?" she asked. "You never told me much about it."

"It was bad, Rachel," Carrie said. "Phil was having an affair. I came home from a business trip and found his girlfriend in our apartment. I guess the bastard was too cheap to rent a motel room."

Rachel suspected this was the reason for her sister's insecurity. "Was she young?" she asked.

"What do you think?" Carrie said bitterly. She remembered the long-legged girl lounging on her sofa in her bra and panties, her youthful face, her slender body. "Anyway, now you know why I never wanted to talk about my divorce. Pretty humiliating, huh?"

"Imagine how humiliated Phil will be when someone mistakes his girlfriend for his daughter," Rachel said, arching an eyebrow. "He'll get tired of babysitting, Carrie. From what I've heard, they always do."

Carrie laughed. "I like your attitude, Sis."

"When you laugh," Rachel said, memories from the past flooding her mind, "you remind me of Mother. She used to laugh just like you."

"Hey, if you want to see our mother," she said, "all you have to do is look at your kid."

"Tracy?"

"Yeah," she said, "she's got Mother's temperament to a tee. She's feisty, opinionated, independent. She's a strong girl, Rachel. You should be proud of her."

"I never saw Mother as strong," Rachel said, returning to her seat and eating one of the orange slices. "She might have been strong-willed, but that's not the same." She offered a slice to Carrie, but her sister shook her head.

"Oh, Mother was strong, all right," Carrie said, hoisting herself onto the counter. "You've just forgotten what she used to be like before she started drinking."

"I don't remember much of anything," Rachel said. "The only thing that stands out in my mind is the day you told me Mother was a prostitute."

Carrie blanched. "I shouldn't have told you," she said, picking up a sponge and tossing it into the sink. "I thought you already knew, okay?

You have no idea how much guilt I carry over that." She stopped and took a deep breath, then slowly let it out. "Now that I'm older, I'm beginning to understand what Mother was all about. It's not such a terrible thing to be a prostitute. She made an honest living. She tried to give us a good home."

"I don't know if I would call it an honest living," Rachel said, a slight tremor in her voice. It was almost as if her mother was in the room, embodied in her older sister's elaborate makeup, her red fingernails.

"Mother must have loved children," Carrie continued. "A person who loves children can't be all bad. She didn't have to have us, you know. She could have aborted us."

"Abortion wasn't legal then."

"She could have given us up for adoption, then," Carrie countered. "People pay good money for babies."

"People didn't pay to get babies back then," Rachel told her. "Before *Roe versus Wade*, there were plenty of abandoned babies around. It was only after people started having abortions that the baby crop dried up."

"Prostitution is a victimless crime."

Rachel said, "Not in the eyes of a police officer."

Carrie slipped down off the counter and returned to her chair at the table, handing Rachel a paper towel to wipe her sticky hands. "Mother was a call girl," she said. "She wasn't a junkie, or a streetwalker. I bet she made big money when she was young. By the time you came along, Rachel, her clientele had dropped down to a lower level, mostly military men. In the beginning, the guys she serviced were all professionals, the majority of them successful businessmen."

"Wouldn't it have been nice to know who our fathers were?" Rachel asked her. "Don't you wonder sometimes?"

"Not anymore," Carrie said, shaking her head.

Rachel refused to accept her sister's sanitized version of their past. Carrie had already left home when things got bad. At the end, their mother had become a cruel woman whose favorite pastime had been venting her hostility on her youngest daughter. "Mother had us for money," she told her. "She'd been collecting aid for dependent children for years. Having kids was similar to a part-time job. She needed a steady income, something that didn't change from month to month. When we became adults and the state stopped supporting us, Mother fell apart. She was too old to turn tricks anymore. She knew the gravy train was about to come to an end. Mother was a lazy, self-indulgent woman. She wanted to drink all night and sleep every day until noon."

"She was a brilliant pianist," Carrie pointed out. "She could have had a legitimate career in music. You know how long a person has to study the piano to play as well as Mother did?"

"Why didn't she get a real job, then? She might not have been able to play at Carnegie Hall, but she could have played in a nightclub."

"Because my asshole father ran out on her when she was six months pregnant," Carrie said, brushing her hair behind her ears. "She started turning tricks right after I was born. Maybe she thought she could get a job somewhere as a piano player when we got older. How could she work at night in a club, Rachel? Who would have looked after us? Her parents were dead. She was alone in the world."

"So are we," Rachel said.

"No," Carrie said, "we have each other. Mother was an only child. Remember all the secrets we used to share, the Saturday afternoons at the movies, the time we spent at Munson's skating rink? Even now, you know you can call me if you have a problem. Mother never had that option."

"I really appreciate what you're doing," Rachel said. "It means a lot right now to know you're willing to look after the kids if I have to—"

"Don't even say it," Carrie said. "This is all going to work out, sweetie. And besides," she added, smiling warmly, "I don't feel depressed anymore. It's nice to be around someone who looks up to you, says comforting things to you. To be perfectly honest, I'd rather be here with you and the kids than moping around an empty apartment."

Rachel fell silent. A few moments later, she said, "I want to talk to you about hiring an attorney."

"Oh," Carrie said, glancing down at a yellow pad where she had made a list of local law firms. "I made a few calls today while you were napping, but none of the attorneys I contacted had handled a case this sensitive before. Tomorrow, I'm going to call the police association and see if they can give me the name of an attorney they've used to defend other officers." She sighed wearily. "If the shooting had gone down while you were on duty, the association would have picked up the tab for your legal expenses."

"I want you to represent me," Rachel said, reaching across the table to touch Carrie's hand. "Don't you understand? If I let you spend your savings on an attorney, what are you going to use to support the kids if I'm convicted and sent to prison? I don't have any money to give you. You'll have to hire someone to look after Joe while you're at work, maybe even move to a larger apartment. Why squander our resources needlessly?"

"I'm a civil litigator," she said. "I don't know enough about criminal law to act as your attorney."

"It can't be that complex," Rachel argued.

Carrie knew her point made sense. She made a good living, but her pockets weren't that deep. Sometimes the cases she handled dragged on for years, and many of them were taken on a contingency basis. If she was forced to care for Tracy and Joe, her whole life would change. She might not be able to travel as much, and her income could suffer as a result. Many of the cases her firm handled were tried outside of San Francisco, and she sometimes had to be gone for weeks at a time.

Could she defend Rachel? Carrie wondered. If she did, she would have to begin preparing immediately. "Are you certain you're willing to take this kind of chance?"

"I trust you. You're my big sister," Rachel said. "Why should I hire a stranger?"

"You'll have to listen to me," Carrie said, looking stern. "You'll have to do whatever I decide is best for your case."

"Fine," she said. "As long as you don't ask me to lie or insist that I allow Tracy to perjure herself, I'll go along with anything you suggest."

"This is survival," Carrie shouted, slamming her fist down on the table. "The cops are lying through their teeth, trying to railroad you. Are you going to throw your life away rather than put a dent in your principles?"

"Why don't we worry about Tracy's testimony when the time comes?" Rachel said, scooping up the rinds from her orange and depositing them in the trash can. "Look, it's getting late. I'd better go."

Joe began crying in the other room. "Go," Carrie said. "I'll take good care of Joe. Rent yourself a nice hotel room. Maybe you can get a decent night's sleep for a change." She walked over and pressed a handful of cash into Rachel's palm, then handed her a stack of envelopes. "Drop these in a mailbox, okay?"

Rachel looked through the envelopes, recognizing some of the addresses. "These are my bills. I can't let you pay them."

"Let me do this for you," she said, clasping her hand. "Are you going to deny me the right to help my own sister?"

"No," Rachel said, dropping her eyes.

"Since I'm going to represent you, maybe I can find a way Tracy doesn't have to testify. As soon as they arraign you, I'll file a discovery motion and find out exactly what kind of a case they've got. They may have a lot less than we think they do."

Rachel embraced her. "What's going to happen with your job? Weren't you working on a big case?"

"Already resolved," Carrie said. "A job is a job, Rachel. If they decide to fire me, I can always find another position. A sister is a lot harder to replace."

With a scarf tied over her head, Rachel backed Lucy's station wagon out of the driveway and squealed off down the road, slipping past the unmarked police car on the corner.

She had not stayed in a hotel since her honeymoon. She drove down Main Street in Oak Grove thinking she might get a room at the new Ramada Inn, then jumped on the 101 freeway. When she reached the exit for Ventura, she steered the car to the off ramp and headed up Victoria Boulevard. The drive was calming her. She was used to driving for long periods of time on her job. For the first time in days, Rachel felt some semblance of normalcy.

Passing Ventura College, she saw Mike Atwater's street. She had been rude to him that morning, and he seemed to be doing everything he could to help her. She drove past his residence, then made a U-turn at the end of the street and returned. The lights were still on in the living room. She parked and walked to the front door, quickly tucking her shirt into the waistband of her jeans.

"What's wrong?" Atwater said when he opened the door. He was dressed in a tank top and running shorts. He looked anything but pleased to see her.

"Don't worry," Rachel told him, stepping into the entryway, "I'm going to surrender myself in the morning."

This announcement startled him. "Did they contact you?"

"No, but you told me they were coming to arrest me tonight. Carrie insisted I get a hotel room. She didn't want me to have to spend the night in jail."

Atwater grabbed her arm, jerking her away from the door and locking it. "You have no idea what you just said," he told her, leading her toward the back of the house. "If you tell anyone else I told you that, I could be brought up on criminal charges. It's against the law to leak information about an impending warrant. The suspect could flee, destroy evidence."

"I'm not going to flee," Rachel said, annoyed that he was treating her like a criminal.

Atwater passed through the living room, opened the French doors leading into the backyard, and stepped out. Rachel walked up behind him. "I'm sorry about yesterday morning," she whispered. "Is your thumb okay?"

"I'm not upset about that, Rachel," he said, not turning to face her. "I'm afraid that the things you told me about Grant assaulting you may be used against you. Besides providing you with a motive, the fact that you withheld information regarding the assault when we interviewed you on the morning of the shooting will make you look suspicious in the eyes of the jury."

"It's okay, Mike," she said, placing a hand on his shoulder.

Not responding, the prosecutor walked down the stone path to the gazebo and stretched out in one of the lounge chairs. It was overcast, the moon hidden behind low-hanging clouds, the air heavy with moisture. Rachel glanced at the sky, seeing the clouds moving like a dark shadow over her head. Combined with the dense foliage, the scent of the air made her think of a tropical forest. "It's going to rain," she said, taking a seat beside him in the matching recliner. The white canvas covering the gazebo was billowing out in the breeze, then slapping back against the columns.

"I'm appalled at what Grant Cummings did to you," Atwater said, a slight catch in his voice. "I saw the photographs. I know how viciously this man beat you. If only you'd called me the night it happened, I would have had Cummings arrested immediately and prosecuted him to the full extent of the law."

"Laws don't mean much to me anymore," Rachel told him. "I'm not saying I don't believe in honesty and integrity. The people who write laws are politicians, though. They only write laws to please their constituents." She watched as a bolt of lightning lit up the sky. "If the people who make the laws are insincere and the people who enforce them are corrupt, where does justice come in?"

Atwater shook his head in disagreement. "Not every police department is like Oak Grove. There are thousands of decent cops out there, people willing to risk their lives for the good of the community."

"Nothing's going to change," Rachel said, reaching her hand outside the canopy and feeling a drop of rain strike her palm. "It's only going to get worse."

"Why do you say that?" he said, turning his head.

"Because I know," Rachel said. "Cummings, Townsend, Miller, Ramone, Hitchcock. Even if they all get fired, others just like them will take their place. It's the authority. It's like a drug, a sickness. Cops begin to think they're beyond the law, that they *are* the law. Then the job itself squeezes you and squeezes you. Someone spits on you. Someone flips you the finger. You save someone's life, and for gratitude, they try to kill you." Rain started pelting the canvas top of the gazebo. "A police officer can't socialize with normal people. They don't understand the things you go through, the constant fear, the horror. You start spending all your time with other cops. Before you know it, every civilian becomes the enemy. It's similar to an army run amuck."

"I guess that's why they ask for the chief's resignation in situations like this," Atwater said. "Anarchy begins where leadership ends."

Rachel smiled. "Catchy phrase."

"It's more than that. Because you came forward, Rachel," he said, "things will change at the Oak Grove Police Department. Give yourself credit. Not many people would have the courage to go up against this army run amuck, as you so aptly described them."

"I'm not a courageous person, Mike," Rachel said. "I'm not even a very good police officer. I didn't set out on this road thinking I could eradicate police corruption or bring about radical change. I get up every morning just like everyone else does. I work. I sleep. I try to be the best person I can possibly be, whether it's as a parent or a police officer. I don't believe in lying, stealing, or intentionally hurting people. Those are the only goals I set for myself." She looked at him and smiled. "Not too sophisticated, huh?"

Atwater fell silent, pondering the things she had said. "If everyone took your approach to life," he said, "the world might be a better place. There's great beauty in simplicity, Rachel."

"I have to go," she said, standing.

"It's raining," he answered. "Why don't you stay?"

Rachel walked out into the rain, tilting her head and letting the drops splash against her face. She felt purged. She had done what she had set out to do. She had told the truth, made a stand for what she felt was right. If she never accomplished another thing for the rest of her life, she could feel a measure of pride. Sergeant Larry Dean would be pleased. She looked up at the heavens, wondering if he was watching. A year after Rachel had moved away from San Diego, she had read about his death in the newspaper. He had died in the line of duty, shot and killed by a robbery suspect. She had driven to San Diego to attend the funeral. The officers had all worn black armbands. They had marched behind Larry Dean's coffin in their dress uniforms. Every police agency in the state had sent a contingent of officers to pay their respects. Sergeant Larry Dean had served his community valiantly, died bravely, and been buried with dignity.

Where had all the heroes gone?

"Come out of the rain," Atwater said, stepping up beside her. "You're getting drenched."

"I love it," Rachel said. "I feel like I've been swimming in sewage for two years. This is the first time I've felt clean."

Atwater felt a stab of guilt. Rachel had trusted him, looked up to him. "There's something I have to tell you," he said, raising his voice so Rachel could hear him over the rain. "I befriended you thinking I could use you to advance my career. I'm not the person you think I am, Rachel. I'm a self-serving asshole."

"I don't understand," she said.

Atwater explained about the Brentwood case, along with the other incident he had handled involving Jimmy Townsend. "Police corruption is a hot ticket," he told her. "I thought if I could get you to cooperate, I might end up with a sensational case on my hands."

Rachel was hurt. "I guess you got what you wanted," she said, turning to walk away.

Atwater caught her arm. "After I got to know you," he said, "my feelings for you became genuine. Please believe me, Rachel. What we shared that night was real."

Rachel spat out a mouthful of rain. So much had happened since that evening, their lovemaking had almost vanished from her memory.

"You're not responsible for my predicament," she said, her anger evaporating. "When my husband and I first met, I was working at a nursery. He said he flirted with me hoping I would forget to charge him for some of the plants." She smiled, remembering that day. "Everyone has something they want from a relationship."

The attorney reached for her, then dropped his arms back to his sides. "If you hadn't been involved with me, Rachel, you might not have gotten in over your head. Someone else might have pointed out the dangers to you, or at the very least, tried to shield your identity from the other officers." A crack of thunder rang out, and Atwater stopped speaking. A few moments later, he continued, "I should have assigned one of our investigators to watch your house from the second you decided to press charges against Grant Cummings. If I had, the sick bastard wouldn't have been able to get his hands on you."

"It's okay," Rachel said.

"How can you say that?" he said, unable to let go of his guilt. "You're about to be arrested."

"It's funny," she said, "but I'm not really afraid. Right now I feel good. I can't explain it exactly, but I feel almost peaceful in a way."

"I'm going to get you off," Atwater said, "even if it costs me my position at the agency."

They were separated by several feet. The rain was coming down now in transparent sheets. Rachel took a step toward him and then stopped. Atwater did the same. When they were face to face, she rested her forehead against his. "Hold me," she said, taking his arms and placing them around her waist.

They stood still, their bodies like statues. Rachel finally raised her head, grabbing onto his wet hair and pulling him closer. "You came to me at just the right time," she whispered. "You came when I needed you."

"Oh, Rachel," he said, overcome with emotion. He wanted to tell her that he had needed her, too, that his life had lost meaning. He had gone through the motions, told himself he was content. In reality he had been lonely, his life empty outside of his work.

Rachel had already slipped out of his arms, though, and was jogging through the rain to the back of the house. She turned around and waved at him through the glass doors, then disappeared.

chapter

TWENTY-NINE

Ted Harriman reported for duty early Tuesday night, wanting to speak to Captain Edgar Madison before he left the station. Due to budget cutbacks, they no longer had a captain assigned to the graveyard watch, and Madison generally left the building around eight. Standing in the door to his office, Harriman said, "Can you spare a few moments?"

"I was about to leave," Madison told him. "What's going on, Ted?"

Harriman stepped into the office, then looked behind him. "If you don't mind," he said, "I'd feel better if we spoke with the door closed."

"Fine," Madison said, watching as Harriman closed the door and took a seat in one of the chairs facing his desk.

Because there were only a few African-Americans in the department, Edgar Madison and Ted Harriman regularly socialized outside of the department. On Thursday evenings, they bowled in a league together, and every month or so they would go out to dinner with their wives. "I think you have a major problem on your hands," Harriman said. "The things Rachel Simmons has been saying may be true. You know I'm not one to speak out against my fellow officers—"

"Spit it out, Ted," Madison said, knowing Harriman was a straight shooter.

"Cummings is a bad actor," he told him. "I didn't see him use the

Hillmont boy as a shield, but I wouldn't put it past him. And I don't believe Rachel shot him."

"When you say Cummings is a bad actor, exactly what are you refer-ring to?"

"Got a few hours?" Harriman said, grimacing. "He's stolen arrests right out from under me. Happened again just the other night. And Townsend, Hitchcock, and Ratso are charter members of Grant's little gang. Nick Miller is one of the ringleaders as well. I guess you could say Cummings runs the watch the same way he runs the parties."

Madison leaned back in his chair. Chief Bates was still recovering from gallbladder surgery. He was not scheduled to return to work until the following week. The deputy chief, Clinton Dowd, was buried under a mountain of paperwork, having taken on the chief's duties during his absence. The chief had been communicating with Madison by phone, though, and had assigned the captain the task of investigating Grant Cummings's shooting, along with the allegations Rachel had made about the Majestic Theater incident. "What makes you think Rachel is innocent?"

"Around the time Grant was shot," Harriman explained, "I was parked outside the back door to the station. I remained in the car for about fifteen minutes finishing one of my reports. If Rachel left through the back of the station after she shot Cummings like Ramone said, why didn't I see her?"

"Maybe you looked away for a moment," the captain answered. "You said you were working on a report."

"That's what I originally told myself," Harriman said. "The hinges on the back door are rusted from the rains we had last month, though. Every time someone opens the door, it makes an irritating sound. Even if I looked away for a moment, my window was down and I would have heard the door making all that racket."

"If Rachel didn't shoot him," Madison said, "who did?"

"I have no idea," Harriman said, shaking his head. "Something else happened that I think you should know about. I saw Ramone carrying a large package out of the station the other night. I asked him what it was, and he told me it was evidence he was taking to the crime lab. The problem is, the watch had just started. Even if Ratso had picked up some kind of evidence from the night before, why didn't he take it straight to the crime lab?"

Madison contemplated his friend's statements for a long time. "You might be onto something," he said. "How big was this package?"

"About four times the size of a briefcase," Harriman said. "If I remember correctly, it was wrapped in newsprint."

"I'll look into it," Madison said. He would have to call his wife and tell her he wouldn't be coming home until later. The information Harriman had told him was critical. Once he confirmed his intentions with the chief, he would start with Nick Miller and work his way down. "Thanks for coming forward, Ted. If you stumble across anything else, let me know immediately."

Captain Madison, Sergeant Nick Miller, and two lieutenants were assembled in the conference room at the police station at 10:15 Tuesday evening.

Captain Madison was seated at the head of the table, addressing the men. "Chief Bates feels with the intense media interest Simmons has generated, it's better for him to remain on the sidelines until he officially returns to work next week. If the allegations this woman has made turn out to be valid, the chief's afraid the City Council may ask for his resignation."

"I don't think it's going to go that far," Miller said. "If Rachel hadn't shot Cummings, we might be in some deep shit. No one's going to believe all this crap she said on television once we bust her for attempted murder."

The captain leveled a finger at him. "You're the one in deep shit, Miller. Didn't you know Grant Cummings was a rogue cop? Can't you control the men who work under you?"

"My men haven't done anything wrong," Miller lied, his shoulder twitching with nervous energy.

"What about the Hillmont matter? Did you try to intimidate Rachel Simmons into doctoring up her report?"

"Of course not," he said.

"How come her report isn't on file?" Madison asked, his voice a deep baritone. "I looked through all the crime reports on the Majestic shooting prior to this meeting. What happened to Simmons's report?"

"I don't know," Miller said, pulling his collar away from his neck. "I guess she never got around to finishing it."

"You guess?" the captain barked, leaning forward over the table.

"Her report should have been turned in at the end of the watch. It's department policy."

"Hey," Miller said, throwing up his hands, "what can I tell you? Shit happens."

"Were you involved in the incident at the beach?" Madison continued.

"I was there," the sergeant answered, beads of perspiration popping out on his forehead. "Nothing happened, Captain. I swear."

"Grant Cummings didn't try to rape her?"

"No," he said, shaking his head. "We were all drinking. Rachel seemed to be having a good time. Then all of a sudden she just went ballistic. Sometimes alcohol affects people the wrong way."

Madison tipped his chair back until the legs came off the floor, his double chin resting on his chest. The two lieutenants studied Nick Miller. "Mike Atwater informed me that Simmons asked the dispatcher to call me out a few nights back," he said. "I was never informed of that request. He said the woman was in trouble, and the other officers on her watch refused to respond for backup. Is this true?"

"I didn't know this was going to be an inquisition," Miller said, squirming under Madison's hot glare.

"Answer the question," Madison said, pressing his fingers to his temples.

"I didn't see a need to get you out of bed at five o'clock in the morning," Miller said quickly. "The situation was under control. There was nothing for you to do. Anyway, my people didn't fail to respond when Simmons called for backup. They were tied up on legitimate calls. They got there as soon as they could." He wiped his mouth with the back of his hand. "The broad just panicked, okay? She didn't belong in a uniform. Look at the last performance evaluation I did on her if you don't believe me. You guys hire these ditzy women and expect us to turn them into competent officers. With this chick, it was too much of a stretch."

Madison pressed on. "Why didn't you inform Internal Affairs of the missing drug money? They weren't aware of the situation until Atwater called and told them."

"I-I didn't . . ." Miller stopped stammering. He hadn't known IA had been informed of the missing money. He wasn't prepared.

Madison waited in stony silence.

"Okay," the sergeant said, his uniform soaked in perspiration. "We're not even certain that money was ever there, okay? No one saw it but Rachel Simmons. Why open a can of worms? I didn't want the department's reputation to be sullied in the media."

Another bout of silence ensued, the air thick with tension. "The performance review you submitted on this woman was out of line," Edgar Madison told him. "I reviewed Officer Simmons's personnel jacket today. I've also spoken to several of our top detectives. They consider Simmons an excellent candidate for advancement. Her reports are some of the finest in the department. They're concise, well-written, and extensively detailed."

"Sure, she can write," Miller said. "All women can write. That doesn't mean she can perform in the field, though. She's not a detective. She's a patrol officer."

Madison picked some reports off the table and flipped through them. "Why was this woman's name not submitted for a commendation after the homicide on Maple Avenue?"

"Excuse me," Miller said, jerking his head back. "She fucked up the case, that's why. She entered the house without a warrant. Tony Mancini thinks there's a possibility that everything we pulled out of that house will be excluded."

"Humph," Madison said, squaring his shoulders, "as I see it, Officer Simmons bravely defended herself against a knife-wielding suspect, a murderer to be precise. When one of our people performs an act of heroism, we generally like to reward them publicly, let the community know the good work we do." He pinned Miller with his eyes. "I've decided to suspend you pending further investigation of these allegations."

"You can't do that," Miller said, leaping to his feet.

"It's only temporary," Madison said. "We have to take action, don't you see? The public will demand it. By early next week, the feds will be crawling all over this place. Everything Chief Bates has tried to do for this department will be destroyed."

"As long as I get paid," Miller said, snickering nervously. "Hey, I know you've got to play along with Rachel's little games. As long as I know you guys are behind me, I won't make waves. All we have to do is hang tough until this shit blows over. We're a team, right?"

Madison said, "The suspension will be without pay."

"What about Simmons?" Miller shouted, flying into a rage. "She shot one of my men. Why am I taking all this heat? I didn't shoot anyone."

"Grant Cummings is dirtier than hell, Miller," Madison barked. "Not only that, you've got a thief on your watch. Fifty grand is not small change. If you'd done your job correctly, you would have seen these problems and helped us to rid ourselves of these rotten apples. That's what being in a supervisory capacity is all about."

"This is a crock of shit." Miller ripped his badge off his uniform, hurling it at the captain. They were making him the sacrificial lamb, and he refused to take it lying down. In only a matter of weeks, he was scheduled to take the lieutenant's exam.

"Your service revolver," the captain said, plucking the badge out of his lap and placing it in his pocket.

Yanking his gun out of his holster, Miller slammed it down on the table. "Can I go now?"

Madison nodded, watching as Miller walked out the door of the conference room. Nick Miller would be the first of many. Every officer involved would have to be terminated. If they acted swiftly, Chief Bates had told him, they might be able to regain the confidence of the community. If not, Madison was certain his head would roll along with the rest of them.

After removing his personal effects from his metal desk, Nick Miller advised the dispatcher to call Jimmy Townsend and Fred Ramone on the radio and have them meet him in the police parking lot. It was 11:20, and the two men had already cleared the station.

Approximately fifteen minutes later, the two officers pulled along-side Miller's Honda Civic and got out of their cars, speaking to him through the open window. "What's going on?" Townsend said. Ratso stood beside him.

"They suspended me without pay," Miller said, still reeling in disbe-lief. "I need those pictures."

"What pictures?" Townsend said.

"The ones Ratso took at the beach that day," he said, glaring at the dark-skinned man. "Grant was supposed to give me the proofs, along with the negatives. He never did. I can't have them floating around."

"I don't have them," Ratso said. "I gave all the pictures to Grant as soon as I got them developed."

"You piece of dog shit," Miller hissed, trying to grab Ratso through the window. "I want those pictures. If I don't destroy them, I'll end up in jail. Rachel will claim I tried to rape her along with Grant."

"They weren't so bad, Sarge," Ratso said, stepping back out of the sergeant's reach. "All you were doing was playing with her tits."

"This woman is poison," Miller said, cracking his knuckles. "I curse the day she was hired, let me tell you. That's the problem with fucking women. You never know what they're going to do, when they're going to start running off at the mouth. Both of you are going to get shit-canned too, you know? It's only a matter of time."

Ratso didn't believe what he was hearing. How could there still be a problem? Why would anyone believe Rachel after what he had told them? "Grant will take care of it," he said. "He will not allow them to fire me, not after I saved his life."

Both of the other men laughed. "You're a moron, Ratso," Townsend said. "Grant can't walk. What's he going to do? Get out of his hospital bed and run over Rachel with his wheelchair? The gig is up, man. We blew it. Wait till my wife hears I'm about to lose my job. Without a paycheck, she'll toss me out on my ear."

"Of course," Sergeant Miller said, arching an eyebrow, "we still might have time to stop this. The engine pushing our lives over the cliff is Rachel Simmons. If she disappeared, all of our problems might go away with her. Get my drift?"

Townsend understood immediately. Ratso, however, was a little slow. "Where would she go?"

"I told you he was a moron," Townsend told Miller. "Go back to work, Ratso. I'll explain everything later."

Ratso dropped his head. When he raised his eyes, the look on his face was frightening. "I'm not a moron. If you want Rachel to disappear, I'll be glad to kill her for you."

Sergeant Miller choked on a toothpick. Townsend looked as if he had seen a ghost. For a long time, no one spoke.

Finally Ratso went on, "I've killed before. It was a long time ago. In Pakistan, things are different than they are in this country. There are many people. Life does not have as great a value. People sometimes have to kill to stay alive."

"Ah," Townsend said, as if Ratso's little speech explained every-thing. He'd always thought the man was Italian. The revelation that he was from Pakistan was almost as shocking as his statement that he had killed someone. "If you don't mind me asking, who exactly did you kill?"

"He's full of shit," Miller said. "What about that incident last year, Ratso? You choked, man. You couldn't pull the trigger. If Grant hadn't stepped in, that asshole would have killed you."

"That was different," Ratso said. "I didn't choke. I waited too long to fire. I wanted to make certain the gun was sighted correctly."

"Who did you kill, huh?" Townsend said, chuckling. "Are you sure you didn't step on a cockroach, Ratso?"

"I don't think that's any of your business," Ratso said, walking back to his police car.

chapter

THIRTY

At 6:20 Wednesday morning, Carrie was feeding Joe his breakfast at the kitchen table. "You could sleep until eight," she told him. "You don't have to get up at the crack of dawn."

"I don't want eggs," Joe said, banging his spoon on the table. "I want Froot Loops."

"Froot Loops aren't good for you," Carrie said, placing a mound of scrambled eggs on his plate, then heading back to the counter to get his toast.

Joe stuck his spoon in the eggs, then flicked them onto the floor. He looked over at his aunt and giggled. "Froot Loops."

"Yeah, right," Carrie said, making a face at him. "You'll get Froot Loops over my dead body, kid. Eat the damn eggs."

"I don't like you," Joe said, frowning. "I want my mommy. You're mean."

Carrie sighed. Parenting was not easy. Her son was eighteen now, and she had forgotten what it was like to care for a child. Her own life was relatively easy. She had a lovely apartment on Russian Hill, one of the nicer sections of San Francisco. She took most of her meals out. She had a maid come in once a week.

Rachel's house was clearly a children's home. Dirty laundry was stacked in the hall. Toys were scattered all over the place. Carrie had tripped on a toy fire truck coming down the hall. How had her sister

255

managed all this while holding down two jobs? Rachel was amazing. The phone rang and she went to the wall phone to answer it.

"My name is Sherry Lafayette," a woman's voice said. "Is this Rachel Simmons?"

"Are you a reporter?"

"No," the woman said. "I saw you on television yesterday. I heard the things you said about that officer."

"What officer?"

"Grant Cummings."

Carrie started to say she was Rachel's sister, then stopped herself. She wanted to hear more. "Do you know him?"

"I don't want to talk over the phone," Lafayette said. "Can we meet somewhere?"

Carrie had no idea what hotel Rachel had stayed at the night before, and the plan was for her to surrender herself at the DA's office before ten o'clock that morning. Carrie wanted to get to the courthouse before her sister, thinking she could introduce herself to Mike Atwater and see if there were any new developments in Rachel's case. "Sure," she said. "Name a location and I'll be there."

"There's a Catholic church at the corner of Adams Road and Parker. Can you be there in fifteen minutes? I'll meet you inside. They leave the doors unlocked."

"I'll try like hell to be there," Carrie said, glancing over at Joe. The boy was still in his pajamas. Getting his clothes on was like wrestling with an alligator. Last night, she had gotten his pajama top stuck on his head, and Joe had sunk his teeth into her hand. She started to ask the woman to give her more time, then realized she was listening to a dial tone.

After depositing Joe, still dressed in his pajamas, next door at Lucy's via the backyard, Carrie returned to her sister's house to retrieve her purse off the living room sofa. When she walked out the front door, she saw a car parked a few doors down at the curb, the man inside sleeping. The second she gunned the engine of the Pathfinder, he jumped out of the car and raced over. "I'm with the *Globe*," he said. "We want to buy exclusive rights to your story."

"Shove off, idiot," Carrie said, prying his hand off the window and quickly rolling it up.

"We're prepared to pay a lot of money," the man yelled, waving what looked like a contract.

Carrie threw the gearshift into reverse and stepped on the gas. He chased the car down the driveway, the paper fluttering in his hand.

Arriving at the church a few minutes after the appointed time, Carrie hurried inside. The church was dark and musty. A dim light filtered through the stained glass windows. She smelled incense and candle wax, the rich oil they used to rub down the wood in the pews. Clothing rustled near the altar. Carrie headed down the center aisle to the front of the church. Seeing a figure in a black raincoat kneeling inside one of the pews, she entered the row and took a seat beside her.

"Who are you?" Sherry Lafayette said, panicking. "You aren't the woman I saw on television."

"I know," Carrie said, taking hold of her arm so she wouldn't flee. "I'm Rachel's sister, Carrie Linderhurst. She couldn't come because she's tied up with the cops. Please, tell me what you know about Grant Cummings."

At thirty-two, Sherry Lafayette was an attractive woman. Her hair was dark and wavy, her body slender inside the raincoat. She remained silent for a few moments, then seemed to accept Carrie's sincerity. "It happened last year," she began. "It was the week before Christmas. My family owns a small toy store in Oak Grove. I stayed late to take inventory and clean up the stock room. I guess my father accidentally set the alarm when he left, out of habit. When I was ready to leave at around eleven that evening, I forgot to look at the alarm panel and just pushed the button we use to arm the system as I walked out the door. When the system is already armed, I discovered, that button sends a signal to the alarm company that we're being robbed." She stopped and took a deep breath. "It's hard for me to talk about this," she said. "I haven't spoken of that night since it happened."

"Please," Carrie said, lightly touching her hand.

"The audible alarm didn't sound," the woman continued, "but a police officer stopped me just as I was about to get into my car in the rear parking lot. He had his gun drawn on me. Once I told him who I was and showed him my identification, he returned to the store with me so I could reset the alarm. He was handsome and talkative, charming in a sort of overbearing way. He asked me to go for a cup of coffee with him, but I declined, telling him I needed to get home. The

Christmas season is exhausting in our business, and I was under a lot of stress. My father is in his late sixties, and the main responsibility for the business had fallen on my shoulders. The police officer seemed put off by my rejection. He kept insisting until he made me angry. I told him to fuck off. That was a mistake, a bad mistake." She cut her eyes to Carrie. "He wrestled me to the floor. He beat me senseless. He made me perform oral sex on him, then sodomized me."

"Why didn't you report this?" Carrie said.

"I was too afraid," she said. "He told me no one would believe me. He said people always take the word of a police officer over that of an ordinary citizen. He said if I tried to report what he had done to me, he would come back and kill my entire family. He said he had the power to monitor my phone calls, have me followed. No matter where I went, he could always find me."

"Are you certain this man was Grant Cummings?"

"Are you kidding?" Lafayette said, her eyes flashing. "I've seen him many times since the attack. He stops by the store. Sometimes he parks outside and watches me through the front windows. Other times the bastard comes inside and shoots the breeze with my father, as if nothing ever happened between us."

Carrie's eyes went to the crucifix. "He maintains control that way. That's what rape is all about, forcing your will on someone, making them feel they're powerless." Yet beyond the sympathy she felt, excitement at what this might mean to Rachel was rising. She had to get Lafayette to come forward. "Will you talk to the authorities now?"

"I don't know," Lafayette said, her hands trembling. "He's a police officer. How can I go to the police?" She turned to slip out of the pew, but Carrie grabbed an edge of her raincoat.

"The man's paralyzed," she said, her voice echoing in the sanctuary. "He can't hurt you anymore. If you come forward, it will confirm what he did to my sister. If not, she may go to prison."

"I'm too afraid," she said. "Who would I talk to?"

"I'll handle it," Carrie said, reaching into her purse for a pen and a scrap of paper. "Write down your address and phone number. I'll contact the DA's office and arrange for them to take down your statement."

Sherry pushed the pen and paper away. "I can't handle a trial," she said, burying her head in her hands. "How can I tell this story in an open courtroom, read about it in the newspaper? For so long, I've felt so weak, so contemptible. I let him brutalize me and get away with it. If I had come forward and told the truth, I could have stopped him, prevented him from hurting other women. I was a coward." She looked at Carrie in a plea for understanding. "I couldn't do it. I was certain if I did, he'd come back and kill my family."

Carrie draped her arm over the woman's shoulders. "There's nothing to feel guilty about," she said. "You might have been right, Sherry. If you had reported the assault when it occurred, Grant's buddies at the police department could have covered it up. Now that Rachel's come forward, though, you have nothing to fear. You'll never have to talk to a police officer. I promise."

Comforted, Sherry Lafayette wrote her address and phone number down on the paper, then handed it to Carrie. "I respect your sister for what she's done," she said. "I'll try my best to help her."

Ratso gave Jimmy Townsend a ride home in his dilapidated Chevy Nova, pulling to the curb in front of his house shortly before eight Wednesday morning. "Forget what Miller said last night about Rachel," Townsend told him. "He was talking out of his asshole. Nobody's going to kill anyone."

"Why?" Ratso said.

"Look, pal," the hefty officer continued, "I like you, okay, but some of the things you say are a little strange. Why didn't you tell me you were from Pakistan? What's the big secret? Why would you want people to think you're Mexican?"

"I didn't want the officers in the department to look down on me," Ratso said, gripping the steering wheel with both hands. "You think because I'm from Pakistan that I'm an inferior human being. People in this country have more respect for black gangsters than they do for people like me."

"Well," Townsend said, thinking the man had a point, "I don't look down on you, Ratso. I don't give a shit where you came from. We're all the same, you know. Just because your skin is different doesn't mean you're an inferior person. I'm not like that, man."

Ratso's eyes shone with pleasure. "You are an honorable man," he said. "I will be your friend for life. I have never heard words so eloquent."

Townsend glanced at his watch. The nurse he had hired still had another hour left on her shift. "Tell you what. Why don't we get ourselves some breakfast?"

"Of course," Ratso responded, honored that the man wanted to eat with him. No one but Grant had ever asked to share a meal with him. Most of the time he passed the night without food, cooking his meal when he got to his apartment.

Townsend cracked open his wallet, finding only a few bills inside. "You got any money on you?"

Ratso smiled, depressing the gas pedal. "I will pay. I have money. For a friend, I always have money."

Rachel stepped up to the reception desk at the DA's office Wednesday morning at 9:33. She had not brought a change of clothing when she had left the house the night before. By the time she'd finally checked into the Marriot around midnight, she'd been so drained, she had passed out on the bed without removing her clothes. Her shirt was wrinkled, and her jeans felt as if they had shrunk on her body after being soaked by the rain. Her hair had dried into a mass of tangled red curls. "I need to talk to someone," she said.

"Oh, my God," the receptionist exclaimed, "you're Rachel Simmons." She glanced down at her desk. "I was just reading about you in the newspaper. Isn't that a coincidence?"

"Do you know which DA has been assigned to my case?" she asked politely. "I'm here to turn myself in."

The woman picked up the newspaper and placed it on the top counter. Rachel saw her picture on one side of the front page. Smaller photos of Cummings, Miller, Townsend, and Ratso were encased in a black-bordered box on the opposite side, under the caption, "*COPS IN THE HOT SEAT.*"

"Would you sign your name across your picture?" the woman asked, looking on her phone list for Blake Reynolds's extension.

"I'd rather not," Rachel said.

"Why?" the woman asked. "Now that you're famous, your autograph might be valuable."

Rather than make a scene, Rachel wrote her name across her picture. The woman thanked her, then buzzed her in through the security doors. "Blake Reynolds will see you. His office is the third door on the left," she told her. "I'll ring him and tell him you're here."

People stared at her as she passed through the open area where the clerical staff worked. She bowed her head, her face burning in shame. Before this was over, the world would know everything there was to know about her. Her past, her mother's occupation, the fact that she had once been kidnapped and held hostage, the things Grant had done to her. Once you passed into the public domain, people thought they had a right to ask you for your autograph, invade your privacy, hound you relentlessly. She ducked into Blake Reynolds's office. He was speaking on the phone. When he saw her, he quickly hung up. Dennis Colter was slouched in a chair facing his desk. Seeing Rachel in the doorway, he craned his neck around to look at her.

"Didn't we go to high school together?" Colter said, smiling.

"Yes," Rachel answered, focusing on Blake Reynolds as if no one else was in the room.

"You're the girl who was kidnapped, right?"

Rachel ignored him, speaking to Reynolds instead. "I came to turn myself in."

"I spoke to Mike Atwater early this morning," Reynolds said, motioning for Rachel to have a seat in the remaining chair. "He's been looking for you. Something has turned up regarding Grant Cummings that might have an impact on your case."

"Like what?" Rachel asked, although her voice held no excitement.

"If you don't mind," Reynolds said to Colter. "I think it would be better if I spoke to Mrs. Simmons privately."

"But we're old friends," Colter said, eager to cash in on his acquaintance with Rachel now that she was front-page news. "Didn't I ask you to dance one time and you refused? I think it was the Valentine's dance at school. You had on a red dress with a bow in the back."

"I didn't go to dances," Rachel said. She had walked the halls of her high school unnoticed, afraid of her own shadow. Colter had been a football player, one of the most popular boys at the school. In the three years she had attended high school with him, he had never said one word to her. "I think you have me confused with someone else."

"No," Colter insisted, "I remember your red hair. I'm certain you attended that Valentine dance."

"That's enough, Dennis," Reynolds said, coming from behind his desk to shoo him out of his office. Turning back to Rachel, he said, "I'm sorry. This is so big now that everyone wants to get in on the action."

Celebrity lawyers. Famous criminals. Rachel shook her head, sucking a portion of her lower lip into her mouth. What was happening was ugly and tawdry. Why would people want to become involved? "What were you talking about earlier? You mentioned a new development."

"Oh, yes," Reynolds said, returning to his desk and putting on his reading glasses. The young attorney had a baby face—small nose, large eyes, smooth skin. The heavy frames on his glasses made him look older and more professional. "Your sister received a call this morning from a woman by the name of Sherry Lafayette," he said. "We have someone on the way to her house right now to take a statement from her. She says Grant Cummings raped and sodomized her last year around Christmas."

Rachel leaned forward, her heart pounding in her chest. "I knew he was a rapist."

"Well, it looks as if you were right," Reynolds said, making a little clicking noise with his mouth. "I'm also looking into the other incidents you mentioned, the attacks that occurred in the orange grove near your house. One of the victims committed suicide last year. The other woman moved out of the state. We're trying to track her down."

Rachel felt a heavy sensation in her chest. "You mean, this Sherry Lafayette is not one of the women from the orange grove?" Her mind was spinning. How many women had Grant brutalized?

"No," he said. "Cummings attacked her while he was on duty, after she accidentally set off a holdup alarm in her father's toy store."

"He threatened to kill her if she reported it, right?"

"More or less," Reynolds said, pressing his glasses into his nose. "We spoke to the family of the woman who killed herself. They say she never got over the attack. She became agoraphobic, refusing to leave the house. She gassed herself by letting her car run in a closed garage."

Rachel gasped. A few moments later, she said, "How will this affect me?"

"The status of your case might be better discussed with a defense attorney," he told her. "All I can tell you legally is it certainly can't make matters worse for you. Sherry Lafayette coming forward is a huge break. It confirms everything you've said about Grant Cummings, about the threats and intimidation he made to you following the assault."

"It doesn't clear me, though," she said.

"I can't give you legal advice," Reynolds said, doodling on a yellow notepad. "But I will tell you one thing to give you at least some insight into your present legal dilemma. With what we've learned this morning, you're moving closer to vindication."

Rachel's eyes expanded. "Does that mean you're not going to arrest me?"

"No," he said, dropping his pen. "If the case is going to go down, Bill Ringwald wants it to go down in the courtroom. When we get to the preliminary hearing stage in a few weeks, the judge could put a stop to it then. He could refuse to hold you to answer in superior court." Rachel's face fell at this news, and Reynolds moved on brusquely. "Who's going to represent you?"

"Carrie Linderhurst," she said. "She's my sister."

"You need a competent defense attorney," Reynolds said. "I know most of the attorneys who practice criminal law around here. I've never heard of your sister."

"Her practice is in San Francisco," Rachel said, deciding it made no sense to tell him that Carrie didn't specialize in criminal law.

Reynolds opened his drawer and pulled out a tape recorder. "I have to advise you of your Miranda rights," he said, reading them off a plastic card. When he was finished, he added, "You really should have your attorney present during the questioning. Once I record your statement, I'll have to take you down to the court and have you arraigned. Is your sister here or is she still in San Francisco?"

"Carrie's supposed to meet me here at ten," Rachel said. "She's been staying at my house." She was afraid of being taken into custody. Correctional officers were just like cops. Everyone in uniform knew the jail was *their* domain, that once the metal bars slammed shut, terrible, despicable things could happen.

"Then I suggest you call and find out where she is," the attorney said, glancing at his watch. "It's 10:15."

"May I use your phone?"

"Be my guest," Reynolds said, pushing it to the corner of his desk. He tested the tape recorder and discovered the batteries were weak. Walking toward the outer office where the supplies were kept, he glanced back from the doorway. "Oh," he said, "I almost forgot. I need to get a statement from your daughter. Ask your sister to bring her along."

Rachel's hand flew to her chest. "Tracy's in school."

"Well," he said, "I guess your sister will have to drop by the school and pick her up. I'm sorry, but we really need to take care of this today. Since Atwater says your daughter can substantiate your whereabouts at the time of the shooting, her testimony will play a major role in this case."

Rachel's fingers trembled as she dialed the number to her house. This was the moment she had dreaded. When Carrie didn't answer, she sighed in relief. "There's no answer," she told him. "My sister must have already left."

"Give me the name of your daughter's school," Reynolds said. "I'll send one of our people over to pick her up."

"You don't have to speak to Tracy," Rachel said. She would tell him the truth. She would rather go to prison than allow her daughter to perjure herself.

"What's this about Tracy?" Carrie said, stepping up behind the attorney in the doorway. She was dressed in a tailored off-white suit, nude hose, and high heels, and her hair had been freshly washed and styled. Her makeup was impeccable, and large gold earrings were clipped to her ears. "I'm Carrie Linderhurst, Rachel's sister," she said, extending her hand. "You must be Blake Reynolds. Mike Atwater says you're an up-and-coming star around here. I've been in his office discussing the rapes."

The young attorney's eyes flashed with pride. "Coming from Mike, that's quite a compliment," he said, shaking her hand. "As to the kid, we need to talk to her right away. I was going to have you bring her down with you, but since you're already here, I'll arrange for someone from our office to pick her up at school."

"Not today," Carrie said, looking over at Rachel. "Tracy has exams all day. If you yank her out of school, the poor kid may fail her courses."

"Fine," Reynolds said reluctantly, "but we'll have to talk to the girl in the next day or so."

"No problem," Carrie said, taking a seat next to Rachel. As soon as the attorney walked into the outer office, she leaned closer to her sister. "I know how strongly you feel about Tracy testifying, Rachel," she whispered. "If we can positively link Grant Cummings to these rapes, we may be able to clear you without using her. We'll stall as long as we can. If the state puts together a strong case, though, I'll have no alternative but to call Tracy as a witness. Since Grant claims he saw you standing behind him in the men's locker room at the time of the shooting, proving he was involved in these crimes will make his testimony less credible."

"But the police say they have another eyewitness in addition to Grant," Rachel said.

Reynolds walked back into the room, and Carrie stopped speaking. Rachel watched as he inserted the new batteries in the tape recorder, then pressed the record button. She focused on the blinking red light, perspiration dampening her armpits. Other than the candy bar she had stolen as a child, Rachel had never broken the law, yet she was about to be marched into a courtroom as a criminal defendant.

The nightmare was now a reality.

chapter

THIRTY-ONE

When Rachel followed Carrie into the courtroom at three o'clock that afternoon, she saw Mike Atwater sitting in the front row. As soon as he saw Carrie, he stood and smiled, drinking her in with his eyes. Rachel regretted her T-shirt and jeans. Next to her sister's polished perfection, she felt disheveled and shabby.

"Did you tell Rachel the news about Sherry Lafayette?" Atwater asked.

"Yes," Carrie said.

"It's a major break," the attorney said with enthusiasm. "We found Alice Rooney less than an hour ago. She's the other woman who was raped in the orange grove. She's living in Colorado Springs now. I have an investigator on the way to the airport as we speak. He's going to show her a photo lineup containing Grant Cummings. If she identifies him as her attacker, we might be able to clear you and get your job back."

Her job? Rachel was standing in a courtroom about to be arraigned for attempted murder, and Atwater was foolish enough to think she might be reinstated as a police officer. She didn't want to develop false hopes. Joe had taught her to be optimistic, holding on to the belief that everything in life happened for a reason, that bad experiences could be turned into something positive. Had she not accepted this premise, she could never have lived through his death. If Grant had done nothing else to her that night in the orange grove, he had made her look at life more realistically. As Tracy had always told her, bad things were simply bad. There was no underlying good in Grant Cummings, nor in any of the other officers who had wronged her. "Even if they agree to take me back," she said, "I don't know if I could ever work there again." She looked over her shoulder, seeing Blake Reynolds take his seat at the prosecution table.

"Of course you can," Carrie said. "That's what this is all about. We're going to undo all the wrong these people have done to you. You shouldn't have to sacrifice anything. You're a victim in this ordeal." She turned her attention to Atwater. "Take off your jacket."

"Why?" he said, taken aback.

"Because I want Rachel to wear it."

Atwater scowled, but he did as she asked, slipping off his gray Armani jacket and handing it to Rachel. "It doesn't matter how I look," Rachel said. "This isn't a beauty contest, Carrie."

"You want to make a good impression, don't you?" her sister said. "Put it on, Rachel. You'll be sitting down. No one will know you have jeans on. Right now, you look like a criminal."

After Rachel slid her arms into Atwater's jacket, she felt small and vulnerable. She took her seat at the counsel table beside her sister. Atwater was almost a foot taller, and the jacket engulfed her, making her feel like a child in an adult's clothing.

"All rise," the bailiff said. "Division Twenty-two of the Ventura County Municipal Court is now in session, Judge Robert Sanders presiding."

The judge took his seat on the bench in a swirl of black robes. With salt-and-pepper hair and eyes the color of slate, Sanders was a diminutive man in his mid sixties with a scratchy voice and a stern demeanor. "*The State of California versus Rachel Simmons,*" he said, calling the case. "Are the parties all present and accounted for?"

"Yes, Your Honor," Blake Reynolds said, standing stiffly.

"Carrie Linderhurst for the defense," Carrie said, organizing her hastily prepared notes on the table. After Rachel had given Reynolds her statement, her sister had asked the district attorney to postpone the arraignment until later in the afternoon. Reynolds had been gracious enough to let Carrie use the agency's law library to prepare. At this stage, things were not that complex, but as the case moved along, she would have to conduct extensive research to familiarize herself with criminal procedure.

"All right, then," Judge Sanders said, slipping on his bifocals. "In case number A358965, the defendant has been charged with the crime of attempted murder, as set forth in section 664(a) and section 187 of the California Penal Code. How do you plead?"

"Not guilty, Your Honor," Carrie said.

"Fine," the judge said. "This matter is set for preliminary hearing two weeks from today. Does April fifth fit your schedules, counselors?"

Reynolds and Carrie said the date was fine.

"As to the matter of bail," he continued, "would the People like to present their position?"

"The defendant voluntarily surrendered," Reynolds said, cutting his eyes to Rachel. "The People feel bail in the amount of fifty thousand dollars is appropriate."

Carrie pushed herself to her feet. "Your Honor, my client has been through hell. I'm not sure you are aware of all the facts in this case, but the man she is charged with shooting brutally battered her." She turned around and whispered something to Atwater, waiting while he removed an envelope from his shirt pocket and handed it to her. "May I approach the bench?"

Judge Sanders nodded.

Carrie walked up and handed the judge the contents of the envelope: the photographs taken of Rachel at the hospital. "Mr. Reynolds, have you seen these photographs?" the judge asked, scowling as he stared at the images.

"Yes, Your Honor," he said. "We're aware Mrs. Simmons was battered, but at present we have no proof that the victim in this matter perpetrated this assault. Not only that, but the beating appears to be intrinsically linked to the shooting. After Mrs. Simmons was allegedly battered by Officer Cummings, evidence shows she went to the police department and shot him in retaliation. For these reasons, I don't believe the court can use the defendant's injuries as a reason to negate setting an appropriate amount of bail in this matter."

"Miss Linderhurst," Judge Sanders said.

"My client has no previous criminal record, has maintained a residence in Oak Grove for many years, and has two minor children in the home," Carrie said, her speech clipped and articulate. "This is a complex situation, Your Honor. My client is a young mother, a widow to be precise, a person who has dedicated her life to serving her community. She has attempted to do the right thing, both morally and legally, by bringing to light serious misconduct by her fellow officers. Because of her actions, she has placed herself in great danger. Her fellow police officers abandoned her, left her trapped in a room with a murderer and a partially decapitated corpse. These same officers entered her home illegally and set up unsanctioned surveillance equipment. Mr. Cummings has made specific threats to harm her daughter. As we already pointed out, this man violently assaulted my client. Should the court now assault my client by locking her up and restricting her from seeing her children?" She stopped and shrugged. "There's no need for bail in this case, Your Honor. If Mrs. Simmons had wanted to flee, she would have already done so. Instead, she came in of her own volition. We respectfully ask the court to release the defendant on her own recognizance."

"No bail in an attempted murder case?" Judge Sanders said, shifting in his seat. Captain Madison had already contacted him, insisting that he hold Rachel without bail. He had been deluged by phone calls from the press, asking if the court proceedings would be televised. Under this kind of public scrutiny, he could not afford to make a mistake. "These charges are too serious for me to release your client on her own recognizance. If she's in the kind of danger you seem to suggest, Miss Linderhurst, perhaps your client will be safer in jail than she would be if I released her into the community."

Carrie's face flushed with anger. "That's ridiculous," she blurted out without thinking.

"Are you addressing the court?" Sanders said, giving her a scalding look.

"No, Your Honor," Carrie said, slouching down in her seat. "Forgive me, I spoke out of turn." Something else came to mind, and she straightened up. "May we schedule an evidentiary hearing? I'd like to file a discovery motion."

Sanders picked up his pen and scribbled something in the file, then began speaking. "Bail will be set at fifty thousand dollars. Until the defendant posts bail, she will be remanded into the custody of the Ventura County Sheriff's Department. As to the evidentiary hearing, we'll schedule it for ten o'clock Friday morning if Mr. Reynolds has no objection."

"That will be fine," the district attorney said, already packing his briefcase to leave.

"This hearing is adjourned." The judge tapped his gavel, then disappeared from the bench.

Rachel had a strange, empty feeling in the pit of her stomach. The bailiff waited while she removed Atwater's jacket and walked over to return it to him. "I think you need to hire another attorney, Rachel," he whispered. Carrie was still looking over some paperwork at the counsel table. "Not only is your sister not familiar with criminal procedure, but she doesn't know the idiosyncrasies of the players. Judge Sanders is a prickly old goat. If she speaks out of turn again, he'll slap her with contempt charges."

"Carrie will be fine," Rachel said.

As soon as the bailiff handcuffed her, Carrie stood, a downcast look on her face. "It's too late to get the money transferred for your bail," she said. "I'm sorry, Rachel. I thought I could get them to release you on your own recognizance. I should be able to get the money together by tomorrow or the next day. Just hang tight and don't panic. I promise I'll get you out of jail." Carrie was beginning to have second thoughts about representing her sister. Seeing Rachel in handcuffs made her feel as if she had already failed. If her sister suffered a conviction, the guilt might be overwhelming. She watched as the bailiff led Rachel out of the courtroom, then picked up her paperwork to leave.

"I'll help any way I can," Atwater said, walking down the aisle beside her. Both were tall, and they easily fell into step together.

"Great," Carrie said. "Can you stop by the house tonight around eight? If you've got a spare copy of the California Penal Code and a volume outlining standards on criminal procedure, I'd appreciate it if you would bring them. I'm going to have to hit the books and see if I can bring myself up to snuff. I don't have a whole lot of time, so I need to began preparing immediately."

"Who's watching Rachel's kids?" Atwater asked, inhaling a whiff of her cologne. It was fresh, lemony, and feminine.

"Joe's at the neighbor's house," Carrie said, pushing open the doors to the courtroom. "I flew down here to look after the kids. Now it looks as if I've got a trial on my hands. I can't be Mary Poppins and F. Lee Bailey at the same time. Tracy's waiting at school for me to pick her up. I promised I'd be there by three-thirty, and it's almost four now."

"Why don't I take you to dinner later this evening?" he asked, his eyes roaming up and down her slender frame.

"I don't need food," Carrie answered. "What I need right now is some peace of mind. My sister's being framed for a crime she didn't commit." She stopped walking and rubbed her forearms, experiencing a sudden chill. "Have you ever had a feeling that something terrible was about to happen? This thing with Rachel and the police department is giving me the creeps. Instead of trying to expose all this stuff, why didn't she simply turn in her resignation and walk away?"

"I guess this is important to her," Atwater said, taking off down the corridor at a brisk pace.

Carrie stopped at a flower shop to purchase a dozen roses. When she arrived at Tracy's school, she saw the girl sitting by herself on the steps. She opened the door to Rachel's Pathfinder and got out, holding the flowers behind her back. "What happened?" she said. "Don't keep me in suspense here. Weren't you supposed to find out if you made cheerleader today?"

"I made it," Tracy said, smiling. "Sheila made it too."

"Congratulations," Carrie said, handing her the flowers.

Tracy sniffed the roses. "How did you know I would make it?"

"You're my niece," she said, pulling her into her arms. "You've got good genes."

Tracy climbed into the passenger seat as Carrie circled around to the other side of the car. "I may have to let it go," she said, staring at the bouquet in her lap.

"I don't understand," Carrie asked, tilting her head.

"How can I practice every day after school? I have to watch Joe so Mother can sleep." She handed Carrie a piece of paper. "Look at how much the uniforms cost."

"Everything will work out," Carrie said, glancing at the notice and then handing it back to her.

"Nothing ever works out," Tracy said, slumping in her seat. "The outfits cost five hundred dollars. Mother doesn't have that kind of money. I should have never tried out. Now I'll have to tell the coach to give my slot to one of the alternates."

Carrie felt a tug on her heart. The girl had suffered enough hardship. She thought of her own son and how uncomplicated his life had been. "Look," she said, "I've been thinking about making some changes. I'm burned out on San Francisco. It's no place for a single woman like me. What would you say to me moving down here?"

"Are you serious?" Tracy said, her eyes expanding. "That would be great. But what about your job and your friends?"

"I'll make new friends," Carrie said. "And affiliating with another firm shouldn't be a problem. If your mother and I split the rent, she should have enough money to put Joe in day care and pay off the rest of your father's hospital bills."

"We don't have enough room as it is," the girl said. "It won't work, Carrie."

"We'll make it work," Carrie told her, smiling. "Your mother's only renting right now. If we pool our resources, maybe we can buy a house large enough for all of us."

Tracy was entranced by the picture Carrie was painting, but she didn't want to get her hopes up only to be disappointed. "Why would you do this?"

"I've made a lot of mistakes in my life," Carrie answered. "Your mother wasn't much older than you when I left home. I abandoned her, Tracy. It wasn't right to leave her alone with our mother. I knew what was going on, how bad Mother's drinking problem had become. I only thought of myself." She cranked the ignition and pulled away from the curb. "Let me give you a piece of advice. You can never escape from a problem. You may think you've escaped, but until you confront it and do the right thing, that problem will always be lurking in the shadows."

Tracy leaned over and kissed her on the cheek. "I love you," she said. "I think it would be wonderful if you lived with us."

Because Rachel was a police officer, she was placed in a cell by herself in the protective custody wing of the jail. By the time the booking process was complete, it was past six and dinner had already been served. "I can see if I can get you a sandwich from the kitchen," the female jailer told her.

"It's all right," Rachel said, dropping down on a corner of the bare mattress. "I'm not hungry."

The Ventura County Jail had been erected in the early eighties. When it had opened for business, the new jail had been a model of sophisticated technology, one of the first correctional facilities in the

Unites States operated solely by computer. The regular cells were located in quads, opening up into a large room containing a television and several stainless steel tables. During the day, inmates in the quads were allowed to wander in and out of their individual cells and congregate in the activity room. Even though the men's section was showing wear and tear, the women's wing was still in excellent condition. It even had an aerobics room, and several times a week an instructor came in to teach classes.

Rachel collapsed on the thin mattress, pulling the coarse blanket over her body. She balled up the lumpy pillow, then placed it under her head, the plastic cover making a crunching sound. Curled up on her side, she inhaled the stagnant jailhouse air as she stared through the metal bars into the corridor.

Visiting hours started at eight o'clock. Not long after, Rachel was led to the common room and took a seat inside a small partition facing a wall of glass. She picked up the phone to speak to her daughter. "Did you come by yourself? Where's Carrie?"

"She's working on your case," Tracy said. "I got a ride down here with a friend."

"What friend?" Rachel asked, puzzled. "You keep talking about getting rides, Tracy, but you've never told me which one of your friends has a driver's license."

"I met a boy," she said timidly. "His name is Matt, and he's really nice. He's the person who gave me a ride home from Sheila's house that morning."

"How long have you known this boy?" Rachel asked, wondering why Tracy had never mentioned him before.

"About a month," Tracy told her. "I met him at the arcade by our house. He's not my boyfriend or anything."

"Have the police tried to talk to you again?"

"No," Tracy said. "But don't worry, Mom, I've taken care of everything." Matt was waiting outside in his car. She had promised to have sex with him after she concluded her visit with her mother. She wanted to make certain the boy would support her mother's alibi before she told the police he had given her a ride home the day of the shooting.

"You have to tell them the truth," her mother said. "Promise me you won't lie."

"Why?" Tracy said. "Carrie thought what I did was really smart. She said not many girls my age could think on their feet the way I did."

"I forbid you to lie," Rachel said. "You're only fourteen. Perjury is a serious crime. Please don't let Carrie talk you into doing this. If you do, you'll live with it the rest of your life."

"I'm doing it for you, Mom," she said. "If I don't tell them you were with me, they'll send you to prison."

"Forget the alibi," Rachel said. "As soon as you leave, I'm going to call Sergeant Miller and tell him the truth, that I was alone inside the house when Grant Cummings was shot. It's over, Tracy. There's nothing more to discuss."

Tracy shook her head in frustration. "Why did you have to go on TV and say all these things about the police department?" she said. "I see dope deals going down at my school all the time, but I don't go running straight to the principal. Everyone knows what happens when you snitch. If I snitched off a drug dealer, he'd probably come back and shoot me." She glared at her mother. "Is that what you want me to do, Mom? Isn't that the same as what you're doing? If I don't report things I know are wrong, does that make me a bad person?"

"Let me explain something," Rachel said. "If you decided you wanted to carry a gun for your own protection, the police could arrest you and charge you with a felony. Is that right?"

"I guess," she said.

"When you drive over the speed limit," Rachel continued, "can the police stop you and give you a ticket?"

"If I had a driver's license," Tracy said, having no idea where her mother was going.

Rachel pressed on. "Police officers have the right to handcuff you, take away your freedom, have you brought up on criminal charges. Don't you understand, Tracy? Along with the authority a police officer is given comes responsibility. And it's far greater than that of an average citizen." She sucked in another breath. "When a police officer breaks the law, or fails to perform his duties in the community, it has an enormous impact on society."

"I understand," Tracy said. "I know someone should speak out about what those police officers did. I just don't understand why that person has to be my mother."

Rachel decided to change the subject. "How's Joe?"

"He misses you," her daughter said. "He doesn't know where you went. I told him you were on a vacation. I don't know if he believes me or not. I'm not sure he knows what a vacation is since we've never gone on one."

Rachel overlooked the veiled barb. "What happened with the cheerleading tryouts?"

Tracy's face brightened. "I made it, Mom. But you haven't heard the best part. Carrie's going to move in with us. Friday morning after the court hearing, she's going to fly to San Francisco to get some of her stuff and put her apartment up for sale."

"You and Joe could stay with her in San Francisco," Rachel said, surprised at this new development. "Why would she leave her job?"

"Carrie's tired of living in San Francisco," Tracy told her. "She's going to get another job here. She says we can get a bigger house if we all live together. She doesn't want me to have to change schools now that I made cheerleader."

Rachel saw the look of excitement in her daughter's eyes. Placing a palm against the glass, she said, "I'm sorry for all the pain I've caused you. I've been thinking about Joe. You were right, honey. It wasn't fair for me to get pregnant when your father was dying. It was a selfish thing your father and I did. We didn't think about the future, that the responsibility of caring for Joe might fall on your shoulders. I wanted to give your father a son. I thought if we shared the joy of bringing a new life into the world, his death might seem less frightening."

At the mention of her father's death, Tracy's voice dropped to a whisper. "How could a baby have anything to do with Dad's death?"

"It's part of the cycle of life," Rachel told her. "You're born. You live. You die. We're terrified of death because it represents the unknown. Death is a natural process, even though it sometimes doesn't appear that way. In many ways, birth is similar to death. Maybe if we believed we were going on to a new life, we'd celebrate death in the same way we celebrate birth."

"I'd rather be born than die," Tracy said, bitterness sparking behind her eyes. "Besides, there wasn't anything natural about what happened to Dad. I was there, remember?"

"Everyone eventually dies," her mother said. "No one escapes, Tracy. The only difference is how long you have on earth, and what you manage to accomplish with the time you are given."

"Whatever," Tracy said, frowning.

Rachel realized she should have had this conversation with her daughter years ago. The buzzer sounded, signaling that visiting hours were over. A voice came out over the loudspeaker issuing the five minute warning, and Rachel panicked. Everything she had wanted to do as a mother was slipping away from her. She remembered the day Tracy had been born, holding her in her arms for the first time, all the promises she had made. How many of them had she broken? She had vowed that she would never disgrace her child, never hurt her, never abandon her. She would teach her daughter values, have long discussions with her, provide a role model she could emulate. Here she was sitting in jail, surrounded by criminals.

She had broken every vow.

Rachel thought of her own mother. Were they really that different? Had Frances set out on the road to motherhood with the same lofty aspirations? She remembered her mother taking them to church every Easter Sunday, buying them pretty clothes to wear. When she led her daughters into the church, people had whispered and stared. Frances had accepted their scorn because she wanted her daughters to have a normal life. Before the kidnapping, the house had been filled with music and laughter. She realized Carrie had been right. Her mother had not always been a monster.

Rachel saw the guard motioning to her. "I love you," she said. "I'm so proud that you made cheerleader. I'm going to come to every game. I promise, baby. Once we get through this, we'll know we can survive anything."

"I love you too," Tracy answered. As her mother stood to leave, she traced the outline of a heart on the glass.

"How did it go?" Matt asked when Tracy opened the passenger door to his Datsun.

"Fine," she said, getting in and fastening her seat belt. "Where are we going to do it? There's no one at my house right now, but my next-door neighbor might see us. The last thing I need right now is for my mother to find out. She told me she was going to call the police and tell them the truth about what time I got home, but I don't think she was serious."

Matt's eyes flashed with excitement. "There's an abandoned shack not far from my house. A few of my friends have gone there with their girlfriends. They say it's a little spooky, but we won't have to worry about anyone spying on us."

Tracy curled up by the window as Matt cranked the ignition and took off. When he pulled into a dark, wooded area and parked, she saw a rundown building about the size of a toolshed. The windows were boarded up, and the roof was made of tar paper. "Maybe we should just do it in the car," she said, fiddling with the buttons on her blouse. "There could be rats in that place."

Matt yanked his T-shirt over his head. "Anywhere is fine with me."

"I bet," Tracy said, giving him a harsh look. "You're going to do what you promised, right? If you go back on your word, I'll tell the cops you raped me."

"I won't go back on my word," he said, scooting over beside her.

"Did you bring a rubber?"

"Of course," Matt said, patting his jeans' pocket. He leaned over to kiss her. Instead of connecting with her mouth, his lips touched the end of her nose. "You've got a runny nose," he said, pulling back. "Do you have a cold?" A few moments later, he realized she was crying. "Damn," he said, slapping the steering wheel with his good hand, "I knew this was going to happen."

"It's okay," Tracy said, wiping her nose with the edge of her shirt. "It's not about your hand, Matt. I'm worried about my mother." She paused, knowing it was more than that. "I always said I wouldn't have sex until I got married. I guess that's silly, huh? Nobody waits until they're married anymore."

Matt pulled her into his arms, feeling how badly she was shaking. For a long time, he just held her. "It's not such a terrible thing to wait until you're married," he said, stroking her hair. "Who knows? Maybe we'll get married some day. My mom was only sixteen when she met my dad."

"Right," she said, looking up at him. "Once we have sex, you'll probably never see me again. I know how it works. Guys are real sweet until they get what they want, then they dump you and tell everyone you're a tramp."

"I have an idea," Matt said, smiling. "Give me a kiss and we're even. But it has to be a really big kiss, not just a little peck on the lips. We're talking tongues and everything."

"And you'll still tell the police you left me at the house before seven?" she asked, straightening up in her seat.

"Yep," he said.

"You promise?"

"Scout's honor," he said. "Do we have a deal?"

"Kiss ahead," Tracy said, closing her eyes and giggling.

A wine bottle sat on Rachel's dining room table, along with two half-empty glasses and several open law books. Mike Atwater was reading through the lab report on evidence found in the police locker room while Carrie finished preparing her discovery motion. It was after ten, and Tracy and Joe were in bed.

"Can I take a look at that report?" Carrie said, her leg brushing accidentally against Atwater's under the table. They both flinched, but when she looked up he was smiling.

"Not until you file your discovery motion," he told her, turning the report face down on the table. "If Blake Reynolds finds out I'm helping you, he'll run straight to Ringwald."

"Look," Carrie argued, "I'm going to get the report in the next few days anyway. Don't you want to help Rachel? What does it say?"

"Not much," Atwater said, stretching his arms over his head. "You're a lot like Rachel, you know."

"Oh, really?" Carrie said, taking a sip of her wine. "Come on, Mike, what does the report say?"

"I'm not going to let you read it," Atwater said, scratching the side of his face. "But there is one thing I find peculiar."

"Shoot," she said.

"The lab didn't find Rachel's fingerprints inside the locker room."

"Of course they didn't find her prints," Carrie said, scowling. "She was never inside the men's locker room. You don't believe she actually shot this man, do you?"

"No," Atwater said. "The evidence is pretty compelling, though."

"She didn't shoot him," Carrie said, her voice escalating. "I know my sister, Mike. She would never shoot a man in the back."

"Okay," he continued, placing his palms on the table. "There's something else I find intriguing. This man they call Ratso—"

"Frederick Ramone," Carrie said, tapping her pen against her teeth. "What about him?"

"His assigned locker is number 489, but the lab found his fingerprints inside locker 212."

"What does that mean?"

"Locker 212 is directly adjacent to Grant's locker. If you will recall, he was standing in front of his locker at the time he was shot."

"Ah," Carrie said, her eyes lighting up as she considered the ramifications of what he was saying. "Rachel accused Ramone of brutalizing one of the boys involved in the Majestic Theater incident. He was also one of the men on the beach. But why would Ramone shoot Grant Cummings? From what I understand, Cummings and this man were bosom buddies."

"I interviewed an officer this afternoon by the name of Chris Lowenberg," Atwater said. "He said Ramone was basically the whipping boy for the graveyard shift. Cummings was constantly belittling him."

Carrie's eyes roamed around the room. "Do you think Ramone could have shot Cummings so he could implicate Rachel?"

"Possibly," he said. "Fred Ramone is the only plausible suspect I can think of besides Jimmy Townsend. Townsend has a partial alibi, though. His wife and kids swear he arrived at his house only minutes after the shooting went down."

"What about Nick Miller?"

"That might work," Atwater said. "Miller claims he was in his office at the time of the shooting, but no one saw him there."

"What do we know about Ramone?"

"Not much," he said. "Don't worry, I'm a step ahead of you. After I left you this afternoon, I put in a call to Internal Affairs and asked them to check Ramone out."

"Good," Carrie said. In her exhaustion she rubbed her hands over her face. A few moments later, she leaned back in her chair. "Why doesn't your agency dump this stupid case against Rachel and concentrate on convicting these corrupt cops?"

"Hey," Atwater said, "I'm all for it. Even Ringwald would like to dismiss the charges against Rachel. As long as the PD continues to pressure us, however, we don't have a choice. A crime was committed, and there appears to be ample evidence that Rachel committed it. Of course," he said, a sly look on his face, "I think you can manage to discredit this eyewitness without a problem. The first thing I'd ask him is why his prints were found in the wrong locker."

Carrie wanted him to clarify his statement, but she knew to remain silent. The attorney had just leaked important information. If Fred Ramone was the state's star witness, as Atwater had just implied, then he was the person who had reported seeing Rachel with the gun in her hand inside the men's locker room. Because Ramone had been implicated in the attempted rape at the beach, Carrie knew his testimony would be tainted. If she pressed hard enough, she might be able to impeach this man and by doing so, create reasonable doubt in the eyes of the jury. "Could this locker have been assigned to Ramone at an earlier date?"

"Not according to the information the police department provided," Atwater told her. "Locker 212 hasn't been used in almost a year. Since the recent budget cutbacks, the department has been downsizing."

"Hot damn," Carrie exclaimed. "Where exactly did the lab lift the prints from? Were they on the door itself or inside the locker?"

"Inside the locker," Atwater said, standing to leave. "Two full sets were lifted from the right interior walls."

"How big are these lockers?"

"They're narrow, but they measure close to six feet in height."

"How big is Ramone?"

"You ask a lot of questions," Atwater said, chuckling. He liked this woman. They spoke the same language. "At the time of his last physical, Frederick Ramone measured five-eleven and weighed in at one hundred and fifty-eight pounds."

"I see," Carrie said, standing to walk him to the door. "I understand Jimmy Townsend is a large man."

"That's an understatement," he said. "I don't think Townsend could fit one leg inside that locker, let alone his whole body. Nick Miller is not a small man either. He may not be as big as Townsend, but his shoulders are extremely broad."

"And Ramone's shoulders?"

"Narrow enough to fit inside a locker," Atwater said, winking as he stepped through the doorway and left.

chapter

THIRTY-TWO

"It's over, Townsend."

When Jimmy Townsend reported for duty Thursday night, Captain Madison was waiting by his locker. Townsend was already dressed in his uniform, having worn it from home. He opened his locker to retrieve his nightstick, but Madison banged the metal door shut with his fist.

Townsend decided to deny everything and remain cool. "What's over? Are you talking about the Lakers? Shit, I thought they were playing good this year."

Madison leered at him, his lips curling back to expose his gum line. "You broke into Rachel Simmons's home, pal. You planted surveillance equipment. That's illegal wiretapping, along with breaking and entry. Internal Affairs has asked for your resignation."

"Fuck Internal Affairs," Townsend said. "I'm not resigning. I didn't do anything wrong. I've never been inside that woman's house in my life. I'm not even sure where she lives."

"The crime lab lifted your fingerprints from her door," Madison growled. "Cut the bullshit, Townsend. We've got you cold. The DA's preparing charges against you."

"It was a setup," Townsend said, his facial muscles jumping. "This whole thing has been nothing but one crazy lie after the other. You have to believe me. I didn't do anything to Rachel Simmons. Before she shot Grant, Rachel and I were friends."

"Here," Madison said, shoving a paper into Townsend's hand. "Hand over your badge and gun. I don't have time to stand here and listen to this crap."

Jimmy Townsend read through the termination order with growing panic. He'd been a cop for over ten years. Where was he going to work? How could he support his wife and kids? Crushing the paper in his fist, he pulled out his gun and slapped it into Madison's open palm. Yanking his badge off his chest, he tossed it in the air. It struck the linoleum floor with a metallic ping.

"I'd suggest you get yourself a good attorney," Madison said. "You're going to need one."

"The police association will provide me with an attorney, right?" Townsend could see the legal fees adding up in his mind.

Captain Madison ignored him, bending down to scoop Townsend's badge off the floor as he made his way out of the locker room.

Once Jimmy Townsend and Captain Madison had left, Ratso stepped out from behind the row of lockers. He was in the clear. If the brass had intended to fire him, they would have already done so by now. Besides, he told himself, what had he done? He had poured sand down Rachel's jeans, but no one except Grant and the other men at the watch party could possibly know that. If Internal Affairs questioned the other officers, he was certain they would cover for him. It was one of the things he liked about police work. In many ways, the department was like an extended family. His parents had died many years ago. He had been sixteen at the time, and he and his sisters had been forced to live on the streets in their home town of Peshawar. Realizing they would perish if he didn't take action, Ratso had stowed away on a tanker to the United States a few months before his seventeenth birthday.

But the United States was not the land of opportunity people thought it was. Foreigners were treated with suspicion, delegated to the most menial tasks. Without specific job skills or proper work papers, Ratso had to work as a laborer for disgustingly low pay. He had picked avocados for five years in the blazing sun alongside illegal immigrants from Mexico, ending each day with an aching back and barely enough money to feed himself, let alone send home to his sisters in Pakistan.

When he had responded to an ad in the newspaper for a phony birth certificate, it had provided him with his first real chance to get ahead. Not only did he get a birth certificate, but for an extra thousand dollars, he was told, he could receive a complete new identity. Using the birth certificate to secure a job in a mini-mart, he had saved assiduously until he had enough money to purchase his new identity. The phony documents had worked perfectly. No one knew he was in the country illegally, that he had never become a citizen. The police department had hired him during an affirmative action campaign, believing he was Hispanic, as his documents showed.

Chris Lowenberg stuck his head in the locker room. "Captain Madison is looking for you," he said. "He's out in the squad room."

"What does he want?" Ratso asked.

"I have no idea, but heads are rolling around here. He just fired Jimmy Townsend. I saw him on his way out. Poor bastard. At least our watch is still intact. You guys don't even have a sergeant now that Miller has been suspended."

Ratso remained in the locker room after Lowenberg left. Captain Madison found him there an hour later, crouched in a corner. When they told him they were terminating his employment, Ratso broke down and cried.

"But I saved Grant's life," he protested. "How can you fire me?"

Madison looked down at him, wondering how the recruiters had ever hired such a man. Fred Ramone was not qualified to carry a badge and gun. Any fool could tell that. "Based on Rachel's statement, the DA may bring charges against you for bashing that kid's head against the pavement during the riot at Majestic Theater," he said. "But that's only half of your problems, pal. Internal Affairs has some questions to ask you about the drug money that disappeared from Maple Avenue."

Ratso stopped sobbing. How could he get the money out of the country now? His plan had been to sit on the cash until his scheduled vacation the following month, then smuggle it into Pakistan in his luggage. If IA filed criminal charges against him, though, he would not be able to use his fictitious documents to get a U.S. passport. "Did Rachel say I took the money? I don't understand."

"You don't have to understand," the captain said. "All you have to do is hand in your equipment, then get the hell out of my police station."

"Can't I come back?" Ratso pleaded, pulling his knees to his chest. "Rachel may take back the things she said about me. If she does, won't the department reinstate me?"

"Not in this lifetime," Madison snapped. Tired of wasting time, he reached down and snatched his gun out of the holster, then plucked his badge off his chest. "You've got thirty minutes, Ramone. Start cleaning out your locker. If you're here when I come back, I'm going to mop the floor with you."

Jimmy Townsend stopped at a pay phone once he had left the station. Calling Grant's room, he asked Carol Hitchcock to meet him in the parking lot of Presbyterian Hospital in an hour. He left the phone booth and returned to his Jeep Cherokee carrying a brown grocery sack. Plunging his hands inside, he pulled out a Twinkie and shoved it into his mouth. Since the problems with Rachel had developed, he had packed on another ten pounds. His uniform shirt was straining, and two buttons had popped off in the past week. Before he had come to work that evening, his wife had replaced the thread holding the buttons in place with elastic.

He slouched down in the seat and glanced around the parking lot. He only binged when no one was around. People became disgusted when they saw an overweight person eating. His weight problem had started as a child. Shoving a Snickers bar into his mouth, he remembered the kids heckling him, calling him fatty and Porky Pig. He had shown them, though. He had become a cop.

He ripped into a bag of potato chips, remembering the day he had arrested Freddy Newman, an asshole lowlife who had tormented him during his childhood. The look on Newman's face when he snapped on the handcuffs had been priceless.

What would Newman say now? And worse, what about his father?

Jimmy Townsend had lived in Oak Grove almost his entire life. When his parents had seen the newspaper article listing him as one of the officers caught up in the corruption scandal, his mother had almost had a heart attack. Townsend had called his father before coming to work, and the man had refused to speak to him.

He shoved a handful of chips into his mouth. Reaching his hand into the sack, he popped the lid on a soda and guzzled it down. Wrappers and food particles were scattered all over the interior of the car. He tossed the empty soda can into the back seat.

When had the nightmare started? He had been riding shotgun with Grant Cummings the previous year. It had been slow that night, and Grant was bored. Spotting an old rusted Plymouth crawling down the street, Grant had turned to him and smiled. "We got us some warrants up ahead, Jimmy boy. Now's the time to get those arrest stats up."

"How do you know they've got warrants?"

"Look at that piece-of-shit car," Grant told him. "People who drive old rattletraps like that always have warrants for something. You know, expired registration, bald tires, faulty emissions, parking tickets. If they can't afford a better car, they can't afford to pay their fines."

"We don't have cause to stop him," Townsend said. "The car's not weaving. The plate isn't expired. The tires look like they have plenty of tread. He may have warrants up the kazoo, Grant, but we can't pop him if we can't stop him."

Grant gunned the engine on the police car and rammed the back of the slow-moving vehicle, shattering both of the taillights. "No taillights," he snickered. "Guess we'll have to give this jerk a citation. Then we'll run him through the computer and see if we hit the jackpot."

A small Hispanic male was in the driver's seat. He appeared to be in his early thirties. As soon as he opened the door to exit the car, Grant seized him by the arm and tossed him to the pavement. "What are you doing in this neighborhood at this hour?" he shouted, kicking the prostrate man with the tip of his boot. "This ain't no beaner town, buddy."

The man groaned, but he knew better than to move. He was face down on the asphalt, his hands positioned on the back of his head.

"Where's your fucking license?" Grant yelled. "Did you think you could drive over here and rob someone? You got a shooter on you?"

The man sat up, reaching into his pocket for his wallet. Townsend thought he was going for a gun. It all happened in a matter of seconds. He whipped out his gun and began firing, the bullets entering the man's leg and hip. His body jumped a few feet off the ground as the bullets seared into his flesh. Every time he moved, Townsend squeezed off another round.

"That's enough," Grant said, grabbing Townsend's arm. "You don't want to kill the bastard."

The man was unconscious, his clothing soaked in blood. They searched him, but there was no gun. "What are we going to do?" Townsend was frantic. He had overreacted, shot an unarmed man. Grant pulled a small revolver out of his boot and wiped it down with a handkerchief. Holding the gun inside the handkerchief, he pressed it into the man's right hand, then watched as it tumbled to the pavement. "Shit, Jimmy," he said, "you're a hero. I'll bet you'll get a commendation for shooting this scumbag. Now go call an ambulance before the guy croaks on us."

Jimmy Townsend surfaced from the past. A woman was staring through the front window of the Jeep, watching as he shoveled a chocolate chip cookie into his mouth. He rolled down his window and stuck his head out. "What are you looking at?" he shouted, causing the woman to back away. The front of his uniform was covered with crumbs. The cream filling from the Twinkies was smeared across his cheeks. His stomach was so bloated, he felt as if he couldn't breathe. Groaning, he undid his belt and opened his pants.

The man he had shot was Luis Mendoza, a thirty-year-old orderly employed at a nursing home in Simi Valley. Mendoza had never been arrested before, nor did the computer turn up any outstanding warrants. He had seven children. Mendoza was presently in prison, serving a five-year sentence for assaulting a police officer and carrying a concealed weapon.

With the illegal wiretapping and breaking and entering charges hanging over his head, Jimmy Townsend had to believe that Internal Affairs would start looking into his past arrests. The officers assigned to IA were sadistic bastards who loved to dig up dirt. Would they find out the truth about Mendoza? There were other discrepancies, but Mendoza was his greatest fear. The man had done absolutely nothing. When Grant had decided to stop him, he had not even been exceeding the speed limit.

Carol Hitchcock climbed into the passenger seat of Townsend's Jeep Cherokee at 11:46. Prior to meeting her, he had stopped at a trash can and tossed out all the food wrappers and garbage. He was still too bloated to close his pants. It was dark inside the car, though, and Carol didn't notice. "Why did you want to see me? Grant needs me now, Jimmy. Why couldn't we talk inside the hospital?"

"They fired me," he said. "They're probably going to fire you, too. Anyone who had anything to do with Grant is history, Carol."

"That's insane," Carol said, her head jerking to one side. "They can't fire me."

"I thought the same thing," Townsend told her. "You're wrong. Miller said the chief is trying to save his own neck. If he cleans house, terminates all the people Rachel implicated, the City Council might not ask for his resignation."

Carol took this news in silence. She was preoccupied with her lover's condition. "You know what they did to Grant today?" she said. "They drilled holes in his head, then put him in this awful contraption that looks like a halo. They're afraid if he moves his neck, more damage will be done to his spinal cord."

Townsend tried to look sympathetic. "How is he taking it?"

"He's in excruciating pain," she said, her face contorting. "It's pathetic, Jimmy. He's like a child. He cries all the time. He rants and raves about Rachel. He panics every time I leave the room, even if it's only for a few minutes."

"They're going to send me to jail," Townsend said, gripping the steering wheel. "They found my fingerprints inside Rachel's house. She must have discovered the monitoring devices. Grant wanted to scare her, make her think we were listening in on her calls." He was almost talking to himself. "I don't even think I wired the damn things right. It was more like a prank than anything. We never intended to actually monitor her phone."

Carol remembered the things Rachel had said in the parking lot the other night. "Bugs. That's what Rachel was trying to tell me. You bugged her house, Jimmy? Please, tell me I'm not hearing this."

"It wasn't my idea. Grant told me he wanted to trick Rachel into believing we were monitoring her phone calls," he said. "I stole some surveillance equipment from the storage room, then set it up inside her house. This was during the time Grant supposedly beat her in the orange grove. They can charge me with wiretapping and breaking and entering. I'm dead, Carol. If they send me to prison, one of the people I've put away will kill me."

Carol was stunned. Even though she had broken out the window at the hardware store, the things Townsend had done were far worse.

"Didn't you realize how serious something like that was? Why did you agree to do it?"

"Grant blackmailed me," Townsend said. His head dropped to his chest, his chin engulfed in rolls of fat. "He said he would tell them I drugged Rachel's beer at the beach. When we left that day, Grant took the empty beer can Rachel had been drinking from with him. He said it was to protect us, but I found out the truth later. If I didn't do what he said, Grant threatened to turn the beer can over to the crime lab, knowing they would be able to find traces of Valium in it along with my fingerprints."

"What Rachel said really happened?" Carol cried, seizing Townsend's arm. "Everyone told me it was a lie, that Rachel made that story up. Grant said when he refused to respond to her advances, she wanted to get back at him by saying he tried to rape her."

"Hey," Townsend said, jerking his arm away, "what do you want from me?"

"Try the truth, asshole."

"Grant had the hots for her," Townsend said, staring out the front window. "He was determined to have her, one way or the other. All the guys knew it. There were other women too. Face it, Carol, Grant was a player. I don't think he could ever be faithful to one woman. You know how broads were always throwing themselves at him. I guess some of them were too good to turn down."

Carol slapped him hard across the face. Townsend balled up his fist and slugged her. They wrestled in the front seat of the car, sweating and cursing. "You bastard," she screamed, pinning him against the driver's door with her feet. "You lied to me. If I had known the truth about Grant, I wouldn't have broken the window at the hardware store."

Carol's legs were like steel rods. Her feet were pressing into the center of Townsend's abdomen. Food bubbled back in his throat, and he was certain he was about to vomit. "Let me go," he moaned. "I didn't do anything to you."

"You lied to me," she screamed. "Everyone lied to me."

A car pulled into the parking space beside them. They stopped fighting, and both turned to look at the driver. Carol got out of the car and slammed the door, stomping back toward the hospital.

* * *

Carol could hear Grant screaming from the end of the corridor. "What's going on?" she asked the officer guarding his room.

"I don't know," he said. "He's been calling for you."

"I bet he has," she said, flinging the door open.

Grant's head was encased in a metal halo. "Why did you leave me alone?"

"I was talking to Jimmy Townsend in the parking lot," Carol said, still panting in anger. "You lied to me. Rachel didn't make up what happened at the beach party because you refused her advances. You tried to rape her. And you didn't just rough her up a little the night I covered for you. I saw the bruises on her body. You beat the crap out of her."

"She's lying," Grant said. "The woman shot me."

"Oh, yeah," Carol shouted, grabbing onto the metal railing and shaking the bed. "We don't even know if that's true, now, do we? Jimmy told me you bugged Rachel's house. He said you drugged her beer on the beach. What else have you done? I'm probably going to lose my job because of you."

Grant's face locked in a mask of fury. He seized her arm, digging his fingernails into her flesh. "Look at me, bitch," he said, the words hissing out between his teeth. "I may be trapped in this bed, but I refuse to let you talk to me in that tone of voice. I'm in pain, damn it. Whatever they're giving me isn't working. Go find the nurse and tell them they'll have to give me something stronger."

"Shut the fuck up," Carol said, prying his hand off her arm and bending it backward until he cried out. "You don't want them to have to reattach the halo, do you? If you don't stop making trouble, they'll withdraw your pain medication altogether. I'll tell them the drugs are making you violent. Maybe they'll transfer you to the mental ward."

"I don't need this shit," Grant barked. "Get out of my room."

"Fine," she said, turning to walk away.

All of a sudden his hostility drained away. "No," he said, the fierceness disappearing from his voice. "Don't leave me, Carol. I don't want to be alone in this place. The nurses don't come when you call them. The food is disgusting. My head feels like someone hit me with a sledgehammer."

Carol had a smug smile on her face when she turned around. "You want me to stay?" she said. She could own him now. After putting up with his rages and tolerating his beatings for so long, she felt a measure of satisfaction. Even though he had yet to realize it, he had just fallen into the hands of the enemy. "What's it going to be, Grant?" she said. "If I stay, it will be on my terms."

"You're all I have, Carol." His eyes held a mixture of fear and pain.

"Okay," she said. "Now that we understand each other, I'll find the nurse and see what she can do about increasing your medication."

chapter

THIRTY-THREE

Carrie called Rachel from the pay phone outside the courtroom Friday morning. "I just got out of the evidentiary hearing," she told her. "The judge refused to give you ten percent privileges, so I'm going to have to fly to San Francisco to get the money to post your bail. Most of the money I have is tied up in investments, Rachel. I don't have fifty thousand in cash. I'll have to arrange a loan, and the bank won't let me do it over the phone."

"How long will you be gone?"

"I'll try to make it back tonight," she said. "If everything goes as planned, I should be able to get you out of jail by tomorrow morning."

"What about the kids?"

"Lucy's going to look after them."

"Tracy told me you were thinking of moving in with us," Rachel said. "That would be great, Carrie. But I'm sorry to be causing so many problems for you."

"Gotta go," Carrie said. "If I don't get to the airport, I'll miss my flight."

Bennie Underwood reported for work Friday night at ten o'clock. She had been a police dispatcher for over fifteen years. As soon as she turned fifty the following year, she planned to submit her retirement papers. She was a tiny woman with crinkly eyes and an easy smile, her frizzy hair the color of syrup. Since Bennie and her husband were childless, the men and women on the force had become like her kids. She had known most of the current crew from the day they had first put on a uniform. When Bennie's lyrical voice came out over the police radio, the officers in the field knew they were in competent hands.

Now that they dispatched via computer and 911 calls came directly into the switchboard, Bennie seldom talked to complainants over the phone as she had in the old days. After the 911 operators typed in the details of the call, the computer would automatically classify it as to priority and the appropriate unit numbers would pop up on Bennie's computer screen. The only calls that came directly into her headset were Class One calls—emergencies of a life-or-death nature.

The radio room was set up in four individual work stations, the long black console lined with rows of buttons and blinking lights. The four dispatchers were chatting at 11:05 when Bennie suddenly stiffened, a finger pressed against her earplug. Almost simultaneously, the details of the call flashed on their computer screens, and the other dispatchers turned and stared at Bennie. Tears were streaming down her face. "Please help me," she exclaimed. "I don't know what to call it."

Ted Harriman was driving down Front Street when he heard the emergency tone signal, followed by Bennie's familiar voice. The experienced dispatcher was perpetually calm, even in the face of chaos. What he heard tonight made the hairs on the back of his neck stand up. Only one thing caused Bennie to lose her cool. Harriman knew what she was going to say before she even finished the transmission. He had already flipped on his lights, and his finger rested on the toggle switch of his siren.

"Officer down," Bennie repeated, her voice cracking. "3980 Orrville Road. Ambulance and fire have already been dispatched."

Harriman didn't wait for her to assign units. They would all be responding, with or without permission. "4A is en route," he yelled into the microphone mounted into the visor. "My ETA is five minutes. I'm six blocks away."

Every unit on the street began to check in, giving their locations and estimated response time. They were talking on top of each other, and Bennie hit the tone signal again to gain control of the radio. "4A, 6A, 7A, respond code three. All other units remain on your beats. I repeat, no other units respond other than those who have been dispatched. If you do, you'll be subject to disciplinary action."

"4A, station two," Harriman barked. "Is there a suspect?"

"No suspects, 4A," Bennie responded.

Harriman had no idea what kind of situation he was walking into, but like everyone else on the street, he knew who resided at 3980 Orrville Road.

Jimmy Townsend.

Lindsey Townsend had gone into premature labor at 9:40 Friday evening after her husband informed her he no longer had a job, and was about to be brought up on criminal charges. She was six months pregnant.

Jimmy had carried her to his car in the driveway, afraid to wait for an ambulance. When his wife began gritting her teeth and bearing down, he knew they would never make it to the hospital in time. He delivered a three-pound baby girl in the back seat of the car.

Ted Harriman squealed to a stop and leaped out of his car, racing over to the Jeep. The paramedics had already arrived and were working over Lindsey in the back seat. Bystanders were lined up on the sidewalk, watching the tragedy unfold. Some of them had to be neighbors, Harriman thought, seeing one of the women sobbing.

"Inside the house," one of the paramedics shouted. "He took the baby. The woman with the blond hair lives next door. She saw Townsend run into the house with the infant in his arms. She was out here during the delivery. She thinks the infant might have been stillborn."

Harriman checked with the station over his portable radio. He didn't understand why Bennie had dispatched it as an officer down. "Who called this in?"

"One of Townsend's children," Bennie said, not wanting to tell him what the child had said over an open frequency. "Check the bathroom off the master bedroom."

Townsend's wife tried to sit up. "He took the baby," she wailed, tears streaming down her cheeks. "My baby, my baby. What's wrong with my baby? She didn't cry. She—"

Harriman raced inside the house. The bathroom door was locked. "Let me in, Jimmy," he yelled. "Open the damn door. Don't be a fool, man. Let us take the baby to a hospital."

Met with silence, Harriman slammed his shoulder into the wood frame. Once was not enough. He continued ramming the door until the lock finally sprang.

The scene inside the bathroom was the most gruesome and disturbing sight he had ever seen. At first he assumed Townsend had swallowed his gun, but there was no blood. The officer's body was crammed between the commode and the sink. The tiny infant was resting in his lap, wrapped in a dish towel. The floor of the bathroom was covered with debris. Food containers. Cereal boxes. Bread wrappers. Soda cans. Townsend's head was slumped forward onto his chest, the front of his shirt covered in vomit.

Stepping over the litter on the floor, Harriman bent down and checked the infant's pulse. Nothing. He had known the baby was dead from the moment he had seen it in Townsend's lap. The infant's skin was blue. It appeared to have died from lack of oxygen.

Lifting Townsend's head, he realized he must have choked on a piece of food. Either that, or he had drowned in his own vomit. How could he eat with a dead baby in his arms? Why would anyone want food at a time like this? Harriman shivered in revulsion.

He turned around, wanting to get out of the room before he became ill. Three adorable little girls were huddled together in the doorway, staring at their deceased father and the tiny bundle of flesh that would have been their baby sister.

He would never forget the horror of that moment.

Quickly closing the door behind him, Harriman dropped to his knees. "You didn't see that," he said, picking up the smallest girl in his arms. Pushing the other children in front of him, he herded them down the hall to the front of the house.

Once she realized she was not going to make bail until Saturday, Rachel asked to be transferred from protective custody to the main jail population. If she had to spend another night in jail, she didn't want to do it in solitary confinement. In a quad, she could eat her meals with the other inmates and watch television. Now that she was caught up on her rest, Rachel was becoming restless and claustrophobic.

Seated in a metal chair next to the three other women, Rachel was laughing at an old Amos and Andy movie.

"I love comedies," a woman with flowing black hair said. "My favorite is Lucy, though. This movie is older than my mother."

The movie was interrupted for a news bulletin. "One of the officers caught up in the corruption scandal inside the Oak Grove Police Department died approximately an hour ago after his wife gave birth to a premature infant in the back seat of the couple's Jeep Cherokee," the female news anchor said. "The baby was stillborn. Department sources . . ."

Rachel bolted upright. "Turn up the volume."

"There's no volume control," the woman with the black hair said. "Say, you look like that cop I saw on TV, now that I think about it. What's your name?"

Rachel rushed over to the television so she could hear better. She knew it could only be Townsend. When the news flash was over, she simply stood there for a long time. Even though Jimmy had made mistakes, he had been her friend.

What had she done?

She felt as if she had pulled a string and unraveled the universe. Something inside her snapped. She stood in the middle of the room and screamed and screamed. Her shrill cries echoed down the corridors, the cells, through the speakers mounted in the ceilings, like a siren's call of despair. Other women answered her with their own tortured wails. Finally the guards came and carried her out of the quad.

chapter

THIRTY-FOUR

When a female correctional officer unlocked the door to her cell in protective custody Saturday morning, Rachel was sleeping. After the commotion she had caused the night before, the guards had taken her to the infirmary, where they had given her a shot of Valium, then deposited her back in her original cell. "Your attorney is here to see you."

Rachel sat up on the bed. Her mouth tasted like cotton. She didn't realize where she was until she saw the bars. A breakfast tray was on the floor by the door. "What time is it?"

The jailer, a middle-aged woman with short curly hair, glanced at her watch. "A few minutes past ten."

The dream was still fresh in Rachel's mind. Frances had been holding the china doll in the pink satin dress. Even now, she could hear her mother's voice, smell her cologne, something with lilacs. Both Rachel and her mother were happy—smiling, hugging. "Isn't she beautiful? Look at her dress, baby. This is a doll for a real princess."

Rachel remembered the clothes she had been wearing: a white cotton dress with a ruffled skirt, white tights, and black patent leather pumps. She squeezed her eyes shut, but all that came to mind were yellow marshmallow bunnies. Had it been Easter? The mind was a strange thing, she decided, pushing herself to her feet. She had dreamed about the china doll repeatedly, but she had never experienced a dream like this one. What was her mother doing with the doll? In her previous dreams, it had always been in the hands of Nathan Richardson.

She recalled her conversation with Mike Atwater the first night she had visited his house. Was there a greater significance to the doll? Possibly along the lines Atwater had suggested?

The jailer looked impatient. Rachel forced the dream out of her mind. Even though it seemed like a memory, she knew it was only the imaginings of a distraught mind.

Walking over to the sink, she tried to run the plastic comb through her hair, but it was too tangled and the comb broke. She asked the jailer if she had time to brush her teeth.

"Go ahead," the woman said, "you've already kept me waiting." Bending down and picking up Rachel's breakfast tray, she saw the food had not been touched. "Guess you're used to sleeping late, huh?"

"All the time," Rachel said. Once she was finished brushing her teeth, the jailer led her through a maze of corridors.

Carrie was seated at the small round table inside the interview room. She stood and rushed over to embrace her sister. "Are you okay?"

"Jimmy Townsend is dead," Rachel said flatly.

"I know," she said. "Listen, the jail is processing the paperwork for your release. You should be out of here within thirty minutes."

"Jimmy wouldn't be dead if it wasn't for me," Rachel told her, taking a seat at the table. "He was a good father, Carrie. Nothing in the world meant more to him than his kids."

"The man broke into your house, Rachel," Carrie said. "He knew you didn't shoot Grant Cummings, but he was more than willing to let you go to prison. How can you possibly grieve for this person? Besides, you didn't cause his death. He died from an eating disorder."

"I should have helped him," Rachel said, wrapping her arms around her chest. "I knew Jimmy had a problem with food, but I never knew it could be so serious. I thought it was only women who developed eating disorders."

Carrie waited until her sister calmed down, then took both her hands. "Let me explain how we're going to proceed."

"You can't use Tracy," Rachel said, a determined look in her eyes. "I've already told her she must not lie. I won't allow it."

"I'm not going to fight you, Rachel," Carrie said patiently. "Believe me, I adore this kid. I don't want Tracy to perjure herself any more than you do. I've decided to approach this from another direction."

"What do you mean?"

"I've been giving a lot of thought to your situation," she continued. "I suddenly realized we were doing ourselves an injustice by not cooperating with the police."

Rachel's eyes flashed. "The police? What are you saying?"

"Relax," Carrie said. "I think we may be able to gain some ground. Internal Affairs has launched a major investigation into the allegations you've made. Without your help, they won't be able to put all the pieces together. I spoke to Captain Madison this morning and arranged for you to meet with an officer from Internal Affairs. We're going to put everything on the table, Rachel. If things go as well as I think they will, we may be able to get the charges dismissed."

Rachel braced her head in her hands. "Why would they believe me?"

"The witness who claims he saw you in the locker room with the gun was Fred Ramone. He may very well be the man who shot Grant." Rachel's head shot up, and Carrie nodded. "The crime lab lifted his fingerprints from the interior walls of the locker adjacent to the one assigned to Grant. When people use a locker, Rachel, their prints might be on the handle or the door, but ask yourself why they would place their hands on the interior walls." She stopped speaking and shrugged. "It wasn't even his locker. He was hiding in there, that's why. Nothing else makes sense."

The jailer unlocked the door to the interview room. "Her release papers just came through," the guard told Carrie, "but I can't let her leave with you. Prisoners have to be released through Central Booking."

"I'll meet you in the parking lot," Carrie said. "We'll drive straight to the police department."

Fred Ramone lived in an apartment in Oak Grove. Located in the older section of town, the complex was constructed of stucco and contained ten units, all of them badly in need of repair. The interior of the apartment was cluttered and filthy. Newspapers, food wrappers, and soda cans were strewn here and there.

Ratso was curled up on the bed. Every few moments, his shoulders would shake and he would start sobbing again. Jimmy Townsend had been his friend, one of the few men in the department who had genuinely accepted him.

The day before, he had applied for a job as a security officer. The company had refused to accept his application on learning he had been terminated from the police department. He wiped his eyes with a corner of the bed sheet. His friends were gone. He would never be respected again, never feel he belonged again.

The phone rang. He let the answering machine pick it up, fearing it was another reporter.

"This is Lenny Schneider with Internal Affairs," a man's voice said. "We need to speak to Fred Ramone."

Ratso raced over and picked up the phone. They were going to give him his job back. "This is Ramone," he said.

"Good," Schneider said briskly. "We were going over your personnel file and we came across something peculiar. We'd like to set up an appointment for you to come down and discuss it, say ten o'clock tomorrow morning."

"What's peculiar?" Ratso said, his pulse pounding in his ears. Tomorrow was Sunday, and if Internal Affairs wanted him to come in over the weekend, he knew it had to be serious. "I don't understand."

"Where did you go to school?"

Ratso's mind went blank. He couldn't remember the name of the school his papers said he had attended. "Modesto," he said finally.

"That's the town," Schneider said. "I asked you the name of your high school."

Ratso didn't answer. He gripped the phone with both hands.

"On your application," Schneider continued, "you listed the school as Freemont High."

"Yes," Ratso said, "that's right." The carefully memorized details of his false identity were coming back to him. "I graduated in 1975, then I went on to community college."

"You didn't graduate from Freemont High in 1975, friend," Schneider said, staring at the data flashing on his computer screen. "Freemont High burned to the ground in 1973. The school district elected not to rebuild it, as the area in Modesto where the school was located was turning commercial and the property was too valuable.

They sold the land, then later erected a new school a few blocks away on Coldwater Drive."

"Yes," Ratso said. "I went to the new school."

"What was the name of the new school?"

"Coldwater High," Ratso said, improvising.

"Then why does your high school diploma read Freemont High?"

"They made a mistake."

Schneider looked over at his partner and smiled. "I don't think so, Ramone," he said, chuckling. "The new school was named Piedmont High, not Coldwater High. Your diploma is a forgery. First thing tomorrow morning—"

Ratso let the receiver fall from his hands.

They knew.

It was over. They would deport him, send him back to Pakistan. He walked over and picked up a Remington 30.06 caliber rifle. He had bought it to go deer hunting with Jimmy Townsend and Grant Cummings the year before. Opening his bureau drawer, he pulled out a box of Black Talon ammo, loading four rounds into the chamber. Carrying it back to the bed with him, he placed the butt on the floor, then opened his mouth wide and lowered it onto the muzzle. His finger trembled on the trigger. He could not go back to Pakistan.

For fifteen minutes he remained in the same position, his mouth sealed on the rifle. Finally he realized he could not do it. Letting the weapon tumble to the floor, he fell back onto the bed and stared at the ceiling. After a while, the water spots came to life, forming the image of a woman's face. A sign from Allah, Ratso told himself, slipping off the edge of the bed and touching his forehead to the floor. He had been selfish, thinking only of himself instead of his friend. Now that he could no longer find a way to get the stolen money to his sisters, he would give it to Lindsey Townsend. He had seen his friend's little girls on numerous occasions. This would be his final tribute to an honorable man.

Picking the rifle up off the floor, he placed it beside him on the bed, stroking the barrel as if it were a lover. He had been given a new mission, a way to redeem himself. Once he completed his mission, he would be granted the courage to end his life.

Lieutenant Lenny Schneider was an attractive man, with neatly trimmed blond hair and steely gray eyes. Generally he didn't work on weekends, but since Internal Affairs was in the midst of a major corruption probe, he had been working around the clock. He was wearing a limp white dress shirt, dark slacks, and red suspenders, and his face was covered with several days' growth of stubble. When Rachel and Carrie stepped through the door to his office, he asked his partner to leave and walked over to close the door.

"Have a seat," he said. "I'm pleased you've decided to cooperate with us. Things will move faster that way."

With Carrie's prompting, Rachel talked for over an hour, painstakingly detailing the events she had witnessed inside the police department. She began with the Brentwood case, explaining how she suspected Townsend had planted the gun on the used car salesman. She told how she had awakened to find Grant Cummings on top of her at the watch party, then moved on to the riot at the Majestic Theater. She said she had seen Grant use the Hillmont boy as a human shield, and additionally witnessed Ratso using excessive force on another young man during the same incident. She described the pressure Sergeant Miller had applied to keep her from speaking out, along with the horror she had been subjected to inside the house on Maple Avenue when her fellow officers failed to respond for backup. She told of officers milking overtime, the use of sap gloves and steel-toed boots, blatant sexual harassment, evidence tampering, and filing false reports. She ended by telling the investigator about Grant's vicious attack in the orange grove.

Schneider reached over and hit the stop button on the tape recorder. "We're investigating Fred Ramone from several angles," he said. "Once the court issues a search warrant for his residence, we may be able to determine the extent of his involvement."

"What are you searching for?" Rachel asked, finding it hard to believe there would be evidence inside Ratso's apartment from the shooting.

"Oh," Schneider said, "nothing much. Just fifty grand in drug money."

Rachel knew she had seen Ratso at the house on Maple Avenue, but only briefly. "What makes you think Ratso stole it?"

"Ted Harriman saw Ramone carrying a package out of the back of the station the day after the money vanished from the crime scene," he told her. "When Harriman quizzed him about what was inside the package, Ramone told him it was evidence. We looked over his activity sheet from the previous night and found no mention of any kind of evidence."

"Are you prepared to tell the DA what you've just told us?" Carrie said. "If you're targeting Fred Ramone as the shooter, why isn't he in custody?"

"Talk to Bill Ringwald at the DA's office," Schneider said. "He doesn't want us to arrest Ramone on probable cause. He wants the judge to issue an arrest warrant, and for that, we need more concrete evidence. With Cummings's statement that Rachel was the shooter, Ringwald's afraid the case might fall apart in the courtroom."

"What about Ratso's fingerprints?" Carrie said. "The lab lifted them off the locker adjacent to Grant's."

Schneider placed a hand inside one of his suspenders. "Ramone could easily explain the prints," he said. "He could say his padlock got jammed one day, and in his rush to get out of the station, he simply shoved his gear into one of the vacant lockers."

"The prints weren't found on the door handle," Carrie told him, "they were lifted from the interior walls."

"So?" Schneider said, shrugging. "The floor in the men's locker room is often wet. Ramone can say he lost his footing on a slippery tile, and had to brace himself by placing his hands against the interior walls of the locker."

Carrie shook her head. Rachel was right about the police department, she decided, wondering if her decision to cooperate with them had been a mistake. Schneider was slick. He seemed to have an explanation for everything.

"Ringwald wants us to dig up every piece of dirt we can find on Ramone, then use it to draw out a confession," he said. "The longer we rattle his cage, the better chance we have that Ramone may crack during interrogation." Schneider covered his mouth and yawned. "The only reason we came to suspect Ramone is the statement Ted Harriman gave us. He claims Rachel couldn't have fled out the back of the station because he was parked right outside the rear door at the time of the shooting. She could have slipped past him, though, so I'm not sure how much weight we should attach to Harriman's statement. The man was coming off a graveyard shift, and for all we know, he might have dozed off for a few moments around the time of the shooting."

"I want Rachel reinstated," Carrie barked, her nerves frazzled. "Don't you think you've put my sister through enough hell? She's been locked up in a cell for the past two days for something she didn't do."

"Just hang tight," Schneider said calmly. "The preliminary hearing won't be held until April fifth. I'm digging into Ramone's past right now, and I've already discovered some major discrepancies. All the men who were involved in this have been either suspended or terminated, so you can't accuse us of not taking action."

"You said men," Rachel said. "Carol Hitchcock was involved. She provided Grant with an alibi during the time he attacked me in the orange grove."

"Right," the investigator said. "That's something else we're working on. We think we might be able to charge Hitchcock with filing a false police report, maybe even breaking and entering. We replayed the tape recording of the caller who reported the hardware store burglary. We can't be certain until the lab performs a voice analysis, but we're fairly certain it's Carol Hitchcock's voice on the tape."

Rachel's jaw dropped. She knew Carol had covered for Grant by saying he was at the hardware store, but from what she was hearing, the woman had taken it a step further. "Are you saying the burglary at the hardware store was a fraud?"

Schneider took a sip of his coffee. "That's the way it appears," he said. "Hitchcock must have tossed a rock through the window, entered the store, then called in the report once she verified the owners were out of town. Since department policy states that the reporting officer must remain at the location until the building is secure, she provided Cummings with enough time to assault you in the orange grove."

"When will we know something?" Carrie asked, standing to leave. "My sister needs a paycheck so she can support her family. If she's not reinstated by early next week, I'll be forced to file a lawsuit."

Lenny Schneider snapped to attention. "On what grounds?"

"Sexual harassment, false imprisonment, emotional trauma." Carrie gave him a cold stare. "Do you have any idea what this story is worth? Look at her," she said, glancing over her shoulder at Rachel. "The tabloids are camped on her lawn right now. She's the perfect whistleblower. Her appearance, her sincerity, the fact that she's a young widow struggling to support her children. With the information Rachel just provided, she could turn this department inside out. Your officers will come across as the slimiest bastards on earth by the time we're finished. Shit, Schneider, we might even make the cover of *Time* magazine."

"You've made your point," Schneider said. "I'll speak to Captain Madison and Chief Bates sometime this weekend. You'll have your answer by Monday."

THIRTY-FIVE

Jimmy Townsend's funeral was held at nine o'clock Monday morning. Rachel and Carrie were glued to the television set in the living room. Even though Townsend had been terminated prior to his death, the chief had decided that he should have an official police funeral. Ted Harriman, Nick Miller, and Carol Hitchcock were among the pall-bearers. Rachel looked for Ratso's face in the crowd. When she failed to find him, she wondered if he had already been arrested. Following on the heels of the corruption scandal, the media coverage was extensive.

When the phone rang at one o'clock that afternoon, Carrie was unpacking some of her belongings in the kitchen. Once she had concluded the phone call, she stuck her head out the door and yelled at Rachel in the living room. "Get dressed," she said. "Lenny Schneider just called. They want you to come down to the police station right away."

"Lucy isn't home to watch Joe," Rachel said, stretched out on the floor coloring with her son. "She went to the doctor for her six-month checkup."

"I'll stay with Joe until she gets back," Carrie said. "I've already called Mike Atwater. He's on the way to the police station with Bill Ringwald and Blake Reynolds. If Lucy doesn't come back in the next hour, I'll jump in a cab and bring Joe with me."

* * *

Ratso walked through the back door into Jimmy Townsend's kitchen, carrying a tattered brown suitcase. An older woman was pulling a casserole out of the oven. "I'm Lindsey's mother," she said, eyeing the suitcase. Her daughter had told her one of Jimmy's college buddies was flying in from Chicago. "You must be Sammy Cohen."

"Yes," he said, hearing voices in the other room. "I'd like to speak to Lindsey privately."

"She's resting, but I'm sure she wouldn't mind if you popped in for a few moments," the woman told him. "Her room is at the end of the hall."

After he had spoken to Lenny Schneider, Ratso had left his apartment and driven to a secluded spot high in the hills above Oak Grove. He had spent Saturday night locked inside his Chevy Nova. By Sunday morning, he had convinced himself that Internal Affairs would not arrest him on the basis of a few suspicious documents. He headed back to his apartment, thinking he could shower and catch a few hours sleep. As soon as he turned the corner onto his street, he saw a string of police cars parked in front of his complex. Sunday night he had locked himself in his car high in the foothills again, but he had been too distraught to sleep. Now that his worst fears had been confirmed, he knew he had to find a safe haven. If he tried to get out of town, the authorities would apprehend him. Reaching into his pocket, his fingers touched a metal object. Grant had given him the key to his townhouse so he could wash his car and clean his gun collection.

The mourners had congregated in the living room. Knowing some of the officers he had worked with might be there, Ratso slipped out of the kitchen and darted down the hallway. When Lindsey Townsend saw the dark-skinned man in the doorway of her bedroom, she pulled the covers up over her chest.

"I came to offer my condolences," Ratso said. He was dressed in a white dress shirt and a crumpled tan suit. "Jimmy was my friend."

"Thank you," she said. "The doctor wants me to stay in bed. There's food in the kitchen. Please help yourself, Fred."

"I no longer need food," Ratso said. "I have a gift for you and your daughters."

"What kind of gift?"

"You must not tell anyone that I have given you this gift," he continued. "If you do, they will ask many questions."

The look she saw in his eyes was alarming. Before her last two children had been born, Lindsey had worked as a nurse in a mental hospital. She wondered if the man was psychotic. His pupils were dilated, his movements stiff and mechanical. Psychotics sometimes believed they possessed supernatural qualities, that they no longer needed to eat, drink, or sleep. She watched anxiously as he placed the suitcase on the floor beside her bed, then turned and walked out of the room.

The conference room at the police department was filling up with people. Rachel was waiting outside on a metal chair. She was an outsider now, not even allowed to be present during the meeting that might determine her future.

Mike Atwater and Blake Reynolds stopped briefly by Rachel's chair before rushing into the meeting. When Atwater realized several of the parties had not yet arrived, he came back outside to speak to Rachel. "Judge Sanders issued an arrest warrant for Ramone in the Cummings shooting," he told her. "Ringwald met him for breakfast Sunday morning and finally got him to sign the paperwork."

"Is Ratso in jail?"

"Not yet," Atwater said tensely. "Lenny Schneider called him on Saturday at his apartment after stumbling across some discrepancies in his background information. When the men tried to serve the warrant Sunday morning, the bastard had already skipped. They found some of his clothing, but there was no sign of the missing cash. Ramone probably used the stolen loot to buy an airline ticket."

Rachel's chest rose and then fell. "Are you saying Schneider tipped him off intentionally?"

"The man's an idiot," Atwater said in anger. "I worked with Schneider on several cases when he was assigned to Homicide. Back then, he had a pretty good head on his shoulders. Since he was transferred to IA, he gets his kicks making people squirm."

"He told me it was Ringwald who wanted to make Ratso sweat," she said. "He said the longer they squeezed him, the greater chance there would be that he might confess."

"Bullshit," Atwater said. He stuck his head inside the conference room. "Who are we waiting for?" he asked Blake Reynolds.

"The attorneys from the AG's office," Reynolds told him.

Atwater returned to his conversation with Rachel. "Chief Bates was behind this, not Ringwald," he told her. "Since you were the person who went on TV and made the corruption accusations, Bates knew if he arrested the real shooter, the public would have no choice but to take your allegations seriously."

Two men in dark suits walked up behind Atwater. He directed the attorneys from the Attorney General's office into the room, then followed behind them and took a seat at the long table.

The atmosphere inside the room was along the lines of a wartime conference between opposing factions. The contingent of high-ranking police officers took seats on one side of the long oak table, next to Lenny Schneider from Internal Affairs. The district attorneys and the two men from the Attorney General's office were seated at the opposite end of the table. Although Chief Bates generally dressed in a suit and tie, he had arrived in his dress uniform after attending Townsend's funeral. With his service medals pinned to his chest, he resembled a general.

Mike Atwater was seated next to Blake Reynolds. The two men had been working around the clock, preparing indictments, subpoenaing evidence, interviewing witnesses. Grant Cummings would be tried on two separate counts of rape, as well as aggravated assault for the attack on Rachel in the orange grove. They had squandered valuable time on Townsend. The complaints for wiretapping and illegal entry had already been typed. Nick Miller would be charged with conspiracy in the attempted rape. Fred Ramone, once he was apprehended, would be charged with attempted murder in the shooting of Grant Cummings, along with the theft of the missing drug money. They were also considering filing charges against Ratso for using excessive force during the Majestic Theater incident.

"This is where we stand as of today," Bill Ringwald said, projecting his voice so the men at the end of the table could hear. "We have two women willing to testify that Grant Cummings raped them. This is in addition to the offense committed against Rachel Simmons. Not the attempted rape," he continued, "as we've decided to set that case aside. In light of the more serious crime Cummings committed in the orange grove, there appears to be no reason to pursue the earlier offense."

"The men involved in this have all been terminated," Chief Bates said, directing his statement to Ringwald. A distinguished man in his early fifties, Bates had silver hair and bushy white eyebrows. While recovering from surgery he had lost close to twenty pounds, and his once round face was now gaunt. "I've called a press conference for this afternoon to let the public know where we stand."

"Have you dealt with Carol Hitchcock yet?" Atwater said, tapping his fingernails on the table. "The lab confirmed it was her voice on the recording."

The chief sighed, then removed a handkerchief to blow his nose. Of all the women on the force, he had considered Carol Hitchcock one of the most competent. "Are you going to file against her?"

"Yes," Atwater said. "Probably illegal entry on the breaking and entering, along with filing a false police report. She'll also be charged with conspiracy to commit rape as to Rachel Simmons."

"What are you filing on Miller?" Captain Madison asked.

A plainclothes officer opened the door and motioned for Lenny Schneider. The investigator stood and rushed out of the room.

"The AG may pick him up in their case," Atwater answered. "Soliciting a false report on the Hillmont matter." He glanced over at a grim-faced attorney from the AG's office.

"It's a little premature at this point," Stan Ramirez said. "We're not going to jump in this with both feet, Atwater. We need to go slowly, build our case, then make our determination as to what violations we want to pursue. It's the overall picture that counts."

Bill Ringwald cleared his throat to get the other men's attention. "I want an all-points bulletin issued for Fred Ramone. Make certain it goes on the national system. Notify security at LAX, along with the bus and train terminals."

"We're not a bunch of ignorant hicks," Chief Bates said, annoyed that the district attorney thought he had to tell him how to do his job. "We notified every law enforcement agency in the country as soon as the warrant was issued."

"Tomorrow morning," Ringwald continued, "we intend to withdraw the charges against Rachel Simmons. If you don't want the department to be sued, Bates, I suggest you give the woman her job back."

"You can't threaten me with a lawsuit," Chief Bates said, standing up behind his chair. "This woman plunged my department into chaos. Why would I consider reinstating her? Until Fred Ramone is proven to be the shooter, Rachel Simmons will remain on suspension."

Chief Bates dropped back in his chair. The room was rife with tension, so still he could hear his watch ticking on his wrist. The City Council had already notified him that they would be taking a vote on his status as chief of police. Larry Hillmont served on the City Council. Bates knew the man would push for his resignation. A number of large developers were also up in arms, concerned about selling homes in a city plagued by police corruption.

Lenny Schneider walked back into the room, bent over and whispered something to the chief. "Excuse us for a few moments," Bates said, stepping to the back of the room.

"There's no doubt now that Ratso's our man," Schneider told him quietly. "I just got off the phone with Lindsey Townsend. As a condolence gift, he gave her fifty grand in a suitcase. I guess we found our missing drug money."

"Where is Ramone now?"

"Your guess is as good as mine," Schneider said, his brows furrowed. "As soon as I spoke to Lindsey, I rolled every unit we had to the area. We're shorthanded today because of the funeral, though, and I had to yank officers off other calls. By the time we got there, Ramone was long gone."

"Even if Ramone took the money," the chief pointed out, "we have no proof that he shot Cummings outside of the prints found inside the adjacent locker."

Lenny Schneider frowned, more concerned with damage control than the fact that they had let a potentially dangerous man slip through their fingers. "Whoever conducted the background investigation on this man was either drunk or out of their mind," he said in disgust. "Almost all of Ramone's documents are forgeries. Some of them aren't even good forgeries. The birth certificate looks like it was designed on a computer and printed on a laser printer. Didn't the idiot who checked it realize they didn't have laser printers twenty-odd years ago? To be honest, I think we might have hired an illegal immigrant. I have no idea who Fred Ramone really is. The way Lindsey Townsend described him just now, it sounds like we handed a gun to a psychopath. This is our shooter, Chief."

"Do you think Cummings could have been involved in the theft of the drug money?"

"I have no idea," Schneider said, shaking his head.

The chief felt his chest tightening. Now the department would be accused of improperly screening applicants. If he didn't get out from under this stress, he was going to drop dead of a heart attack. He turned and walked back to the table.

Some of the men were conversing in one corner of the room. When the chief sat down, they returned to their seats. "I've given greater thought to your earlier request," he told Ringwald. "It seems the best thing for me to do at this point is to reinstate Mrs. Simmons's status as a police officer. Then maybe we can pull our people together, and try to get back to work."

"When will you reinstate her?" Atwater asked, triumph flashing in his eyes.

"As soon as possible."

Mike Atwater leapt out of his chair, racing out of the room to get Rachel. "They want to speak to you," he said, taking her hand and leading her into the conference room.

Rachel stood at the front of the room. Atwater stood next to her, a smile playing at the corners of his mouth.

"Mrs. Simmons," Chief Bates said slowly, "I'm reinstating you. When you leave this room, stop by the supply office. They'll reassign you some new equipment. You can come back to work tomorrow if you'd like. If not, make arrangements with Captain Madison."

Rachel's mouth fell open. For a moment, she thought she was hallucinating. "You're joking."

"Nope," the chief said. He fiddled with his hands in his lap, then stood and smiled. "Welcome back."

Captain Madison walked over and pumped Rachel's hand. "I'm putting you up for a commendation for the way you handled the situation on Maple Avenue," he said. "After looking over the reports you submitted over the past two years, I think you have an excellent opportunity for advancement. How would you like to work in Internal Affairs?"

"Good match," Atwater said.

Captain Madison scowled. "I didn't mean right away," he said. "I meant somewhere down the line, Atwater. Officer Simmons needs to perfect her patrol skills before we can promote her."

Rachel's body felt light enough to float to the ceiling. Bill Ringwald walked over and shook her hand. "Good work, Simmons. You've made some changes in this town. It was about time we cleaned up our police department."

Rachel's mind was churning. Had the world suddenly righted itself? She looked up at Atwater. "Is this real?"

"Absolutely," he said, smiling again.

"But what about my court case?"

"We're withdrawing the charges, Rachel," he said, quickly embracing her. "It's over."

For approximately fifteen minutes, Rachel stood at the front of the room as if in a receiving line, as each man stopped on his way out to say a few words and shake her hand. The chief darted out of the room, then returned a few moments later with a photographer from the local paper. "If you don't mind," he said almost timidly, "the paper would like to take some pictures of us together."

"It's okay," Rachel said, smoothing her hair down.

The photographer said something to the chief. "It might be better if you were wearing your uniform," Bates told her. "Perhaps the supply office has an extra one you can borrow."

While she was in jail, Carrie had picked up her cleaning. "I have my uniform in the car," she told them. "If you'll give me a few minutes, I'll run out and get it."

"I'll send someone to the supply room for your badge and gun," Chief Bates told her.

Rachel was out of breath when she entered the ladies room a few doors down from the conference room. She ripped open the plastic and crushed the uniform to her chest. It might be nothing but black fabric, but to Rachel, it was her cloak of honor. She removed her clothing and slipped it on, then stared at her image in the mirror. She had reclaimed her integrity. Tears streamed down her face. "I did it, Joe," she said, raising her eyes to the ceiling. "I finally accomplished something on my own."

Once she had washed the tears away with tap water, she thrust her shoulders back and stepped out of the bathroom.

"Stand over there, Officer Simmons," the photographer said, indicating a spot by the window. "The light's perfect."

She stepped up beside the chief. Sunlight danced around her head, changing her hair from red to gold. Bates leaned over and attached her shield to the front of her shirt. "You're one determined lady," he whispered, handing her back her service revolver. "I'd appreciate it if you would report any future problems to me, though, before you go running to the media."

Rachel closed her eyes, wanting to seal the moment in her memory. When she opened them, she looked into the camera lens and smiled.

chapter

THIRTY-SIX

Mike Atwater had brought a case of champagne. Carrie had made chicken and barbecued ribs on the backyard grill. Tracy had blown up dozens of balloons and tied them to the overhang on the porch. Lucy and her husband were present, along with the couple's four children.

"You're not really going to go back to the police department?" Lucy asked, seated in a plastic chair on the patio.

"Of course I am," Rachel said. "Don't worry, Lucy, I'm not going to ask you to watch the kids. I'm going to work days now. Captain Madison told me it wasn't a problem."

"Who's going to watch Joe for you?"

"I'm going to put him in day care," Rachel told her. "Carrie is going to live with us and split some of the expenses. Since she already borrowed the money to put up my bail, we're going to use it to put a down payment on a larger house."

"What about that?" Lucy said, tilting her head. Carrie and Mike Atwater were standing side by side on the opposite side of the yard, chatting and laughing.

"Oh," Rachel said. "I know what you mean. I don't mind, Lucy. Mike and I are just friends."

"I wasn't referring only to Mike," her friend told her. "Isn't Carrie a little overbearing now and then? Are you certain you can live together?"

Rachel laughed. "Carrie's a pistol, all right, but I adore her. Everything will work out just fine." She watched as her older sister grinned at something Atwater had said. "It's funny, but I really don't mind not having a man in my life. I have my career, my family. I had a lot of time to think when I was in jail. I could never love another man the way I loved Joe. If I married someone else, it wouldn't be fair to him. You can't give a person just a piece of yourself. Good relationships require total commitment."

"That's because you won't let go," Lucy said, popping a potato chip in her mouth. "Everyone needs a companion, Rachel. You're a young woman. You can't go through the rest of your life alone. Why do you think I took Glen back?"

Rachel didn't agree. "If you really love someone," she said, "you love them forever. I'm married to Joe as much now as I was when he was alive. Just because he isn't physically present doesn't mean he isn't still around somewhere. I feel like he's been with me through this whole ordeal."

A chilly breeze developed, and the balloons began swaying back and forth over Rachel's head. One came loose, and she watched as it floated out into the yard, then vanished into the night sky.

Excusing herself, Rachel went inside the house. Since her release from jail, personal freedom had taken on new meaning. Being able to eat when she wanted, sleep when she wanted, go where she wanted— so many things she had taken for granted. Before her incarceration, she had often seen her life as drudgery. Now she realized there were simple pleasures all around her, something to be gained from each moment, each day, each experience. She had her children, her friends, her career. She vowed to fill the new house with happiness and laughter.

Carrie had her belongings strewn all over the house. Rachel stopped, seeing several photo albums on the dining room table. Her sister had always been good at preserving pictures. Picking up one of the albums, she carried it to the living room and settled into a recliner.

As Rachel flipped through the pages, memories flooded her mind. The photos were like a road map of her life. All of them gathered around the Christmas tree in their pajamas. Her mother mugging for the camera. Susan was so skinny in some of the pictures, she looked like a spider monkey. Rachel pulled the book closer to her face. She had never realized she had that many freckles.

At the bottom of one page, she saw a spot of white. As her eyes focused on the image, her body stiffened. She was seated in a chair in their living room, a box of yellow marshmallow bunnies in her lap. She was wearing the white dress she had dreamed about inside the jail. She studied the date on the photo. It was Easter Sunday and she had been three years old that year.

Next to her in the chair was the china doll with the pink satin dress, the same doll she had seen in the hands of Nathan Richardson seven years later.

Rachel's guests had gone home. It was late, and Tracy and Joe were in bed. Rachel sat at the kitchen table, her head buried in her hands. "Why didn't you show me this picture? You had to know about the doll. You were old enough to hear us talking about the doll the kidnapper had."

"I knew about *a* doll," Carrie said tensely. "How would I know it was the same doll Richardson had? Dolls aren't unique, Rachel. There could be all kinds of those dolls floating around out there. They probably manufactured hundreds of them."

"It's the same doll," she insisted. "Mother couldn't afford to buy me a doll this expensive. This is a collector's doll, Carrie. See the china face, the dress?"

"Look," Carrie snapped, "I don't know, okay? Let it go, Rachel. We're supposed to be celebrating. I don't know why you wanted to look through those old pictures anyway. I only brought them to show Tracy what we looked like when we were children."

Rachel opened the album and removed the photo from the page to study it more closely. She had not been seated in a chair, as she originally had thought. Her mind had simply created that image out of fragments from the kidnapping. When the picture in her hands had been taken, she had been seated on the sofa in the living room of their house in San Diego. She could see a few strands of her mother's hair in one corner of the picture, a portion of her dress, her long red fingernails. Suddenly she saw something else she had failed to see before. Her mother was holding someone's hand. She saw the dark hairs on the forearm, then spotted the outline of the tattoo. "Good Lord, Carrie," she said, her heart pounding in her chest, "it's the same tattoo Richardson had on his hand. It's a heart with an arrow through it. He was in our house. He was sitting on the sofa with me when this picture was taken."

Carrie rushed over and stood behind her. "You're crazy," she said. "Why would Nathan Richardson be in our house? You were only three years old in this picture. Besides, he was a doctor at one time. Most doctors don't have tattoos."

"He got his medical training in the service," Rachel said, recalling the things Sergeant Dean had told her. "I remember now," she continued, her eyes expanding. "He was Mother's friend. He took us to lunch that day after church. He bought us all Easter baskets and marshmallow bunnies."

"No," Carrie said, "that couldn't be. Mother would have told us if she had known Richardson before the kidnapping. You were only three when that picture was taken. How could you possibly remember that day?"

Rachel remembered everything now. Richardson had looked different when she had seen him in the market. After spending seven years in prison, he'd been pallid and thin, only a shadow of the robust man he had once been.

"He took the doll back," she said. "The doll was a bribe, Carrie. When he came to see Mother, he would give me the doll to play with so I would leave them alone. He always took it with him when he left. He said I couldn't keep it because it belonged to someone else."

"If you knew this man," Carrie countered, "then why don't I remember him?"

"Because he came to see Mother when you were in school," Rachel explained. "If I was three when this picture was taken, Carrie, then you were nine."

Her sister's hand flew to her chest. "You think he was one of Mother's customers, right?"

"More than that," Rachel said. "I think Nathan Richardson was my father."

Carrie shook her head, denying this idea. "Why would you say that?"

"Because it makes sense," Rachel answered. "Mother got pregnant, then she probably tried to extract money from him. If Richardson paid child support, she would have had to let him see me from time to time. Mother probably had no idea that Richardson went on to become a pedophile. She might not have known his real name. Most men don't tell prostitutes their real name."

"I refuse to believe this," Carrie said, walking around in a circle. "Why would he molest his own daughter?"

"Why would he molest any child?" Rachel said. "Before he kidnapped the other girl, Nathan Richardson was a successful pediatrician. When he took my clothes off, it was almost as if he was examining me."

"I don't understand," she said. "The man was a pedophile. He tricked you into walking over to his car, locked you in the trunk, took you to that sleazy motel room. If he didn't molest you, Rachel, what the hell was he doing?"

"Don't you see?" Rachel said. "Richardson was probably molesting children for years under the guise of giving them an examination. When he got to the point where touching no longer satisfied him, he kidnapped that girl and raped her."

Carrie picked up the photo and studied the picture again. The longer she looked at it, the more familiar Richardson's face became. "You might be right," she said, setting the picture back down on the table. "One of Mother's customers used to give me the creeps. He gave me money to buy candy, but I always had to kiss him on the lips first. He never tried to bribe me with a doll, though."

"After he molested me," Rachel said, the final piece of the puzzle snapping into place, "he sat me in a chair and took pictures of me. Maybe he wanted to compare them to pictures of himself as a child. He could have thought Mother lied to him, and he wanted to confirm that I was really his daughter."

"If what you are saying is true, it might explain Mother's disintegration after the kidnapping."

"Exactly," Rachel said. "It was as if she hated me, Carrie. Every time she looked in my face, she must have been reminded of Nathan Richardson. She blamed herself, don't you see? She brought this man into our lives. She demanded money from him. When they told her about the doll, she must have freaked, terrified I would remember seeing Richardson all those years ago in our house."

"That cop hanging around all the time probably didn't help," Carrie said, taking a seat at the table. "What was his name?"

"Sergeant Larry Dean."

Carrie snatched the photo off the table, walked over and dropped it in the trash can. "Forget it," she said, turning to face Rachel again. "The past is over. Whatever happened, happened. You'll never know the truth now. Mother's dead. Richardson's dead."

After Carrie headed to the master bedroom to go to bed, Rachel removed the green rubber pitcher from under the sink and occupied herself by watering her plants. She caressed a leaf on the potted fern in the dining room, feeling its delicate texture between her fingers. Joe had insisted that plants could somehow experience emotion. Was the fern trembling in fear? By touching it, was she molesting it? Rachel knew that the world was far more mysterious than people realized.

After she finished watering her plants, she went to check on the children. Joe was curled up in a tight ball, sucking on his thumb. She gently slipped his thumb out of his mouth, then kissed the damp hairs on the top of his head. Tracy was sleeping on her back, her arms stretched out at her side, her chest gently rising and falling. The girlishness was disappearing from her face, and Rachel knew her daughter would soon be a beautiful and confident woman. Positioning the sheet over her sleeping form, Rachel slipped out of the room.

She removed a fresh uniform from the hall closet, placed her shiny black shoes on the floor next to the sofa, oiled down her leather. Carrying her badge in her hand, she set it on the end table, then nestled down on the sofa to go to sleep.

As Rachel's eyes closed, she expected the nightmare of Nathan Richardson chasing her with the china doll to return. When she awoke the next morning, however, she felt refreshed and energetic. For twenty-four years, her subconscious mind had shielded her from the truth. Now that it was out in the open, she knew the dream was gone forever.

The picture of Rachel and Chief Bates was on the front page of the morning newspaper. Tracy rushed to the corner market and bought a dozen copies for her friends at school. "I'm so proud of you, Mom," she said, hugging Rachel before she left for work that morning. "You showed them all. Wait until my friends see this. I have a famous mom now. I'm going to spend all day bragging about you."

Rachel chuckled, bending down to pick up her son. "You're not going to give Aunt Carrie a hard time today, are you?"

"Sandbox," he said, clapping his hands in delight.

Carrie was washing dishes at the sink. "We've come to an understanding," she said. "If Joe eats his eggs every morning, I've promised to buy him his own sandbox." She shook her finger at him. "No more Froot Loops, guy. You don't want your teeth to rot."

Joe giggled, squirming in Rachel's arms.

Rachel covered his face with kisses, then placed him back on the floor. Carrie said she was going to work on her resume and begin contacting some local law firms. "I couldn't have made it through this without you," Rachel said, walking over to embrace her. "Are you certain you want to do this, Carrie? We're fine now. If you want, you can go back to San Francisco. All your friends are there. Brent's at Berkeley. Don't you want to live close to him?"

"Brent has his own life now," her sister told her. "Besides, it's only a short plane ride away. Since I lived in San Francisco the entire time I was with Phil, it's kind of exciting to start fresh in a new town."

Rachel wondered if Carrie was staying because of her attraction to Mike Atwater, but it didn't really matter. Already Joe and Tracy had grown very attached to her. Since they didn't have a father, Rachel decided, a little extra help in the parenting department might work out just fine. Waving to them, she headed to the front of the house to go to work.

Rachel felt like a celebrity when she entered the station that morning for the watch meeting. Sergeant Harry Blackmore, who supervised the day shift, walked over and pumped her hand. One of the female officers stepped up and congratulated her. Some of the men were standoffish, but they knew better than to harass her. The picture of her in the newspaper with the chief had served her well.

Once the watch meeting was over and they all headed out to their units in the parking lot, several of the male officers walked over and mumbled a few words to welcome her. Whether they were sincere or not didn't matter. Rachel smiled and shook their hands.

She spotted Ted Harriman exiting the back of the station in his street clothes, and walked over to speak to him. "I guess I wouldn't be back on the job if it wasn't for you," Rachel said. "Thanks, Ted, it took a lot of courage to speak out the way you did."

"Yeah, well," Harriman said, shuffling his feet, "I wanted you to know that we're not all bad guys around here, Rachel. Oak Grove has some outstanding officers."

Rachel started to extend her hand, but a handshake didn't seem adequate. She moved closer to embrace him. It was one of those awkward moments when intent slips away and emotion takes over. With her arms at her side, Rachel simply leaned into his chest, her cheek pressed against the cotton fabric of his shirt. Instead of the casual embrace of a friend, Harriman became a father comforting a child. She felt his hand touch the back of her head, felt the warmth of his body through his clothing. She remained still for several moments. "I'm sorry, Ted," she said, laughing nervously. "I hope I didn't embarrass you. I guess I needed some reassurance. First day back, you know."

Harriman's face spread in a wide grin. "Hey, any time I can be of service."

Rachel walked off to find her unit in the string of police cars, then turned and waved as Harriman took off across the parking lot. The sky was overcast and gray. She had to get used to the morning fog now that she was working days. Locating her unit, she quickly ran through her checklist, then headed out to her assigned beat.

The hours clicked off. Rachel issued several traffic citations for speeding in a school zone. At a little after ten, she was dispatched on a residential burglary and ended up waiting over two hours for the crime scene unit to arrive. After lunch, she parked and worked on some of her paperwork.

"2B3," the dispatcher's voice squawked over the radio, "respond to 589 Rosemount Drive on a report of a suspicious person possibly casing the neighborhood."

"Station one," Rachel asked, depressing the foot pedal for her microphone, "can you advise a description of the suspect?"

"The caller didn't give his name, 2B3. Just make a pass by the house and see if you spot anyone. Suspect should be a white male dressed in dark clothing."

Rachel placed her unfinished report back in her briefcase, started the engine and sped off. Rosemount was only a few blocks away. Normally when this type of call came in, the suspicious person was gone by the time police arrived in the area. Slowing as she turned onto Rosemount, she glanced at the houses on either side of the street. The development was one of the most prestigious in the city. Unlike most of the homes in Oak Grove, the houses on Rosemount had been custom built to the owners' specifications, the lots well over an acre. Most of the structures were set back from the street, and the yards were shaded with mature trees.

Rachel drove to the end of the block, then turned around and returned, looking for the complainant's address so she could make contact. Finding the number 589 painted on the curb, she steered the car over. She was parked next to a large oak tree and birds were perched on the limbs, chirping away. She sucked in a breath of fresh air. Someone must have just mowed their grass. She could smell its fragrance in the air. Picking up her clipboard off the seat, she glanced at her watch so she could note the time on her activity sheet.

The morning haze had finally blown away. Opening the car door, she stepped out into the sunshine. The light burned her eyes. Turning around, she reached back into the front seat to get her sunglasses from the visor.

A loud explosion rang in her ears.

Rachel felt something strike her back with enormous force. She tumbled forward onto the front seat, her feet still grazing the asphalt. At first she thought someone had thrown a baseball at her, possibly one of the kids in the neighborhood. She had trouble catching her breath, but she felt no pain. Blood oozed out onto the seat, then spilled over onto the floorboard of the police car. Rachel did not try to move, nor did she call for help.

She felt strangely peaceful, as if she were floating outside her body. Her wedding day passed through her mind. She saw Joe smiling at her in his tuxedo. They were standing at the altar in the church. He pushed back the lace veil from her face and kissed her on the mouth. "Come on," he said, tilting his head to let her know it was time to walk down the aisle as husband and wife.

"I can't go," she told him. "I have to stay here with the kids."

"The kids are fine," he said, firmly clasping her hand. "Look, Rachel, everyone is waiting for us."

She didn't hear Ratso's heavy footsteps racing toward the car, the urgent sounds of his rapid breathing. When the swarthy man raised the rifle to his waist and blasted away at the prostrate form draped over the front seat of the police car, Rachel had her arm linked in her husband's as he proudly escorted his new wife from the church.

EPILOGUE

Six months had passed. Carrie had gained ten pounds, but instead of making her look heavy, the extra weight made her look shapely and radiant. Her dyed hair had finally grown out, leaving a halo of lively brown curls. Dressed in a royal blue suit, she was standing beside Mike Atwater in front of the police station, dabbing at her eyes with a Kleenex. It was December 20th, but the day was unseasonably warm. "If only Rachel could have been here today," she said, gazing at the bronze plaque on the front of the building bearing her sister's name.

The ceremony had been covered by the media. Tracy and Joe were posing for photographs with the mayor and Chief Bates. Tracy held a framed photograph of her mother in her police uniform in front of her chest. Joe was dressed in a miniature three-piece suit, clutching a white rose someone had handed him. His face had grown more slender over the months, but his legs were still chubby.

Tracy looked every bit the young lady. Her hair was swept back in a French twist. She was wearing a white dress with a shawl collar, hose and white pumps. She looked over at Carrie and the attorney with a trembling smile on her face. She would not cry. This was her mother's day, and she knew her mother would not want them to cry. Her mother was a hero. Tracy had to be strong, dignified, proud. Everyone knew who she was, what her mother had done, how she had sacrificed her life for her community. Even the kids at her school looked up to her now.

Carrie had filed a civil lawsuit against Grant Cummings for attempted rape and aggravated assault. Cummings's parents had left him a sizable inheritance, and the jury had awarded Rachel's children a large sum of money.

Tracy's eyes fell on Mike Atwater. He had become a reassuring presence in her life. Every day after work, the attorney stopped by the house and they went running together. If she kept her grades up, Atwater was certain she would be able to get into Stanford, the college he had attended.

On the opposite side of the lawn, the district attorney draped an arm around Carrie's shoulder. "Maybe Rachel is here, you know?" he said, a slight catch in his voice. "Tracy looks more like her every day."

Fred Ramone had turned the rifle on himself after shooting Rachel. He had died instantly from a massive gunshot wound to the head. His body was found on the street next to Rachel's patrol car. The Black Talon bullets had pierced her bulletproof vest. The coroner's report said the first shot had killed her, passing through her back to shatter her heart.

Sergeant Nick Miller had been tried and later acquitted on the charge of conspiracy to commit rape, but the department had refused to rehire him. Grant Cummings was in prison and would remain there for twenty years, having been convicted of four counts of rape, along with numerous other violations, including the manslaughter of Timothy Hillmont. Carol Hitchcock had been convicted of breaking and entering and filing a false report. She had served thirty days in jail, and was presently employed by a private security company. She had married Grant Cummings before he had been shipped off to prison in a ceremony conducted by Judge Sanders in the courtroom the day of Grant's sentencing hearing. Twice a month she traveled to the prison medical facility in Vacaville to visit her husband.

Luis Mendoza, the unarmed man Jimmy Townsend had shot, had been paroled from prison due to Mike Atwater's intervention. The attorney had also filed a petition with the governor to grant Mendoza a full pardon.

With a solemn look on his face, Ted Harriman stepped up beside Carrie and Atwater. He had finally realized his goal to become a sergeant, taking the slot left open by Nick Miller. "Your sister was a courageous woman," he said, shaking Carrie's hand. "Her death was not without meaning. The police officers in this county will think twice before they step out of line again."

"I hope you're right," Carrie said.

"The department's screening process was sloppy and outdated. Applicants will be checked more thoroughly now." Harriman coughed in an attempt to keep his emotions in check. He could not forget the morning of Rachel's death, standing in the parking lot with her head cradled to his chest. "I'm sorry we weren't able to pick up Ramone sooner. No one suspected that he might be holed up in Grant's townhouse."

Once Harriman walked away, Carrie turned to Atwater. "Brent is coming for Christmas. I haven't even bought a tree yet. I just can't do it, you know? How can we celebrate Christmas without Rachel?" She covered her face with her hands. "I knew something terrible was going to happen to her. Remember the first day we met? I told you how I felt when we were walking out of the courtroom."

"Brent is coming for Christmas, huh?" Atwater said softly. He stood quietly for a few moments, then smiled. "You wouldn't have an extra seat at the table, would you?"

He had taken Rachel's death hard. Even though he had spent a great deal of time with Tracy and Joe over the last six months, he had consistently resisted Carrie's advances. "The kids will be thrilled." Throwing her arms around his neck, Carrie planted a big kiss on his mouth. "I'm going to get you, you know," she whispered. "It's only a matter of time."

"Do tell?" Atwater said, laughing. "What makes you so confident?"

"I can see it in your eyes," Carrie said, taking his hand and leading him across the lawn.

"Where are you taking me?" Atwater said.

"We have to tell Tracy and Joe," she said. "I want them to know you're going to spend Christmas with us. Now maybe I'll feel like putting up a tree."

Tracy, Joe, Mike Atwater and Carrie stood in a tight huddle. Atwater picked up Joe, then stretched his free arm around Carrie and Tracy. "If I come for Christmas, we have to enter into an agreement that we won't be sad. That means singing carols, making popcorn balls for the tree, all that corny stuff. Understand?"

"I think we can handle that," Tracy said.

"Listen," Carrie said, playfully punching him in the shoulder, "I'll make popcorn balls as long as you agree to clean up the mess."

Atwater did a double take. "Maybe I'm getting in over my head here." He looked at Joe. "We're men, big guy, and don't you ever forget it. We can't let these girls push us around and turn us into sissies."

Before they left, Tracy walked over with Joe and placed her mother's framed photograph in the middle of the flower arrangements. "It's too small," she mumbled, staring at the bronze plaque bearing her mother's name.

"Mommy," the boy said, pointing at the picture.

"Don't worry, Joe," Tracy told him, leading him across the lawn. "We're not poor anymore. We don't have to settle for their stupid little plaque. We'll buy Mom a big monument, a statue maybe. We'll make them put it right here where everyone will see it."

Joe broke away from her, running over and leaping into Carrie's arms. Tracy stood in the center of the lawn, imagining how the statue of her mother would look. The spot she had picked was surrounded by trees. She could almost hear her mother's voice whispering among the leaves.

· A NOTE ON THE TYPE ·

The typeface used in this book is a version of Goudy (Old Style), originally designed by Frederick W. Goudy (1865–1947), perhaps the best known and certainly one of the most prolific of American type designers. He created over a hundred typefaces—the actual number is unknown because a 1939 fire destroyed many of his drawings and "matrices" (molds from which type is cast). Initially a calligrapher, rather than a type cutter or printer, he represented a new breed of designer made possible by late-nineteenth-century technological advances; later on, in order to maintain artistic control, he supervised the production of matrices himself. He was also a tireless promoter of wider awareness of type, with the paradoxical result that the distinctive style of his influential output tends to be associated with his period and, though still a model of taste, can now seem somewhat dated.